Music

&

Meaning

Music

Meaning

A Theoretical Introduction
to Musical Aesthetics

BY

WILSON COKER

THE FREE PRESS

NEW YORK

COLLIER-MACMILLAN LIMITED

LONDON

Collier-Macmillan Canada, Ltd., Toronto,
Ontario
Library of Congress Catalogue Card
Number: 72–142358

Printing Number 12345678910

To my wife, Donna

Contents

Preface

Musical aesthetics beckons for study of its rich content: the study provides one with both foundations for musical understanding and a wider view of relationships between musical disciplines traditionally pursued in isolation. Aesthetics is the one academic musical study that integrates the great insights of composition and theory, performance, history, and appreciation while tieing them to the other arts and humanities.

Although the importance of musical aesthetics to musicians and laymen seems self-evident, collegiate courses in the subject do not abound. Toward cultivation of the subject's study, the Tanglewood Symposium in 1967 of the Music Educators National Conference called for training in musical aesthetics for music educators. But already numerous courses in the professional curricula draw heavily on aesthetics for much of their content, *e.g.*, studies of music appreciation, composition, graduate theory, performance courses stressing interpretation, courses in criticism and philosophy of education, and historical studies not limited to bald surveys of style trends, masterworks, and biographical trivia. Even so, music educators face a pressing need for books and articles dealing with musical aesthetics. A good sign appears with the inauguration of *The Journal of Aesthetic Education*, supplementing the established *Journal of Aesthetics and Art Criticism* and the British *Journal of Aesthetics*. It is hoped that the present book will help fill existing needs and assist further research.

Although the general field of aesthetics has a vast literature, the musical branch has not had the largest share of attention. And yet many philosophers and musicians have given us a valuable legacy of thought.

Not the least of those earlier authors have been Plato, Aristotle, Aristoxenus, Boethius, Gioseffo Zarlino, Nicola Vincentino, Vincenzo Galilei, Claudio Monteverdi, Johann Mattheson, Jean Philippe Rameau, Jean Jacques Rousseau, Herbert Spencer, Richard Wagner, Eduard Hanslick, and Edmund Gurney. In more recent times a number of outstanding books have appeared: *Philosophy in a New Key* and *Feeling and Form* by Susanne K. Langer, *The Musical Experience* by Roger Sessions, *A Composer's World* by Paul Hindemith, *Music as Metaphor* by Donald N. Ferguson, *Emotion and Meaning in Music* by Leonard B. Meyer, and *The Language of Music* by Deryck Cooke. Of those it seems that only the work of Langer, Meyer, and Sessions delve very far into the central issue challenging musical aestheticians—the problem of musical meaning. It is not, however, my purpose to review the literature here or to give in this book readings from major sources.

The works bearing strongly upon the present theory are listed in the bibliography, and many are cited in notes to support the chief points of view propounded. Some of the writers who most influenced my opinions are relatively silent on the subject of aesthetics—*e.g.*, Bertrand Russell, George Herbert Mead, Ludwig Wittgenstein, Rudolf Carnap, Alfred J. Ayer, and Willard Van Orman Quine. The greatest impetus for this study has been my desire to learn more about music, its composition and functions. Several of my teachers contributed greatly to shaping my ways of thinking and spurred interest in aspects of music and philosophy that led to the book, particularly Hubert Kessler, Quincy Porter, Paul Hindemith, Aaron Copland, Milton Babbitt, Charles Leonhard, Leonard Linsky, and G. J. Warnock. And through feedback in and out of the classroom many students gave me excellent instruction.

The chapters of this book may be searched in vain for discussions of beauty and for criticism of music. The ideas presented here may easily lead one to opinions on the obvious aesthetic relevance of delighting the senses and intellect. However, the notion that the theories of beauty and aesthetics are materially equivalent has so long been cast aside by composers as quaint rubbish that "the beautiful" as such gets no direct consideration in the text. I believe it is sufficient to say here that among the meaningful responses to music one may make is included that of recognition of beauty along with many other interpretations, not the least of which is grasping as relevant, ugliness and a host of other qualities music may exhibit. Similarly, critical theorizing or criticism of specific works is not characteristic of the text. The approach of the book is not dominated by representing important properties of individual works and subjecting them to evaluation. By using the aesthetic theory I have introduced, a critic should be better equipped to make judgements of artistic worth. I have regarded the field of musical aesthetics along lines suggested by Charles Morris as comprising ways in which one may interpret the significance and significations of music. I cannot claim to have investigated every way of so interpreting music. Still, I may lay claim to having given attention to the more pressing problems of current musical aesthetics, and grounds have been given upon which to stand in wrestling with the more arcane aesthetic dilemmas.

Music and Meaning offers a fairly comprehensive theory of musical meaning designed to lead musicians and laymen alike to a richer appreciation of musical experience. It tries to bring out the elements of musical meaning and pursue their main ramifications. Without dwelling upon other theories, the book points ways toward solutions of problems discussed in the literature. The reconstruction needed for an adequate aesthetic is set forth in a positive manner rather than by way of rehashing well known difficulties in other theories. Even so, I am quite aware that my efforts will at best constitute but another step in search of knowledge about the art of music.

In certain areas of musical aesthetics this book may be found to offer some contributions in emphasis or outlook. The most obvious of these would include application to musical aesthetics of the general theory of signs and the germinal concept of music as gesture. The ideas advanced may be described as a semiotic-gestural theory of music and musical experience. It follows that there are extensive accounts of indexical, iconic, and logical signs, including musical propositional attitudes. Through the semiotic approach adopted, the separate functions and relatedness of congeneric and extrageneric kinds of musical meaning are shown, and bases for developing a theory of musical truth are considered. The sonorous motion of music and expressive characters supporting its significations are singled out and related to matters of verbal discourse and paraphrase of musical meaning. In the course of advancing views, certain terminology and ideas, some drawn from semiotics and logic, are introduced with an eye to adding conceptual tools and efficiency to theoretical vocabulary and analytic discourse. Without any intentional ethnological or historical musical bias, the examples have been chosen primarily because of the reasonable clarity they bring to instantiating general concepts, sometimes because of their probable familiarity to readers, and because the author has found them of interest. For very useful and scholarly criticism of many features of the approaches to aesthetics taken in the book, the reader should examine carefully Monroe C. Beardsley's *Aesthetics: Problems in the Philosophy of Criticism*, especially chapters VII and VIII.

I wish to extend particular thanks to certain people at The Free Press who encouraged my effort and saw it through publication—to Craig Anderson, who first suggested the possibility of publishing a book; to William Whitford, who critically read and improved the manuscript; to V. H. Webb, who was most patient about a number of matters, including deadlines; and to Shirley Covington, for her excellent editorial help. The seemingly endless chore of typing the material was most ably done by Mrs. Josie Jenkins. The reductions of scores and preparation of examples were greatly facilitated by the work of Patrick Castle.

Wilson Coker
Fresno, July, 1970

Acknowledgments

I am grateful for the privilege of using copyrighted material from the sources listed below.

George Allen and Unwin Ltd.
  Bertrand Russell, *An Inquiry into Meaning and Truth*, © copyright 1940 by George Allen and Unwin Ltd., used by permission.

American Institute of Musicology
  René Descartes, *Compendium of Music*, translated by Walter Robert, © copyright 1961 by Armen Carapetyan, used by permission.

The Bobbs-Merrill Company, Inc.
  From Aristotle: *On Poetry and Music*, translated by S. H. Butcher, copyright © 1948, 1956, by The Liberal Arts Press Division of The Bobbs-Merrill Company, Inc.
  From Eduard Hanslick: *The Beautiful In Music*, translated by Gustav Cohen, edited by Morris Weitz, copyright © 1957 by The Liberal Arts Press Division of The Bobbs-Merrill Company, Inc.

Boosey and Hawkes, Inc.
  Recollections and Reflections by Richard Strauss, English translation by L. J. Lawrence, copyright 1949 by Atlantis-Verlag, Zurich, English translation copyright 1953 by Boosey and Hawkes Ltd., reprinted by permission of Boosey and Hawkes, Inc.
  Orpheus by Igor Stravinsky, copyright 1948 by Boosey and Hawkes, Inc. reprinted by permission.

The University of Chicago Press
  George Herbert Mead, *Mind, Self, and Society*, edited by Charles W. Morris, copyright 1934 by The University of Chicago, The University of Chicago Press.

J. Curwen and Sons Ltd.
> Frederick Delius, "At the Crossroads," *The Sackbut I*, copyright 1920 by J. Curwen and Sons Ltd., used by permission.

Victor Gollancz Ltd.
> Igor Stravinsky, *Chronicle of My Life*, copyright 1936 by Victor Gollancz Ltd., used by permission.

Harvard University Press
> Rudolf Carnap, *Introduction to Semantics and Formalization of Logic*, © copyright 1942, 1943, by the President and Fellows of Harvard College, used by permission.
> Morris Weitz, *Philosophy of the Arts*, © copyright 1950 by the President and Fellows of Harvard College, used by permission.

Journal of Aesthetics and Art Criticism
> Carroll C. Pratt, "The Design of Music," *Journal of Aesthetics and Art Criticism*, XII, 3, copyright 1954, the *Journal of Aesthetics and Art Criticism*, used by permission.

The Macmillan Company
> A. J. Ayer, *The Concept of a Person*, © copyright 1963, Macmillan and Company Ltd., used by permission.
> Bernard Bosanquet, *A History of Aesthetic*, © copyright 1932, The Macmillan Company, used by permission.
> Albert Schweitzer, *J. S. Bach*, © copyright 1935, The Macmillan Company, used by permission.

McGraw-Hill Book Company
> From *The Meaning of Music* by Carroll C. Pratt, copyright 1931, McGraw-Hill Company, Inc. Used by permission of McGraw-Hill Book Company.

Mills Music, Inc.
> Ernst Toch, *Third Symphony*, © copyright 1957, Mills Music, Inc., used by permission.

The New York Times
> Aaron Copland, "A Modernist Defends Modern Music," *The New York Times Magazine* (December 25, 1949), © copyright 1949 by The New York Times Company. Reprinted by permission.

W. W. Norton and Company, Inc.
> James L. Mursell, *The Psychology of Music*, © copyright 1937 by W. W. Norton and Company, Inc., used by permission.
> Oliver Strunk, *Source Readings in Music History*, © copyright 1950 by W. W. Norton and Company, Inc., used by permission.

Oliver and Boyd Ltd.

G. W. Wyburn, R. W. Pickford, and R. J. Hirst, *Human Senses and Perception*, © copyright 1964 by G. M. Wyburn, R. W. Pickford, R. J. Hirst, used by permission of Oliver and Boyd Ltd.

Oxford University Press

Plato, *The Dialogues of Plato*, translated by B. Jowett, © copyright 1953 by Oxford University Press, used by permission.

Theodore Presser Company

Charles Ives, *Majority*, © copyright 1935 by Merion Music, Inc.;

Oliver Messiaen, *Oiseau Exotiques*, © copyright 1959 by Universal Edition Ltd., London;

George Rochberg, *Duo Concertante*, © copyright 1960 by Theodore Presser Co.;

Anton Webern, *Konzert*, opus 24, copyright 1948 by Universal Edition A. G. Wien; all used by permission of Theodore Presser Company.

Princeton University Press

Roger Sessions, *The Musical Experience of Composer, Performer, and Listener*, © copyright 1950 by Princeton University Press, used by permission.

G. P. Putnam's Sons

John Dewey, *Art as Experience*, copyright © 1934 by John Dewey, used by permission of G. P. Putnam's Sons.

Revue Internationale de Philosophie

DeWitt Parker, "The Nature of Art," *Revue Internationale de Philosophie*, I, 4 (July 15, 1939).

Éditions Salabert

Arthur Honegger, *Pacific 231*, © copyright 1924 by Éditions Maurice Senart, Paris, used with permission of Éditions Salabert, 22 rue Chauchat, Paris, France.

Yale University Press

Ragnar Granit, *Receptors and Sensory Perception*, © copyright 1955 by Yale University Press, used by permission.

I

Semiotic:
Signs
and Meaning

Semiotic is a term to describe the scientific study of a general theory of signs. It concerns signs in every conceivable manifestation—signs as involved in the individual or the social lives of men or animals, in linguistic or pre-linguistic behavior, in all sorts of psychological and physiological ramifications. Semiotic, as a general theory of signs, is the foundation for all studies of what we call "meaning," whether one's particular approach be by way of information theory, psycholinguistics, metalanguages, or as in our case, the arts and music in particular.

According to the authority Charles Morris, *semiosis* is the process in which something acts as a sign for some organism.[1] The field of semiosis may be regarded as the five-way relation between (1) any stimulus that calls out (2) in some person or organism (3) a disposition to respond in some way to (4) another object or event (5) under certain conditions. The elements in the semiotic field, then, are the (1) sign (stimulus), (2) interpreter (organism), (3) interpretant (disposition to respond), (4) the signification (object or event), and (5) context (conditions).

Several conditions on such a formulation of semiosis are noteworthy. For one, the presentation does not itself give a definition of "sign." Moreover, one notes that both mediated (rationally taken) and im-

Notes to this chapter are on p. 9.

mediate (instinctually felt) stimuli are included within the field. In addition, while behavioral in orientation, the formulation is fully open to objective study of sign behavior. And still signification is not itself something hardened into a concrete object. The context of semiosis, although studied with respect to some specific sign situation, admits other signs being present also. And last, the interpretant should not be supposed to have any essentially subjective nature, since it is surely a matter of objective scrutiny in the most rigorous empirical ways.

A musical phrase or even a tone has, as any musician or layman interested in music knows, many possible kinds of signification and significance—i.e., "meaning." To get at any object's meaning we have at least three avenues of approach which correspond to the main divisions or dimensions of semiosis. These dimensions include the studies of semantics, syntactics, and pragmatics. The dimension of *semantics* concerns the relations of signs to their contexts and to what they signify. The kinds of signs, their ordering, and their relations to one another are the dimension of *syntactics*. And the dimension of *pragmatics* treats the relations of signs to their interpreters. To discuss the meaning of something is to consider the object of interest in terms of its relations in one or more of the dimensions of semiosis. To give a full explication of an object's meaning obviously requires that the whole complex of dimensions be considered. Thus, to regard a phrase as it refers to another phrase or as it suggests an extramusical object or event is to consider the semantic dimension of the phrase. The syntactical dimension of that same phrase would concern such matters as the kind of formal unit it is, its ordering, and the mode of its connection to or separation from other formal units. The effects the phrase has on its composer, its performer, or one who listens to it are in the realm of its pragmatic dimension.

Just what is a sign? For our purposes let us say a *sign* is a stimulus that directs or influences some organism's behavior in relation to something that is momentarily but not necessarily the dominant stimulus in the situation. Subjectively, something (A) is a sign of something else (B) if an organism (O) behaves in the presence of A in a manner appropriate to B. Objectively, something (A) is a sign of something else (B) if and only if in fact A accompanies, follows, or refers back to B. With respect to music it should be obvious that even a single fleeting sound or silence may be a sign. Indeed, even a single quality of sound—a quality of pitch, timbre, duration, or intensity—may act as a sign. What matters in a sign situation is that whatever acts as a sign in some way or ways causes an interpreter to take account of an object or event. The sonic and rhythmic properties of music have effects on us; they produce dispositions to respond: they potentially are signs.

To be comprehended at all adequately, the whole concept of meaning as a property of signs must be understood as being of the most fundamental—the biological—order of things. The very fact that some organism tends to respond or does respond to a stimulus meets the basic condition for attaching meaning to that stimulus. Thus, any attitude—feeling, emotion, or desire—any anticipation, any action, or any state of consciousness is significant only insofar as it is a response or a disposition to respond to some stimulus within the internal or external environment of the organism. Stimulus–response, the physiological level of existence and experience: this is the essence of sign functioning and meaning. Moreover, this set of facts requires us to acknowledge that *all* signification and meaning involve an affective (*i.e.*, "emotional") component, because all sensory perception, the cognition and recognition of stimuli as significant, brings attitudes and the affective processes into play. The primary function of any object as a sign is emotional, and all other significatory effects of a sign are dependent upon this prior affectivity.[2] There is, furthermore, an inseparable bond between the affective-instinctual and the rational sides of meaning such that, although meanings of signs may be affective alone, a meaning may be rational and intellectual only along with being emotional to some extent. So we must find that the meaning of anything acting as a sign includes along with its semantical, syntactical, and pragmatic dimensions an affective or emotional component ("charge") as well. However, where the situation leads to interpretation emphasizing semantical and especially syntactical dimensions, the affective force of the sign-object may be weakened (*e.g.*, as in constructs of symbolic logic). But it seems unlikely that there ever is no affective force to anything significant.

Two characteristics of signs and their functioning now bear preliminary attention. The first is that the signification of a sign may vary widely due to differences in possible interpretation. What is taken account of by means of a sign may be different for different interpreters. Thus, the signification of a musical phrase taken as a sign may be for one interpreter another prior or subsequent musical phrase. Yet to another interpreter (or the same interpreter at a different time) that same phrase may be significant of gentle motion, a mood of calmness, and the like. In short, different interpreters or the same interpreter at diverse times may find varied significations for the same object which acts as a sign.

A second characteristic of signs and sign functioning is that the signification is best regarded as a class or set of objects, and as such may have no members, one or more members. Hence, the hypothetical phrase posed just above admits varied significations. But the key point now is to recognize not only the possible plurality of significations but that what is signified may be an existent object or it may be a non-existent object, especially the hypothetical object of thought. Accordingly, as a sign a musical motive or phrase may have as its signification such abstract objects as "desire" or "yearning" as in Wagner's *Tristan and Isolde*. Similarly, in the case of words as signs the significations may vary and be either concrete things or abstractions. The word "independence," for example, may have such obvious significations as the town in Missouri or the concept of freedom.

For the purposes of this book we must acknowledge that signs have temporal and spatial dimensions. There are three temporal dimensions that a sign may have. A sign may be *predictive*—causing an interpreter to look forward in anticipation or expectation toward what is signified—as lightning may signify an impending clap of thunder. Conversely, a sign may be *retrodictive* and cause an interpreter to reach back in memory to recall or recognize what is signified. And, too, a sign may be *juxtadictive*; it may cause an interpreter to take account of something that is present now but not necessarily present earlier or later—as a telephone bell signifies someone now on the line. The temporal and spatial significations of signs will call for our attention again when we turn to discuss various types of signs such as indices, icons, and logical operators.

The foregoing observations lead us to notice that an object taken as a sign is affected in its signification by its context, by its situation with respect to other objects, and more particularly now by its temporal and spatial circumstances. Accordingly, the interpretant and signification of an object taken as a sign vary with the surroundings of time, space, and relative intensity of the object as a stimulus within those surroundings. Thus, at one time or place but not another the same object may be significant. Also, at one degree of intensity relative to other stimuli present the same object may be significant or not, more or less significant by comparison or contrast. A ring of the doorbell may, for instance, attract our attention to a caller in most cases, even if we are asleep or out in the backyard. But the same door ring may pass unnoticed while we listen to a powerful passage of, say, Varese's *Arcana* just a few minutes after the earlier bell ring. And still a few moments hence the bell ring—now heard however dimly—would be significant again. Moreover, not only do significations vary with time, place, and intensity but so do interpretants. For, if one is asleep rather than awake, the ring of a doorbell can easily cause a disposition to considerable irritation it often would not provoke. This sort of observation may easily be followed out without further comment here. But before closing this discussion of variations in meaning due to context we can note that the same categories of variance (time-space, intensity) also have relevance to the sign objects as such and to their significations. Thus, either signs (sign objects) or their significations are more or less persistent in time, more or less extensive in space, as well as relatively intensive as stimuli.

A sign may be used by its producer for many purposes, to attain one or another goal. Naturally the test of the adequacy of a sign, therefore, is its effectiveness in helping achieve a goal, which will always be a matter of degree. Some signs may be more adequate than others to use in attaining a given goal. Signs may be used in at least four main ways. These four uses of signs may be classed as (1) informative, (2) evaluative, (3) incitive, or (4) systemic according to Morris' categories. In informative use a person uses a sign to inform others or himself about what has been, is, or will be. In such cases the producer or an interpreter uses the sign to cause himself or another to act as if some object or situation had certain properties. If a sign is used evaluatively, then the producer seeks to cause preferential behavior by interpreters toward certain objects or events. He may try to use a sign to establish a liking or a distaste for the signification. In an incitive use the producer of a sign attempts to guide the interpreter to some specific response pattern, *i.e.*, the producer attempts to persuade the interpreter to do or think this in particular as opposed to that. Lastly, when a producer intends to assist an interpreter to organize his behavior toward the sequence, grouping, connection, or separation of other signs, then the use of the sign is systemic.

Among the uses a composer may make of a given musical phrase he composes is to inform us about the character of the phrase itself or what it points to. He may use the musical phrase to exhibit a set of qualities, perhaps those of a tensing action, or an impulsion and stressing, or a place of repose and relaxing. And similarly he may use that phrase to call attention to another phrase's chracteristics—its contour, way of moving, or such. Inasmuch as the given phrase is used evaluatively the composer strives to entice the listener to adopt an appraisive attitude toward the phrase so as to like it and be attracted or to be repulsed by it, say. In an incitive use of that phrase, the composer seeks to call out a specific response pattern from us. Through his shaping of that phrase the composer asks us to do something—say, to find a similarity between this phrase and another or between the phrase and an extramusical object, to be surprised, delighted, or disappointed. And if the same phrase is used systemically, the composer initiates, extends, or closes some larger formal segment, and as well he attempts to cause listeners to expect some relatively specific kind of consequent musical event or to grasp a retrospective link to a prior musical event. In all, the use made of a phrase is an effort to guide the listener toward an appropriate organization of responses which constitute the meaning—the signification—of that phrase.

Another important distinction to make about using signs is that between what commonly are called "symbols" and what may be called for want of a better term "signals" or "informal signs." When regularly used as a sign by some group of people so that it acquires a definite set of conventional significations, a sign-object is a *symbol*. As a symbol, a sign may substitute for or be replaced by any other synonymous symbol. Thus, symbols are the formalized signs used in language systems. The signs used to notate music are symbols—*e.g.*, the great staff, the pitch and durational notes, the dynamic and phrasing or articulation marks, and so on. Synonymous symbols often replace the traditional great staff notational system, as in the cases of stringed instrument or keyboard tablatures (ancient and modern) and as in recent stabile, mobile, action, or theatre piece notations used in aleatory music. The bugle calls of the military are sets of phrases used as symbols for verbal commands. Thus, the bugle call "reveille" symbolizes the pain-provoking order to get up in the morning, for which that music is a synonym.

By contrast to symbols, *signals* or *informal signs* are objects or events that are momentarily taken as signs on some occasion but which have no regular use or conventional set of significations. A signal is an informal sign in the two senses that it is only temporarily significant and that it is significant only to some member of a group but neither necessarily or ordinarily to others. Thus, a signal may be some object which you or I take as significant now under certain conditions but which you or I do not take as significant at some other time under similar conditions, or which under different conditions you or I would not find significant either then or now. As an informal sign, a signal is momentarily and provisionally a sign. Thus, an improvized phrase on a bugle may seem significant of something to you but not me, to us but not our group, now but not later when played back on a recording, whether conditions are essentially the same or not, and so on. Signals or informal signs are not parts of a language system. And now it is the language system to which we need to attend.

A *language*, as Rudolf Carnap describes it, "is a system of sounds, or rather the habits of producing them . . ., for the purpose of communicating with other persons, *i.e.*, of influencing their actions, decisions, thoughts, etc. Instead of speech sounds other movements or things are sometimes produced for the same purpose, *e.g.*, gestures, written marks, signals by drums, flags, trumpets, rockets, etc. It seems convenient to cover all these kinds of systems of means of communication, no matter what material they use."[3] The criteria for a language may be listed for our purposes in this way.

1. A language consists of a complex of symbols.
2. The set of significations for each symbol is shared in common, at least to some extent, by the members of the linguistic community.
3. The symbols can be interpreted and usually produced by the normal members of the community.
4. The set of significations for each symbol is conventionally fixed, *i.e.*, it is relatively constant with respect to appropriate spatio-temporal contexts of use.
5. A language has, or in principle is capable of having, a dictionary listing each symbol and its synonyms or the set of its significations.
6. A language has a syntax: it has structural rules for the kinds, the ordering, and the connection of symbols into permissible combinations.

In a nutshell, the purposes of a language are, as Bertrand Russell says, ". . . (1) to *indicate facts*, (2) to *express* the state of the speaker, (3) to *alter* the state of the hearer."[4] The functional unit of language is, as we saw above, the symbol. The fuller functioning of a language involves the interconnection of symbols in expressions. The obvious explanation for the emergence of a language as a system of symbols is in the observation by a group that on the one side of experience events are interconnected and on another side that organic actions and dispositions are interconnected.

On the basis of the foregoing foundations, we can now distinguish meaning and knowledge of two kinds. On the one hand we can speak of *acquaintance* meanings and knowledge, and on the other hand we can speak of *discursive* meanings and knowledge.[5] The former corresponds to the instinctual-affective aspect of signs as informal signs or signals, whereas the latter corresponds to the rational-intellectual aspect of signs as the symbols of language systems.

Those things we find significant and know by *acquaintance* we directly and intuitively grasp by feeling and without the mediation of thought. Our acquaintance includes all that is apprehended in sensory perception: sensations, our affective and conative life (feelings, emotions, moods, desires), our mental states (belief, doubt, expectancy, that we are conscious and attentive), our memory, most universals (general objects of thought shared by diverse particulars), properties of objects (qualities and relations), and the inferential process itself. In this connection it is most important to recognize that most musical properties are known by acquaintance: *i.e.*, the sonic qualities of tone or noise (pitch, loudness, and timbre), the rhythmic and temporal properties (tempo, the cyclic accumulation of energy, release of stress, relaxation), and the regional qualities of sonorous motion. All these things are significant to us by being known at first hand. No one can give us or tell us one of their meanings—say, what "loud" is or "fast" is. Either we grasp such meanings immediately in direct experience or they remain unknown to us.

Discursive meaning and knowledge, in contrast, is secondhand, indirect, derivative by means of thought. Whereas we become acquainted with things by feeling, we know things discursively by noticing, analyzing, and using our wits to think. Discursive knowledge includes whatever is significant about other selves and their mental states, historical facts (events, places, times, persons, and the like) and scientific knowledge (hypothetical constructions and theories involving inference and abstraction)—most of which consists of symbolic meanings of propositions and indicative statements (concepts, descriptions, and definitions) such as those I am presently advancing. Discursive meanings involve, and discursive knowledge is acquired by, inference. The significations essential to discursive knowledge are acquired by passing from belief in one or more given expressions or premises to belief in a further expression or conclusion, the validity of which is either guaranteed by a logical structure (deduction) or made probable by the validity of the premises (induction). The meaning of discursive symbols can always be explained by verbal description or definition, as one learns the meaning of such symbols as the formal design of a sonata form, the chords which comprise an authentic cadence, or a basic set of twelve pitch-classes. One recognizes, then, that most knowledge and most of what is significant in formal education is discursive. Moreover, one recognizes that what we call thought or thinking takes place by means of symbols and is discursive in nature. That is, we think in terms of discursive symbols. And last, we note that a language allows us to discuss by discursive symbols what we know either by acquaintance or discursively.

Notes

1   Charles Morris, *Signification and Significance* (Cambridge: M.I.T. Press, 1964), pp. 1–34. Also see Charles Morris, *Signs, Language and Behavior* (Englewood Cliffs, N.J.: Prentice-Hall, Inc., 1946); ———, "Foundations of the Theory of Signs," *International Encyclopedia of Unified Science*, ed. Rudolf Carnap, Otto Neurath, and Charles Morris (Chicago: The University of Chicago Press, 1955).

2   Charles Sanders Peirce, *Philosophical Writings of Peirce*, ed. Justus Buchler (New York: Dover Publications, 1955), pp. 233, 237–38, 258 and 276–77. Also see James Hillman, *Emotion* (London: Routledge and Kegan Paul, 1960), pp. 193–94.

3   Rudolf Carnap, *Introduction to Semantics and Formalization of Logic* (Cambridge: Harvard University Press, 1961), p. 3.

4   Bertrand Russell, *An Inquiry Into Meaning And Truth* (Baltimore: Penguin Books, 1962), p. 194.

5   William James, *The Principles of Psychology* (New York: Henry Holt and Co., 1890; citations refer to the Dover Publications reprint, 1950), vol. 1, pp. 221–22. Bertrand Russell, *The Problems of Philosophy* (London: Oxford University Press, 1912; citations refer to the reset printing of 1946), pp. 46–52, 68–72, 93, 101–9.

2

Gesture and Meaning

The outline of the general theory of signs presented in the previous chapter will be one foundation for the developments of this book. There is another foundation which consists in viewing gesture as basic to the origins of human communication and languages. A fairly careful survey of that view will lead us to grasp not only the semiotic foundations but the gestural features which are basic to musical meaning. With that goal in mind, let us turn to the gestural theory of communication developed by George Herbert Mead.

According to Mead, language must be considered in terms of gesture, conduct that has existed prior to definite language and out of which language develops.[1] Gesture itself arises at the most rudimentary level of biological behavior.

A gesture may initiate complex social acts. The attitude, movements, or sounds of one organism affect another; the gesture (signal) of one organism is the stimulus to adjustive behavior (signification) of the other. Indeed, each response may become a reciprocal gesture to the opposite organism, creating a series of interactions, adjustments, and changes of attitude. Mead calls this developing series of attitudinal and postural changes a "conversation of gestures."

Note to this chapter is on p. 15.

An important element in the conversation of gestures is the unreflective immediacy of response. One adjusts himself quickly, instinctively, and without thought to the attitude of the other. Thus, we find that even at unreflective and instinctual levels of behavior, gestures carry attitudes with them. There are the attitudes one holds in making a gesture and the attitude as an observer sees it. Quite obviously the attitude of one organism might or might not be recognized as it is by another organism, but always an attitude lies behind a gesture and is carried with it. Among the most elemental are those emotional ones of fear and anger which are carried with gestures of flight or fight. When we see that an animal is angry (its spine stiff with hair erect), we expect it to attack.

An important distinction lies in the matter of whether an attitude accompanying a gesture is held with a self-conscious awareness, whether the idea of a gesture is in one's mind before or while he makes the gesture. The distinction that Mead marks off with his discussion of attitudes is the distinction between the pre-linguistic or biologic level of behavior and the linguistic or rational level of behavior. At the pre-linguistic level, nothing reflective or contemplative is involved in an organism's gestures, nor is there an awareness of self, of one's own attitude, or the attitude others take toward one's gestures and attitudes. Instead, there is only affective behavior without thought, only attitude and reaction to stimulation. However, at the linguistic and intelligent level of conduct a most important difference is involved: the social awareness of the attitude of others toward one's own attitude and gestures. At this level one is self-conscious and conscious of other's attitudes; he selects his own attitudes in view of the bearing of others, and he makes gestures because he wishes to affect the deportment of others with them just as he knows the gestures affect himself.

At the biological level of behavior, an angered man strikes out at another in a flash of emotional rage but without thought or intention, without expectation and awareness of what the attitude of the other will be or of what consequences might follow. At the rational level of behavior, an angered man strikes out at another with foresight, he anticipates what the other's attitude to his aggression will be, he selects or reinforces his own attitude, with awareness of the quality and nature of his act, and goes ahead deliberately.

Mead points out that only when attitude and gesture reach the stage of being employed voluntarily to affect others as they affect one's self is language possible.

Gestures become *symbols* (linguistic signs) when they implicitly arouse in the individual making them the same responses that they arouse in the other individuals to whom the gestures are addressed. A gesture becomes symbolic—conventional—within a social group by standing for a particular act, a particular response: the gesture explicitly elicits on all appropriate occasions of use the same response from the individual addressed with the gesture as it does from the one who makes the gesture. The symbolic gesture stands for the act from the perspectives of all participants. One person raises and draws back his clenched fist as he envisions the other in the situation retiring; the other does move back. The gesture has been used linguistically, because the gesture evoked the same response from the other as it had implicitly in the one who employed it.

In a conversation of gestures, some phases of the total social act become stimuli—gestures—that prompt the individuals involved to carry out their own parts of the act. A phase of the act influences more or less specific individual behavior toward the completion of the act. And in a sense this earlier phase of the act carries with it the completions of the act; the initial gesture implicitly calls out in individuals involved the immediate responses that fill out a sequence of adjustments. In this situation the initial gesture may be indicative of the entire act, for it carries with it the import of the act as a whole. As Mead observes, the clenching of a fist by one offers up to another the threat of violence, and that clenched fist is the stimulus to the other to prepare for defense or to flee. The clenched fist conveys the immediate sense of danger but also calls out the direct responses of the observer to fight or run.

The *symbolic gesture*, occurring at the mental level of behavior, indicates to the individual making it just what it indicates to others. What language involves is the use of sets of symbolic gestures, for if there is to be communication, the gestures of the individuals in a social situation must—and do—mean the same thing to all.

Mead places great emphasis upon the vocal gesture. The importance lies mainly in this fact: *vocal gestures* are social stimuli that tend to affect the one making them in the same way that the same gestural sounds affect him when they are made by another. In order to make a certain sound, one arouses in anticipation within himself a particular tendency to respond to the sound. And in the production of a given vocal gesture, one effects the appropriate character of sound by coaxing forth something of his own disposition to respond, something of the attitude he wants to evoke from others. This calling out in one's self what he wants to get from others' responses gives an emphasis to one's gestures. Indeed, the very meaning of our gestures is in the tendency to respond to them—our own tendency and the tendency of others. If we want to intimidate another by some bullying statement, we find in ourselves something of the weakened or cringing feeling we hope to create in others in order to command the tone of voice that will instill fear. Mead maintains that it is only our vocal gestures that can equally affect others as they would tend to affect ourselves—and it is this power that makes vocal gesture so peculiarly fitted to act as a linguistic symbol for communicative purposes. In arousing in ourselves the particular responses we desire from others, we are importing the attitudes of others into our own behavior in order to influence both our and others' behavior. The importation is an enlargement of ourselves, and it is a critical step in linguistic development. Thus, the action we are going to take bears upon what we are doing now. This is to say that our nervous systems are selective and integrative in their functions, and that they can sustain at once and organize various competing tendencies seeking expression. Sets of responses can be organized so that we can selectively order attitudes and action. In this connection Mead notes the behavior of boxers, when one boxer feints a guarding reaction in order to draw out the thrust of his opponent. By feigning, the one boxer has already started within himself something like the blow of the other as well as his own reaction, but the "reaction"—the guarding feint—alone appears. The feint is a stimulus to the opponent to make him strike.

Mead explains that initiating an organized set of responses corresponds to what is called the *idea* of something, or a *concept*. Such an organized set of responses involves imagery—bringing something into one's mind that is of the expected future or the past as an extension of the immediate environment. The imagery reaches out into the structure of objects and cues one to the adjustments necessary to meet objects, events, or gestures that are not present. The imagery allows selection and organization of action by enlarging the field of objects and related potential responses available to one.

As to the meaning of "thought" then, it consists of our capacities to anticipate the responses of others to our attitudes and gestures, to use the anticipation to stimulate ourselves, to control and organize sets of competing impulses, and to select the gesture that will affect others as it tends to affect ourselves. The key function—arousing in ourselves the tendency of response we want explicitly from others—is aptly called "taking the role of the other" or, more simply, *role taking*. When the participants in a social act are severally carrying out and controlling their actions with regard for that act, their common response, which is the stimulus to each, becomes the symbolic meaning of, the thought about, that act (or of the object the act concerns). Again, the implicit attitude (the disposition to respond) on the part of one making a gesture is of central importance in the emergence of thought. The implicit attitude of one making a gesture must correspond to the overt response (attitudinal adjustment) to the gesture by another individual.

Mead describes meaning as emergent from the threefold relation between phases of the social act. Within the context of the social act, the members related in the development of meaning are the gesture of one organism, the resultant of the social act, and the response of another organism to the gesture. The threefold relationship involved is that of the gesture to the first organism, of the gesture to the second organism, and of the gesture to the resultant of the social act. The gesture stands for ("means") the resultant of the social act—a resultant to which each organism makes a definite response. Because the individual organisms make certain responses to the resultant of the social act, meaning is stated in terms of responses. Thus, meaning is an emergent of the social act. And since meaning emerges from the social act, it is always implicit in the relationship among the phases of the act.

Consciousness (in the sense of awareness of one's self or discursive mental activity) is not necessary on the part of organisms in a social situation in order for meaning to arise. The mechanism of meaning is present in the social act prior to the emergence of consciousness itself, and hence prior to one's consciousness of meaning. The adjustive response of the second organism to the gesture of the first within a social act constitutes the meaning of that gesture.

Through social process and the nature of the organism objects come to have meaning for us. In any situation objects exist in our field of perception. The objects present become stimuli that draw out our tendencies to response. We develop attitudes toward these objects, and the attitudes determine the environment: what becomes real to us is picked out by the response we make to it. Moreover, the meanings objects have to us are our responses to them.

Inasmuch as objects may be part of our social situation and stimulate us, they have gestural meaning. Objects call out tendencies of behavior in us. The precise meaning of an object is, on the one hand, what we are going to do with it or, on the other, what the object can do to or for us. For example, what we call a chair is something on which to sit, a knife something with which to cut. What we call an insect is something that causes displeasure by biting or crawling on us. Thus, the meaning of an object arises in the organization of our response to the particular character of the thing as it affects us.

Music, as we shall soon see, is most clearly an object with gestural meaning. But for now it is important to note that music enters into our experience and has meaning as "music" because it is in each instance an object in our environment. Music is an objective sound stimulus that acts as the control object for experience. Thus, the meanings conveyed by the sound stimulus reside in our blocking of instinctual reactions to the sound stimulus and, rather, responding by listening to the stimulus as "music." In listening to music and recognizing the sound stimuli as "music" we grasp the fundamental discursive meaning which music has, that is, its object-meaning as music. Moreover, as we just saw, it is as a stimulus that anything acquires not only its object-meaning but its gestural force as well. Thus, as the object "music" calls out dispositions and responses in us, we properly speak of the gestural meaning of music.

Note

1   George Herbert Mead, *Mind, Self And Society*, ed. Charles W. Morris (Chicago: The University of Chicago Press, 1934), p. 17ff. See also George Herbert Mead, *The Philosophy of the Act*, ed. Charles W. Morris *et al.* (Chicago: The University of Chicago Press, 1938), pp. 68–69, 375–76, 446–47, 660–61.

3
Music as Gesture

Music enters into our world of meaningful things and experiences as a stimulus. It subsequently gains for us the status of an object and still later the status of the object "music," and so on for specific experiences and pieces. And yet, however sophisticated the music, the person, or the experience, music as an object is a stimulus above and before all else. But what may this imply for our conception of music?

Objects, musical or otherwise, require certain dispositions and responses from us. They curtail or forestall others. A cushioned arm chair, for instance, is made for comfortable sitting, so we speak of its inviting us to sit down. That implicit invitation is an objective and functional meaning of the chair. By the same token, the chair impedes or discourages our making other possible responses to it, say, one such as eating the chair. So we see that insofar as inanimate things exist in our situation they elicit or tend to elicit certain kinds of behavior from us, because as stimuli they facilitate and inhibit dispositions and responses. And so it is with music: the music stimulates; we are disposed this or that way, and we respond.

In the most strict sense, then, we speak of inanimate things as stimuli requiring behavior from us, we describe them, and we discuss our dispositions and responses to them. Our attention is attracted to objects, we

Notes to this chapter are on p. 23.

notice and scrutinize them. We recognize objects as something particular or as of a kind and suitable for this or that use. We observe immediately the properties of objects and speak of their qualities, their internal or external relations. In short, objects—including music—are significant to us in many ways and we talk about their variegated meanings.

As an object, music or any other thing may take part in our social situation. And, as Friedrich Kainz points out, for many primitive people and children this leads them to take account of inanimate objects in special ways; they tend to credit virtually every perceived object, animate or not, as living and attribute to it, however confusedly, human form, feeling, will, or thought as needs be.[1] In such cases not only is the object taken as being in one's social situation—as it is—but it is personified. The wind is a living god. The doll is a close friend, who talks and says such nice things. There are many other examples. But avoiding such a simplistic philosophy, we must acknowledge that as social beings we do respond and interact not only with other people but with inanimate objects in our social situations. Moreover, those objects do draw out dispositions and responses from us, much as people do. Furthermore, for mature people, there is a considerable gain in insight and knowledge in regarding objects as having what Mead called gestural force to elicit behavior of a social orientation. This is especially so in cases of inanimate objects which move and which make sounds. Nonetheless, we take such a view without necessarily confounding the animate and inanimate as a child might. We need not attribute life itself, human form, emotion, motive, or thought to an object if we notice the obvious—that something has the characteristics of motion or sound, as many machines do, as a waterfall does, or as music does.

If an object moves or has characteristics of motion, we can properly comment on those just as we must have responded to the characteristics initially to recognize them as motion. Similarly, we correctly comment on the sounds and qualities or relations of sounds an object makes. Thus, if an object moves into our path, we stop, step aside, remove the object, or the like. We say it "popped up" or it "slid over" or whatever. If a machine loudly shrills a sudden noise, we say so, just as we already have reacted to it instinctively and emotionally.

Music appears as an inanimate object of sound with the properties of motion. Moreover, music has the properties that other sound stimuli have, which obviously makes music potentially significant of any object or being which is also sonorous, which moves, or which produces sounds while in motion. It is in this comprehensive sense that we appropriately refer to the stimulus object "music" as having the gestural force of resembling objects, animate or not. Music is a complex sound stimulus which controls experience and elicits dispositions and responses from us while it is within our social situation. By extension through analogy, then, we legitimately adopt the root metaphor of the sonorous object as a sound-producing "organism " and, hence, we speak of the "gestures" (sonorously moving structures) made by that "musical organism." And none of this entails any misapprehension, nor does it involve us in any supposed emphathic or pathetic fallacy, any bogus doctrine of anthropomorphism or animism. On the contrary, with an awareness of its firm foundation in signification, our way of viewing musical experience opens up to us profound perspectives. It enables us to apprehend the basic objective significance of music, and it allows us insight into mani-fold meanings of human behavior and experience, which music is par-ticularly well suited to signify and communicate.

Therefore, the musical art work, although it is literally speaking a sonorous-rhythmic sign object, is regarded as an organism. Thus, our musical experience is social in nature, because it involves us as listeners with that musical organism; listener and musical organism interact and affect one another. The attitude of the listener determines what he will be responsive to, how he will select and organize stimuli. And the gestures of the musical organism act causally as controlling stimuli for the responses of the listener. As we can see, the basis for the aesthetic ex-perience with music is the gestural activity of the musical organism. Each musical gesture affects the conduct of the social act in two ways: it affects the listener; but it also affects, and is affected by, the subsequent behavior of the musical organism itself.

What is a musical gesture? A *musical gesture* is a complex stimulus to the response of composer, performer, and listener as well as to further musical development: it comprises a recognizable formal unit and consists of a selection and organization of sonic and rhythmic pro-perties in sonorous motion, which signifies other purely musical objects or non-musical objects, events, and actions. Like the basic phonemes and word units of speech, the musical gesture on different occasions of appearance may be used with distinctive expressive force, or sense and reference.[2] As with other kinds of signs, a musical gesture is capable of many different significations, which are explicated by refer-ence to its semantic, syntactic, or pragmatic dimensions. And, too, a

gesture will always carry with it an affective charge. Also, because of
differences in interpretation, what is taken account of by means of the
gesture will vary from time to time with the same or different interpreters.
In this connection it is good to remember that a gesture may have different temporal directions of reference, being variously predictive, retrodictive, or juxtadictive. Moreover, as suggested above, the situations in
which the gesture appears and the diverse contexts in which it is composed, performed, or heard influence its meanings. Furthermore, a
musical gesture may have many uses, including those that are evaluative,
incitive, informative, and systemic. Besides those uses, a gesture may
function either as a symbol or as an informal sign: it may be linguistic or
it may be immediately communicative. In later discussions these
numerous qualifications of musical meaning will be given attention. Just
for now a few prominent characteristics of musical gestures most need
consideration.

Here at the beginnings of our discussion of musical gesture, let us
notice that musical gestures tend to be much more a doing of something
than a saying of things about something. *Gestures are performatives.*
This is, of course, inherent in the nature of much gesture, for gesture is a
making of sound or movement. Gesture is active. In contrast, telling
about something is derivative and often passive—a report of what has
happened, what is or will be happening. Whereas a gesture is an event
itself, the telling about something is a secondhand substitute. In its active
doing of something, a musical gesture directly puts significant events
before us and gives us the straightforward stimulus of immediate experience. So, in acknowledging the performative character of musical
gesture, we notice also that we have acquaintance with gestures.
Musical gestures are there—or rather "here"—with us in our situation;
they are right before us bearing attitudes and stimulating us.

The simplest musical gesture surely is a single sound without more of
rhythm than a sole pulse of emphasis. Such a kind of gesture—with
harmonic enrichment, to be sure—opens and recurs in the first movement of Stravinsky's "Symphony of Psalms." Gestures nearly as simple
may employ only a tone reiterated, or perhaps several sounds, together
with a single rhythmic foot. The fragments contrived by primitives for
their chants, in which the gestures are almost incessantly repeated, are
familiar instances of this second sort of simple gesture. With primitive
musical gestures comparatively restricted, employment of variety in the
dimensions of sound and rhythm restricts as well the interests of the

music. But a complex manipulation of virtually every dimension occurs in sophisticated cases of simple gestures such as we find in Webern's "Variations, Op. 27"[3] or in the opening of Beethoven's famous "Fifth Symphony."

Such basic forms of musical gesture as we have just mentioned are usually labeled "figures" or "motives." And anything more than a cursory perusal of musical form will reveal that the conventionally distinguished formal units and groupings of units correspond syntactically to gestures or sequences of gestures.[4] Indeed, we shall avoid further exploration of correlating gesture and formal units, for syntactical analyses of music abound in which one may easily note the parallels to which we allude. Suffice to say a motive, phrase, theme, section, or even a movement may be taken as a single gesture.

Momentarily the more pressing matter of the attitudes of musical gestures concerns us. For, as we have already seen, each gesture an organism makes may be expected to carry with it an attitude. And by *attitude* we mean an organism's affective, conative, and cognitive disposition, the character of its readiness to respond, especially as concerns the organism's belief, expectancy, and interest regarding its situation.[5]

J. W. N. Sullivan has suggested that what music brings to us is attitude, an attitude originally taken by the composer as he conceives his work and which is embodied in the work, to be intuited by the listener.[6] His point is well taken. Especially so since the attitude conveyed by musical gesture is important as it is recognized by the listener, because it then is a stimulus prompting the listener's adjustment of his own attitude. Therefore, in the course of the aesthetic experience with music what takes place is a series of attitudinal adjustments by music and listener, and these may be viewed as constituting a conversation of gestural attitudes.

The conversation of gestures takes place on differing levels of behavior, levels that imperceptibly pass over and back from one to the other. Some behavior occurs at a biological level and is instinctual, whereas other behavior is rational and self-conscious. The listener's behavior especially concerns us, although what we now say applies very much to the apparent behavior of the music, not to mention that of performer and composer.

To the extent that the listener is unreflective, he adjusts his attitudes in more or less immediate responses to the recognized attitudes of the music without being much aware of the shifts in attitude made by the music or himself. The listener tends to respond impulsively and involuntarily, liking or disliking what he hears, feeling tendencies and their fulfillments or frustration. However, in contrasting, self-conscious responses, the listener chooses his own attitude and heeds the attitudes and changes of attitude shown by the gestures of the music. He savors the feeling-tone of each gesture. He thinks about the attitude the musical gesture reveals or seems to conceal. And, too, the listener stays aware of his own disposition, noting the attitudes the music's gestures tend to draw from him. Moreover, if he wishes to grasp fully intentions behind musical gestures, the self-conscious listener will adopt the role of the musical organism in order to feel and to think over the attitudes of the music.

In concentrating on musical gestures and listener responses we have passed over the obviously momentous role of the creator of the music. And, to be sure, it is the composer who gives life to the musical organism, just as it is the performer who nourishes and sustains the vitality of the music. The composer, in conceiving the aesthetic object, has already gone through a complicated artistic process. But the role of the performer shall be but mentioned as a mediating one, which must surmount the compounded difficulty of integrating the activity of composer and of listener.[7]

We may expect that in the complex creative process the composer repeatedly assumes the role of various sorts of listeners (the professional musician, the layman as rational listener and as instinctual listener), so that he knows, in the only way possible, what the force of each musical gesture is and what attitude each gesture may seem to present to various listeners. By taking the role of listeners the composer anticipates the impact gestures will have on others, and he isolates thereby gestural stimuli and responsive sequences that he desires. And in this way the composer at once exerts control over the probable behavior of listeners and determines the meaning of his music. So we see that the composer may be expected to move through the entire range of responses of which he is capable—now instinctual, next rational—and he does so quite self-consciously and over and over again (in different roles) to obtain exactly what he wants in the music's personality.

The importance of role taking is that, when practiced by people involved with the musical work, it makes communication possible. In exchanging roles the composer and listener utilize the music's gestures as a medium. The situation is not unlike the use of oracles by priests, whereby attitudes are transmitted largely in one direction. In musical experience the composer, by taking the roles of performers and listeners, shapes his creation so that it will implicitly arouse in himself a sort of response he envisions for the others. In this way he determines the expressive force of musical gestures and embodies that expression in the music. Communication of that expression will be achieved to the extent he has aptly gauged the responses of others and to the extent that listeners and performers make corresponding efforts to take the role of one making the gestures heard.

True, a composer may care little or not a whit about the reactions of others to his music. It may be that he only writes music, nothing more; he expresses himself, he puts down what he feels. And by the same token, the performer or listener may have little or no concern for what the composer did, how he felt, or what he intended. But for communication to occur the cooperative exchanging of roles becomes relevant to everyone involved with the music. Hence, a self-conscious approach to the musical experience is implied if it is to be communicative. This is, of course, not to say that musical aesthetic experience requires exchange role taking, or role taking at all by the listener. It does not. Only the interaction of art work and listener are necessary. However, in defining an art work, it may be that one would feel that an artist would have done considerable role taking.

We see, then, that the attitudinal conversation of gestures can lead to a communicative situation. When a composer meets the challenge of that situation, he insists upon securing for each gesture a form with definite expressive force, a stimulus that implicitly arouses in himself a respnose he can expect from his listener. Only then do his music's gestures carry intended attitudes and attain the level of conventional expression. And only when others in the musical situation carry out their corresponding role-taking parts can they tell what musical gestures are meant to transmit. The musical gesture that is tested by exchange role taking thus comes to stand for, to imply, the social act it initiates, because that gesture can be expected to point to the act from the varied perspectives of all its participants. In effect, the early phases of acts imply the later phases. Thus, the completions of a tested early phase become implicit in that phase: the later phases of the aesthetic act are contained in the tendencies started in the early gestures.

Now let us turn to a more explicit statement of what we can regard as the aesthetic meaning of musical experience.

We may say that the aesthetic meaning of experience with music results from the interaction of listener and musical organism in social acts. Musical meaning is an emergent implicitly present in a threefold relation between phases of social acts. The phases include aesthetic gesture by the musical organism, response of the listener, and resultants of the act. The relational matrix consists of the relation of gesture to the musical organism, the relation of gesture to the listener, and the relation of the music's gesture to resultants of the act. The meaning of the musical gesture is the set of resultants, the adjusive behavior of the listener and the musical organism, which emerges in response to the stimulus of the gestures.

Notes

1 Friedrich Kainz, *Aesthetics the Science*, trans. Herbert M. Schueller (Detroit: Wayne State University Press, 1962), p. 169.

2 J. L. Austin, *How To Do Things With Words*, ed. J. O. Urmson (Oxford: Oxford University Press, 1962), pp. 6–7.

3 See Peter Westergaard, "Webern And 'Total Organization': An Analysis of The Second Movement of Piano Variations, Op. 27," *Perspectives Of New Music* 1, no. 2 (1963): 107–20.

4 *E.g.*, see Percy Goetschius, *Lessons In Musical Form* (Philadelphia: Oliver Ditson Co., 1914); Hugo Leichtentritt, *Musical Form* (Cambridge: Harvard University Press, 1951); R. O. Morris, *The Structure Of Music* (London: Oxford University Press, 1935). For adept analysis of the uses of formal schemata, see De Witt Parker, *The Principles of Aesthetics*, 2nd rev. ed. (New York: F. S. Crofts and Co., 1947) Chap. 5.

5 Bertrand Russell, *An Inquiry Into Meaning And Truth* (Baltimore: Penguin Books, 1962), p. 18. C. I. Lewis in *An Analysis of Knowledge And Valuation* (La Salle, Ill.: The Open Court Publishing Co., 1946), pp. 438–41, distinguishes three basic attitudes: one of biological sensitivity and receptivity to any given stimulus (the "aesthetic"); another of interest directed toward fulfilling desires and gratifying affective states (the "active" or "moral"); and that of thoughtful interpretation of present stimuli as significant of absent objects, which will be valued positively or negatively and intrinsically or extrinsically on appearance (the "cognitive"). See Leonard W. Doob, "The Behavior of Attitudes," *Readings in Attitude Theory and Measurement*, ed. Martin Fishbein (New York: John Wiley and Sons, Inc., 1967), pp. 42–50 and Gordon W. Allport, "Attitudes," ibid., pp. 1–13.

6 J. W. N. Sullivan, *Beethoven His Spiritual Development* (New York: Alfred A. Knopf, Inc., 1927; citations refer to the Vintage Books reprint 1960), p. 16. See also I. A. Richards, *Principles of Literary Criticism* (New York: Harcourt, Brace, and Co., 1924), pp. 267–68, 272–73.

7 See Roger Sessions, *The Musical Experience of Composer, Performer, Listener* (Princeton: Princeton University Press, 1950), for most penetrating comments on all three roles.

4
Aesthetic Relevance

We have just seen that aesthetic experience involves gestural meaning. But aesthetic experience should not be regarded as a completely different realm to be contrasted with other experience.[1] To do so makes it difficult to define. Presumably aesthetic experiences differ, at least in the sense that various art works offer us different experiences. Yet the process of sensory perception—which through elaboration allows for distinguishing character, stimuli, situation, and self—surely is the same for all experience. So it is difficult, if not absurd, to speak of the perception of art works as a unique attitude or mode of experience. And consequently the sense we can give "aesthetic experience" is molded and distinguished best in terms of its connection with the art work, which acts as the controlling stimulus-complex for the situation.[2] It is not necessary to digress far in defining "art work," because we tend to accept it as a somewhat open term.[3]

We may hazard, however, a definition of music, consistent with our semiotic-gestural point of view. As a kind of art, *music* is a product of human skill the medium for which consists of characteristics of sound and rhythm, which are selectively organized into sonorous motion that signifies—as well as affects—organic attitudes and other objects and

Notes to this chapter begin on p. 28.

always added

values, either musical or otherwise. The explication of the definition is, or course, embodied in the present book.

By extension from the musical definition, one may expect that any work of art will be a skilled human product, although as computer technology advances this provision might come into profound question. Moreover, we would expect that an art work have a material medium or substance in which that skilled product is embodied. In addition, we shall expect an art work to be a formed object in the sense of having its qualities and relations selected and organized at least to some extent. That form may take variant configurations, including those of structure (the ways in which the elemental parts and qualities are related to each other within the whole), the shape (the outlines or contours of strands of events or main features), and the design or pattern (the planned or resultant schemes and procedures of resembling and contrasted parts or sections). And last, we would expect an art work to have signified content or subject matter consisting of a pluralism of attitudes or dispositions, of tendencies and facts or values, which may be within or without the art work itself.

Part of the problem of defining aesthetic experience lies in the compass of what "experience" means to us. Experience is basically related to the behavior of the particular individual as he interacts with his environment[4] and is constituted largely by the conditions of sign functioning.[5] An essential character of experience is awareness or consciousness—the state in which one becomes an object unto himself so that he can refer stimuli and situations to his own attitude and being. The situation giving rise to experience is to be interpreted in terms of the reciprocal relation between (a) the causal effects of environment on the individual and (b) the individual's sensory-perceptual selection and organization of the environment. Whatever causes an experience is in some respect part of, or it involves, acquaintance—most particularly qualities, relations, what we call the logical constants, and what we have in memory.[6] And, in addition, we may say that experience is related to the formation of habits: the effects of experience continue in the individual's behavior after stimulation ceases. In light of the foregoing comments we can understand more fully the ordinary use of "experience" to mean what we undergo or do and our observation of events, considered as leading to knowledge.

Another part of the problem of defining "aesthetic experience" comes in saying what is meant by "aesthetic." At least two main senses of the word can be given, one of which we shall dub "slender" and the other, "large."[7]

A slender sense of aesthetic is discussed by C. I. Lewis.[8] According to Lewis, aesthetic values are a sub-class of inherent values. Inherent values are regarded as goodnesses which are findable immediately and are, on disclosure, unmistakable. All aesthetic objects have such values. The inherent values may be further described as having no distinct ingredients and as being contextually unspecific and without straightaway location. Being the objects of conation and affection, inherent values are what we desire and avoid, like and dislike, and what we have feelings about. Inherent values are of the essence of *here* and *now*—the "specious present": they are what is apparent to and immediately in contact with our senses. Since reality is apprehended only by appearances, inherent values are presupposed by, hence beyond the pale of, the objective-subjective distinction.[9] And yet, inherent values are not merely functions of perceptions, for they also are resultants of their contexts (*i.e.*, products of "organic sensation and conditioning," of "anticipatory associations, . . . habitual or explicitly cognitive," and of subjective "free associations.").[10]

In short, we might characterize such a slender sense of aesthetic as being, in the main, equivalent to acquaintance. Accordingly, we would say, in terms of the slender sense, that whatever is aesthetic either must be known by, or it must involve, acquaintance.[11]

Another connotation of aesthetic experience (with a slender sense assigned to aesthetic) is the observer's "contemplative attitude," which means a reflective pause, suspension of active involvement, and a complete meditative absorption in which appears as immediate. Explicitly the contemplative attitude is a rejection of any distraction of fixed attention from directly present stimuli. In a contemplation of the immediate object, one's attention supposedly does not move beyond the content of awareness here and now. Consequently expectation, especially self-conscious expectation, is not at all involved in the contemplative attitude, hence, in the slender sense of aesthetic experience. This means, moreover, that highly cerebral interpretation of immediate stimuli—thought involving discursive meanings—is held in abeyance, if not excluded. However, the contemplative attitude, so much as it is deliberate, may be said to verge toward the cognitive and self-conscious, even though the contemplative attitude is at its height when most unself-conscious.

In closing our examination of the slender sense of aesthetic, we note that many philosophers hold a view, as does Lewis, that aesthetic experience is necessarily, or at least fundamentally, sensory (*i.e.*, immediate and directly given).[12] Thus, aesthetic experience in that sense is constituted wholly or predominantly by acquaintance. And so we acknowledge here one basic point that can be drawn into our definition: objects that we know, or that are knowable, by acquaintance are of primary importance to our aesthetic experience.

R. G. Collingwood outlines a "large" sense of aesthetic.[13] For him, aesthetic experience lies between the poles of pure sensation on one side and abstract intellectual activity on the other. Acquaintance is of basic import. But in addition, aesthetic experience involves a shifting between and combination of varied levels of response to art works; instinctual levels meld together with the most abstractly intellectual levels.[14]

Support for adopting a large sense of aesthetic is found in Mead's contrast of biological (instinctual) with social (rational) behavior. According to Mead, these two sorts of conduct generally are not distinct but rather are in flux, one to the other.[15] Whereas instinctual behavior is clearly sensorial and impulsive, rational behavior grows out of instinctual behavior where impulsive behavior breaks down. The instinctual and rational forms of conduct "are not on separate planes, but play back and forth into each other, and constitute, under most conditions an experience which appears to be cut by no lines of cleavage."[16] Obviously, if this is so, and we believe it is, then no restriction such as Lewis aims at need be maintained. Instead, a much more broadened conception of "aesthetic" seems in order. Starting by accepting the involvement of an instinctual-rational flux in our conception of "aesthetic experience," let us list reasons for an extension of sense, as well as what else may be included.

The etymology of "aesthetic" suggests both "sensing" and "perceiving", *i.e.*, both instinctual and intellectual levels of response.[17] And, too, the view of sensation versus preception held by leading physiologists seems to support us in that "sensory perception" is preferred usage by them now rather than the dichotomous "sensing" and "perceiving."[18] Moreover, in current usage "aesthetic" may refer to appreciation of the beautiful in nature or art without a complete limitation to sensuous impressions alone.

The slender sense of aesthetic experience can stand further expansion in regard to the meaning that the inescapable contemplative attitude has. The passive absorption of attention in the immediately present, the retreat from active and self-conscious involvement seems infelicitous. A more apt sense of contemplative can retain the force of absorbed and continuing attention to the stimulus object and also include self-conscious and alert expectancy. For although some phases of aesthetic experience may at times be a passive and bemused involvement with sensuous objects of acquaintance, still other phases need not be so restricted. They may be participative, self-conscious and inferential. Both passive and active contemplation may be involved in the large sense of aesthetic. Indeed, this large sense of aesthetic experience is the one we shall accept, and furthermore, it seems to correspond to our descriptions of aesthetic meaning and our coming definition of congeneric meaning.

Before continuing let us tie up a few points. The slender sense of aesthetic seems to exclude self-conscious expectation and may effectively preclude thinking. In contrast, our large sense of aesthetic clearly admits unself-conscious, instinctual responses as well as the self-conscious expectancy and reflective responses of thinking. Thus, while a slender sense of aesthetic confines aesthetic experience to acquaintance meanings, our large sense includes both acquaintance meanings and discursive meanings. We may summarize and generalize this by expressing several facts about semiosis considered in relation to the present context. We shall accept that aesthetic relevance is properly characteristic of sign functioning.[19] And so we recognize that there are aesthetic and non-aesthetic uses of signs. "Aesthetic" simply refers to the uses and interpretation of signs in art works. Moreover, both acquaintance and discursive meaning may have relevance for aesthetic experience when involved in response to the stimulus of a work of art. But we would note that while art works can signify in all dimensions of semiosis to some degree, not all art media equal the semiotic capacity developed in scientific discourse.[20] And last, we would remember that an affective component is involved in any sign situation and therefore, most definitely in aesthetic sign situations.

Notes

1   John Dewey, *Art as Experience* (New York: G. P. Putnam's Sons, 1934; citations refer to the Capricorn Books reprint, 1958), pp. 3–25. See also Charles W. Morris, *Signs, Language and Behavior* (Englewood Cliffs, N.J.: Prentice-Hall, Inc., 1946), pp. 192–96; and F. E. Sparshott, *The Structure of Aesthetics* (London: Routledge and Kegan Paul, 1963), pp. 264–66.

2   See Dewey, *Art as Experience*, pp. 3–25; and Stephen C. Pepper, *The Work of Art* (Bloomington: Indiana University Press, 1955), chap. 4, especially pp. 90–95, 117.

3   Morris Weitz,"The Role of Theory in Aesthetics,"*Journal of Aesthetics and Art Criticism*
    15, no. 1 (1956): 27–35. Monroe C. Beardsley, *Aesthetics: Problems in the Philosophy
    of Criticism* (New York: Harcourt, Brace and Co., 1958), p. 59; and for bibliography
    on definition of 'work of art,' 'aesthetic object' etc., see Beardsley's listing, pp. 73–74.
    For a clear summary of perspectives (and their problems) of defining 'work of art' see
    Sparshott, *Structure of Aesthetics*, pp. 35–41, and for elaboration, chaps. 5–7.

4   George H. Mead, *Mind, Self and Society*, ed. Charles Morris (Chicago: University of
    Chicago Press, 1934), p. 112; and Dewey, *Art as Experience*, p. 22.

5   Mead, *Mind, Self and Society*, p. 112; and Bertrand Russell, *An Inquiry Into Meaning
    and Truth* (Baltimore: Penguin Books, 1962), pp. 11–12.

6   Russell, *Inquiry Into Meaning and Truth*, pp. 278–83.

7   These terms are suggested by the "thin-thick" terminology of John Hospers, *Meaning
    and Truth in the Arts* (Chapel Hill: The University of North Carolina Press, 1946).
    pp. 13–15. Hospers seems to say something like what I shall. However, his emphasis
    on *importation* of "life values" into a work's aesthetic meaning seems to give a lop-
    sided value to his "thick" sense of aesthetic. He appears to slight the possibilities in-
    herent in the equally meaningful *exportation* of "artistic values" to experience—which,
    too, is aesthetic.

8   Clarence I. Lewis, *An Analysis of Knowledge and Valuation* (La Salle: The Open Court
    Publishing Co., 1946), chaps. 13 and 14.

9   Ibid. Cf. Theodore M. Greene, *The Arts And The Art Of Criticism* (Princeton: Princeton
    University Press, 1940), pp. 4–6, 14–15; also see Theodore M. Greene, *Moral, Aes-
    thetic, and Religious Insight* (New Brunswick, N.J.: Rutgers University Press, 1957),
    pp. 24–27, 86–87, in which Greene says that demonstrations of aesthetic value are
    impossible. But he also argues that aesthetic values are fully "objective," because they
    meet Kant's test of objectivity by being coercive, public, and orderly in appearance.

10 Lewis, *Knowledge and Valuation*, pp. 426, 429–30. These admissions seem to open up the
    possibility of a more expansive sense of "aesthetic."

11 Cf. Dewey, *Art as Experience*, p. 119: "It cannot be asserted too strongly what is not
    immediate is not aesthetic."

12 Cf. L. A. Reid, *A Study in Aesthetics* (New York: The Macmillan Company, 1954),
    pp. 68–73; and Dewey, *Art as Experience*, pp. 73–103, 119–23.

13 R. G. Collingwood, *The Principles of Art* (New York: Oxford University Press, 1938;
    citations refer to the Galaxy Books reprint, 1958), chap. 8.

14 Ibid. Also see Carroll C. Pratt, *The Meaning of Music* (New York: McGraw-Hill Book
    Co., Inc., 1931), pp. 5–6, 24, 29, 35–37.

15 Mead, *Mind, Self and Society*, p. 347.

16 Ibid. Pratt, too, (*Meaning of Music*, p. 6) says the difference between instinctual and
    rational behavior is, in musical experience, ". . . not so much in kind as in degree."

17 Henry D. Aiken, "Some Notes Concerning the Aesthetic and the Cognitive," *Journal of
    Aesthetics and Art Criticism* 13 (1955); citations refer to the reprint in Morris
    Philipson, ed., *Aesthetics Today* (Cleveland: The World Publishing Co., 1961), p. 256.

18 *E.g.*, see Ragnar Granit, *Receptors and Sensory Perception* (New Haven: Yale Univer-
    sity Press, 1955), p. 37: "There may be some foundation for distinctions along such
    lines in that sensory experiences can be more or less elaborated depending upon the
    significance for the organism of the information delivered. On the whole, however, the
    distinction between sensation and perception has lost its validity. . . ."

19 Charles W. Morris, *Signs,—Language and Behavior* (Englewood Cliffs, N.J.: Prentice-
    Hall, Inc., 1946), pp. 134–52 and 192–95.

20 Ibid. See also Morris Weitz, *Philosophy of the Arts* (Cambridge: Harvard University
    Press, 1950), pp. 134–52.

5

The Iconic Sign,
Value, and
Congeneric Meaning

If we regard aesthetics in terms of semiotic, then an art work may be considered as a sign or as a structure of signs.[1] The type of sign that appears to be centrally important in art works, although other types of sign are also involved, is the iconic sign. The *iconic sign* (or, as we sometimes call it, the *icon*) has a property or properties in common with whatever it denotes; hence, an iconic sign in some respects resembles the object it denotes.

Iconic signs, involving similarity as they do, refer to their signified objects in a rather primitive way. They signify objects by explicitly exhibiting properties common to them and their significations. A single quality or relationship may suffice for the iconic sign function, but usually a set of such properties does. The icon displays the significant characters. And because the iconic sign does place certain properties before us for our observation, it does not explicitly assert a proposition *about* its object. The significant characters are there *in* the sign vehicle itself. Thus, a house plan exhibits the wall, door, the open room space; it doesn't *say* anything about the house (unless additional sign systems are used, such as words and numbers), but it does *show* things about it.

An iconic sign may signal, or it may symbolize, or at once it may do

Notes to this chapter begin on p. 36.

both. That is to say, the iconic sign causes an immediate and instinctual apprehension of relevant properties, or it may require a mediated taking into consideration, by our thinking, of important characters. For instance, a siren may convey as a signal a feeling of alarm simply because the noise a siren makes has a loud and piercing wail. The siren directly gives us the expressive qualities in extension and intensification of a cry of anguish, pain, and fear; it both emits emotive signals and evokes an instinctual level of emotional response. But again, a siren is sounded also as a symbol, warning us of an emergency situation involving certain specific possibilities and demanding our thoughtful action. We are to expect an ambulance, a fire truck or police car, so we must clear the road; we are to expect an air raid, so we must seek shelter. So the siren acts in two ways at once—immediately, it is a signal presenting affective stimuli and evoking emotional response, and mediately it is a symbol standing for explicit situations and calling for reflective behavior. Because of its power to display two or more sets of properties at once, the iconic sign is said to be the only sign capable of directly communicating either ideas or feeling.[2]

There are various sorts of iconic signs, because the similarity of sign and significations may appear in a number of different ways. Sign and signified object may share some striking characteristic, say the quality of peacefulness so common to some religious icons, in which case one speaks of an *image*. In another case relations are signified, being exhibited, as in a *diagram*, within the sign vehicle itself and found accordingly exactly so disposed in the signified object. We call an iconic sign a *metaphor* where there is an extended parallelism of qualities and relations in both sign vehicle and the signified objects. Music is often properly described as a structure of metaphors.[3] Examples of iconic signs include mathematical formulas (relational structures), photographs, representational paintings, designs, scientific models, hieroglyphics, much aboriginal sign language, and literary metaphors.

In closing these preliminary comments on iconic signs, let us note that iconic signs may be said to involve "partial identification" and accordingly are somewhat "open."[4] Thus, although an iconic sign may be extensively similar to its denoted object, as in a portrait or a photograph, the sign need not in addition materially resemble its object in terms of physical embodiment. A portrait is wood, canvas and paint, not flesh, bone, blood, and nerve. This observation should be borne in mind particularly when one considers musical signification. And the resemblance itself need not be extensive. For in a diagram only characters for open terms and relations are needed, and in a blueprint only a few lines indicate a structure without much else needed. And, too, in the case of some metaphors only a bare quality in the writing can evoke and carry the import of complex feeling and mood. Thus, a sign is iconic to the extent that it has the properties of its signified objects: being an iconic sign is a matter of degree.

Value. The significations of iconic signs in art works often, though not always, are values or value properties.[5] Hence, among a wide range of potential significations of icons, values apparently inhering within the work of art may be signified. In speaking of signs that mean a value, it is useful to use the term "significance" to denote the signified value. It is the icon's semantic capacity of designating value that gives rise to various pronouncements of autonomist aestheticians about "self-contained" or "embodied" meaning, which seem largely to derive from Kant's famed doctrine of "purposiveness without purpose."[6] The partial truth claims of autonomists may be brought into more coherent understanding by brief explication of what value and the signification of value mean for aesthetic experience.

Value arises within an act, within which a property of an object or situation, in relation to someone, consummates or frustrates his interest; hence, value elicits positive or negative preferential behavior.[7] Within an act, value has reference to a participant or participants, an object or a situation, relations within the act, and the future character of the object or situation in its capacity to determine one's responses toward it.[8] The future character of the object or the situation implies tendencies seeking fulfillment and the effects—pleasurable or painful, exciting or depressing —which accompany and follow the act. The values belong to the whole complex. In a sense, they are embodied, are objectively *in*, the situation, and yet the values are felt and perceived by the participants as interests and the qualitative termination (fulfillment, frustration; pleasure, pain, and so on) of the interests.

At the risk of repetition, we note that there are the aspects of both signal and symbol in the iconic sign situation; both feeling and thought are involved in a direct grasping of values along with a reasoned observation of value properties. Moreover, the values or value properties, as meaning, belong to the complex whole of the sign situation (interpreter-sign-significance). But when we question in a less analytic way how value comes about, we may speak about the "value of," our "interest in," our "desire for," or "feelings about" *something*. Then the focus of our attention is on something; and we tend to impute value to that object. Thus, when value is most straightforwardly considered, it appears to be characteristic of the object of our attention. *What* we are interested in, *what* we have feelings about, *what* we desire or need *has* value. And so it seems that from this peculiarity of natural expression we get the notion of value as embodied *within* an object. Although it is not entirely accurate, since it states a partial truth, there may be little harm in that restricted usage. However, it seems best to express ourselves in terms of the aesthetic experience whenever possible and say that value belongs to the experience of some act and is the significance of it. That act will be an interaction or transaction between ourselves and an art work.

In attending to a piece of music, we perceive series of gestures, distinctive in quality and structure, which are intertwined as strands in a texture and which lead our attention on and on from one aspect of the whole to another and another. The surface qualities and relationships heard, as well as the emerging character of the formal gesture for which we listen carefully, are stimuli. And part of our responses elicited by the strands of gestures are feelings of need and desire or preference for certain other events and continuations. We find the gestures setting up both in ourselves and in the work itself tendencies which seek fulfillment through the appearance of other strands of gestures. Some stimulating characteristics whet our appetites for more or for other sounds, while still others tend to offer us satisfaction. They are preferred. But in offering us satisfaction, the work, it is hoped, holds out more and we demand more. Each strand of the work, then, leads us on, stirring tendencies, prompting expectations we hope are to be consummated by still other strands. But sometimes not every tendency is fulfilled, not every expectation is wholly or even partially met. Some events occur which thwart desires or unpleasantly negate expectations. They are not preferred, momentarily at least.

Now, what is important about this process is that the texture of gestures is woven into a whole piece because we can experience in feeling and thought each part of the work as signifying another part. It is in this context that the iconic sign holds its central place (although others such as the index play prominent roles), for the gestures are iconic signs. The very tendencies and expectations exhibited and aroused by the work signal and symbolize fulfillment or frustration and realization or denial

which are positive or negatively preferred value properties. We intuit and
we discern these tendencies, expectations, and their various consummations in the work (the sign vehicle) and in our experience of it. On one
side, under the control stimulus of the work's structure and qualities,
we experience desires and needs of our own interests. On the other side,
through observation of the structure and quality of the music as the control stimulus, we experience the tendencies and consummations of the
gestures as they are objectively displayed in and signified by the work
itself. The value or significance of the work or a portion of it is the resultant meaning of this experience.

Congeneric Meaning.   An important feature of aesthetic meaning is
related to one aspect of the semantic dimension of iconic signification.
In an iconic sign situation both the sign and its significations are objects
which share a common property and which may be in some respect of a
class. And so the iconic sign and its referents may be, but not always are,
the same kind of thing. Whenever the two are of the same kind, they are
congeners. Sets of numerals are congeners and so are the twelve pitch-
classes or tones of music, as well as materials of other arts (*e.g.*, paints and
canvas in painting; stone, wood, and metal in sculpturing and in architecture). Whenever iconic signification involves reference between congeners, we have a congeneric meaning. *Congeneric meaning* grows out
of an iconic sign situation in which an observer interprets one element of a
work (such as a relation, quality, value property of a gesture) as referring
to another such element in either that work or a different work in the
same medium. If the congeneric sign and signified object appear within
a single work, the reference is *intrafluent.* If the two occur in different
works (or in different movements, acts, or autonomous parts of larger
forms), the reference is *interfluent.* Congeneric meaning is just one
semantic dimension of aesthetic meaning. Later on we shall differentiate
it from what we shall call the "extrinsic" or "extrageneric" meaning of
art works.

The syntax of works figures prominently in considerations of congeneric meaning, for it is largely because we respond to the stimuli of a
work's structural characters that a work has significance for us.[9] And in
order to make form statements about syntax, we use words such as
"structure," "relations," "internal relevance," and "intrinsic." But mere
mention of these words calls forth suggestions of the well known autonomistic doctrine of the self-enclosed nature and meaning of art works. It

should be no surprise, therefore, to point out that our concept of congeneric meaning is akin, but not restricted to, that doctrine. Both share
an affinity through mutual emphasis on the relevance of internal relatedness for aesthetic experience. Congeneric meaning includes the concepts
of that doctrine.

The *autonomistic doctrine*, applied to the arts in general and music
in particular, is aptly summarized by DeWitt Parker:

> . . . in the case of a work of art, there is no relation of parts to an en-
> vironment, but only of parts to parts within a whole. . . . In a work of art
> . . . there are internal relations only; a part refers to other parts, within the
> whole, in accordance with the idea that is expressed there, but does not
> refer to anything outside itself. It is a microcosm, a self-sufficient little
> world of embodied, interrelated meanings in need of nothing to give it life
> and significance, save only the mind of the spectator.

> . . . Absolute music is the best example, for there all form is intrinsic
> form. The rhythmic and harmonic structure of music is effective and intel-
> ligible wholly by itself; we understand why certain harmonies are present
> or certain dissonances resolved without any reference to the objects and
> events in nature or human life.[10]

We must recognize that what we call congeneric meaning is of great
moment to aesthetic experience. It may be the indispensable feature.[11] At
the very least, one must grant that the internal structural relatedness of
elements in art works and the perception of that relatedness are important to aesthetic experience. This is the burden of the autonomistic doctrine. Sources asserting the autonomistic doctrine (in some form) as the
dominant characteristic of art, or of particular arts, are numerous,[12]
and they perhaps form a preponderance of opinion about what is
aesthetically meaningful.

The internal relationships in art forms which are integral to congeneric meaning received great stress in the aesthetics of philosophers
writing during the later eighteenth and the nineteenth centuries. Close
attention was given to the importance of structural organization in art
forms by Schopenhauer (1788–1860), Lotze (1817–1881), Schelling
(1775–1854), Herbart (1776–1841), and the critical writers Hanslick and
Gurney.[13] Most of those writers gave us versions of the autonomistic
doctrine which appear to stem from Immanuel Kant (1724–1804).[14]

For our explanation of congeneric meaning as central to aesthetic
experience, what is important generally in Kant's work is his consideration of an art object as autonomously and intrinsically significant.[15]

More particularly we find interesting Kant's conception of the apparently paradoxical "purposiveness without purpose" as the main value of the art object. Kant's expression may be said to mean that there are objects in which one may find purposiveness without being pressed to recognize an extrinsic utilization for them. Art objects accordingly may be said to embody "purposiveness without purpose," may have inherent objective purpose.[16]

There actually may be no paradox in Kant's expression as it concerns art, provided that "purposiveness without purpose" may be interpreted as description of the value properties involved in congeneric meaning. Anything that is purposeful is meaningful because whatever has purpose also has intent or aim and so points to goals. It is in nature a matter of significance and value. And when purpose is intrinsic to an object and serves no ends beyond its own being, then the meaning involved need not have external reference but may have internal significance instead. But, as we indicated, such is a part of the case in the congeneric meaning of art works.

Now, in the next chapters, let us examine more specifically the features of congeneric and extrageneric musical meaning.

Notes

1   Charles W. Morris, "Esthetics And The Theory of Signs," *The Journal of Unified Science,* ed. Rudolf Carnap and Hans Reichenbach (Chicago: The University of Chicago Press, 1939–1940), vol. 8, p. 131.
2   Charles S. Peirce, *Philosophical Writings of Peirce,* ed. Justus Buchler (New York: Dover Publications, 1955), p. 105.
3   See Donald N. Ferguson, *Music As Metaphor* (Minneapolis: University of Minnesota Press, 1960).
4   Isabel Creed Hungerland, "Iconic Signs and Communication," *Journal of Aesthetics and Art Criticism* 3, nos. 11–12 (n.d.): 15–21.
5   Morris, "Esthetics and the Theory of Signs," p. 134. See also Charles W. Morris, "Science, Art and Technology," *Kenyon Review,* I (1939), pp. 406–23; citations refer to the reprint in Eliseo Vivas and Murray Krieger (eds.), *The Problems of Aesthetics* (New York: Rinehart and Co., 1953), p. 110. See also Isabel Creed Hungerland, "Iconic Signs and Expressiveness," *Journal of Aesthetics and Art Criticism* 3, no. 11–12 (n.d.); citations refer to the reprint in Vivas and Krieger, p. 237.
6   Morris, "Esthetics and the Theory of Signs," pp. 136–37. See also Immanuel Kant, *Critique of Judgememt, First Book, Analytic of the Beautiful* trans. J. H. Bernard (New York: Hafner Publishing Co., 1951), p. 55ff.
7   Charles W. Morris, *Signification and Significance* (Cambridge; M.I.T. Press, 1964), chap. 2; Louis Arnaud Reid, *A Study in Aesthetics* (New York: The Macmillan Company, 1954), pp. 61–62; George Herbert Mead, *The Philosohpy of the Act,* ed. Charles W. Morris et al. (Chicago: University of Chicago Press, 1938), pp. 462–63. For discussion of the background of value formation, see Benbow Ritchie, "The Formal Structure of the Aesthetic Object," *Journal of Aesthetics and Art Criticism* 3, nos. 11–12 (n.d.): 5–14.

8   George Herbert Mead, *Mind, Self and Society*, ed. Charles W. Morris (Chicago: University of Chicago Press, 1934), p. 5n; Morris, "Esthetics and the Theory of Signs," pp. 134, 136–37; Bernard C. Heyl, "Relativism Again," *Journal of Aesthetics and Art Criticism* 5 (1946): 54–61.

9   Kurt Koffka, "Problems in the Psychology of Art," in *Art: A Bryn Mawr Symposium*, ed. Richard Bernheimer, Rhys Carpenter, Kurt Koffka, and Milton C. Nahm (Bryn Mawr, Pa.: Bryn Mawr College, 1950), pp. 187, 197–98.

10 De Witt H. Parker, "The Nature of Art," *Revue Internationale de Philosophie*, Brussels, Première année, no. 4 (1939): 684–702; citations refer to the reprint in Morris Weitz, *Problems in Aesthetics* (New York: The Macmillan Co., 1959), pp. 74–75.

11 However, for a dissenting voice cf. Curt John Ducasse, *The Philosophy of Art* (New York: The Dial Press, 1929), p. 89.

12 See Lucius Garvin, "The Paradox of Aesthetic Meaning," *Philosophy and Phenomenological Research* 8, no. 1 (1947): 99–106; reprinted in Susanne K. Langer, *Reflections on Art* (Baltimore: Johns Hopkins Press, 1958); Theodore M. Greene, *The Arts and the Art of Criticism* (Princeton: Princeton University Press, 1940), pp. 29–33, 127–28, 140–42, 214–17, 263–68, 333; Vernon Lee, *The Beautiful* (Cambridge: University Press, 1913), pp. 29–54; David Prall, *Aesthetic Analysis* (New York: Thomas Y. Crowell Co., 1936), pp. 39–42; Herbert Read, *The Form of Things Unknown* (London: Faber and Faber Ltd., 1960), pp. 49–63; Louis A. Reid, *A Study in Aesthetics* (New York: The Macmillan Co., 1931), pp. 37–45, 66–73. For material about the plastic arts, see Walter Abell, *Representation and Form* (New York: Charles Scribner's Sons, 1936), pp. 21–24, 33–35, 39–51, 68–69; Clive Bell, *Art* (London: Chatto and Windus Ltd., 1913; citations refer to the reprint, New York: G. P. Putnam's Sons, Capricorn Books, 1958), pp. 26–30, 38; Roger Fry, *Transformations* (Garden City, N.Y.: Doubleday and Co., 1926; citations refer to the Anchor Books: reprint, 1956) pp. 4–5, 10–11, 30; Herbert Read, *The Meaning of Art* (Harmondsworth: Penguin Books Ltd., 1931), pp. 15–16, 20–21. Works bearing upon congeneric meaning and/or the doctrine as related to verbal arts (drama, poetry, and literature) include Kenneth Burke, *Counter-statement* (Chicago: University of Chicago Press, 1931; citations refer to the reprinted second edition, 1957), pp. 54–55, 77, 123–46 especially; Northrop Frye, *Anatomy of Criticism* (Princeton: Princeton University Press, 1957), pp. 71–82; Sidney Zink, "Poetry and Truth," *Philosophical Review* 54, no. 2 (1945): 134–52. The standard references dealing in the autonomistic doctrine and music are Eduard Hanslick, *The Beautiful in Music*, trans. Gustav Cohen, ed. Morris Weitz (New York: The Liberal Arts Press, 1957), and Edmund Gurney, *The Power of Sound* (London: Smith, Elder and Co., 1880).

13 Bernard Bosanquet, *A History of Aesthetic* (New York: The Macmillan Co., 1932: citations refer to the reprint, 1957), pp. 363–76.

14 For further discussion of Kant's and post-Kantian aesthetics as they relate to music, see Julius Portnoy, *The Philosopher and Music* (New York: The Humanities Press, 1954), chaps. 6 and 7.

15 See Israel Knox, *The Aesthetic Theories of Kant, Hegel, and Schopenhauer* (New York: The Humanities Press, 1936), p. 3; Immanuel Kant, *Critique of Judgement*, p. 55ff.

16 Katharine Everett Gilbert and Helmut Kuhn, *A History of Esthetic*, 2nd ed. (London: Thames and Hudson, 1956), pp. 337, 343.

6

Factors Supporting the
Signification of Music:
Sound, Rhythm, and Sonorous Motion

Sound. As a stimulus, *sound* is physiological sensation received by the ear. As an object in itself, *sound* is vibratory motion which is caused by energy being imparted to an elastic material, such as air, through which it is transmitted as longitudinal pressure wave motion.[1] When the vibratory wave motion is irregular or random, the sound is *noise*; and when the wave motion is regular and periodic, the sound is *tone*. For scientific talk, the dimensions of sound are amplitude, frequency, and wave form; and for ordinary talk their correlatives are, respectively, loudness (or intensity), pitch, and timbre (or "quality").[2] Our discussion will be mainly in terms of the more ordinary correlatives.[3] To the three main dimensions of sound a fourth may be added: volume (mass or size), which appears as a function of the combination of pitch and loudness.[4]

The ear is, as we know, one of the main sense organs (the other, the eye) that orients the organism to spatial and temporal characters of the external environment. The ear allows us to take sounds as signs of things and events. We hear something, we then turn to look, to touch, or to act otherwise.

The ear contains the organs for hearing and, quite separately, those for equilibrium and acceleration as well.[5] In hearing, the ear gathers,

Notes to this chapter begin on p. 57.

transmits, and ultimately transforms sound wave motion acting as stimuli into afferent impulses to the brain, where sounds are interpreted.[6] The essential pathway the impulses take via the auditory nerve is exceedingly short and direct to both the rational and the affective (emotional) centers of the brain, which are activated.[7] Without further ado, I wish to stress the utmost importance of recognizing these apparently indisputable facts: auditory stimuli generally have inherent affective force, they definitely activate emotional patterns of behavior, and they decidedly activate the highest cerebral sorts of behavior.[8] Response to sound, hence musical sound, involves the complete range of human behavior from the biological to the rational; it gives rise to both emotion and thought.

The properties of sound, which in specific gestures become significant, are loudness, pitch, volume, timbre, and duration. Let us consider the first for now.

Loudness generally seems to increase according to the relative energy carried by the wave amplitude.[9] But loudness also depends on pitch. The same amount of energy applied to lower frequency sounds gives more loudness than when it is applied to higher frequency sounds, and it gives most loudness with middle frequency sounds.[10] And, too, noise grows in loudness more rapidly than does tone when a fixed amount of energy is used in sound production.[11]

Pitch refers to the degree of sound elevation, the positional relation of sounds to one another as higher or lower. The correlation of pitch to frequency of wave motion is that the more wave vibrations there are per second, the higher is the pitch.[12] But loudness affects pitch in that a low-pitched sound tends to drop in pitch when it is made increasingly louder, and the inverse holds for increasing the loudness of relatively high-pitched sounds.[13] A concomitant peculiarity of hearing the pitch of tones is the recognition that tones appear in classes with a distinct periodic similarity at the octave that gives twelve pitch classes ("c-ness," "c♯-ness," and so on).[14]

The quality of size and mass—*volume*—appears as a function of loudness and pitch. Generally volume seems to increase in relation to the energy applied in sound production, with the understanding that only a slight increase in loudness results in considerable apparent extension of mass for the lower pitches, whereas great increase in loudness for higher pitches adds comparatively little or even no apparent size.[15] The idea of volume clearly involves spatial connotations, just as pitch does.

The correlative of wave forms is *timbre*, which we hear as the peculiar quality of the voice or instrument making a sound. Different instruments generate for any given frequency relatively distinct combinations of fundamentals and partials in varying intensities.[16] An oboe's quality of sound differs from that of the violin or bongo, and so on. Timbre, moreover, appears affected by devices and articulation—by such as mutes, bowing (over the bridge or the fingerboard) or plucking, staccato or legato tongueing, soft versus hard hammers and the like.

Rhythm.   The second major component of music is rhythm. When we speak of *rhythm* in a general sense, we mean the temporal relations and qualities involved in a cyclic flow of energy through three successive phases of accumulation, discharge, and relaxation and recovery.[17] The periods of accumulation (arsis phase) are characterized by excitation giving rise to mounting tension or to strain. In turn, the most dynamic phase (thesis phase), discharge, arrives with that moment of greatest stress when impulsion forces an emphatic release of energy. The loosening of tension in the subsequent phase of relaxation (stasis phase), which eases back to a recovery of strength, may subside into a period of complete exhaustion or even depression. The rhythmic process as a whole, then, represents a movement emerging from incipient tendencies striving for fulfillment and continuing through a consummation, and so on. We would find in what we call rhythm the essence of formal value and of life as it is felt.[18] Tensing, emphasizing, relaxing, preparing again: these rhythmic characteristics are fundamental facts underlying signification generally and musical signification in particular.

It is interesting to note that the basic patterns of rhythm are well known, especially to poets and musicians, as the "poetic" or "metrical feet." Most rhythms can be given by the schema of emphasized and unemphasized elements (*not* long or short values) in sets of twos and threes and their several combinations.[19]

Of course, we recognize that relative emphasis is a dominant characteristic of rhythm. Rhythm involves the felt values of "more than" and "less than." But we also should pay heed to other important characters that are implicit in rhythm—order (before and after; together and apart), similarity and contrast (like and unlike), repetition (again), as well as the tempo of events (faster than and slower than). Moreover, rhythm as action implies motion.

Nature and life abound with instances of rhythmic activity for us to observe. Perhaps most remote among examples might be geological and biological evolution. Both, we are told, exhibit in their larger phases, covering hundreds of thousands of years of unfolding, a definite, if jerky, rhythm: major changes of form have occurred in relatively short but explosive bursts of activity, which are coupled with much longer periods of preparatory quiescence.[20] Similarly, we read of "biological clocks" such as "relaxation oscillation" that appear to be rhythmic just as do the other basic functions of organisms: during surface quietude, physiological systems build up states of intensity to a critical point at which a rapid discharge of energy automatically takes place, followed by a repetition of the process. The migration of birds, coloration of fiddler crabs and other cold-blooded creatures, and the flowering of plants exhibit this phenomenon. In the case of man, we note the obvious rhythms of sleeping and waking, respiration, heart beating, digestion and elimination, and sexual acts.[21]

Our awareness of rhythm arises in our most basic sensory experience; it originates with our general sensitivity to the stimuli of pleasure and pain; it develops with our kinaesthetic feelings of excitement, tension, effort, and fatigue in adaptive movements as we seek pleasure, relaxation, and gratification of desires.[22] And just as we intuitively know the meanings of before-after, more-or-less-than, recurrence and similarity, and the quality of motion, so surely we know rhythm by direct acquaintance.

Rhythm is not infrequently acknowledged as the necessary element of art works.[23] And, more specifically for the case of music, rhythm—or as Hanslick called it, the "main artery of the musical organism"—is what organizes sound and gives vital form to music.[24] Indeed, I shall insist here that we recognize the dominant importance of rhythm for musical aesthetic experience. For rhythm not only creates form in organizing sound, it is the foundation for the more impressive organic analogues.[25] Thus, rhythm shall be seen to bear directly upon musical value and iconic signification. It is the felt quality of rhythm that I wish to emphasize. For not only is rhythmic form essential to congeneric musical meaning, experimental evidence suggests that rhythmic signs most generally are the stimuli for extrageneric meanings in a musical experience.[26]

The cogency of the foregoing material brings us to the fact that rhythm constitutes the most fundamental grounds for the iconic significance of aesthetic experience. As we saw, rhythm is a dominant characteristic of basic, life-sustaining functions of organisms. In addition, rhythm appears in inorganic processes, such as geologic evolution. And in the case of art work generally and music particularly, rhythm is again an essential property. Thus, rhythm is to be recognized as a basic property of art works as well as of organic and inorganic processes. Since rhythm is a commonly shared property of both aesthetic and extrageneric objects, it becomes a basis for the reciprocating iconic significance of art for life and life for art. And so, rhythm constitutes grounds for applying organic metaphors to art works, especially the naming of art works as "aesthetic organisms."

We should be clear not to confound rhythm with time or its related ideas. Rhythm is the generic phenomenon. Time is concerned with characteristics of rhythm, but in a particular way. Time measures the duration, the lengths of emphasis, respose or such in relation to a set beat unit, its multiples and subdivisions. Thus, time becomes the rationalized form of rhythm. Time pertains to self-conscious constructs, whereas rhythm is a matter of the immediate feeling of phases of tension, stress, relaxation, and repose.[27] Hence, we equate time with cerebral and symbolic meaning and rhythm with our intuition and feeling of the flow of energy. Knowledge of time is discursive, and knowledge of rhythm is by acquaintance.

Sonorous Motion. *Sonorous motion* is recognizable as difference in qualities or relations of successive sounds and silences, whether the sounds are tones or noises. The qualitative differences in sonorous motion involve contrasts and changes in the *local* sonic and temporal characteristics of each separate sound; that is, the dimensions of pitch, timbre, loudness, and duration vary moment to moment and create movement in sound. Of course, the contrasts may appear as changes within a single sonic or temporal dimension while the others remain stable. For instance, sonorous motion may occur essentially as change in the timbre(s) of relatively steady pitches in a sustained line or harmony. Or the local sonic characteristic of loudness may offer change in contrast to fixed pitch, timbre, and duration. Similar observations may be made about motion restricted to differences of pitch or of duration. But in every instance of sonorous motion, we shall notice, at least two characteristics are needed to produce change or difference necessary to the motion.

In its most familiar forms, musical movement usually involves complexes of qualitative and relational differences. The qualities of timbre, loudness, and pitch along with duration relations appear in groupings. And as the music's sounds succeed each other, the local sonic and temporal charactersitics continually present new groupings. Thus, the differences which make sonorous motion are polymorphic combinations: pitches, timbres, intensities, and durations of sounds are heard in ever varied arrangements with several—or even all—of those characteristics changing together.

From the flux in the sounding characteristics and their manifold groupings the regional properties of music emerge. The *regional properties* are characteristics belonging to the whole of a complex set of sounds rather than to any particular sound or relatively elemental part of the complex. Melody and harmony are such regional characteristics. What concerns us here will be, for the most part, the regional characteristics of melodic strands and those of melodic strands simultaneously combined in contrapuntal textures. Foremost among the regional characteristics of melodic strands are force, tempo, momentum, continuity, and direction.

Ordinarily force is regarded as a push or pull which tends to produce change of motion. And we also may regard a force as a quantity. Quantitative forces requiring both (1) specific direction and (2) magnitude or degree are sometimes called vector or regional qualities. The force imparting motion to music is such a quality. For our purposes we shall define *musical force* as the potential energy possessed by sounds by virtue of (1) the position of the sonic and temporal characters within their respective dimensions and (2) the energy expended, or amount of work done, as the sonic and temporal characters are displaced from one position to another. The displacement will have both direction and degree.

In a general sort of way we shall notice that the *amount of energy* expended is proportional to the degree of the displacement from one position to another within the various sonic or temporal dimensions. The greater the degree of displacement, the greater the force represented and vice versa. This is perhaps most easily understood in terms of performance, which musical notation, in a very explicit sense, symbolizes. For instance, let us discuss the force imparting motion in the dimension of pitch (assuming loudness, timbre, and duration remain constant). We can notice that the production of sound by voice or the orchestral wind and stringed instruments requires a certain effort. And to move in a given direction from a fixed pitch by a large interval normally is to use more energy for that pitch displacement than is required to move in the same direction from that pitch by a smaller interval. Thus, ascending a seventh is expending more energy than ascending a third, and accordingly the ascent of a seventh has greater force than the ascent of a third. So we tend to regard the displacement of pitch by larger intervals as more forceful than the displacement of smaller intervals, other things being equal.

We should, however, note a qualification of the foregoing observation, for most often in vocal and orchestral performance to ascend in pitch from a given point by a certain interval is to expend more energy than to descend from that point by the same interval. Thus, for a soprano to sing d^2 or f^2 after c^2 is more taxing than to sing $b\flat^1$ or g^1 instead. And similar comments apply to most other performance of ascending as against descending intervals. Hence, in the main, we come to regard displacement by the same interval in ascent as more forceful—using more energy—than displacement of the same interval in descent.

And by way of combining the general observations made in the previous two paragraphs, we can imagine with very little difficulty that the relative force of a small ascending interval may be counterbalanced by the force of a larger descending interval.

In a similar vein of thought, an observation can be made about the relation of force to intensity or loudness. Briefly stated, the guide rule is that, from a given level of intensity, displacement to a greater level has more force and spends more energy than a similar increased displacement to a lesser level. And so, the greater the loudness, the greater the force; the less the loudness, the less the force.

We can best consider the relation of force to duration by first taking up another regional property of sonorous motion, that of tempo. *Musical tempo* or velocity is the temporal rate of displacement, the pace of change in position of sonic qualities. We are accustomed to sensing and thinking of tempo in relation to pulse, the underlying beat about which sounds appear to be grouped. And when given an established and relatively constant pulse beat as a unit of value, the flow of groupings of durations may be comparatively referred to that unit. So we find that when a preponderance of shorter durations occurs, greater force is at work and more energy is being used up than when there is a preponderance of longer durations. Thus, relative to a fixed pulse unit, shorter durations represent a rapid flow of energy and greater force; longer durations represent a sparing release of energy and lesser force.

Momentum in sonorous motion is a distinctly dynamic vector quality, which perhaps is best conceived as the amount or quantity of motion. We can analyze the quality of musical momentum in terms of the interrelated complex of (1) the mass of sonic qualities present, (2) the tempo of their changes and (3) the durations of the sonic qualities. Thus, we can see that momentum is a complexly variable quality, emergent from the proportionate balance of sonic mass, tempo, and duration. Rather than take time here to ring the changes on some of the more obvious blends of sonic mass, tempo, and duration which are possible, let us go ahead to some more general points. In brief, we find that the greater the sonic mass, the shorter the durations, and the quicker the tempo, then the greater the musical momentum. And conversely, the smaller the mass of sound, the longer the durations, and the slower the tempo, then the less the momentum. Musical momentum, then, is a matter of degree, and it may vary greatly from being the bare suggestion of impetus to being a powerful thrust.

Sonorous motion also has *direction*, which is revealed in the tendencies of sonic qualities—especially pitches—to move from and toward one and another. Pitches not only follow one and another, they move through and about points of reference. The way in which directional tendencies are distributed (their extent, intension, and order) gives rise to differences in sonorous motion, and these differences may be viewed analytically as constituting *tonal shape* and *rhythmic shape*.

The *tonal shape* of sonorous motion may take on one or both of two main forms: (1) melodic (linear) succession of single tones, or (2) harmonic (simultaneous) successions of sets of tones sounding at once. Let us deal briefly with harmonic successions before turning to our main concern, linear successions.

Harmony in Tonal Shaping.   The *tonal shape of a single harmony* or chord appears in terms of its dimensions of mass, volume, density, and tension. The *mass* of a chord is its aggregate of sounding qualities—the quantity of pitches, timbres, and intensities—as well as durations, which as an aggregate may be a more or less unbroken expanse and which, accordingly, may offer greater or lesser resistance to change or motion. Obviously, a larger mass sustained over a longer time offers considerably more resistance to change (*i.e.*, is more static) than a smaller mass only briefly held.

The *volume* of a chord refers not to its loudness, as many mistakenly suppose, but rather to the measure of the chord's bulk or the musical space occupied by the pitches. Thus, whatever the loudness of the tones may be, the volume of a chord is the area it covers or encompasses. And for a chord of any given number of tones, that volume may be vast, not so big, or tiny.

In considering the next dimension of harmonic tonal shape, density, we shall notice that a given volume may be more or less densely filled. For *musical density* is the mass of sound within a given volume. In considering the density of a chord, we examine the spacing or compactness of chord members, seeing how close to each other the tones are. Again, given one of the previously considered volumes, we may find that volume relatively sparsely filled and of low density, or it very well might be jammed with sound and of quite a high density.

The *tension* of a harmonic shape is the inherent tendency toward motion as exhibited by the degree of consonance or dissonance generated by the interaction of the chord tones as a conjunction of intervals. And consonance and dissonance are value properties of sound combination, especially of tones, whether the sounds occur harmonically or melodically. The consonant or dissonant quality of sound combinations appears to be, in large part at least, a stable quality inherent in the stimulus (as gauged inevitably by our responses) and consequently is largely independent of training.[28] Possibly because of neural functions in hearing, we seem to apprehend the consonant combinations more easily than the dissonant ones.[29] In any event, the intrinsic value of sound combinations primarily depends upon the immediate sensuous appeal of the combination, that is, upon the affective and conative force of the stimulus.[30] Thus, speaking generally, we tend to accept a combination of sounds as being immediately and directly either agreeable and satisfying (consonant) or disagreeable and unsatisfying (dissonant). Indeed, apparently most people rather consistently tend to group the twelve basic interval classes (or more loosely speaking, "intervals") into a pleasant-consonant set (the diatonic thirds, sixths, octave, fourth, and fifth) and an unpleasant-dissonant set (the tritone, diatonic seconds, and sevenths.)[31] Intervals of the consonant set are taken as relatively pleasant, restful, and stable, whereas intervals of the dissonant set are heard as relatively unpleasant, unstable, and tense. Moreover, within each set of intervals, the stability or tenseness is taken as a matter of degree.[32] By grouping pairs of complementary interval classes, intervals may be put in order on a scale of increasing harmonic tension. The scale, from most consonant or relaxed intervals to most dissonant or tensed intervals, would be: unison or octave, perfect fifth or perfect fourth, major third or minor sixth, minor third or major sixth; tritone, minor seventh or major second, and major seventh or minor second. The greater the tension of the interval(s), the greater the tendency toward motion.

Not only is the tension of intervals a matter of degree, but so is the tension of chords. For *harmonic tension* is a summative quality, and accordingly we find that—other factors being neutral—the larger the number of dissonant intervals in a chord, the greater its cumulative dissonance and tension. Hence, in successions of chords, there can be a flux of tension with one chord being more or less tense than its neighbors. And we should note that the degree of tension (relative consonance-dissonance) of a combination stands in relation to its neighboring sonorities. Thus, in one context a chord may sound relatively pleasant and consonant in comparison to its surroundings, and in another context the chord might appear clearly to be a dissonance.

In closing the comments on tonal harmonic shape, we should note that in succession chords may give use to great variation in total shape as the several dimensions of mass, volume, density, and tension can offer up many fluctuations.

Melody in Tonal Shaping.   In the case of melodic strands tonal shape occurs most noticeably as *pitch contour*, which a melodic gesture outlines as it traverses musical space. A melodic contour can be analyzed in terms of three basic directional possibilities of intervals: ascending, descending, or leveling. The simplest contours conform in the main to one overall direction of movement, such as rising, hovering about an axial pitch, or going downward.

Within any overall direction of movement further important distinctions may be noted. For one, we see that contours may vary in the *extent* of their directed motion. That is, the total distance covered in musical space is a matter of degree and may be very little or quite a lot. In addition, the extent of directed motion varies with the number of tones involved. And, furthermore, the extent of movement in a direction depends on the time taken.

We can discriminate further regarding the *intensity* of motion in a single direction, in the sense that from a given level the movement describes an angle of ascent or descent. The *angle* of a single directional movement is a function of the number of tones essential to the outlining of the pitch contour and the distance between the extreme pitches at the top and bottom of the line. The angle of ascent or descent in a single direction is potentially greatest or least when but two different pitches are involved. And accordingly, with increasing numbers of contrasting pitches moving in the same direction, the angle is diminished. So we can observe that movement in a given direction may be more or less sudden or gradual, and consequently it can exhibit characteristics such as gentle sloping or precipitous plunging.

The more complex melodic strands are given their tonal shape by any of the many possible combinations of the basic directional tendencies already noted. Many contours of contrapuntal motives and subjects may be rather simple variants of the more obvious combinations, such as an ascent with a descent and its inversion, or a descent and leveling and its inverse curve. Still more complex tonal shapes are developments of further directional combinations.

And in the shaping of complex directional contours the placement of the uppermost and lowest points as well as planes is of utmost importance. These positions command a listener's attention. They act as indexical signposts for directed motion in the outlining of gestures. Moreover, the placement of these focal points represents relative phases in the flow of energy within the gesture. The distribution of energy as melodic gestures unfold is the heart of melodic activity. We must, then, bear in mind that the peaks, dips, and leveled places are structural points of melody. Not only do they do the most to determine contour, they also act as the salient moments of departure and arrival for teleogical movement. Thus, a sharp angle of ascent followed by a leveling off, say, effectively answers to a sudden expenditure of force and gaining of momentum in driving to a goal, the arrival at which may indicate lessened force and momentum.

In counterpoint, where distinctive and comparatively independent melodic strands are woven together, the strands themselves give rise to harmonic implications, and combined strands explicitly outline or create chords. Consequently, contrapuntal texture can be analyzed in terms of (1) the harmonic implications of separate lines and (2) the resultant chordal shapes and progressions generated by the combination of several lines. Hence, what has been predicated of harmonic shapes may be applied *mutatis mutandis* to contrapuntal strands and textures. Let us see briefly what this means.

Even a single contrapuntal strand carries with it unmistakable connotations of mass, since the collection of its pitches, timbres, intensities, and durations may be grasped as a single object or configuration. Similarly, several melodic strands in counterpoint constitute an aggregate or mass of sound. And the total musical space traversed by the gesture of a single melodic strand connotes an occupancy of—or at least an influence in—the spatial bulk it covers. Although the boundaries of a contrapuntal texture expand and contract in various patterns, the two outermost parts of the texture encompass determinate areas. Moreover, within the area outlined by a contrapuntal melody the sounds may be densely compact or sparsely spaced. And, much more obviously, within the musical space bounded by the highest and lowest strands of a texture any other strands are more or less tightly compressed together, just as the strands of a two-part frame are in greater or lesser proximity to each other. Furthermore, contrapuntal strands often tend to have sets of their tones—single intervals as well as a number of intervals—grouped into implicit harmonies which exhibit degrees of tonal tension in the flux of relative consonance and dissonance. Again the same holds true for combined melodic gestures, for they, too, both imply and explicitly express a flux of harmonic tension. And last, in this vein, both single contrapuntal lines and composites of them are comparatively coherent and continuous in activity or show degrees of fragmentation and discontinuousness.

Besides being created by pitch contour, which we have been according considerable attention, tonal shape is also a function of the dimensions of intensity, timbre, duration, and tempo. This is so because there are differences of quality or relation expressible within each of these dimensions. Thus, they, too, may act separately and in coalition to shape tonal direction.

Contrasts in levels of intensity, such as terraced loudness and fluctuation in the variables of crescendo and decrescendo, are determinates of tonal shape. Besides those forms of intensity shaping there also is the series of determinants involved in articulation of sound, *i.e.*, the envelope consisting of manner of attack and decay together with the steady state of each sound. Thus, for instance, music is shaped by attacks such as the *forte-piano* (fp), the *sfororzato* (sfz), the *forzando* (fz), the "normal" attack, the "hair-pin" $\prec$ $\succ$ and analogous forms of release or sound decay.

Similarly, changes in timbral qualities affect tonal shape. In the cases of a melodic strand carried by a single voice or instrument, the quality which the sound source imparts to pitches changes sometimes in subtle ways and at other times drastically as the melody moves into extreme registers. For instance, a descending passage for flute may become quite open and light in timbre as it approaches the instrument's lowest tones, whereas the same passage for oboe produces a marked coarsening of quality. A myriad of distinctions of this sort might be made, space permitting, but for now I can only point out the influence of timbre in tonal shaping. Another important source of timbral shaping of music arises from the "color-melody" device of passing separate tones or small groups of them in a single melodic strand from one sort of instrument to another. Thus, we can see that the changes of timbre may give direction to tonal shapes, in that sounds may be made that are more or less penetrating or smooth in quality or the like by virtue of the timbres the tones have.

As I mentioned, duration and tempo also bear upon tonal shaping, but we shall best be able to consider their effects in the discussion of rhythmic shapes.

Rhythmic Shape.   The several local characteristics of sound share in the shaping of sonorous motion. And each bears on the relative energy imparted to that motion, affecting the force, momentum, continuity, and direction achieved. Indeed, the full expressive character of sonorous motion is itself a complex emergent—regional quality—of the interaction of the many sonic and temporal characteristics within an overall rhythmic organization. Hence, it is the concept of rhythm that is of central importance in gaining insight into the form and shape of musical movement.

We have spoken of rhythm as a generic concept entailing other qualitative—accentual and relational—temporal concepts. By means of the rhythm concept we refer to the selection and organization of sonic qualities and temporal relations. And we have defined *rhythm* or the *rhythmic shape* of sonorous motion as the flow of energy in recurrent phases of accumulation, impulsion, and relaxation. Moreover, we noted that our awareness of rhythm arises in our most basic sensory experience: it originates with our sensitivity to the stimuli causing pleasure and pain; it develops with our kinaesthetic feelings of excitement, tension, effort, and fatigue in adaptive movements as we seek pleasure, relaxation, and gratification of desires. And just as we intuitively know the meanings of order (before-after, more-or-less-than), recurrence and similarity, and the quality of motion, so surely do we know rhythm directly by acquaintance. And in sonorous motion, rhythm is what organizes sound and gives vital form to music.

We must take care, as I have said above, not to confound rhythm with time and other temporal concepts. Time is concerned with rhythm but in a particular way. Let us define *time* as the principle of measuring components of rhythm with reference to an assumed unit of fixed duration called a pulse or beat. Time measures the duration and tempo of events. Thus, time becomes the rationalized form of rhythm; it pertains to abstract constructs, whereas rhythm is more a matter of the unself-conscious and immediate awareness of phases of tension and accumulating energy, accentual impulsion, and relaxation. And so whereas we may equate time with the cerebral and symbolic meanings of measuring rhythms, we may equate rhythm with the intuited and felt meanings of cyclic flows of energy. Hence, time is inferentially derived from our acquaintance with rhythm; the abstract constructs of time are based on our prior instinctual grasp of rhythm.

Before turning to the analysis of rhythm let us clarify some important factors involved in that analysis. The unit of temporal measurement is the *pulse*, a regularly recurrent release of energy which often is called a beat. To a listener the pulse of sonorous motion is probably felt more than conceptualized, for pulse is most often associated with one's acquaintance with the physiological facts of either the stride of walking at normal relaxed paces (*i.e.*, pace = ca. 76-80 m.m.) or the heartbeat when one is engaged in normal activity (*i.e.*, beat = ca. 68-72 m.m.).

Tempo (the velocity or rate of sounds in motion) takes on its shades of meaning in comparison to pulses. Slower tempos have pulses falling below the norm of about 68 to 76 beats a minute, whereas faster tempos move at more pulses a minute.

Inasmuch as our minds apparently tend to apprehend successions of pulses in patterns, it is not surprising that the sonorous motion of musical works most often is organized by composers in terms of pulse groupings. *Meter* is the concept of measured groupings of pulses into regularly recurrent patterns. The idea of meter is an abstract temporal construct for the measuring of species of rhythm and sonorous motion. A specified meter denotes the organization and measurement of (1) the number of pulses within the recurring unit grouping (*i.e.*, measure or metrical foot), (2) the unit duration representing the pulse, and (3) the relative accentual stress given one or another pulse. Consequently, the notions of meter and metrical patterns schematically treat of (1) three *qualities* of sonorous motion, pulse, quantity of pulses, and stress as well as (2) the relations holding between those qualities when they are grouped in patterns.

For our next task of analyzing the component phases of rhythmic action in music, the quality of accentual stress, the shadings of it, and the relations between shadings of accent will most concern us. *Accent* or *stress* involves an unusual flow of energy. It is the emphasis and prominence given to one sound (*i.e.*, one set of sonic qualities) or combination of sounds in relation to others within a patterned context. Accent occurs when a selected sound is brought to attention more than others in terms of—either singly or in combinations—its (1) pitch (tonic accent), (2) intensity (dynamic accent), (3) timbre (timbral accent), (4) duration (agogic accent),[33] or (5) serial place value (ordinal accent).

To those ways of accentuation we should add accent as a function of harmonic or contrapuntal factors. Accentuation may result from (6) the marked contrast of monody, polyphony, or homophony (textural accent) as well as (7) the marked contrast of harmonic characteristics (mass accent, volume accent, density accent, and tension accent).

We can analyze the cycle of an act of rhythmic shaping in terms of three phases—the arsis (∪), thesis (↗), and stasis (~). In the *arsis* phase the energy of the music accumulates faster than it is expended. Even though the flow of energy increases all the while, the overall force of motion amasses. And, too, the arsis is a highly motivated phase: the sonic and temporal dimensions of sounds develop tendencies of direction which strive for, but do not yet achieve, fulfillment. The dimensions exhibit growing excitation as they take directional shape. And yet excitation and energy are contained; there is a certain resistance to the striving of the tendencies for release. Hence, the arsis characteristically reveals mounting tension and conflict between the mustering of force and the resistance to its release. So we see that an arsis phase acts as an upbeat effect preparatory to a coming event of greater importance.[34]

The *thesis* phase gives the moment when impulsion overwhelms resistance and forces an emphatic release of pent-up energy in accentual stress. Tendencies that strained for fulfillment find consummation as in a downbeat effect. The expression of force marks sonic and temporal characters for attention as they arrive at goals. And although this moment of greatest prominence and emphasis may be brief, the impulsive force of the moment impels the musical motion onward and produces subsequent changes in momentum.

The activity of the *stasis* phase brings a loosening of tension and relaxation; it affords respite and a moment of recovery from preceding conflict and stress—however fleeting or prolonged that moment may be. The stasis begins immediately after the moment in which the thesis releases its great energy, and it is carried on as an afterbeat effect caused by impulsion. Thus, in the stasis energy flows more gently than before as the tendencies emerging in the arsis and consummated in the thesis now have their denouement and unravel in ebbing motion.

We should qualify our comments on the several phases of rhythmic activity by noting that the phases do not always appear sharply defined. This proves true most often in the case of the thesis-stasis connection. For it is easy to lump the two together and overlook the facts that an impulsion usually is a brief moment and that the aftermath of the impulsion may extend a much longer time. Moreover, a similar problem exists for the case of a stasis-arsis connection. It is not everywhere clear that at this or that point the music ceases relaxing and begins tensing. And furthermore it is not uncommon to find that a stasis phase is virtually suppressed altogether as the music rapidly draws itself up into another arsis just after thesis.

In both larger and smaller formal contexts Wagner's familiar "Prelude" to *Tristan and Isolde* presents well known rhythmic cycles. The "Prelude" in its entirety is, of course, a partial cycle, a single orchestral arsis leading into the first scene. However, within the "Prelude" the larger design delineates a full rhythmic cycle: an elongated arsis wells up —albeit with tenuous respites along the way—to the grand climax of the thesis measure (m. 83), the impact of which gives way at once to the relative calm of the stasis segment that closes the "Prelude." Similarly, the very first three measures of the "Prelude" also display a full rhythmic cycle in the conjunction of the confession of love motive and the desire motive (Example 6-1). The first three tones (a–f^1–e^1) of the confession of

EXAMPLE 6-1   Richard Wagner, "Prelude," *Tristan and Isolde*, mm. 1–3

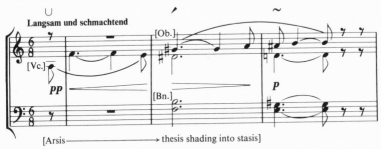

love motive in the cellos crescendo in a pronounced arsis, and simultaneously with the arrival on the fourth tone (d♯^{1}), the thesis point, the doublereeds and clarinets enter, giving further harmonic, dynamic, and timbral impulse to the thesis. The impact comes just at the moment of overlap between the cellos and the winds. The thesis shades into its following stasis as the desire motive is drawn out by the diminishing tones of the oboe.

Tensing, accentuating, relaxing: these characteristics are fundamental to the rhythm of sonorous motion just as they are essential features of organic activity and form.[35] The rhythmic process as a whole, then, represents a movement that emerges from incipient tendencies of direction fulfillment and continues on through consummation and denouement.

Rhythm, in the generic sense used here, has the far-reaching structural function of organizing the various elements and parts of a work into a whole organic form. By analysis of music we can see that each formal unit is shaped by rhythm. Whether the formal unit of interest be a figure or motive, phrase, section, or movement, analysis will reveal that some element has the rhythmic function of an arsis and that others will act as thesis or stasis. Moreover, each formal unit may be classed with others of the same kind (figures, motives, phrases, and so on) so that a hierarchy of formal contexts is envisioned for an entire work. And within each class of formal units the organizing shaping of rhythm can be found. Thus, each larger context subsumes under it and gives over all rhythmic shape to several smaller contexts, as several figures or motives are given rhythmic shape by a phrase grouping, as themes are grouped by a major section, and the like. Accordingly, rhythm forms the work into an organic unity. Each element is a necessary part of a larger rhythmic action; the sweep of rhythm creates a total cohesion by relating the elements at the levels of larger and larger contexts to each other.

Musical Syntax and Punctuation.   *Musical syntax* is, as our discussions have implied, gesture construction and gesture ordering. As gesture construction, musical syntax is concerned with the arrangement, according to principles or rules, of elements in sonorous motion. It deals with the structure of possible serial orders which may be given to characteristics of sonorous motion in order to form musical gestures. And as gesture ordering, musical syntax is concerned with the possible arrangements of any conceivable set of musical gestures. Although we shall treat construction and ordering of gestures later, we need to mention the syntactic functions of cadence and caesura here, since they are of importance to completing our survey of sonorous motion.

Cadence and *caesura* are characteristic ways of ending gestures so that a particular degree of completeness or incompleteness is specified. Both are forms of musical punctuation, but *cadence* refers to the *sounding* manner of closure given to a gesture, whereas *caesura* refers to the *pause* or *silence* which either follows a gesture or separates two gestures. Cadences and caesuras may be either *terminating* or *mediating*; they may either mark off gestures as fully separate or they may tie gestures together in varying degrees of closeness.

The distinction between whether a cadence or caesura is either terminating or mediating depends largely upon the rhythmic function of distinct gestures involved within their contexts. When a gesture acts as a discrete stasis (or as a tight-knit thesis-stasis), it may be marked off readily by terminating punctuation. By contrast, an arsis gesture rather clearly tends to have mediating punctuation, which can both loosely bind it to and separate it from its subsequent thesis. And, somewhat similarly, a distinct thesis gesture may be closed by rather complete punctuation when it entails a stasis gesture which is itself either individual enough in character or prolonged.

Musical Properties and Description of Music.   The foregoing survey has called attention to the point that the materials of music are the local and regional properties of sound and rhythm and the regional properties of sonorous motion. We shall have occasion later to call all of them the "sensuous surface" or surface qualities of music. All are known intuitively by acquaintance, being apprehended in direct experience. They are the very properties which comprise gestures and make the gestures significant as they move in characteristic ways and reveal tendencies of motion. Furthermore, they are the value properties to which one responds with positive or negative preference. In sum, then, the local and regional properties of sound, rhythm, and sonorous motion are what constitute musical character and disposition; they overtly display musical attitude. (In later discussions we shall return to the consequences of these matters as they concern musical expressivity.) Now we need only to remark that these properties are the atomic elements of music itself. They are perceived as *in* the music; they are recognized as the very stuff of music.

In consequence of the preceding discussion of musical properties, we may go on to examine in a simple way the relation of one facet of sensory perception to the naming of the properties and the use of the naming words in describing music.

As we know, our senses of hearing, sight, touch, and the rest differ according to the objects that stimulate them. We can taste the flavor of an orange, but we cannot hear it; we can see the light of a star, but we cannot touch or smell it. So in sensory perception each sense organ does some things that others cannot do.

However, that is not always the case, not most of the time. Indeed, we find frequently that several different senses detect the same properties (qualities and relationships). For instance, we both see and touch the sharpness of a needle point. Or, too, we hear and feel ("touch") the sound (vibratory motion) of an explosive detonation of dynamite. And we can hear the relationships of "before" and "after" or "more" and "less" between sounds, just as we can see these relationships in other events or touch-feel them in still others.

This latter sort of experiencing properties concerns us here. For we notice that our responses to many different stimuli, perceived by different sense organs, feel or seem to be similar. That is, our various senses often share in common experiences we have. Our responses to stimuli may appear closely alike when different senses are involved, so that there is a noticeable cross-sensory participation in a common response to variegated stimuli. The same quality or relationship, occurring over and over in different forms, affects several sense organs in a way enough alike to have the same name. We call this phenomenon of perception involving cross-sensory participation *sensory isomorphism*.[36]

Usually we use certain words to name the feelings or appearances of similarity that we sense in different ways. Words that do this are among *universals*.[37] The names for properties are universals. A universal names a kind of response that we make in common for various particular instances. The response is universal, but each stimulus is particular. So, when we say something such as, "a melodic line has the property of roughness," we are naming a certain kind of response to a particular, a response we might make in experiencing other objects as well. We might find roughness in many stimuli: we might touch or see a file that has the property of roughness, just as we might hear that the melodic line has a roughness in it, too. Thus, we use the same word to describe many different objects that involve a similarity of feeling in our responses.

These facts are most important for our being able to talk about music. For the same words used to describe objective properties when they appear in non-musical objects and events are exactly the same words used to discuss those properties when they occur in music. That is, our metalanguage for description of music is essentially our common language, amplified, of course, by technical terms and symbols such as "dominant seventh" (V^7) and so forth. Accordingly, use of descriptive words for properties of sound and motion generally applies also to musical discussion. Moreover, it is not only appropriate but necessary for adequate musical analysis. Pointing out the agitated or the calm character, the underlying tension or the surging power of musical gestures is the properly founded use of names for universals, characteristic properties of motion *per se*. Such use involves neither questionable subjectivity nor dubious metaphor, so long as one observes such properties before reporting on them and so long as another person can have the same experience and verify the report. All that is necessary usually for proper observation and translation of musical experiences to words is that there be a sufficiently long segment of experience to establish the relevant facts and discourse upon them.[38] With these matters well in mind we can proceed to more specific aspects of congeneric meaning.

Notes

1   E. B. Uvarov and D. R. Chapman, *A Dictionary of Science*, rev. ed. (Baltimore: Penguin Books, 1951), p. 201; Ernest Glen Wever and Merle Lawrence, *Physiological Accoustics* (Princeton: Princeton University Press, 1954), p. 16.

2   J. C. R. Licklider, "Basic Correlatives of the Auditory Stimulus," *Handbook of Experimental Psychology*, ed. S. S. Stevens (New York: John Wiley and Sons, Inc., 1951), pp. 1002ff.

3   For information on the specific correlations, see Licklider, "Correlatives of Auditory Stimulus"; G. Révész, *Introduction to the Psychology of Music*, trans. G. I. C. de Courcy (London: Longmans, Green and Co. Ltd., 1953), chap. 1.

4   Licklider, "Correlatives of Auditory Stimulus", pp. 1004–5; James Mursell, *The Psychology of Music* (New York: W. W. Norton and Co., 1937), pp. 63–64; Hans Heinz Dräger, "The Concept of 'Tonal Body'," *Archiv für Musikwissenschaft* 9, no. 1 (1952): 68–77, reprinted in Sussanne K. Langer, *Reflections on Art* (Baltimore: Johns Hopkins Press, 1958).

5   Hallowell Davis, "Psychophysiology of Hearing and Deafness," in Stevens, ed., *Experimental Psychology*, p. 1117.

6   For details, as well as they are known, about how this occurs see Georg von Békésy and Walter A. Rosenblith, "The Mechanical Properties of the Ear," in Stevens, ed., *Experimental Psychology*; Davis, "Psychophysiology of Hearing," pp. 1116–22; John R. Pierce and Edward E. Davis, Jr., *Man's World of Sound* (Garden City, N.Y.: Doubleday and Co., Inc., 1958), and Ashley Montagu, *Anatomy and Physiology* (New York: Barnes and Noble, Inc., 1959), vol. 2, pp. 171–77.

7   See Davis, "Psychophysiology of Hearing," pp. 1116–22, T. C. Ruch, "Sensory Mechanisms," in Stevens, ed., *Experimental Psychology*, pp. 126, 144, 186–88; Donald B. Lindsley, "Emotion," in Stevens, ed., *Experimental Psychology*, pp. 487–88, 495–500, 504–9. The pathway from the inner ear is from the organ of corti on the basilar membrane to the nuclei in the lower brain stem, the reticular formation, the cerebellum, the inferior colliculus, the medial geniculate body, and the temporal lobe (auditory area) of the cerebral cortex.

8   Davis, "Psychophysiology of Hearing," pp. 1116–22. See also James Hillman, *Emotion* (London: Routledge and Kegan Paul, 1960), pp. 100–103.
9   Révész, *Psychology of Music*, p. 6.
10 Licklider, "Correlatives of Auditory Stimulus," p. 1003.
11 Ibid., p. 1016.
12 Révész, *Psychology of Music*, p. 9.
13 Paul E. Sabine, "Acoustics," *The Encyclopedia Americana* (New York: Americana Corporation, 1956), vol. 1, p. 97.
14 Licklider, "Correlatives of Auditory Stimulus," p. 1003; Révész, *Psychology of Music*, pp. 57–59.
15 Licklider, "Correlatives of Auditory Stimulus," p. 1003; Mursell, *The Psychology of Music* (New York: W. W. Norton and Co., 1937), pp. 176–77; Hans Heinz Dräger, "Concept of 'Tonal Body'," pp. 68–77.
16 Licklider, "Correlatives of Auditory Stimulus," p. 1019; Révész, *Psychology of Music*, pp. 10–12.
17 Cf. G. J. Whitrow, *The Natural Philosophy of Time* (London: Thomas Nelson and Sons, Ltd., 1961), pp. 53–73; Raymond Bayer, "The Essence of Rhythm," *Revue d' Esthétique* vol. 6, no. 4 (1953), pp. 369–85 (citations refer to the reprint in Langer, *Reflections on Art*, pp. 186–201); and Otto Baensch, "Art and Feeling," *Logos*, Vol. XII (1923–1924), pp. 1–28 (citations refer to the reprint in Langer, *Reflections on Art*, pp. 25–27.)
18 John Dewey, *Art as Experience* (New York: G. P. Putnam's Sons, Capricorn Books, 1958), p. 136; Susanne K. Langer, *Feeling and Form* (New York: Charles Scribner's Sons, 1953), pp. 328–31.
19 See James Mursell, *Psychology of Music*, pp. 176–77. Also see Grosvenor W. Cooper and Leonard B. Meyer, *The Rhythmic Structure of Music* (Chicago: University of Chicago Press, 1960), chap. 3 especially.
20 Whitrow, *Natural Philosophy of Time*, pp. 15–16.
21 Ibid., pp. 69–70. (But man's supposed *sense* of rhythm is sometimes attributed to the entirely unobvious "alpha rhythm" of the central nervous processes—a rhythmic electric current generated by the brain which has a frequency of eight to twelve cycles per second.)
22 Whitrow, *Natural Philosophy of Time*, pp. 52–55.
23 Bayer, "Essence of Rhythm," p. 193; Baensch, "Art and Feeling," pp. 25–27.
24 Eduard Hanslick, *The Beautiful in Music*, translated by Gustave Cohen, edited by Morris Wietz, 8th ed. (New York: The Liberal Arts Press, 1957), pp. 47–48; Langer, *Feeling and Form*, pp. 126–27.
25 Deryck Cooke, *The Language of Music* (London: Oxford University Press, 1959), pp. 94–98, 177–81; Donald Ferguson, *Music As Metaphor* (Minneapolis: University of Minnesota Press, 1960, pp. 14, 47, 59, 67–69, 73, 87; Paul Hindemith, *A Composer's World* (Cambridge: Harvard University Press, 1952), pp. 18, 20, 42–44; Roger Sessions, *The Musical Experience of Composer, Performer, Listener* (Princeton: Princeton University Press, 1950, pp. 11–12, 15, 17–20, 62–63, 73–78.
26 C. W. Valentine, *The Experimental Psychology of Beauty* (London: Methuen and Co., Ltd., 1962), pp. 229–46.
27 Whitrow, *Natural Philosophy of Time*, pp. 36, 47, 53–55, 81–82.
28 Otto Ortman, "Types of Listeners," in *The Effects of Music*, ed. Max Schoen (New York: Harcourt, Brace and Co., 1927), pp. 42–48.
29 Paul Boomsliter and Warren Creel, "The Long Pattern Hypothesis in Harmony and Hearing," *Journal of Music Theory* (April, 1961), pp. 14, 18, 28. Cf. James Mursell, *Psychology of Music*, pp. 82–89, 97.
30 Cf. Willi Apel, "Consonance, Dissonance," in *Harvard Dictionary of Music* (Cambridge: Harvard University Press, 1944), pp. 180–82.
31 Ortman, "Types of Listeners," pp. 42–48; Valentine, *Experimental Psychology of Beauty*, pp. 210, 217–18.

32 Ibid.

33 We must avoid the common error of identifying duration or durational patterns (long-short schemata) with rhythm. For, as I have tried to show above, duration is best considered as one of the species of accent which contributes to the establishment of rhythm. It is not rhythm itself.

34 In order to designate the several phases of rhythmic shaping, we may adopt the diacritical symbols of the breve (∪) to denote an arsis, the acute accent (✓) to denote a thesis, and the tilde sign (∼) to denote a stasis. For the more limited, but often referred to, cases of durational relationships we shall reserve the traditional macron (–) for length and the point (·) for shortness.

35 Dewey, *Art as Experience*, p. 136 and Langer, *Feeling and Form*, pp. 328–31.

36 Carroll C. Pratt, *The Meaning of Music* (New York: McGraw-Hill Book Co., 1931), pp. 152–53, 180–85; Paul Henle (ed.), *Language, Thought, and Culture* (Ann Arbor: University of Michigan Press, 1958), pp. 179–91, 205; Wolfgang Kohler, *Gestalt Psychology* (New York; Liveright Publishing Corp., Mentor Books, 1947), pp. 88–90, 179, 201, 209.

37 H. H. Price, *Thinking and Experience* (Cambridge: Harvard University Press, 1962), pp. 10–13.

38 See Willard Van Orman Quine, *From a Logical Point of View* (second edition, revised; New York: Harper and Row, 1963), pp. 56–63, and Willard Van Orman Quine, *Word and Object* (Cambridge: M.I.T. Press, 1960), pp. 7–14, 42–57 for illuminating discussion on the metalinguistic problem, synonymy, and translation from one sign system to another.

7

Congeneric Musical Meaning

Congeneric and Extrageneric
Musical Meaning

In virtue of iconic sign functioning we can determine two major classes of aesthetic meanings within the semantic dimension of musical experience. Those classes are congeneric musical meanings and extrageneric musical meanings. Both owe their meaningfulness to the determining characteristic of iconic signification—resemblance or similarity. Speaking objectively, something A_1 is an iconic sign of an object A_2 for someone if and only if both A_1 and A_2 in fact actually share a common set of characteristics which are recognizable as identity elements of both A_1 and A_2. Subjectively, something A_1 is an iconic sign of an object A_2 for someone if he has a disposition to respond or does respond to A_1 as though it either is like or resembles A_2 in some respect.

In order to demarcate congeneric signification from extrageneric signification, a further condition must be met within the iconic sign situation. The distinction sought by the additional condition also is semantic, concerning what is signified by a sign. We need to distinguish between musical and non-musical objects. To do this I advance the criterion of the congener in order to classify all sounds organized into musical works as comprising one kind (*i.e.*, genus) of sound. And I classify all other ob-

Notes to this chapter begin on p. 87.

jects, including sounds not in musical works, as being of a different kind by virtue of both inherent nature for non-sonic objects and use for sonic objects. The criterion of the congener demarcates the difference between congeneric and extrageneric musical meanings. A musical work is one kind of object. Everything else, including sound not organized in a musical work, is of a different kind for our purposes of definition.

Congeneric musical meanings are those resultants of a dominantly iconic sign situation in which someone interprets one part of a musical work as a sign of another part of that same work or a diverse musical work. But on the basis of intuited or conceived similarity, the reference of a musical gesture may be either in one or both of two modes of iconic signification: (1) a musical gesture may point to another musical gesture, or (2) a musical gesture may point to some non-musical object. *Extrageneric musical meanings* are those resultants of the iconic sign situation in which someone interprets a musical work or some portion of it as a sign of some non-musical object, including sounds not then organized as parts of the musical work.

The necessary and sufficient conditions for congeneric musical meaning are (1) that the sign function be iconic and (2) that the sign vehicle and the signification both be musical works or portions of musical works. In contradistinction the equivalent conditions for extrageneric musical meaning are (1) that the sign function be iconic and (2) that the sign vehicle and signification be respectively a musical work or a portion of a work and any other non-musical object (including within the immediate context any sounds not within the style system of the musical work).

Given the basic distinction between congeneric and extrageneric signification, I wish to turn to inspecting the former class of musical meaning in greater detail. However, before proceeding, it must be made clear that the meaning of musical gestures is dependent upon other kinds of signs besides icons. Indeed, we need to understand here and now that musical gestures always are complex objects consisting of a plurality of signs at once. Three main types of signs comprise a musical gesture: the indexical signs, the iconic signs, and the logical or syntactical signs. In anticipation of detailed examinations in later chapters and in order to clarify our next and more immediate investigations, we can glimpse the role of each and the general way in which the three types are involved in gestural meaning. Through the combined functioning of the three types of sign a musical gesture achieves definite significations, character or attitude, and relatedness within itself and in its connection to other gestures. The indices or indexical signs orient interpreters to the structural or configurational properties of a musical gesture. In addition, the indices command one's attention and spatio-temporally locate other signs one must heed in order to grasp the fuller meaning. The iconic signs are characterizing signs which associate resembling properties and exhibit value properties. The syntactical connection of the signs is given by logical signs which express the relationships between and within musical gestures. The indices, then, give specificity of reference, and together the connecting logical signs and iconic signs lend coherence and determinateness to the interpreter's intuitions, retrospections, and expectations.

To return to congenerous signification, we should mark off within it two species of reference—the interfluent reference and the intrafluent reference. We may speak of the *interfluent reference* as one flowing from a sign in one piece to a signification in another work or to a signification in another movement or act of the same larger composition. When the reference flows from a sign to a signification within one and the same piece, the reference is *intrafluent*. For the most part, the species of congenerous reference of musical gestures which one needs to discuss in clarifying the meanings of a composition will be intrafluent ones. For we will speak constantly of a musical gesture pointing to another musical gesture within the same piece or movement. And yet for many compositions the interfluent reference is of great moment, especially in cyclic forms. Take, for examples, the obvious cases of some works which utilize a basic theme that flows throughout a series of separate movements: Josquin's *Missa Pange lingua* and other cyclic masses, the Cantata No. 80 (*Ein feste Burg*) of J. S. Bach or others of his chorale cantatas, Berlioz' *Symphonie Fantastique*, the *Symphony in D Minor* of Franck, and so on.

We should restrict the terms "intermusical" and "intramusical," for they can aptly qualify discussions of different "musics," to which we so often need to speak, as in comparing the different cultural literatures of the orient and occident, the several style systems of distinct historical eras, or of style systems of various composers. Thus, in describing "third stream music" we compare (and contrast) the traditional concert and religious music of Western civilization with the jazz music of our times in order to note an intermusical evolution. By the same means we define a composer's various periods by intramusical references to one or another set of systematic stylistic criteria.

Music certainly is preeminently a temporal art, which requires us to take careful account of the temporal directions in which signs point. Signs may be predictive, retrodictive, or juxtadictive. In a general way this is noticeable readily in the case of Berlioz' *Symphonie Fantastique.* The cyclic theme (*idée fixe*), quite apart from its palpable extragenerous symbolizations, refers interfluently in the first movement ("Reveries, Passions") to implicit variations to come in successive movements— obvious predictive signification. In succeeding movements that signifi- cation is materialized. And in the process other temporal references occur, as when in the fourth movement ("March to the Scaffold") the brief recurrence of the cyclic theme explicitly calls upon our memory of its previous variants in three earlier movements. Besides such retrodictive signification, the *idée fixe* carries all three sorts of temporal reference as a sign in the last movement ("Dreams of a Witches' Sabbath"). The theme points at once back to earlier appearances in other movements, points intrafluently to other subordinate accompanying gestures concurrent with it, and points to a forthcoming restatement of itself in the orgy of sound in the dance section.

The intrafluent mode of congeneric signification commands a domi- nant place in our deliberations, and it now requires fuller consideration of its temporal characteristics. These characteristics may best be under- stood by observing their divarications in a short section of a well known masterwork, the first five phrases (mm. 1–21) of Beethoven's *Fifth Symphony* (Example 7-1). The basic musical gesture is the famous call of fate motive (mm. 1–2). Certain general features of the section are noteworthy. The forceful paired assertions of the basic gesture in octaves opens the work and sets its overall character, in Beethoven's words, of "destiny knocking at the door" (mm. 1–2, 3–4). The first two statements act as complete thesis phrases whereas subsequent statements of the basic gesture are motivic parts of larger arsis phrases. The larger phrases (mm. 6–10, 10–14, 14–21), beginning softly after the unison outbursts, amass harmonic sonorities by intersecting entries of the basic gesture, gradually enlarging the volume of musical space. The imitation—so close at one beat spaces—creates a reverberating effect. While the har- mony is static on tonic in the third phrase (mm. 6–10) and on dominant in the fourth (mm. 10–14), the harmony begins tonic-dominant alter- nation (mm. 15–18), concluding the section with its progression to a half close (mm. 19–21). The entire section exhibits a high order of redundancy through the constant reiteration of the basic gesture and its simple vari- ants.

EXAMPLE 7-1   Ludwig van Beethoven, *Fifth Symphony*, I, mm. 1–21

In all, thirteen assertions of the basic gesture or obvious variants appear (symbolized here: p_1, p_2, . . . p_{13}). Their web of temporal references at once forward and backward is remarkable. To begin p_1 (mm. 1–2) predictively signifies p_2 (mm. 3–4). In turn p_2 retrodictively indicates p_1, and it also points forward to the third phrase consisting of p_3, p_4, and p_5 (mm. 6–10). The gestures $p_{3,4,5}$ in their turn also refer retrodictively as a single larger phrase-gesture to p_2 (and p_1). Whereas the opening gesture outlines tonic harmony, the second gives dominant harmony, and the third phrase unfolds the full tonic chord. The first juxtadictive references occur with the third phrase as $p_{3,4,5}$ point to each other in their intersections within the tonic unfolding. Besides its retrodictive and its own internal references, the third phrase as a single larger gesture also points onward to the fourth phrase. Thus, the third phrase embodies all three directions of temporal reference. The references of the fourth phrase (mm. 10–14) parallel those of the third, with which it intersects (m. 10), but in the fourth phrase harmony alternates between tonic and dominant. The phrase as a whole points fore and aft, to the fifth and third phrases. Furthermore, through their overlappings, the reiterations of variants and the basic gesture weave together the fourth phrase in juxtadictive references of $p_{6,7,8}$ to one another. Last in the section, the fifth phrase (mm. 14–21; $p_{9,10,11,12,13}$) continues the tendencies set in action by the earlier two phrases. Overall the phrase points onward, signifying the section to come, especially by means of the last three chords of cadence and the last motivic gesture, p_{13} (mm. 18–21). More specifically the phrase ties together the whole section with a general retrodictive signification of the prior phrase(s). And again, separate statements of the basic gesture—$p_{9,10,11,12}$—refer concurrently to each other as they intersect (mm. 14–18). In all, the webwork of references established by the motivic gestures link together within the section, and they link together the entire section to the next one. In the musical progress of the section, the weight of sign direction must be noted as ever pointing onward, so that one is always led to feel and believe that more is to come. Taken as a single large gesture, the section is itself a predictive sign of the further action in the ensuing section, a direction of reference assured by the partial cadence on the dominant and the sustained violin I on the dominant scale degree (m. 21). Not only does the section attain meaning congenerically through its web of forward, backward, and simultaneous significations, but it also achieves in large measure its internal cohesion through them.

The importance of the three temporal directions of intrafluent refer- ences is a—if not *the*—most substantial and consequential characteristic of musical meaning. No adequate explanation of a musical work can be given without taking into account the essential aspects of congeneric semantics, which we have identified as the intrafluent designations and temporal directions of gesture signs. Those characteristics are universal in meaningful music, whether composed in full or to various extents improvised or aleatoric resultants. They are not peculiar to any one style system or one music of a single culture. They are based upon the most fundamental processes of human sentience and intelligent behavior, by which anything achieves the status of meaningful experience. Other basic ramifications of congeneric meaning now demand attention, and we must turn to them.

Iconicity, Coherence
and the Sensuous Surface

So far our exploration of congeneric meaning has been through its semantic dimension. Some investigation of the syntactic dimension will reveal much about the nature of musical coherence, although it will leave much to be discussed later. It is, after all, because one part of a piece may iconically signify another that the piece may be endowed by its composer with the larger portion of its coherence. The *coherence* of a composition may itself be regarded as its consistency in integrating each and every gesture or element of a gesture into an organized whole in which (1) no fragment could be omitted without injuriously altering the whole and (2) no fragment stands alone without relation to at least one or more equivalent fragments. A coherent whole sticks together because the whole is implicit in the fragments and each fragment does appear with connection to others. The basis for cohesive connection lies in the correspondence—the agreement of similarity or congruity—between fragments. The cohesion of the whole is made intelligible by its fragments being consistent with each other, by the compatibility of the fragments rather than any of their apparent contrast or opposition. Agreeing in certain properties rather than contrasting, sameness rather than diversity, make for consistency and coherence.

Chief among the roots of coherence are those elemental sonic and rhythmic properties that are shared in common even by fragments that might be diverse in important respects. Frequent recurrence or universality of those sensuous properties—the surface qualities—integrate fragments that otherwise might be divergent. The qualities heard as the sensuous surface of gestures' sonorous motion have three important characteristics: (1) they may be more or less persistent in temporal and spatial extent; (2) they may be relatively intense—strong or weak— stimuli; and (3) they may be comparatively well blended together or not. And for the various elemental properties of a musical gesture we need to consider those characteristics.

The employment of a single tone system contributes to consistency, for it allows the origination of all melodic and harmonic events from a common basic set of pitch classes. A basic set such as a mode, a scale, or a serial set of twelve pitch classes may give rise to horizontal and vertical gestures sharing in recurrent intervallic pitch relationships. Nowhere is this more evident than in the tonal music of the past few centuries: the use of the major-minor scalar system together with mostly three and four note chords built up in thirds provides considerable melodic-harmonic integration—quite aside from the more complex formation rules of syntax for functional tonality. Thus, in the foregoing excerpt from Beethoven's *Fifth Symphony* (Example 7-1) a surface coherence is gained at once for the tone structure in virtue of the persistent basic set of pitch classes in the particular form of the C minor mode used (*i.e.*, c, d, e, f, f♯, g, a♭, b). The dominant melodic intervals are the minor third and scalar seconds. The harmonies, constructed in thirds (the generic identity intervals of the basic gesture), yield the conventional tertial chords. All melodic and harmonic content of the excerpt is derived straightforwardly from the basic set, which allowed the composer to blend the atomistic pitch elements into a cohering surface of sound. It is important to note in this connection that similar melodic-harmonic consistency is generated in more recent times by utilization of a basic set of twelve pitch classes and ordered interval classes in serial music. But whatever the stylistic system, the function of a basic set of pitch classes or interval classes is to confer coherence and comprehensibility upon all simultaneous or successive linear and vertical events. In consequence, successive musical gestures are related sensuously because they are presenting over and over within a context the same basic sets of sounds, however varied the structuring of them becomes.

With respect to timbre, the iconic relation of surface qualities also plays a useful role. The instruments or voices chosen by a composer for a work predetermine a universe not only of audible sounds but of source qualities peculiar to the sound-generating bodies. So even where the other elemental dimensions of sound may or may not vary, a surface coherence can be established by a selection from among the available timbres. And for the whole of a work the extension of timbres within the universe of instrumentation gives a consistent realm of qualities. Again, in the excerpt from the *Fifth Symphony* (Example 7-1), a basic orchestration pervades the section with ease, fusing the whole by the surface quality of dominating string timbres. Similar use of basic agogic patterns integrates durational values. We readily recall in the Beethoven the intense and ubiquitous motivic gesture's agogic formula (· · ·–), which so completely blends together that dimension of the sound. And despite its obvious variance in incompleteness (· · ·) and augmentation, that formula ties the cadential final phrase (mm. 18–21) to the others before it. Dynamic levels and articulation or phrasing, chordal volumes and densities, and textures all have their place, too, in making for coherence through surface qualities. Each may be used to bestow a certain consistency upon even variegated gestures insofar as it remains constant. Note, for example, in the Beethoven the fortissimo grouping the first assertions of the basic gesture, the piano unification of the subsequent phrases, the piano crescendo to fortissimo of the closing phrase. Moreover, scrutiny of the detached articulations shows how a single quality there molds together the whole section. Further coherence for the section's middle phrases, in contrast to its outer ones, is given by their apparent contrapuntal activation of harmonic texture as against the outer phrases' more strictly homophonic texture.

From the foregoing discussion we may draw up three observations about coherence with its roots in elementary musical properties. To the extent that a set of sonic or rhythmic properties *persists* from one fragment to another, then that set of properties acts as fragment-integrating for the sensuous surface of musical motion. To the extent that such a set of properties is *intense* in different fragments, then it acts as fragment-integrating. To the extent that such a set of properties *fuses* together frgaments, then it acts as fragment-integrating.

As one surely should begin to see, the sensuous surface of qualities in musical motion is a most patent ground for musical coherence. Sets of surface qualities may be universal, that is, they may be persistent or intense or fused throughout a composition. Whereas universality of surface qualities confers something of a pandemic coherence, lesser degrees of interpenetration, dominance, and comingling of those sets of qualities give corresponding orders of cohesion to a work's sensuous surface. Within the whole, one fragment—one musical gesture—becomes compatible with another in the proportion that the two display the same or similar sets of surface qualities. Inasmuch as otherwise diverse gestures are made compatible by partaking of common sets of surface qualities, they are consistent with one another. Thus, coherence of the musical work as a whole is in large part a function of the ubiquity of local and regional surface qualities. As the surface qualities from one musical gesture to another are resemblant they permeate, strengthen, and fuse the gesture fragments together, creating a unified and coherent surface of sonorous motion. However, I am not asserting that coherence is a function of iconic signs alone. Far from it, for musical indices (to be considered in the next chapter) contribute greatly to musical cohesion, as do syntactic signs and the logical operators in musical counterparts.

Some Syntactic Relations in Music

In addition to the force of local sonic and rhythmic properties to unify the sensuous surface of musical motion, there remain to be considered the principal cases of relational reference within the syntactic dimension of congeneric meaning. These cases involve us in the logical syntax of musical structures—the kinds of gestures or formal units, their orderings and relations in designs built up by the similarity and contrast of formal segments. In this undertaking we can observe the role of iconic signs in establishing coherence, and we shall see something of the prominent place that diversity has in facilitating analysis. (In a later chapter we shall delve into the operations of the logical constants as they are presented in music. Just now more obvious matters call for attention.)

It is entirely possible that we could hear a whole composition without ever coming to know what even its foremost segments are. That is, an altogether sensuous tone bath, giving us an affective-conative glow is possible. Doubtless some persons at the concerts have such meaningful musical experiences, if one places store in reports of writers such as Vernon Lee and Otto Ortman.[1] We can, in contrast, respond not only to a cohesive aggregate but also to its parts. In this case, by dint of using our wits, we can perceive further that fragmental portions are related. By sufficient application and hearings we can discover parts within parts, their relations to each other and the larger context. It is this latter sort of listening rather than passive hearing that is the indispensable orientation for a comprehension of the larger syntactical meanings of musical structures.

Grasping part-whole relations calls upon us to notice, observe, and analyze. Realizing what the main syntactical meanings of a work are presupposes an interested and attentive attitude. We not only must hear things but notice while doing so. We must perceive and heed what happens as musical gestures occur. We observe carefully, scrutinizing and selectively focusing attention in order to discriminate one gesture from another, one section from another, through comparison and contrast. In this process we analyze the composition to discover parts within wholes and to pair parts in relation. It is noticing, observing, and analyzing that yields meaningful experience of music's syntax. To gain an awareness of a work's significations we must show enough interest to invest sustained attention.

Among valuable things to notice about apparent wholes usually is their divisibility, the cues for which often lie in characteristics of contrast and diversity. For present purposes of ease in handling material, let us examine a relatively short musical "whole," the basic musical gesture used as the subject of J. S. Bach's *Fugue XXII* in B♭ minor from *The Well-Tempered Clavier*, Part I (Example 7-2, mm. 1–4). Several factors allow

EXAMPLE 7-2   J. S. Bach, Fugue XXII, Wohltemperirte Clavier, I, mm. 1–4 (subject)

us to discriminate the main segments within this whole. First, there is a caesura of one quarter's rest which calls attention to a division of the subject into a head motive A and a tail motive B (m. 1 versus mm. 2–4). Also there is a contrast in interval structures and registers between the motives. Motive A is comprised of one interval of a descending fourth, whereas motive B consists of seven intervals in diatonic seconds. Here we notice also that A is shorter by half than B. But a further distinction is readily made about motive B: it divides into two figures B[1] and B[2], a downward scalar movement followed by its transposed retrograde inversion in ascent. Then, too, the motivic gestures contrast in degree by the relatively lower register of A and the higher register of B, marked off by the space of the dissonant disjuncture of a minor ninth between them. In addition, the motives are diversified by the relative length of the tones within each, with those of A being twice as long as those of B. Moreover, the metric placements vary importantly. Motive A is situated metrically as a thesis-stasis (⁄~), and B is a disjunction of arsis-thesis (∪∪∪⁄; ∪∪∪⁄). Dynamics, timbre, and articulation appear uniform, although performance practice suggests further differences in those parameters as well. Although any assumed dynamic is uniformly possible (all p or all mf, and so on), it is equally possible to perform A as louder than B, for example. Similarly, articulation might be equal throughout with all tones played sustained, or taking the clavichord or the harpsichord into account, A might be relatively detached and B more legato. The two are given timbral definition to some extent by virtue of the registral change (and this might even be heightened by contrasts in use of keyboards and registration of stops on the harpsichord).

As we have seen, then, in taking cognizance of simple contrasts we can analyze an aggregate into a number of pieces. Under scrutiny a whole is rationally divisible. And yet the musical whole coheres, despite the diversities it embraces, because the sensuous surface is formed exclusively from basic sets of internally resemblant sonic and rhythmic properties. In the Bach the pitches all belong to a minor mode (b♭, c, d♭, e♭, f, g♭ . . .), the timbres all belong to the clavier, the durations belong essentially to the spondee (– –) and pyrrhic (· ·) agogic schemata, the dynamics and articulating phrasing are uniform or of obvious sets. By partitioning forms into syntactical units and then by comparing and contrasting them as sets of characteristics, remarks of the foregoing kind hold for whatever context of music we choose to submit to analysis. Not simply basic musical gestures are susceptible to this analytic process; so also are the formal units from figures up to entire compositions in several movements.

One relation involved in whole-part analysis, *inclusion* (symbol: ⊂), stands out and requires some contemplation. For our purposes we may say that one formal unit A is included in another B provided that every element of the one A necessarily also is a member of the other B.[2] Thus, in the Bach, for example (Example 7-2), the basic musical gesture taken as the subject S includes within its field the sub-units motives A and B. Moreover, in turn B includes two figures B^1 and B^2. Surely, without too much pondering, we see that the half notes $b♭^1$ and f^1 of A must belong also to S, that the quarter notes $g♭^2 - f^2 - e♭^2 - d♭^2$ of figure B^1 belong to B and also to S as do the remaining quarter notes of B^2, $c^2 - d♭^2 - e♭^2 - f^2$. Three points to glean from these observations so far on inclusion and formal units are implicit but not yet stated. They are: (1) every formal unit is included in itself (*i.e.*, S ⊂ S, a ⊂ a, b ⊂ b); (2) if one formal unit is included in a second, and that in a third, then the first likewise is included in the third (*i.e.*, B^1 ⊂ B ⊂ S → B^2 ⊂ S); and (3) it is not consistent or possible to include a larger formal unit in a smaller one (*i.e.*, although it holds that B^1 ∈ S, it fails that S ∈ B^1). That is, then, the inclusion relation is reflexive, transitive, and asymmetrical. And so we see that in discerning the reaches of the inclusion relation we isolate formal units and find noteworthy ways in which they are involved with each other. Of course, with the inclusion relation of part to whole, genuine signification arises. The included fragment may indicate the totality and vice versa, which gives rise to earlier or later congeneric references of development.

At this juncture we might venture a cursory listing of the main kinds of formal units often identified in simple analyses of musical syntax. Their classification forms a neat hierarchy of inclusions progressing from sets of the smallest to the largest kinds of context, to wit: single sound $\subset$ interval (durational or pitch) $\subset$ figure $\subset$ motive $\subset$ phrase $\subset$ period (or chain of phrases) $\subset$ double period (or chain of periods) $\subset$ section $\subset$ movement (or piece) $\subset$ work of several movements. Rather than the terms "period," "section," or the like, sometimes the terms "theme" and "theme group" are used. In addition, at the level of "movement" the terms for operatic music vary with references to "scenes," which are included in "acts." Our adumbration needs stop short of detailing criteria for each kind of unit, however, so that we may pursue our discussion of other relations of consequence.[3]

Another and most important relation found through attentive listening is that of *equality*, by means of which some kind of identity is displayed. The identity is discovered in musical experience when we think and feel "it again" of a stimulus—whether "it" is a single sonic or rhythmic property, a short gesture, or a large section of music. The mental act is one of recognition. And, indeed, the recognition of identities is fundamental to thinking and to mental evolution.[4] In itself equality is the relation of being the same. Whatever as a musical object is an identity is also an individuality—a set of characteristics that sustains the relation of maximum resemblance so that two or more expressions may be recognized as the same in substance, property, or form.[5] Although complete or total likeness may be an ideal limit not quite attainable in fact, still some pairs of objects will come closer to it than others.[6] (For examples: compare the case of two phonograph records of the same performance, or compare two playings of the same recording and notice that, all other things being equal, the records and the performances are indistinguishable.) Were there "two" objects completely similar to each other in their entire spatio-temporal existence as well as in all other ways, then it would seem inconsistent to think of them as "two" rather than one. For practical purposes we can consider identity conceptually in this or that respect, according to whether specified conditions or a set of determining characteristics are met. Thus, we recognize musical identity if, in the relevant respects, the objects falling under one concept, musical gesture X, are in one-to-one correspondence with those objects falling under the concept, musical gesture Y. Two musical gestures are equal as formal units if and only if they have the same elements.[7]

The most important points to grasp about equality are summed up in the so-called laws of equality.[8] The reflexive law of equality may be stated for musical gestures: every gesture is equal to itself. *I.e.*, $x = x$. Whatever x may be, x is equal to x. The commutative law of equality may be stated for musical gestures: if two gestures are identical, then they are equal to each other regardless of their order. *I.e.*, $(x = y) \supset (y = x)$. Whatever x and y may be severally, x is equal to y in all orderings. The transitive law of equality may be stated for musical gestures: if a pair of gestures are identical and one of them is identical with a third gesture, then the remaining gesture of the pair is equal to the third. *I.e.*, $(x = y) \supset (y = z) \supset (x = z)$. If x and y are equal, and if y and z are equal, then so also are x and z equal.

In due time we shall augment the group of relations necessary for analysis by adding the concept of material equivalence and the principle of substitution or "development." Already there are concepts at hand to follow up, for the inclusion and equality relations help account for much congeneric meaning.

In small contexts comprised of figures, motives, and phrases the inclusion and equality relations are embedded in iconically referential expressions based on the *principle of immediate repetition*—(1) by simple repetition (Example 7-3, Franz Joseph Haydn, *Symphony No. 104*,

EXAMPLE 7-3 Franz Joseph Haydn, *Symphony No. 104*, I, mm. 1–4.

EXAMPLE 7-4 Wolfgang Amadeus Mozart, *Piano Sonata*, K.547a, I, mm. 32–39

EXAMPLE 7-5 George Frederick Handel, *Suite IV*, "Courante," mm. 1–12

I, mm. 1–4), (2) by transposed repetition (Example 7-4, Wolfgang Amadeus Mozart, *Piano Sonata*, K. 547a, I, mm. 32–35 = 36–39), (3) by sequential repetition (Example 7-5, George Frederick Handel, *Suite No. IV*, "Courante," mm. 1–12), and (4) by continuous repetition, as in homophonic accompaniments (Example 7-6, Franz Schubert, "Gretchen am Spinnrade," mm. 1–6), not to mention ostinati such as many primitive and popular musics employ *ad nauseam*. The intrafluent references of gestures in immediate repetition are patently tautologous. Yet coherence of reiterated formal units is a function of just their brute restatement

EXAMPLE 7-6   Franz Schubert, *Gretchen am Spinnrade*, mm. 1–6

or redundancy. By redundancy a gesture is presented more than would be minimally necessary to convey the import of the gesture simply in order to affirm the message and insure that the listener cannot mistake what that message is.[9] Similar remarks apply to immediate repetition of larger formal units such as periods and entire sections, which needs no further comment here. But a more fertile principle of repetition does need attention.

Repetition after intervening departure or contrast of a set of gestures, *the principle of return*, establishes coherence of the larger compositional design. Admitting for minor deviations such as transposition of tonal levels and connective adjustments, the essential identity of sections allows the listener to integrate the whole of his experience. The return of a series of gestures after digression helps to knit together the diverse larger acts by drawing attention to the similarity of major tendencies. It is a fecund principle of syntax. Return yields a great deal more. Although temporal order of gestures does not affect equivalence or equality relations, order in time does bear on the comprehensive sense of the music. Reappearance of identities affords a more general application of redundancy in assuring not only the reception of the message but also opportunity to respond anew because of the insight gained by a now enlarged perspective and acquaintance. These increments in experience enable the listener (as well as the composer and the performer) to adopt new attitudes toward the initial gestures and to probe for additional meanings and allusions which possibly were not perceived on first hearing. Thus, a return of a section gives one room to confirm or deny inferences made earlier about the implications of gestures and the attitudes they seemed to convey. The return permits occasion for recognition, comparison and contrast, reflection and deeper analysis, and discrimination of further inclusions and equalities. In short, a reprise of material opens the doorway for the perspicacious listener to move into a fuller comprehension of the larger act's meaning.

There are relatively few different ways in which musical forms may be ordered in a temporal series with a small but determined number of major sections. Historically the basic procedures and schemes for resembling or contrasting of sections have each yielded a much larger number of types. Two main genera may be indicated: the *homogeneous* kind of design, in which the same basic sections recur in repetition, and the *heterogeneous* kind of form, in which diverse sections are integrated. Each genus may be described as having two main species, and each of those species contains many differentiae. In the homogeneous genera are included the continuous repetition designs and the varied repetition designs. Permutational forms with alternations or interversions of sections are one species of heterogeneous form, and free forms with continuous introduction of new segments constitute its other species. By way of a curtailed listing, the various species might be grouped as follows. Continuous repetition designs (a, a′, a″, . . .) would include among their differentiae such unifying procedures and designs as the ostinato, the fourteenth-century isorhythmic motet, the strophic song, and jazz "blues." The much richer species of varied repetition designs would contain among its differentiae procedures and designs such as those of many thirteenth-century organa, the canon, caccia, the fifteenth- and sixteenth-century madrigal and motet, many suite movements of the late Renaissance and early Baroque, chorale partitas and variations, ground bass and strophic bass, chaconne and passacaglia, ricercare, canzone, fugue and invention, baroque bipartite form, and the theme and variations. By contrast, the heterogeneous forms' permutational species include such differentiae as the binary design ($\|$: A :$\|$: B :$\|$), the rounded binary ($\|$: A :$\|$: BA :$\|$), the simple ternary and aria da capo (ABA), the four part song form (AABA), the five part song form (ABACA), the rondo or rondo-sonata (ABACABA), the sonata form—$\|$: A(a, b, c):$\|$B (devel. A) $\|$ A $\|$—as well as such early bar forms as the fourteenth-century madrigal, the twelfth- to fourteenth-century ballade (AAB or AABB) and virelai (or ballata)—AB (i.e., bb) AA and AB (i.e., bba) ABABA, respectively—the Renaissance chanson, and, in addition, the rondellus and round. Under the rubric of combinatorial or freely compounded forms might be included the earlier medieval organa, through-composed song forms, the recitative, rhapsodies or fantasies, as well as recent aleatory procedures.

The syntactic importance of the two main formal genera does not lie in their classification so much as in their ordering force. With respect to their orderings, both homogeneous and heterogeneous organizations relate well formed sections in predictive and retrodictive significations, which confer coherence upon the formal whole. In homogeneous cases the relatedness and coherence is usually most obvious. A leading species of homogeneous form, the strophic song, displays identities with patent predictive and retrodictive references in terms of the musical repetition setting each successive verse. The tautologous iconic significations virtually guarantee coherence. For example, in "Nähe des Geliebten" of Franz Schubert a short introduction of two measures is followed by four immediate repetitions of the main section, a straightforward strophic setting of the corresponding set of Goethe's stanzas (Example 7-7). The larger coherent relationship, identity of sections, is self-evident: $A^1 = A^2 = A^3 = A^4$. Embedded within the larger scheme of musical tauto-

EXAMPLE 7-7   Franz Schubert, *Nähe des Geliebten*

logies are interesting reverberations of less exact similarities, which also contribute to the taut internal relatedness of the song. The main section includes four phrases of varied but related length. The outermost pair of phrases (1 and 4) are two measures long whereas the innermost pair are one measure each. Moreover, all four of the included phrases share in common other features of importance. Pitch contours of the vocal part are rather alike—descent followed by ascent. Accompaniment figures also in the prevalent triplet repeated notes and essential recurrence (mm. 2–5; 6–9) of the fundamental functional harmonic progression (tonic-subdominant-dominant-tonic function chords). Substitution of pyhrric repeated notes and more extended weaving about of contour (directional inversion of m. 6 in m. 7) make for greater differentiation of the last phrase. In all, then, both at the phrase level and section level coherence is achieved by important resemblances and identity respectively, the one level strengthening the other.

Heterogeneous designs marked by the principle of return contain the chief classic and romantic era patterns, the rondo and sonata form. The sonata form may be taken as the class representative. Through considering it, we can take account of the main syntactic features of congeneric meaning generated by the design class.

The sonata form design may be divided for analytic purposes into an expository section (I), a developmental section (II), and a recapitulatory section (III). In the classic concerto and earlier sonata forms a re-exposition (I^1) may also be included. Each of the three major sections may contain a number of sub-sections, usually distinguished by divergent tonal levels or functions as well as by diverse thematic content most often. (There are, however, monothematic designs in which tonal levels, texture, and the like constitute the main contrasts.) The normal sub-sections within the exposition include the so-called first theme group (p), the second theme group (q), and the closing group (r) (see Figure 7-1). Each sub-section in turn may contain a number of distinct formal segments or gestures. The recapitulation consists of the essential return of sub-sections from the exposition (with the requisite transposition of tonal levels and connective adjustments). The development involves a number of segments that act as a departure from the exposition in order to develop implications of the principal thematic gestures by substitution of variants, expansions, and eliminations (p_x . . ., q_x . . ., r_x . . .). In many cases the three main sections are enclosed by two further segments, an introduction to the expositions and a coda to the recapitulation. In terms of proportions a large number of plans are to be found, wherein symmetries between sections arise on such bases as lengths, textures, orchestrations, tonal levels, and so on. And yet certain more general significations and logical relations in the sonata form design already are evident. Foremost of these are (1) the basic identity of sections in exposition and re-exposition as well as (2) the essential identity of exposition and recapitulation ($I = I^1 = III$). Lesser but very high degrees of resemblance tie the exposition and recapitulation together with the development (I R II I II R II). Similar comments may apply to the introduction and coda as they may be tied to the three principal sections. All

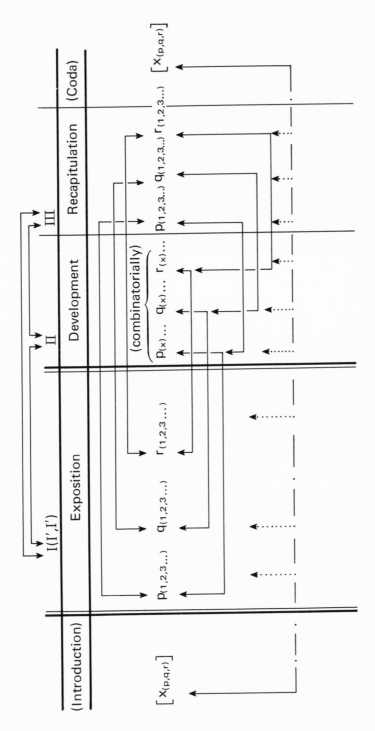

Figure 7-1. Sectional design of sonata form, showing sectional and gestural relatedness (intrafluent references)

these intrafluent references, predictive and retrodictive alike, may be exhibited diagrammatically (Figure 7-1).

Our beginning look into syntax and congeneric meaning would be incomplete if at least one more relation were not given thought, and that relation is *equivalence* (symbol: ≡). For common discourse we tend to use the word "equivalent" to indicate of two (or more) expressions that one has essentially the same value as the other in some respect: that is, one expression has the same result or meaning as another in a given context, even though the two apparently may differ in some other ways. Note, however, that a statement of equivalence does not necessarily denote that two expressions mean exactly the same thing in all respects (*e.g.*, the differences in comprehensive enrichment of meaning due to temporal relationships in earlier and later statements of otherwise equivalent gestures, discussed before). Rather, what is involved in equivalent expressions is that, if one object or set has a relevant property or properties, then so also has the other. Philosophers are wont to make the relevant property the same truth value (*i.e.*, either truth or falsity but not both).[10] This leads us to define equivalence as "material equivalence" or mutual implication. Thus, one expression p implies another q and in turn the latter q implies the former p: $(p \supset q) \cdot (q \supset p)$. Accordingly, p is equivalent to q $(p \equiv q)$. And so we may speak of musical gestures. When each of two musical gestures implies the other, then the two are equivalent. So as we find that there are two or more ways of musically expressing fundamentally the same thing, we are dealing with equivalent gestures.

What is most important about the equivalence relation in music is this: if one gesture is equivalent to another, then the one may be substituted for the other without affecting the aesthetic truth value of the situation. Whenever a composer may use one gesture he also may use the other. And composers do just that. How? Simply by the transformation of a given gesture into one of its variants.[11] That is to say, a musical gesture may be developed. Indeed, the hallmark of a composer with great expressive powers and technical skills is revealed largely in his development of the musical ideas within each work. Musical development itself is unfolding, growth, or working out changes in the character of a basic musical gesture. To develop a gesture is to change it. It is to substitute a new version of a gesture for the original.

We may regard each musical gesture syntactically as a "variable." It may be taken as a symbol or form. And, as a variable form, a basic musical gesture may be replaced in the progress of a composition by any one of its variants. Each variant is obtained by applying one or more developmental operations to the original gesture or to some mutation of the original. In itself each variant is a substitute for the original and related to it by resemblance. Moreover, each variant is marked by its own distinctive expressive character.

In developing a musical gesture, the composer may regard it from a technical perspective as a variable form and substitute an equivalent variant for the original. From an aesthetic perspective, in developing a gesture the composer is regarding it as a basis for deriving a new expressive value to be used to affect listeners in specific ways.

The domain of a musical gesture seems incredibly large: it includes all ways in which that variable may be developed. There are at least ten fundamental ways, ten developmental operations. Therefore, the number of ways to develop a gesture through combined operations is 10! or 3,628,800. That is quite a few more ways than one can expect to occur in any piece. But just what are those ten fundamental operations of development? They are inversion, retrogradation, retrograde inversion, augmentation, diminution, partition, interversion, exclusion, inclusion, and textural change. Each device may be applied to alter properties of a gesture's sonorous motion—i.e., changes in elements of pitch, duration and tempo, intensity, timbre, and the like. Single sounds or silences may be affected, but often it is the intervallic relationships that are changed. On careful inspection it would be seen that the developmental operations do, in the main, correspond to the application of elementary laws and theorems in the theory or calculus of formal logic.[12] But here let us give a brief listing and definition to the main kinds of developing operation.

Inversion is turning upside down, changing position by substituting ascending intervals for descending ones of the same size and vice versa (melodic inversion). Or it is the changing of higher elements for lower ones (harmonic inversion). Or it is the substitution by complementation of larger durations for equivalent smaller ones and vice versa within the combined values of largest and smallest values (durational inversion). *Retrogradation* is the reversed ordering of elements in a series (pitches, durations, dynamics, timbres, and so on). *Retrograde inversion* is the combined reversed order and turning upside down of elements in a series. *Augmentation* is the repetition of an ordered set of intervals with their arithmetic or proportional enlargement (durational, pitched, dynamic, or timbral forms, and so on). *Diminution* is the repetition of an ordered set of intervals with their arithmetic or proportional reduction (durational, pitched, and so on). *Partition* is to divide into parts or fragments, apportioning and distributing the elements by interposed caesuras or cadences. *Interversion* is the interchanging or diverting of events another way on the repetition of a series by changing the internal order of elements. Known also as transposition, interversion utilizes permutation or combinatorial reordering of either sonic or durational elements.

Exclusion or elimination is the shortening, the logical simplification, of a set of events on repetition by selective taking away of elements. Exclusion has many forms, a few of which are: (a) *elision*—cutting out internal or intermediate events, (b) *curtailment*—cutting off the ending, (c) *decapitation*—cutting off the head or beginning, (d) *verticalization*— bringing together at once a former series of events, compressing successive elements into a simultaneity, (e) *ellipsis*—omitting one or more connective elements from an extended sequence of separable but connected gestures, (f) *synopsis*—shortened repetition of a whole in which only the most typical elements occur.

Inclusion or extension is the expansion, enlargement or prolongation of a set of events when it is repeated by the selective addition of elements to the original. Some of the forms of inclusion are: (a) *interpolation*— inserting intermediate elements into a series, (b) *appending*—adding elements to the end of a series, (c) *prefixing* —adding elements to the beginning of a series, (d) *horizontalization*—unfolding successively the elements in a simultaneity, (e) *imitation* or *absorption*—repeating in close succession of a gesture by a different part in a contrapuntal texture, (f) *free absorption*—relegating to the background or accompaniment of a gesture on its repetition while bringing another gesture or variant into the foreground, (g) *corrective interjection*—the interruption of the statement of a gesture to insert an altered fragment within the whole.

Textural change is the representation of a gesture formerly in one texture (monodic, homophonic, or contrapuntal) in another texture.

An example of substitution of gestural equivalents might reveal more directly the nature of developing gestures while retaining coherence. In the *Duo Concertante* for violin and *violoncello* of George Rochberg, which may be described as a heterogeneous design, the main theme group's second period (mm. 9–15) and its recapitulation (mm. 175–182) are equivalent segments (Example 7-8a and 7-8b). Although closely similar, the segments also contrast with each other in many ways. A number of substitutions appear in the return. Among the aurally more subtle are: replacement of sixteenths (m. 9) by quintuplets (m. 175) along with added accent and intensified legato bowing; use of subito piano with variegated pizzicatti and arco attacks (m. 176) for equivalent effects earlier (m. 10). More substantial alterations involve complex durational values in diminutions (m. 179 ≡ m. 13; m. 180 vln. ≡ m. 13; m. 182 ≡ mm. 14–15, and m. 181 vlc.) and augmentations (m. 180, vlc. ≡ m. 13; m. 182, vlc. ≡ mm. 14–15) as well as considerable inclusions (m. 177, vlc. and m. 178, vln. ≡ *mm. 11*) and exclusions (m. 182 ≡ mm. 14–15) along with horizontalizations (m. 178, vlc. ≡ m. 111; m. 180, vlc. ≡ m. 13). Although not all transformations are noted here, at least enough is indicated to show artistically employed operations of development as an equivalent variant is substituted for the original gesture. Despite fairly extended changes in the return, the exposition is clearly in resemblance to it, creating coherence within the larger design by means of symmetrical intrafluent reference of the gestures.

The techniques of variable substitution are numerous, and of those only the more basic kinds of developing operations have been mentioned. For the composer the hoary maxim on when and where to develop a

EXAMPLE 7-8a   George Rochberg, *Duo Concertante*, mm. 9–15

EXAMPLE 7-8b   George Rochberg, *Duo Concertante*, mm. 175–182

gesture has always been, "When restating an idea, vary it." But which kind of replacement is appropriate? From the viewpoint of logical composition, the answer probably is that the variant should be shown to emerge as a clear implicate of the original, by such rewriting of the variable form that the explicit statement of the variant appears as an undeniable conclusion to be drawn. Thus, the only sensible action is to make the substitution that will produce the desired result in terms of self-tested and listener-expected responses. But more specifically the rider of some logicians probably could be attached to the act that, although any equivalent may be substituted whenever desired, the substitution should be made consistently throughout a given context or formal unit.[13] In any event we see that the substitution selected is tied to the need to achieve a certain expressive effect, and this must be done by matching the operational changes to the degree of alteration the effect implies. In addition, the selection is tied not only to the immediate context but also to the ramifications for the larger formal design. The guideline of variation upon restatement is involved with the more basic principles of immediate repetition and return after departure. So when higher coherence is to be achieved, accentuation of similarities to the original gesture is implied along with making smaller and subtle changes in the elemental sonic and rhythmic properties. But if contrast is in order, then bigger changes in replacement are suggested. Furthermore, in consequence of the possible overuse of brute repetition, at least a few further observations are in order. When repetition may threaten to exhaust listeners' interest, the offending gesture must be replaced or the section—even the piece—should be terminated as an act of mercy for devoted audiences. Two kinds of replacement are available: use of a completely new and diverse gesture, or substitution of a differing but equivalent variant. Development being a matter of gradation, when several gestures or sections have ensued, then a "new" idea may be a freshly developed variant of earlier events, particularly those other than the immediately preceding ones. In larger heterogeneous designs especially there is plenty of room for use of development to obtain variety while achieving both new expressive implications and coherence through introduction of equivalents. If the composer wants to give life and organic character to his work, then he must let his gestures grow. He must develop both the basic musical gestures and the overall design of resembling and contrasting sections. Vital things grow, develop, and decay. They change. Development by substitutions makes that possible.

Notes

1 Vernon Lee, *Music and Its Lovers* (London: George Allen and Unwin Ltd., 1932), chaps. 7 and 8; Otto Ortman, "Types of Listeners," in *The Effects of Music*. ed. Max Schoen (New York: Harcourt, Brace and Co., Inc., 1927), pp. 40–43.
2 Usually the account of inclusion is more properly treated in terms of classes and sets. *E.g.*, see Harold N. Lee, *Symbolic Logic* (London: Routledge and Kegan Paul, Ltd. 1962), pp. 8, 52–57; Gottlob Frege, "A Critical Elucidation of Some Points in E. Schroeder's *Vorlesungen Ueber Die Algebra Der Logik*," *Philosophical Writings of Gottlob Frege*, ed. Peter Geach and Max Black (Oxford: Basil Blackwell, 1960), pp. 86–106.

3 For criteria on classification see Wallace Berry, *Form in Music* (Englewood Cliffs, N.J.: Prentice-Hall, Inc., 1966); Douglass Green, *Form in Tonal Music* (New York: Holt, Rinehart, and Winston, Inc., 1965); or Hugo Leichtentritt, *Musical Form* (Cambridge: Harvard University Press, 1951).

4 Brand Blanshard, *The Nature of Thought* (New York: Humanities Press, 1939), vol. 1, pp. 242–43.

5 For discussion of the theory of universals and the theory of resemblance in defining identity, see H. H. Price, *Thinking and Experience* (Cambridge: Harvard University Press, 1962), pp. 1–74.

6 Regarding Leibniz's doctrine of the identity of indiscernibles, which is evoked here, an excellent discussion appears in P. F. Strawson, *Individuals* (Garden City: Doubleday and Co., Inc., 1963), chap. 4; Cf. Price, *Thinking and Experience*, chap. 1.

7 Gottlob Frege, *The Foundations of Arithmetic*, tran. J. L. Austin, 2nd ed. rev. (Oxford: Basil Blackwell, 1959), pp. 58^e–86^e; Paul R. Halmos, *Naive Set Theory* (Princeton: D. Van Nostrand Co., Inc., 1960), p. 2—from whence our definitions in extension derive.

8 Alonzo Church, *Introduction to Mathematical Logic* (Princeton: Princeton University Press, 1956), pp. 281, 301; Clarence I. Lewis and Cooper H. Langford, *Symbolic Logic*, 2nd ed. (New York: Dover Publications, Inc., 1959), pp. 28–34.

9 Colin Cherry, *On Human Communication* (Cambridge: M.I.T. Press, 1966), pp. 19, 42, 120, 186–87; Charles E. Osgood and Thomas A. Sebeok, eds., *Psycholinguistics* (Bloomington: Indiana University Press, 1965), p. 42.

10 *E.g.*, Irving M. Copi, *Symbolic Logic*, 3rd ed. (New York: The Macmillan Company, 1967), p. 29.

11 Cf. Willard Van Orman Quine, *Elementary Logic*, rev. ed. (New York: Harper and Row, Publishers, 1965), p. 66.

12 See Alfred North Whitehead and Bertrand Russell, *Principia Mathematica to* *56, rev. ed. (Cambridge: Cambridge University Press, 1962), pp. 115–26.

13 Lee, *Symbolic Logic*, p. 35.

8

The Musical Index Sign

An *index* is a sign that guides behavior in two ways. It focuses one's attention, attracting then directing attention; and it specifies more or less the location of an object or an event in space or time.[1] An index makes us pay heed, first to itself, then to what it indicates. It acts as a preparatory stimulus inasmuch as it shows us where or when to seek something beyond itself. An index signifies what it brings to attention and locates.

Several peculiarities of indices bear on aesthetic experience. Most important is that stimuli acting as indices tend to have emotional impact. The index sign often, though not always, directs attention by what Charles S. Peirce called a "blind compulsion." An index has great immediacy and can mark emphatically the advent of an object for our experience of it, thus drawing—even forcing—us to heed it.[2] Thus, any stimulus or set of stimuli that startles or surprises may be an index because of its power to mark off two portions of experience and make us notice them. This power to startle is in itself a sufficient condition for affective arousal.[3] In fact, when we notice anything we tend to invest it with significance from past experience, by virtue of which we have come to single out the object. But in primal experience such significance is absent, and then the more vivid and extreme stimuli control attention,

Notes to this chapter begin on p. 108.

tend to leave their traces in memory, and enable us to identify them later.[4] Another peculiarity of the index is implied by the foregoing, for it suggests that the index brings out contrast, drawing attention to the difference between the sign and its signification. Although indices need not resemble their significations, still they may. Another feature of an index sign is that it locates its object by a dynamic connection involving an association by contiguity. An index points to a particular rather than general object—to something immediate, close at hand, and relatively specific, but to one thing at a time. Furthermore, we should be aware that an index also gives rise to primary sensory generalization. That is, an organism tends to be most responsive to a dominant and immediate characteristic of a set of stimuli, responding not to all properties of the object or situation; the organism tends to categorize the object stimulus in terms of its most striking property.[5] That property is an index.

In non-verbal communication pointing gestures such as those of a traffic policeman are instances of indices. Instances of designation such as directional signals on cars, book page markers, clock chimes, and the like are indices. So are such objects as buoys, beacons, or lighthouses that locate a dangerous promontory of land, reef, shoal, or channel. In verbal discourse words used in ostensive definition of egocentric particulars are indices: this, that, I, you, here, there, now, then, past, present, future, and so on.[6] Nearly all words used as indices can be defined in terms of the immediate naming function of "this."

Our conception of an index implies that not all sonic and rhythmic elements in musical gestures are equal in value. Rather, some properties attain greater prominence and immediate value than others within a well defined formal context. Those properties become index signs. We may say that *musical indices* are the salient points within musical gestures and that they mark these points for attention in themselves as well as direct attention to other more or less specific places in the gestures. Collectively sets of musical indices vividly point out the most important properties of a formal unit such as a motive, phrase, period, or section. (Obviously, a hierarchy of indexical values may arise: the greater the extent of the gesture as a formal unit, the more likely, then, that more intensive effects are required to be indices.) By investing a musical gesture with particular points of interest, the indices define the skeletal shape and outlines of the gesture. Musical index signs determine the promontories and relate them to each other; they display the structure of a gesture and give it internal cohesion. From the standpoint of a gesture's sonorous motion the indices' structural functions are to act as the starting points, the salient way points, and the terminal goal points of musical tendencies, which bind together to shape the gesture into a cohesive whole. Within the music itself the tendencies of sonorous motion are just those relatively stable dispositions to behave with apparent purpose, to move in definite directions from positions, through and to other positions or ends.[7] The musical indices give us the structure of the gesture, and by doing so they give us the structure of the gestural tendencies of sonorous motion. Musical index signs outline the boundaries of musical space-time in which the motion takes place. It might be said that the indices are the signposts along the pathway of a gesture's sonorous motion. They provide the performer and listener with a coherent map of the aesthetic experience as they undergo it. They help the listener notice, to perceive and heed, what is important. The index signs guide one's observations, giving him cues to the qualities and relations he should savor and scrutinize. They assist one in analytic discovery and discrimination of the moment. Thus, on a here-and-now, this-and-that basis of signification, the musical index signs play a structural role in forming musical gestures and syntax.

We can enumerate the principal ways in which elemental properties of gestures may appear as index signs. The ways are many, for the sonic and rhythmic properties, either singly or in combinations, may be indices. Within any well formed and defined formal unit the following properties in each of the primary dimensions of sound may be indices or parts of a complex index. In the dimension of successive pitch (melody) the candidates for indexical position are the first, last, top, and bottom pitches, the most dissonant and most consonant intervals, the inflected (tendency) tones in tonal music, and the pitches marking great or sudden register change. In the parameter of simultaneous pitches (harmony) the probable indices would be the first and last simultaneities, the highest and lowest, the most dissonant and consonant sets of intervals, those creating the largest and smallest spatial volumes, as well as those that are the most compact or sparse in density. The durational properties with indexical potential include the values of a gesture that are first, last, longest, shortest, or that in a group present the greatest density of attacks per unit, in addition to the caesura or plain articulating silence. The parallels in tempo are the fastest and slowest areas along with the places of quickening and slowing. Proper characteristics of intensity and loudness, too, such as the loudest or softest and crescendoing or decrescendoing sounds may be indices. Moreover, the qualities of timbre that might become indices include such sounds as the most shrill or piercing (ēē; ĭ), the most nasal or twangy (ā; ă; ă), the most fulsome or rich (oo; ū), noise as against tone, pure sets of qualities (families versus mixed timbres), contrast within source families (*e.g.*, membranes versus metal in percussion), and especially the comparatively unusual effects (col legno, rattling valves, flutter, and the like). Furthermore, qualities of articulation have potential: the most detached or most legato sounds, the slurred in contrast to those, and the fullest body on attack, release, or steady state. In addition, the change of texture (monodic, homophonic, or polyphonic) may signify indexically.

The musical indices may be taken as including those effects corresponding to what theorists call the "structural tones" or "outlining" functions of melody and harmony.[8] But to this observation some qualification is needed: we would not identify the idea of such skeletal tones and chords in the background of music with the musical index, because the concept of musical index admits rhythmic, temporal, textural, timbral, dynamic and other accentual elements on the surface or foreground in addition to tonic accents. However, we may say that the skeletal melodic tones and basic harmonic progressions will often have the force of abstracting from the structural indices a general pitch structure. Hence, the index signs contain and are significant of the structural tones in the Schenker and Hindemith modes of musical analysis.

We should see that indicating the structure and integration of gestures is the force that indices have. The more dynamic elements—those points that jut out melodically and protrude harmonically or that are conspicuous rhythmically, texturally, and so on—are the ones that define and delineate that to which we are to give the most attention. In short, then, musical indices are created by (1) extremes and (2) sharp contrasts of sonic and rhythmic properties. Within the well defined formal context, these structural cues consist of the musical forms of accent (*i.e.*, tonic, volumetric, ordinal, agogic, dynamic, timbral, articulatory, and textural accent).

At this juncture it is valuable to connect several points relating the musical index signs and affection. It should be clear already that the extreme properties and sharp contrasts which define the gestural structure also have affective functions. Indeed, already we have seen that all sign functioning involves an affective component in that instinctual responses (emotional and conative) are brought into play in sensory perception, in the cognition and recognition of any stimulus as significant. The fundamental function of any sign, including musical indices, is emotional. Moreover, we have seen as well that whatever is known by acquaintance, and significant in that sense, is grasped by intuition, by directly felt experience. The elemental musical properties, which include just those properties acting as musical indices, are objects of acquaintance. And furthermore we have seen that one of the sufficient conditions for emotional response to stimuli is that the stimuli are extreme or they offer surprise by great contrast, tripping the brain's startle mechanism. Again, the properties taken as musical indices are just such emotional stimuli.

EXAMPLE 8-1   Charles Ives, *Majority*, mm. 1–8

EXAMPLE 8-1 *continued*

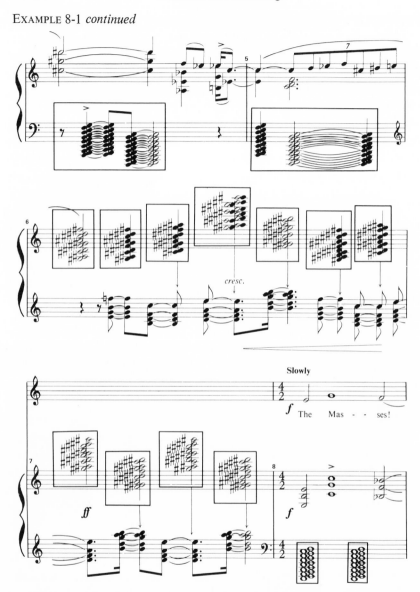

On all approaches noted, then, we find affirmation for the fact that musical indices are potential emotional stimuli.

Surely the best explanation of musical indices is to exhibit a segment of music in which index signs determine the structure of a fairly complex and extended gesture. The introduction of Charles Ives' song "Majority" provides a good example (Example 8-1, mm. 1–8). In the introduction we find tonic, agogic, dynamic, and registral accents all contributing to delineation of the main tendencies of sonorous motion. "Black-key" (mm. 1 and 6) and "white-key" (mm. 2 and 8) tone-clusters play especially prominent roles. Their tonic, volumetric, and mass accents are supported by agogic stress, dynamic stress, and registral contrast. The top tones (as pitch classes) of the black-key clusters are associated in contiguity by a descending scalar tendency leading from a♯ (m. 1), through g♯ (m. 1) and f♯ (mm. 1 and 6), to their goal of e (m. 8), the entry point of the voice. Each of those index tones and clusters forcibly calls for attention, then guides it to the next, which follows a wholetone below. The lowermost tones of the bass chord supporting the black-key cluster at the opening (m. 1) and the conjunctive closing chord (m. 8) of the segment reveal a similar descending stepwise relation, f♯ to e. The outermost tendencies together define the main musical motion. Within the main outlines a number of sub-gestures occur and present lesser but important complementary tendencies of motion in ascent toward the whole section's goal, pitch class e.

Foremost of these is the large lowest register movement of ascent by step from the bass c of the F-major eleventh chord (m. 1) through the white-key cluster built on d (m. 2) to the terminal cluster on e (m. 8). Two other similar tendencies appear in the upper register. The lesser upward tendency from the pitch class a♯ of the first cluster to b, c, d, and e (all in m. 1) should be noticed. Likewise, the top line's movement of pitch classes c♯ to d♯ (m. 4) implies continuation into e (m. 8), while the f♯ (m. 4) also heralds the high black-key clusters topped also by f♯'s (mm. 6 and 7). A more remote possible indexical function of the top g♯ to the second cluster (m. 1) might be observed: it may be taken as pointing to the voice part's entry motive and second tone g♮ (m. 8). Be that as it may, however, it is important to see and hear in the example as a whole that the indices function to locate spatial positions of pitch classes set apart by steps (mostly whole tones). Equally important to recognize is that the indexical pitch classes display a dominant tendency of descent in wholetones into a conjunction with the pitch class (e), on which the voice enters. The secondary indices exhibit the contrasting tendency of line moving upward into the same pitch class. Figures 8-1 and 8-2 display the set of indices and their connected significations. The normal convention of using octave register transfers within pitch classes has been followed (notice arrows in the figures).

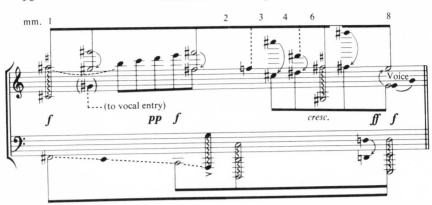

Figure 8-1. Indexical structure of pitch-classes in Ives' Majority, *mm. 1–8*

Figure 8-2. Indexical structure of pitch-classes in Ives' Majority, *mm. 1–8*

In addition to the indexical functions one should observe that the chief melodic tendency as overall contour is a relatively quick ascent (the first and second clusters, *e.g.*) followed by more gradual descent in an unbalanced arch contour. Inspection will reveal that the generalized contour running through the introduction is equivalent to the contour of the basic melodic motive of the voice part (m. 8) as it exclaims "The Masses!" Moreover, the entire harmonic novelty of the introduction, the massive chord clusters, iconically signifies "The Masses" in patent extragenerous reference, as it also is congenerically focal in creating intrafluent references and coherence.

So far we have seen something of the nature of musical indices, of what constitutes an index, and an excerpt of which we analyzed the more important indexical functions. Now it behooves us to examine briefly other facets of index sign situations, especially certain principles of sensory perception along with corresponding structural relations of properties affecting interpretant formation. In this connection, among the fundamentals bearing on interpretant formation, is that whatever is given in experience tends to be interpreted either self-consciously or intuitively in itself as incomplete, as a fragment included in some larger whole or as a strand in an ever-extending context.[9] Obviously, taking anything as part of a whole at even an instinctual level of response involves an implicit inference that such a whole exists and that we either know or are capable of knowing it. To go one step further, another principle of interpretation bearing on experience in general, hence indices, is this: stimuli tend to appear to us as grouped into sets so that configurations of properties are perceived as functional wholes.[10] That is, sets that do contain separate elements are grouped spontaneously during interpretation into sensory fields, foregrounds, and backgrounds. As we have observed, index signs arise and dominate sensory fields so as to structure them. And, according to our most recent several observations, we note that each musical index, too, will tend to be taken as a fragment within some intelligible configuration (*i.e.*, a musical gesture). Moreover, just as local properties appear to be in groupings, so too will sets of those special indexical properties of a gesture tend to be grasped in functionally grouped wholes of their own. Hence it is that we get hierarchies of inclusions for formal units. But, then, we still are led to seek out principles accounting for the interrelation of sets of musical indices that promote sensory groupings and recognition of both inclusions and identification of wholes themselves.[11] At this time we may pursue one or both of two sides of our concern. We may explore the subjective aspects of interpretant formation (*i.e.*, psychology of pattern perception), or we may concentrate on the objective musical properties and indexical sign vehicles as they tend through their objective dispositions to elicit interpretation in groupings. We shall take the latter course rather than the former, for later on we shall be more closely concerned with pragmatic aspects of interpretation.

As we saw above, grouping of a number of indices may stem from the actual *inclusion* of each index as a fragment within a larger complex. Analysis of Ives' "Majority" revealed the part-whole inclusion of each index as a part of the introduction. A second set of relations which may group musical indices consists of *identity*, *equivalence*, and *similarity*. For examples, in the Ives excerpt the black-key clusters in the upper registers were grouped by the identity of the pitch class elements, by the equivalence in function of the clusters, along with the obvious pitch, durational, and dynamic similarity of each. Comparable comments apply to the white-key clusters. A third relation between musical indices that facilitates their coherence as a group is *contiguity*, the contact or proximity of indices in musical space or time. Within the space defined by the outermost sets of indices in the Ives several groupings by nearness were noticed. The first and second black-key clusters and their top pitches adhered in virtue of their temporal contiguity, as did the next to last introductory index (f♯, m. 7) as it connected to the opening index (e, m. 8) of the voice part. Moreover, several of the indices in the interior ascending structure were similarly related temporally. Furthermore, contiguity in musical space related all the indices as pitch classes in "Majority": each index was but a step or half-step away from its next or its prior sign (*i.e.*, a♯ – g♯ – f♯ e; b – c – d – e, and the like). *Joint prominence* may be a fourth principle of grouping—a tautologous way of asserting that an index stands out and that sets of connected indices stand out together, just as the indices do in the Ives. Still another principle of grouping indices may be their *joint movement* or *change* in position, which is exemplified in "Majority" by the resolution of outermost index pitches, f♯ above and d below, into the last index e (m. 8). A sixth principle of grouping is that of *joint utility* or *teleology*. Again in Ives' song each of the index signs shared in a common end; each was disposed to point ultimately toward the goal index of e, upon which pitch class the voice enters. Another complex principle of grouping is that of *economy*, known also as the Gestalt "law of prägnanz" or "good shape." According to this principle, a cohesive grouping of musical indices may arise singly or jointly because of its *simplicity*, its *regularity*, or its *symmetry*.[12] In at least three main respects the indices as a set exhibit simplicity: in their small number, their direct scalar relationships, and their singular fulfillment of scalar directional tendencies. The spatial regularity of scale relationships, exclusively in whole-tones, of the principal indices is itself also quite symmetrical. An eighth principle of grouping is evident in the totality of the indices since they display as a group an *implicit pattern* or configuration. This principle of implicit pattern corresponds to the Gestalt "law of good continuation," according to which a tendency once begun probably will perpetuate itself according to its own rule. This all seems self-evidently the case with the scalar structuring of the indexical pitch classes in the Ives excerpt. Further, as a ninth principle of grouping applicable to indices, we would mention that of *closure*, the termination without further elaboration so that the result is another member within the same

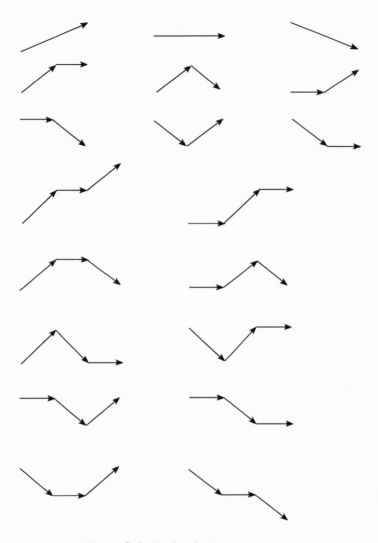

Figure 8-3. Basic pitch contours

Each contour is given as a general form without distinguishing variables of length in duration or range as well as minor deviations in pitches within a directional tendency. The contours are ordered in descending order of energy expressed or required for production—assuming a fixed neutral point of origin and other non-pitched elements as equal. More complex contours may be realized as permutations or combinations of the given examples for one, two, or three pitch intervals.

domain as the others. The convergence on the pitch class e by the contrary moving strands of indices in "Majority" again illustrates the idea. (The closure in this case is coincident with the initiation of a new gesture. Hence, it involves a closure by conjunction.) As a tenth and last principle of grouping we may recall attention to *contrast* or *diversity*, which has effects on closure. And in our example the essential differences establishing the end of one gesture and the beginning of the next is in the entry of the voice part. The addition of a new and primary timbre—not to mention the effect of text—is itself quite a difference in fact. But it is further coupled with the main melodic activity starting up in a register of pitch not well explored so far. Those contrasts signal both conclusion of the old and beginning of the new.

In addition to the most general ways of grouping through which musical indices might attain structural relatedness, there are a few more properly musical ways of systemic grouping. The most important two ways are by schemata of scalar outlining and by schemata of chordal outlining. Together in interrelations these ways of systematic grouping account for the indexical shaping of melodic gestures as pitch contours.

Pitch contours in themselves may be comprised of the permutations of sets of but three directional tendencies, *i.e.*, ascent, descent, and leveling (see Figure 8-3). All contours may be conceived as one of the elemental directional tendencies or as some more or less complex combination of them. Presently it matters only that we consider ways in which indices define contours and are organized into systemic structures.

Grouping pitch indices by scalar schemata organizes contour tendencies by contiguity of pitch classes in conjunct interval classes of semitones or wholetones. Any mode or scale, whether traditional or synthesized, may fulfill this role of a scalar schema. Contiguity in the present sense is spatial. It may or may not also involve temporal proximity of indexical pitch classes. The scalar schema has been remarked upon already in the examination of Ives' "Majority," but another more traditional theme will further clarify the concept. In the main thematic gesture of the Brahms *Violin Concerto*, last movement (mm. 1–8), the contour shaped in the solo part is essentially one of hovering on the mediant degree in the first half followed by scalar descent to the submediant in the second half (Example 8-2; Figure 8-4). Within the essential contour at least one subordinate counter-tendency is important. That is, in the first half, the line makes a scalar thrust upward to the submediant. Here in this theme not every tone is equally important to the contour

EXAMPLE 8-2   Johannes Brahms, *Violin Concerto*, III, mm. 1–8

102

Figure 8-4. Indexical pitch-class structure, Brahms' Violin Concerto, *III, mm. 1–8: scalar outlining.*

outline. The bare essentials are given mostly by the quarter-notes, which are systematically related as members of a scalar schema.

Chordal outlining is our second melodic kind of schema. In chordal outlining of pitch contour, ascending or descending pitch tendencies are organized by structuring pitch classes in recurrent conjunct interval classes larger than wholetones. The contour may be outlined by any recognizable chord form, whether in thirds (or sixths), in fourths (or fifths) or in sevenths. As in scalar outlining the indexical sounds may or may not be next to each other temporally. A fairly straightforward example of chordal outlining is to be found in Ernst Toch's *Third Symphony*, first movement, at the entry of the principal thematic gesture of the agitato (Example 8-3, mm. 37–41). The gesture in the upper part outlines a bowed contour with a long plunge downward and a climb back above the beginning position. The structural shaping of the descent is given by indices that systematically group together in a quartal chord pattern, whereas the ascent is made by more obvious arpeggiation of tertial chords (Figure 8-5). Although the shaping by the quartal chord schema is clear enough, it is equally clear that many non-structural tones elaborate the line, giving it durational vitality and tense intervallic content suggestive of polyphonic solo writing.

Harmony, too, may act as a third kind of schema for grouping indices. Among the index harmonies are the traditional cadential formulae that signify termination of tonal gestures, and these will be examined more carefully later. Most important now for understanding the harmonic shaping of tonal gestures are the schemata called "basic harmonic progressions." In a basic harmonic progression the elemental relationship is between the tonic (I) and dominant (V) harmonies. The basic harmonic progression includes that relationship along with one other structural

EXAMPLE 8-3   Ernst Toch, *Third Symphony*, I, mm. 37–41

harmony, which may be of subdominant function (IV, ii, N . . .) or a mediant (III, iii). The usual list of basic harmonic progressions in tonal music include I . . . , IV . . . , V . . . , I . . . ; I . . . , ii . . . , V . . . , I . . . , and, especially in the minor i . . . , III . . . , V . . . , i . . . . The listing may be varied by the usual substitutions of chords within the function-classes of tonic (I, vi), subdominant (IV, ii, N, Gr.$_6$, It.$_6$, Fr.$_6$ . . .), and dominant (V, vii, iii . . .). The real importance of the basic harmonic progressions is jointly (1) that each member chord is an index sign and (2) these are related in a schema. Delineating part of the outline of harmonic motion and structure of chordal tendencies within a gesture, each index chord acts as a point of origin, or a way point, or a conclusion point for the sonorous motion. These structural chords may stand next to each other, and often the last two harmonies do so. However, they also may be separated and spread out within a gesture. In this latter case any of the index

Figure 8-5. Indexical pitch-class structure as chordal outlining in Toch's Third Symphony, I, mm. 37–41.

harmonies may be more or less generously amplified by surrounding neighboring harmonies or the spaces between structural chords filled by contrapuntally passing chords that flesh out the bare bones of the structure and qualify the directional tendencies of the motion. A gesture's

EXAMPLE 8-4   Robert Schumann, *Piano Concerto*, mm. 12–19

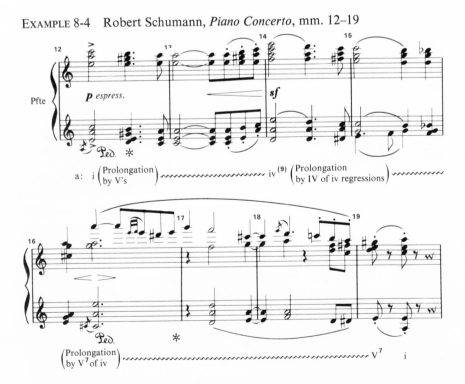

structure of harmonic indices might appear elaborated, say, as I, X . . . ,
IV, X . . . , V, I and so forth, in which the X's represent ampliative chords
with a prolonging function. A fairly simple example of such a harmonic
schema for indices and their prolongation by elaborating chords is found
in the main theme of Schumann's *Piano Concerto*, Op. 54 (Example 8-4,
mm. 12–19). The set of melodic index tones in the upper line is of interest.
Beginning on the mediant, the essential melodic contour is defined by a
chordal outlining in ascent through the dominant degree to the tonic
and a scalar descent through the octave. Our main point is, however, that
the force of harmonic indices provides a schema organizing harmonic
tendencies in functional progression. The overall harmonic tendency of
the gesture is embodied in the schema of harmonic index signs i . . . ,
iv . . . , V^7, i. The first structural chord is amplified by a passing dominant
(m. 12). The second structural chord is elaborated more fully by passing

Figure 8-6. Indexical pitch-class structure, Schumann, Piano Concerto,
mm. 12–19

tonic as well as its applied subdominant and dominant harmonies (mm.
14–18). The general tendency of the harmonic motion moves from the
prolonged tonic (mm. 12–13) through prolonged subdominant. (mm.
14–18) and dominant to the close on the tonic (m. 19; Figure 8-6).

As we have just seen, in addition the melodic index (*i.e.*, either scalar
or chordal outlining) harmony and its successions may offer indices of
sonorous motion. Our analytic example was, to be sure, a preeminently
tonal excerpt. Nonetheless, in atonal music harmonic index signs may
abound for just the same basic reasons of complex accentuation that
create any harmonic index, whether or not it happens to be a basic
harmonic progression. In atonal music the harmonic indices are not

coextensive with such a progression. The difference between tonal and atonal harmonic indices lies not in the means of creating harmonic indices themselves, for those basic means of accentuation are independent of stylistic formation rules. Rather, the difference is merely that atonal music usually does not employ the traditional tonal harmonic functions as formulae for allowable chordal or melodic sequences. Thus, atonal music will utilize harmonic indices but without the added syntactic strictures of tonal music for permissible harmonic formations and successions.

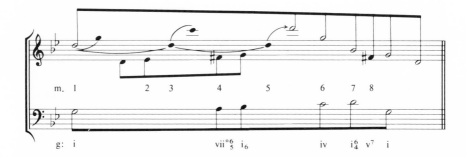

Figure 8-7. Indexical structure of pitch-classes in Haydn's String Quartet in G Major, *Op. 17, No. 5, III, mm. 1–8.*

From the foregoing discussions it should be apparent that the composite set of melodic and harmonic schemata for grouping indices constitutes an outline of the musical space bounding any gesture and its tendencies of pitched movement within that space. For a given gesture this structural framework and outline of tendencies consists of (1) the most important pitch class indices of contour in the principal upper line, (2) the equivalent indices in the lowest moving line, and (3) the chief harmonic indices or the basic harmonic progression in tonal music. Figure 8-7 illustrates such a structural framework of pitch classes in the case of the primary gesture opening the third movement of Haydn's *String Quartet in G Major*, Op. 17, No. 5 (Example 8-5, mm. 1–8). The gesture is shaped melodically and harmonically by five schemata of consequence. One schema is the scalar grouping of pitch classes in the bass line into an ascent from tonic to dominant, which sets up the cadence (mm. 1–7). Another shorter scalar schema leads an upper melodic action through the ascending harmonic minor tetrachord from dominant to tonic (mm. 1–4). This schema is disjunctly coupled with another schema in the highest register and which outlines the principal scale degrees ($d^2 - g^2 - c^3 - d^3$) to arrive on the gesture's high point, the dominant (mm. 1–5). In turn that schema is conjoined to a chordal schema which descends gently through two octaves from the melodic zenith on the

EXAMPLE 8-5   Joseph Haydn, *String Quartet in G Major* Op. 17, No. 5, III, mm. 1–8

dominant to the nadir on the same degree (mm. 5–8). In harmonic support of the entire gesture the last schema is the basic harmonic progression of i . . . , iv, . . . V, i (mm. 1–8). The composite set of schemata form a structural framework of great clarity and control, presenting the several directional tendencies in poised counterpoint to each other within a homophonic texture.

In attracting attention to the structure of gestures the index signs are of considerable value to our analysis of meaningful aesthetic experience. But they also are cues to a great amount of the dual affective force of a composition. The musical indices may be interpreted analytically as a sketch displaying the characteristics (1) that may act as affective stimuli to performers or listeners, and (2) that in themselves may signify the structure of affective content within the work. This is not to say that all affective stimuli in a composition must also be index signs. They need not be. Nor is it to say that all musical properties that can be discriminated analytically as indices are guaranteed to be experienced by performers and listeners as indices. Rather, by analysis we can pick out the characteristics of a work that are likely to be interpreted as index signs. Moreover, those characteristics are in some degree affective stimuli to anyone who is disposed to respond to them as index signs. Accordingly, an analysis of the probable indexical properties in a composition may be interpreted analytically in two ways: they may be conceived as clues to a work's congeneric signification of affectivity, and they may be regarded as potential affective stimuli to auditors. So some considerable portion of a composition's probable affective force may be discovered by analysis of its potential index signs.

By way of tying up the threads of thought in our foregoing investigation we ought to remember at least five main points. First, any of the elemental sonic or rhythmic properties may serve either singly or in complexes as an indexical sign vehicle. Second, as an index a set of properties vividly calls itself to attention as well as focuses and directs the interpreter's attention to a more or less specific location in musical space-time, a location which may be another index. Third, the primal function of musical indices, whether isolated or in groups, is to elicit instinctual affective responses from the interpreter. Fourth, sets of indices have the syntactic function of delineating and bounding the structure of a musical gesture by displaying in outline the overall shape of pitch class tendencies in the sonorous motion of the gesture. Fifth, a number of principles of grouping promote the coherence of musical indices within a gesture, providing objective stimuli to interpretant formation of configurations so as to correspond to psychological principles of sensory perception and subjective patterning.

Notes

1 Charles Morris, *Signs, Language and Behavior* (Englewood Cliffs, N.J.: Prentice-Hall, Inc., 1946), pp. 66, 76.
2 Charles S. Peirce, "Logic as Semiotic: The Theory of Signs," *Philosophical Writings of Peirce*, ed. Justus Buchler (New York: Dover Publications, 1955), pp. 108–10.
3 Donald B. Lindsley, "Emotion," in *Handbook of Experimental Psychology*, ed. S. S. Stevens (New York: John Wiley and Sons, 1951), pp. 507–8.

4 Brand Blanshard, *The Nature of Thought* (New York: Humanities Press, 1939), vol. 1, p. 69.

5 Paul Henle, ed., *Language, Thought, and Culture* (Ann Arbor: University of Michigan Press, 1958), p. 55.

6 Bertrand Russell, *An Inquiry Into Meaning and Truth* (Baltimore: Penguin Books, 1962), pp. 102–3.

7 James Drever, *A Dictionary of Psychology* (Baltimore: Penguin Books, 1952), p. 290.

8 For material on the theories to which allusion is made, see Heinrich Schenker, *Neue Musikalische Theorien und Phatasien*, vol. 1, *Harmonielehre*, vol. 2, *Kontrapunkt*, vol. 3, *Der Freie* (Vienna: Universal-Edition, 1906, 1910–1912, 1935); Adele T. Katz. *Challenge to Musical Tradition* (New York: Alfred A. Knopf, 1946); Felix Salzer, *Structural Hearing*, 2 vols. (New York: Charles Boni, 1952); Allen Forte, *Contemporary Tone-Structures* (New York: Bureau of Publications, Teachers College, Columbia University, 1955); Paul Hindemith, *Craft of Musical Composition* (New York: Associated Music Publishers, 1945), vol. 1.

9 Blanshard, *Nature of Thought*, 1: 111.

10 Wolfgang Köhler, *Gestalt Psychology* (New York: Liveright Publishing Corp., Mentor Books, 1947), pp. 62, 84, 85.

11 The following discussion is drawn from Blanshard, *Nature of Thought*, 1: 124–135.

12 For the best and most extensive pragmatic elaboration for music of this principle and its implicate corollaries, see Leonard B. Meyer, *Emotion and Meaning in Music* (Chicago: University of Chicago Press, 1956), chap. 3.

9

Logical Signs in Music

So far we have explored two large classes of signs, iconic and index signs. In looking into index signs we have seen how some properties of musical gestures are made to stand out, command and direct attention, thereby giving structure to the gesture and cues to what may elicit affective behavior in auditors. In considering iconic signs earlier, we saw how part of a work may signify another part and how much of the coherence of music is created through exhibition of various forms of resemblance. Now we shall turn to a third class of signs, the logical signs, in order to examine what constitutes logical connection of musical gestures and their elements. Because the syntactical structure of a sign system generally involves both objective events and behavior together, in treating logical signs in music we shall refer extensively to matters of pragmatics and semantics as well as syntactics.[1]

For there to be any intelligible combinations of signs seemingly requires still other signs to join together the combinations of signs. Signs that serve to connect, or to indicate the relation of, other signs to each other are *logical signs*.[2] Logical signs comprise such as position or order of sign vehicles (*e.g.*, word-order); diacritical marks, emphasis, and inflection (*i.e.*, speech melodies); pauses and written punctuation devices (*i.e.*, period, comma, colon and semicolon, parentheses, brackets, and so on); and logical words (logical constants), including such as 'is,' 'or,' 'not,' 'if . . . then,' 'and,' 'some,' 'all,' and 'none.'[3]

When present in groups of signs, logical signs alter the signification of the groups. And, although logical signs may not add objects or characteristics to objects in the group, they do affect the interpretants we form of the other signs in that grouping. The basis of the influence which logical signs exert on behavior lies in the propositional attitudes or *relations felt* to exist between significant objects.[4] For there is something of a *feeling of reality* involved in using 'is,' as well as *feelings of* 'and,' 'or,' 'not,' and 'if . . . then,' and these feelings of relation are much of what logical signs signify. So much is this the case that our *concepts of relation* may be said to originate from a more basic experience of the modes of connection that are felt and believed in prior to thought.

The point of our present discussion—that feelings of relation underlie the significance of logical signs—is neither obvious nor trivial. Understanding this point is central to understanding what logical structure is, especially as it concerns aesthetic experience. What is important to remember is that the logical signs that connect meaningful structures of signs have an expressive (pragmatic) function.[5] Logical signs give us the linguistic expression of feelings of relation among events and objects; they express the felt connections between successive interpretants of sign combinations. Indeed, as Arthur Pap observed in *Semantics and Necessary Truth*, pragmatic interpretation is the only kind that reasonably can be demanded for the logical constants.[6] Otherwise, the constants must be accepted as undefined primitive connective terms and their meanings already grasped. However, to ground our understanding of the musical expression of logical signs of connection we first shall explore the pragmatic sense of the logical constants verbally denoted by 'or,' 'not,' and 'if . . . then' and so on.

The disjunctive word 'or' is related to our experience of choosing between, or of questioning, several possible courses of action.[7] 'Or' may express momentary indecision or hesitation, which occurs when we feel at once several competing tendencies, none of which dominates the others. Action is restrained while the tendencies are in conflict. A feeling of suspensive tension accompanies the hesitancy, as a desire to reach a decision accompanies a questioning attitude. Now let us be entirely clear about one point involved here: the states of indecision, doubt, hesitancy, and questioning associated with the use of 'or' are decidedly subjective, and the subjectivity is there no less so when one is involved in highly cerebral ("logical") activity.[8]

In connection with the consideration of 'or,' it is pertinent to say that nearly every statement might be regarded as a potential disjunction simply by our substituting or anticipating different predicates and conclusions to the statement. And, consequently, the emergent effects of a statement can vary widely from giving a feeling of knowledge to creating a feeling of doubt. Thus, by introducing the logical word 'or' into an expression, the weight of meaning may be shifted from that of certainty to that of indecision. From the perspective of aesthetic experience, we would find that non-verbal gestures eliciting responses of doubt or hesitancy about their continuation act very much as the logical constant 'or.'

We note briefly that 'not' expresses rejection, and it derives its meaning from our experiences of turning away from—denying—a possible course of action.[9] In the case of negation, we are in a state of feeling in which impulses seek completion but are inhibited; they either cannot find completion or we will not allow them to reach completion.

Regarding the hypothetical or implicative connective pair 'if . . . then,' we note that 'this leading to that' is equivalent to the logical form of an act. 'If this, then that' is another way of expressing the schema. Moreover, we notice also that the schema involves an interaction of the effects of antecedent and consequent phases of an act upon one another. The consideration of the one affects one's attitude toward the other, so that the later phase of an act influences our conduct in the earlier phases. In the meaning of 'if . . . then' we find again inhibition of impulses and tension. However, the tension seems to vary from that involved in the use of 'or' in that the tension in 'if . . . then' seems to direct or require the movement from antecedent into consequent. The tension seems to be directed from the one to the following rather than to be suspensive between the two. We may say that 'if . . . then' expresses *leading to*, involving a heightening of tension and a preparatory feeling of moving to, a certainty or something emphatic. The force of the 'if ... then' connection is to create more or less definite expectations of a certain kind of experience.

Logical Signs and Primitive Connectives in Music

Music is, of course, replete with ways to signify syntactical groupings through order, emphasis and inflections, or pauses. We may say that what speech does in these respects can be done by music. Furthermore, these rhythmic and temporal articulations of gestures are susceptible in music to extreme degrees of control and shading, largely because in notation and performance music has a highly discriminate set of symbols and conventions for writing and reproducing accent and inflection, phrasing, timing, and tempo of ordered events—which perhaps speech and surely written discourse fail to have in the same high degree of refinement. Just as it does in speech, and as punctuation marks are intended to do in written discourse, cadence in music reveals the nature of connections between syntactical units. So also with the pause or caesura. The cadences and caesurae of speech and music define the ending quality of intensity and inflection that are meant by written question marks, commas, and such. Thus, cadence and caesura not only mark off expressions, they also show qualitative variations in independence or interdependence of simple and complete gestural acts and of compound acts, such as those involving either conjunct simple gestures or antecedent and consequent gestures of implicative acts. Just now we need to observe that caesura and cadence do effectively convey in music all they do in speech and all that is the intent of punctuation in written discourse. Moreover, the logical signs showing the connection and separation of gestures by means of inflection, pauses, and cadential formulae surely account for most uses of logical signs relating separate gestures. It seems that the majority of musical gestures succeed one another by brute repetition of simple, short expressions analogous to the simple sentences of much verbal discourse. Thus, it appears that in musical experience we encounter an almost excessive amount of simple performative expressions with the characteristic attitudes of assertions, exclamations, questions, denials, and such. These sorts of simple gesture by and large seem to be connected or separated effectively enough by cadence and caesura coupled with melodic inflection.

We use the logical word 'is' to express the propositional attitude of belief in the reality of a state of affairs or in the existence of an object. The word indirectly represents; it verbally supplants and expresses belief in a connection between an object and its properties, a relation which one feels to exist or that, he reasons, does exist. The sense of reality about objects, which is conveyed indirectly by the word 'is', finds immediate expression in musical experience through the direct appearance of the objects and their relevant properties in gestures. For musical gestures exhibit attitude in the very quality of their sonorous motion. In actually *doing* something in a certain way, musical gestures present actual states of affairs: their very presentation goes beyond indirect verbalization and assertions about beliefs. Thus, in presentation of properties music exhibits connections—logical connections between objects—that the word 'is' denotes in a less direct way. Musical gestures *do* overtly what 'is' stands for discursively. And what is directly given to observation does not need discourse about it to establish its existence; its reality is there to be apprehended on its appearance. Thus, the musical gesture itself *is* "bold," or it *is* "complex," it intersects with the next gesture, or what have you. Music does not need to concoct locutions about what is: either the music itself presents it, implies it, or must be mute.

Among the meanings music can convey are significations of certain logical relations that bind together elemental sonic properties into single basic gestures and that also connect separate gestures. The relations that link together musical materials may be taken as equivalents of the logical constants, *i.e.*, disjunction (union), conjunction (intersection), negation (complementation), and material implication.[10] In the following pages I shall explore how we legitimately may speak of the logical operators functioning in music, beginning with a conventional explanation of the constants. We shall consider the pragmatic sense of the propositional attitudes associated with each operator. Exemplification will be made of intragestural and intergestural connections. The musical gestures considered at intergestural levels will be treated to some extent as unanalyzed expressions. However, we shall not deal so extensively with truth-functional properties of such gestural expressions as with the overt display in music of the connective operations and attendant propositional attitudes. Following elaboration of the musical sense of logical constants and propositional attitudes, we shall give attention to the matter of artistic truth.

Two simple statements connected by 'or' (symbol: ∨) form a compound statement called a *disjunction*.[11] The two statements (p, q) combined are disjuncts. The sense in which 'or' is interpreted usually is the inclusive one in which it means "either—or—or both." Accordingly, an inclusive disjunction asserts that at least one of the disjuncts is true and that both may be true. The thought schema of a disjunction is symbolized p ∨ q.

The connective operation in set theory corresponding to logical disjunction is union (symbol: ∪). A *union* of two sets (A, B) is the resultant set uniting all those elements which are members of either the one set or the other.[12] If the set A includes as its elements the pitch classes d♭, f, a♭ and the set B includes e♭, g, b♭, then the union of those disjunct sets is the compound set of elements d♭, f, a♭, e♭, g, b♭. The union of A or B would be symbolized A ∪ B.

As we know, a disjunctive feeling of relation between possibilities is denoted by 'or', which brings together for comparison several alternatives—either contraries, opposites, or equivalents. 'Or' may be said to express a complicated attitude of hesitation, a momentary questioning indecision and inactivity in response to 'all these' objects before one while he is selecting one or more alternate courses of action.[13] The attitude, then, involves a certain conflict of impulses, and while neither impulse prevails there may be some degree of tension and discomfort present.

Several musical correlatives, jointly or singly employed, may be expressive of the propositional attitude 'or' signifies. The alternation of gestures may suffice. But also in filler material between gestures a rhythmic figure that is hesitant, one with a halting motion involving delays or pauses, may show the feeling of relation. And, again, the expression of hesitancy may be brought off by vacillations between qualities of pitch, of loudness, or of timbre. The wavering between one tendency of organizing action and another may suffice to indicate the attitude. And certainly tension can be revealed in a prevailing dissonant set of intervals, whereas the conflict of impulses finds correlation in tenuous introductions of contrasting texture or gesture.

A *conjunction* may be regarded as the compound statement formed by joining two simple statements with 'and' (symbol: ·).[14] The simple statements connected by 'and' are conjuncts. A conjunction holds and is true provided that both of its conjuncts are true. We may symbolize the thought schema of conjunction by p·q or simply by the juxtaposition pq.

In the operation of intersection (symbol: ∩) we find the set-theoretic correlative of conjunction. An *intersection* of two sets is the resultant set comprised of those elements of the two sets which are members of both.[15] For instance, if a set A consists of the pitch-classes a♭, c, e♭ and set B consists of d♭, f, a♭, then the intersection of the two sets A and B—A ∩ B—is a♭, their common element. The a♭ conjoins the conjunct sets A and B.

In discourse the logical word expressing the felt relation of conjunction or joining together of objects is 'and.' The elements, gestures, and component propositions that 'and' connects are conjuncts. Just as 'and' joins together components in a series by contiguity, so can musical components—gestures or parts of them—be presented in turn by overlapping or intersecting tones so that the point of arrival for one element or gesture becomes the point of departure for another to express conjunction. But

conjunction is expressed musically another way that also allows a qualitative shading of meaning. Whereas things conjoined in succession may
express a spatial and temporal contiguity of juxtaposition, the simultaneous appearance of musical elements and gestures expresses another
more compact sense of conjunction. However, for an adequate musical
expression of simultaneous conjunction, tonal and rhythmic compatibility or felicitous fitting together is involved. When one familiar with a
style hears two musical properties or gestures simultaneously mesh together, he would be able to feel the appropriateness of the conjunction,
while he also would need to be aware of the distinct identity of the conjuncts. The well known musical locus for this sort of conjunction is what
we call texture. In a polyphonic texture, clearly separate musical gestures
may be joined together (in double counterpoint, possibly) to signify the
logical connection expressed by 'and.' And a homophonic texture would
bring together a dominant gesture with other qualifying properties,
accompaniments, that characterize the gesture.

Within a gesture the pitch interval is the musical unit; it binds together
pitches in a pair or dyad. Horizontal gestures (melodies) may be regarded
as sets of dyads bound together by conjunction, as the links of a chain are,
with each member tone appearing successively. Simultaneities (harmonies) may be regarded as sets of intervals in conjunction binding
together dyads, triads, tetrads, and so on, as a chain strung vertically.
Within a melodic gesture in harmonic setting the intragestural connections for the horizontal chains of dyads and the successions of chords are
easily analyzed. The disjunct tone-members of linear dyads, the conjunct
linkage of those dyads, the conjunct and disjunct sets of pitch classes in
chords are all apparent enough. For example, in a phrase from one of
Bach's settings of the chorale melody *An Wasserflüssen Babylon* one
finds the following intragestural melodic connections: each tone-member

EXAMPLE 9-1   J. S. Bach, *An Wasserflüssen Babylon*, mm. 1–2

of the gesture is disjoined to each other successively, and each dyad is conjoined to its successor and predecessor (Example 9-1, mm. 1–2). The chords harmonizing the melody are sets of pitch classes, too, and they are similarly related. As pairs of chords share pitch classes in common (loosely speaking, "common tones"), they are conjoined, they intersect on the common element(s). Or they may have nothing in common, being disjoined. These intragestural harmonic connections of simultaneities (Example 8-6) might be symbolized as:

$$\text{I} \cap \text{IV}^{-7} \cup \text{V}^{-7} \cup \text{vi} \cup \text{V}_6 \cap \text{I}^7 \cup \text{ii}^{-7} \cap \text{V}_4{}^7{}_3 \cap \text{I}$$

From these opening remarks on logical signs of connection at the intragestural level we may move on to consideration of connection of similar detail at the intragestural level, but we also may go on to the larger connections at the intergestural level. In both directions we find disjunctive and conjunctive operations. For example, in the opening gestural phrase (mm. 1–3) of Anton Webern's *Konzert*, Op. 24, four statements of the basic motivic gesture are given out in turn by oboe, flute, trumpet, and clarinet (Example 9-2). In three pitches the oboe shapes the motive's contour of descent and ascent. As sub-sets within that motive the three pitch classes are related by unions—b ∪ b♭ ∪ d. The two intervals (13

EXAMPLE 9-2   Anton Webern, *Konzert*, I, mm. 1–3

and 4 semitones) bind together the three pitches by intersections—
$(b^2 - bb^1) \cap (bb^1 - d)$. The agogic schema of the same basic motivic gesture is a tribrach, involving the relation by equality of three identical
durations. The dynamic dimension of the motive links all three sounds by
equality of loudness (forte). The set of timbres similarly is uniformly that
of the oboe. The articulatory connection of the three sounds is by slur.
So within the basic motive there are overlappings or common properties
shared in each of the several elemental dimensions of sound—in durations, dynamics, timbre, and articulations. And, although the diverse
pitches are disjunctly related as pitches, they also are connected by intersection with respect to their interval organization. Similar observations
apply to each successive motivic variant within the phrase. With a new
set of pitches the flute presents the retrograde inversion equivalent of
the basic contour together with durational augmentation. Next the trumpet gives the retrograde contour also in durational augmentation. Then
the clarinet concludes the phrase in a durational augmentation and contour inversion of the motive. Each successive variant of the motive connects to its neighbors by union with respect to pitch, duration, timbre,
and articulation. Yet each motivic unit connects to its contiguous
motive(s) by intersection in the dimension of loudness. The four sub-
sets of pitch classes add up in union to a basic ordered set of the twelve
pitch classes. In terms used earlier, we would notice that the phrase
as a whole gesture is highly cohesive because of the many identity and
equivalence relations on the sensuous surface of sound. Moreover,
there is a further subtle coherence embedded in the phrase in virtue of its
use of registers of pitch space. The four motivic statements are made in
three contrasted registers. The oboe, in the axial center, is followed by the
flute in a higher register; the trumpet is the lowest register below the axial
level; and the clarinet is back again essentially in the axial register. The
first three and last three registers, as intersecting sets, outline in registral
contour levels two general reflections of the basic motivic contour, *i.e.*,
the retrograde inversion intersecting the prime (Figure 9-1).

  Disjunctive and conjunctive connections of gestures are observable
in more extended contexts also. In the first movement of Brahms'
Symphony IV, for instance, the closing of the first theme group into the
beginning of the second theme group involves one disjunction and two
conjunctions of larger gestures (Example 9-3, mm. 45–60). Four gestures
are stated in the segment (mm. 45–49, 49–53, 53–57, and 57–60). Without
analyzing the segment in detail we can note that the harmony moves

from the mediant level of G in the first gesture into the dominant minor of b in the second gesture to a prolongation of the secondary dominant level of b in the last two gestures. The second gesture rather clearly extends the expansive sweep of the first by a varied repetition, the two gestures being connected disjunctly (m. 49) in a direct alternation of equivalents: (mm. 45–49) ∨ (mm. 49–53). The second and third gestures overtly overlap (m. 53) with respect to pitch and dynamic qualities as well as woodwind timbral qualities: (mm. 49–53) · (mm. 53–57). This conjunction admits the introduction of the vigorous, fanfare-like third gesture which bridges the end of the first theme group and the opening of the strong and lyric second theme group. A second conjunction of

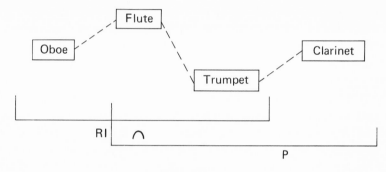

Figure 9-1

gestures follows. In its turn the third gesture closes into the fourth as the second closed into the third. The point of arrival for the second gesture becomes the point of origin for the third, and the termination of the third gesture becomes the beginning place for the fourth. The conjunction of the third and fourth gestures (m. 57) is effected by the intersections of agogic values, and timbral, dynamic, and pitch qualities of the horn and cello parts: (mm. 53–57) · (mm. 57–60). With the foregoing connections Brahms welded together the two main formal sections of the first movement's exposition into a smooth succession of diverse gestures.

The propositional attitude underlying use of the words 'not,' 'no one,' and such terms has its origins in dispositions of displeasure or aversion and in our experiences of rejection.[16] As stimuli deviate from those tending to please and satisfy desires or needs—as stimuli thwart interests—the negative affect, and with it the negative value, arises.[17] The range of negative affect is vast, extending from feelings of anxiety and discomfort to the extremes of distress—anguish, fear-terror, shame-

EXAMPLE 9-3   Disjunct and conjunct connections of gestures, Johannes Brahms, *Symphony IV*, I, mm. 45–60

humiliation, contempt-disgust, and anger-rage. Thus, as tendencies of behavior reject, turn away from, exclude, or spurn some object or some other tendency of behavior the attitude of negation and denial finds its natural expression. In this light we see that the *denial* or *negation* of a statement consists in another statement with the opposite truth value. This is so in the sense that, with respect to some given or anticipated identity, diversity is the negation of that identity.[18] With reference to sets we may say that the negation of a set A is another set ~A, the complement of A, which includes everything that does not belong to A. Similarly in terms of unanalyzed expressions, the range of the negate or complement of an expression G is the class of value assignments not belonging to G.[19]

By complementation of musical gestures, sharp contrast to the point of clear diversity may express the objective negation of one gesture by another, whether in succession or simultaneity. Moreover, in view of earlier comments on negative affect we may say that, to signify negation, the impulse of a musical gesture may be so inhibited that its dominant tendencies are not allowed to reach their apparent conclusion. And within a context the negative propositional attitude is brought out in the music by the implicit disclaimer in music's quitting a teleological movement, by its dropping a progression of qualities toward an expected goal, such as rejecting the completion of a full cadence by a retrogressive or deceptive movement. A denial may be effected musically also by the disavowal implicit in the interruption of a gesture. Denial might be displayed by the obtrusion of a foreign strand in a qualitatively well defined texture, by the injection of a new tonality in a melodic strand, or the forcing in of marked contrasts of timbre, loudness, or agogic patterns.

A good expression of a statement and its negation by another is afforded by the closing of the exposition's second theme group and

EXAMPLE 9-4   Peter Tschaikowsky, *Symphony VI*, I, mm. 153–164

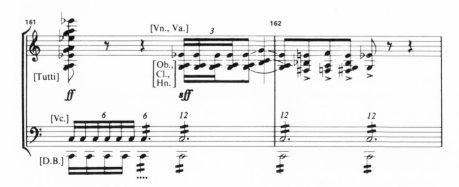

opening of the development in Tschaikowsky's *Symphony VI*, first movement (Example 9-4, mm. 153–164 . . .). The negation consists in
opposition of contrasting sets of sonic and rhythmic characteristics. The
earlier gesture (mm. 153–160) at the end of the exposition is followed by
its negate (mm. 161–164 . . .). Inspection of the main characteristics of
each gesture allows one to hear the necessary sharp contrast and certain
diversity of a denial. The first gestural segment reaffirms the tender
sentiment of the second subject—an extended lyric gesture of wide contour, which here peacefully unfolds in a gradual descent through two
and a half octaves. In its larger rhythmic function the gesture acts as the
stasis unravelling the earlier impulsive tendencies of the exposition.
Within the gesture itself the long anacrusis of seven eighths leading to
longer values is an especially prominent and steadily flowing pattern of
durations. Stable harmonies in basic relationships (*i.e.*, D : I – vii°⁷/V – I –
V⁷ – I) over tonic pedal point move slowly in half-note changes, ending
with tonic reiterations. Very soft levels give way to extremely soft ones
(*ppp—pppppp*). A slow tempo (Adagio mosso ♩ = 60) slackens to a near
halt with a hold on the last eighth-note anacrusis of the segment. All the
while sustaining articulations support the lyric disposition. In timbre
the rich tone of the clarinet is accompanied by the divided strings
(minus double bass). In opposition, the denial of the second gestural
segment (mm. 161–164 . . .) presents an agitated, even stormy, presence.
Beginning abruptly with a strong punctuating chord by the full ensemble
covering extremes of orchestral range, the negate obtrudes with radical
changes of tempo (Allegro vivo ♩ = 144) at steady pace, very loud dynamics, and timbres dominated by horns and lower registers of woodwinds
and strings. Short, choppy thrusts characterize melodic action which is
restricted in contour to motion about axial levels. Conflicting compound
and simple subdivisions offer agogic excitation in cellos and double

basses, upper strings and winds. Prior tonal stability is replaced by ambiguous triads and seventh chords $\left(v{}^{\flat 6}_{5}{}_{\flat 3} \ldots I{}^{4}_{\natural 2} - \flat iii \ldots \right)$, destroying preceding clarity of key. The music displays its "no." Such bold contrasts as these can establish an unquestionable diversity requisite for expression of the musical analogue of negation.

The Musical Conditional
Material Implication, and Inference

Probably the most important logical constant for us is the implicative connective, which usually is expressed verbally by the pair 'if . . . , then . . .' (symbol: ⊃). When two simple statements (p, q) are related by 'if . . . then' to form a compound statement, that statement is called a *conditional*.[20] It also is known as a "hypothetical" or an "implication." If two simple statements take the form of this sentence, then they make a conditional. The first of the combined statements is called the *antecedent* or "hypothesis," and the second is called the *consequent* or "conclusion." We shall consider the conditional in the sense of "material implication." A *material implication* is the connective relation of two expressions such that either the first is false or the second is true ("not-p or q"). Other ways to say the same thing are that the first expression cannot be true and the second false, or that if the first expression is true, then the second also is true. Symbolically, material implication may be defined as: $(p \supset q) = (\sim p \vee q)$. (In terms of sets, implication is the special case where the set A is such that if it contains the subset B it also must contain the subset C.) Saying a compound statement is a conditional, then, is to say that two successive simple statements are connected by a material implication.

The conditional connection of statements gives us the scheme for inference. As we have seen, material implication is a logical relation connecting simple statements in a compound statement, a conditional. Let us digress to say by contrast that *inference* is a repeatable psychological process of reasoning in which we pass from belief in a set of data or expressions taken as true (premises) to belief in a further set of data or expression (conclusion), which either is guaranteed or made probable by the validity of the premises.[21] In *deductive inference* the validity of the conclusion depends solely upon the structure or logical form of the inferential scheme rather than upon its matter—its conclusion not being more general than its premises and the conclusion following necessarily from its premises. In *inductive inference* we expect that unobserved events will be like events already observed, basing our expectation upon the presupposition that the future will resemble the past. Hence, induction has its basis in expectation and our tendency to generalize from past experience; the conclusion, which may be ampliative or more general than its premises, follows from the premises because it represents a probable course of events, a reasonable but not an absolute certainty. An inference is an operation involving mental habits formed in problem solving and is constituted largely by intellectual skill obtained through practice.[22] By way of analysis of the process of inference, we might point out that we reason within the intelligible system of beliefs and knowledge we possess and that systematized experience exerts control over our thought. If the thought A occurs, the thought B may be inferred because of our mental habits. Recognizing A as a fragment within the system of our experience, we seek out B, the developed consequence of A, because our minds tend to proceed along some line of thought rather than others. It is into this situation that the implicative relation and conditional propositional attitude enter.

The essential feeling of relation appropriate to conditionals may be described as one of "this-leading-to-that."[23] But this feeling is compounded of earlier and later parts. The earlier part of an implicative act carries the quality of an 'if-feeling' of some tension and expectancy. And a sustained or intense concentration on the 'if' expression through delay will heighten tensions and bring in doubt and hesitancy. The earlier and the later phases of an implication are pulled together by an underlying attraction we feel that the phases have for each other. And the associated tension to what we feel as that attraction may be released by resolution of the antecedent expression into the consequent. The latter part of an implicative act normally carries with it the 'then-feeling' of fulfillment of expectancy and satisfaction in relief from doubt.

A gestural act by means of which implication is expressed conveys, and is expected to evoke, the feeling that an antecedent gesture and a consequent gesture fit together as accepted condition and resultant. So within a given situation, the force of using an implicative pair of connective signs should be to fulfill expectations and create the feeling that things are as they should be.[24] In an implicative act the set of properties in an antecedent gesture imply and make one expect the set of properties in the following consequent gesture, because together the properties make up a single larger collection.

Since expectation plays an important role in materially implicative acts, let us clarify its meaning. We may regard *expectation* as a form of belief about the immediate future, involving a state of tension and receptivity of the senses.[25] An expectational belief is based on one's experiences in which several events or sets of properties ("x" and "y") have been so closely associated in a situation as to lead one to regard them as habitually associated. So, whenever "x" occurs, "y" is expected. Accordingly, we would say that expectancy arises or is embedded in a situation of a kind with which one is acquainted. It is always an expectation of something more or less specific, even though the expectancy still is unsatisfied. Thus, whatever occurs in consummation of the expectation to some extent either must accord with the belief or not. The specific consummation, of course, may be a disjunction of differing possibilities. Nonetheless, an expectation will be confirmed or denied to some extent, and the conclusion accordingly will be either true or false. That is, the expectation held in following an implicative act involves degrees of confirmation and degrees of entailment of the conclusion.[26] A pragmatic conception of truth seems the only acceptable one for purposes of our discussion. Truth will come into the situation of consummation to the extent that expectations are fulfilled; falsity will appear as the negative value of frustration of expectation or as surprise.[27] The negation of the expectation to an implicative act (p $\supset$ q) is simply the finding of p and not q. (We shall extend our observations on music and truth values at the conclusion of this chapter.)

We should observe that implication is a component of meaning (and sign functioning), which is the more inclusive concept, and therefore implication cannot be limited to connecting propositions that assert discursive meanings.[28] Accordingly, we must find that formal truth values do not constitute implication, since implication extends beyond discursive meanings and is part of meaning in general. Implication has its roots in affective phenomena, in the felt relations that bind gestures together.

Compound musical acts comprised of interdependent gestures in conditional form provide an analogue to the logical connective function of material implication. What we shall call musical implicative connection of gestures is a part of a larger situation which contributes to the comprehensive meaning of the musical conditional expression. In that larger situation the elements that need consideration for our understanding of the musical conditional include matters of musical style and both intuitive as well as inferential levels of response to the conditional.

Musical Style, Inference, and the Conditional

Compositions not only are instances of a composer's output but also are examples of his stylistic traits. The style of one composer may in turn have much in common with larger sets of styles or a style system common to a group of composers. Since implicative connection in conditional gestures is bound up with its setting within a work, a particular composer's style, and usually a larger style system, to explore musical implication we need to be clear about what musical style or a style system itself is.[29] We probably can best grasp the meaning of what is a musical style or a style system by reference to characteristics of linguistic systems or language.

As we saw in the first chapter, a linguistic system may be considered to have its roots in the observations of a group of people that on one side of experience objects and events are interrelated and on another side that organic dispositions and actions are interrelated. This leads to use of symbols which stand for the observed interconnections of both sides of experience. A language, then, becomes a system of sounds habitually produced for the purpose of communication, for indication of facts, for the expression of states of the users of symbols, and for the affecting of the states of the users. A number of criteria for calling a symbol system a language are: (1) a language comprises a complex set of symbols; (2) the significations of each symbol are shared to some extent by members using the language; (3) the symbols can be interpreted and usually can be produced by the normal members of the linguistic community; (4) the set of significations for symbols is relatively constant according to contexts of use; (5) in principle at least, the significations of symbols may be recorded or defined; (6) and a language possesses a syntax limiting the admissible kinds of symbols and their orderings, connections, and combinations in complex symbol structures. Implicative connections occur within linguistic usage and are explainable by reference to conventions of such systems.

We may regard a well defined musical style as equivalent to a special case of a linguistic system and a musical style system as equivalent to a more general linguistic system. The metalanguage to discuss and analyze the musical systems is, of course, our normal English amplified by descriptive technical terms and symbols such as "tonality," "V_7," and the like. A musical style involves use of signs in meaningful complexes, and those signs may become symbols in that persons familiar with the style share knowledge of the tendencies of signification by gestures within the style. Those significatory tendencies can be interpreted on firm acquaintance by the musically knowledgeable, because the significations within works and within common styles are relatively stable contextually—allowing in principle (and in fact) their listing.[30] And a style certainly possesses a definite set of syntactic rules of formation, ordering, connection, and combination for gestures admissible within the style. The appearance of any set of sounds and silences successively or simultaneously is a matter of probability or describable tendency (*i.e.*, inductive inference) according to the style's structure and the context. In short, musical tendencies—linguistic habits, if you will—define a style.

A conceptual key to understanding the notion of style is that of what we have called a tendency. We may take a *tendency*, whether musical or other, to be a relatively constant disposition to behave purposively, as a definite direction of movement toward some apparent goal.[31] Each goal may in turn act doubly as end for one set of tendencies and origin point for another set. In musical experience we find gestures both setting forth tendencies within the work and eliciting tendencies within us. Both sorts of tendency seek fulfillment in relation to what strands of gestures do. However, not every tendency, musical or organic, is consummated. Whereas some are fulfilled and yield positive value, others come to nothing and negative value. And what makes musical tendencies clear to us are the indexical signs. Denoting the points of origin for important musical motion, the salient way points, and terminal goals, the indices define the spatio-temporal shape and outline of musical gestures. They give us the structural tendencies of the aesthetic acts, and this fulfills logical functions.

Two important logical functions are involved in the indexical structuring of tendencies: one function affects us at the intuitional level and the other at the inferential level of response. Sets of indices determine much of the tendencies of sonorous motion made by musical gestures. Moreover, besides shaping gestures the indices also shape much of our affective responses. Indices give coherence both to the gestures themselves and to our successive affective responses to those gestures. Inasmuch as the musical index signs forcibly seize our attention and, as they surprise us and trip the startle mechanism of the brain, they elicit emotional dispositions or behavior. In addition, our primal responses to connections of gestures by negation similarly are affective for the same reasons. So to the extent that we are disposed to an unself-conscious and intuitive mode of response, we are guided by the stimuli of the organized series of effective indices. This is to say, then, that one function of the indexical structure of gestural tendencies is to give logical form to our aesthetic experience at the instinctual level. The function is supported by our intuitions of negations as they relate gestures. Hence, we may say that in intuitively disposed responses to gestures related by material implication, the musical indices (and negations) lead us through their own logical form in stimulus-controlled affective behavior. Indices and negations allow us to follow instinctively in a cohesive experience the sense of implicative acts of conditional expressions. The second valuable logical function of the indexical structuring of gestural tendencies is to display for our reason the logical form of gestures (*i.e.*, intergestural coherence). Intellectually interpreting the organization of indices in a conditional gesture allows us to infer what the probable course of musical events will be. Over and beyond the affective elements in interpretants (*e.g.*, the propositional attitude for 'if-then'), inference from one gesture to another connected by the implicative relation requires one to interpret imaginatively by self-conscious reasoning and expectation. The inferential act depends upon there being definite schematic ordering of indices that clearly delineate musical tendencies. The tendencies outlined by indexical signs objectively define much of the implication binding together the two phases of a conditional. They allow us to extrapolate. As we attend to an antecedent gesture and ascertain the tendencies at work, we can *suppose* what sort of musical tendencies are the reasonable consequence to come. Thus, the indexical structure of the antecedent gesture leads us to predict the nature of the signified referent of that gesture, the ensuing consequent.

Now, the predictions made in hearing a work, like all predictions, pertain to things not yet observed. Moreover, it is most important to see that, as inductive extrapolations, musical predictions in listening simply cannot be inferred as logical necessity from what has been observed. Past occurrences alone do not impose any logical demands on the future.

And so it seems there is little or no sense in speaking of a *necessary* kind of logical connection for matters of fact such as musical gestures. Whatever sense can be given to the notion of a logical connection by implication between musical gestures must rest on ingrained general experiential as well as musical habits of thought and feeling in making inductive inferences while listening. The brutal fact is: *any* gesture *may* follow any other gesture. There is no purely logical necessity for one gesture preceding or following one or another. However, for aesthetic experience it also is greatly important that there are recognizable situations involving recurrent patterns of events and tendencies within music. These may be more or less firmly rooted in our prior musical experience, especially so with respect to systems of styles with which we have substantial familiarity. So in hearing conditional gestures our projective forecasts may be more or less well made because we know that certain kinds of gestural connections are better or less well entrenched than others. More simply, then, in conditional situations within a known style, where a kind of gesture B follows a kind of gesture A often enough, when one hears some gesture of the same kind as A, he is led by simple habit to expect something rather on the order of B.[32] But alone, these observations do not account for the stimuli that lead to conditioning the habits of inferring and accepting as valid the implicative relation of gestures in a conditional. It seems that the roots of musical (and, perhaps, purely logical) implications lie in our most primal instinctual intuitions of the rhythmic flow of experience in the largest sense.

Surely we have seen enough of properties of inference and implication to recognize that the implicative relation of gestures owes much of its meaning to the rhythmic quality of movement from antecedent to consequent. That is, by creating a particular set of conditions, the earlier phase of an implicative act may be said to arouse expectations and a certain concomitant excitement. And the expectations, which draw upon behavior supposed to have been learned already, involve the excitement and tension of initiating tendencies leading toward a specific sort of action. The later phase of the implicative act, arriving as the consequential expression of the conditions present in the earlier phase, consummates the tendencies and expectations of the earlier phase. The action of the whole conditional act, then, may build up tension and nervous energy in the antecedent that may be released in a stress upon the consequent. The conclusion of the act expresses the point toward which the force of the antecedent phase has driven.

It is also possible that a movement from antecedent to consequent may hold an internal position of greater or lesser intensity within a larger conceptual or rhythmic scheme. A complete implicative act might itself articulate only the accumulative phase of a rhythmic movement or only the stress and relaxation phase. Accordingly, in the former case, an antecedent gesture might be preparatory movement leading into a consequent of greater tension; the consequent might sustain or increase tension through its own containment of still more exciting material. Or, in the latter case, the antecedent gesture could be dynamically assertive, yet leading to a consequent gesture which spells out details, draws upon the antecedent's assertion, and more or less gradually exhausts relevant content in a movement in which intensity tapers off.

Our foregoing two paragraphs should have made it clear that rhythm is involved in an essential way with what, in music, compares to implication. And yet one might think that rhythm is more peculiar to music. But what is important is that it gives music an analogue for the psychology of implication, because of the commonage of rhythm in music and implication.

The analogy does not end with rhythm, however. It extends as well to other properties of sonorous motion, especially the cadential connections ending and between gestures and, in addition, to tonal direction and consonance-dissonance. Cadence is of particular importance in musical implication because of its pause or ending quality. Not only does cadence mark off the syntactical units, it also designates, by means of intensity and inflection, the sort of relation the closing gesture holds in connection with its successor. The conclusions of compound acts and complete simple acts tend to have terminal cadences and well made pauses as punctuation. And the articulation of earlier phases of complex and compound acts tends to have intermediate cadences. These sorts of cadence have great variety in intensity. The articulation achieved by intermediate cadences and caesurae are on the weaker, inconclusive, and suspensive side, whereas the terminal cadences are quite clearly conclusive in being either emphatic or fully reposeful, and in suggesting stronger articulation. Thus, the close of subordinate and dependent gestures or interpolated asides may have ending qualities of considerable tenseness, or frailty for that matter—but qualities expressing their inferior relation to their context. But the articulations between conjuncts call for the greater differentiation of more conspicuous caesurae along with a certain suspensiveness, so that the conjuncts sustain their interdependence. It is in concatenations of rhythmic, cadential, melodic, tonal-progressive, and inflective properties that the implicative relation is displayed in music.

We can say a few words about several other points of similarity between verbal and musical forms of implicative acts. One is that in inference there is a movement from one proposition to another in seeking out a goal. There is an effort to advance an argument and to establish an objective as resulting from the force contained in certain conditions. Musical motion has something like this progression of thought in music's directional quality of sonorous motion, in the way melodies and harmonies form gestures that strive to attain points of emphasis. Further support for the teleological tendencies of sonorous motion is generated by degrees of consonance and dissonance in gestures. This is especially true of cadence areas, where the sonorous gestures are made more or less tense and suspensive, resolved and reposeful in their directed motion to a closure. And similarly, background movement behind and between melodic gestures may contribute to unifying a pair of gestures by implication, as it were, into one set of properties, for background motion may cease or continue with cadences to further qualify the nature of the connection between phases of an act.

By way of drawing together what we have been saying about inferential acts and musical analogues, let us add this: the force of inference seems to reside in the expression of an act in several phases leading from one to another. We may say that an inference is a transition or movement to the completion of an act. But such acts may be expressed both in discourse and in other action; they are not limited to discourse alone.[33] Discourse makes a verbal transition to an assertion. It is one way of doing things—an internalization of gesture as a working out of conditional behavior and its consequences. But there is a more direct and active way of doing. The two ways need not be conceived as parallels to each other; discursive thought especially need not be considered an accompaniment of physical activity. Whereas discourse expresses inferential acts in internalized gesture of thought or in written and spoken form, music expresses an inferential act directly in gestural behavior. In music an inferential act is physically worked out in sonorous motion: one musical gesture, with its set of properties, implies and leads to another musical gesture with a set of properties that completes the total act and presents a unified and characteristic group of properties. The pervasive sense of unity conveyed by such an act—whether in discourse or music—has its basis in the conditional feelings of relation that the gestures exhibit and evoke. The drawing of a consequence from certain antecedents feels appropriate, because we have learned that gestures with certain properties fit together under certain conditions, and we habitually expect that they, or similar gestures, will usually do so.

In exemplification of the musical conditional let us examine the connection by material implication of a pair of relatively simple gestures from the familiar work and style of Beethoven. The opening statements of his *Sonata in D Major*, Op. 10, No. 3, for piano provide a classic specimen (Example 9-5, mm. 1–10).

EXAMPLE 9-5   Ludwig van Beethoven, *Sonata in D Major*, Op. 10, No. 3, I, mm. 1–10

The main tendencies of the antecedent (mm. 1–4) include: (1) the overall octaval rise from tonic to dominant, providing a melodically tensing arsis; (2) the steady, staccato quarters; (3) the prevailing soft dynamic; (4) the opening four tones suggesting a scalar thrust downward, which is deferred; (5) a conflicting melodic tendency as the main contour turns upward in tonic arpeggiation, then scalar motion through two octaves from dominant low point (m. 1) to sustained dominant top

(m. 4); (6) the taut dominant peak pointed up by sudden loudness; (7) plus the peak's conflicting metric function as the arsis measure in a trochaic alternation of metric thesis and arsis measures. The most significant predictive tendencies of the antecedent that effect a materially implicative relation are these: (1) the loud interruption of motion by the sustained dominant, which stylistically calls for a tonal continuation of melody to the tonic, (2) the early intimation of downward movement, postponed also at the dominant, and (3) the general rhythmic function of the gesture as an arsis, which implicitly calls for impending fulfillment in thesis or thesis and stasis expression. The implicative connection to the coming gesture holding in virtue of the antecedent's tendencies, the conclusion of the period form follows with tendencies to complete the ties that bind the conditional pair. The consequent gesture (mm. 5–10 with upbeat from m. 4) discloses: (1) the thesis of the contour continued in a conspicuous scalar slope that eases tension in declining to the tonic (mm. 5–8), harmonized in parallel first inversion triads; (2) reiteration and another stress on the former dominant peak (mm. 5–6), dropping to the tonic (mm. 7–8); (3) regular, slurred quarters; (4) soft dynamic again; (5) prolongation of the harmonic dominant on strong beats (mm. 5–7$\frac{1}{2}$) then tonic (mm. 7$\frac{1}{2}$–8); (6) relaxing into a metrically weak cadence on tonic (m. 8), which is extended by intersection with a full cadence formula on tonic (mm. 8–10); (7) the whole consequent standing as a thesis-stasis gesture of obvious stylistic probability. All those tendencies share involvement in display of the relation by material implication of the conditional pair of gestures. Some tendencies are more important retrodictive signs of connection in the relational complex. They are: (1) the recurrence of the top dominant pitch and the fall to the tonic, (2) the ampliative realization of the antecedent's beginning reference to a descending contour unravelling prior directional conflicts and tensions, (3) the assertion and further generalization of expected impulsion on dominant and release into tonic levels melodically and harmonically, which is confirmed by the stasis action of the full cadence on tonic, and (4) the consequent's explicit function in toto as a thesis-stasis gesture that consummates the tendencies of its antecedent. Inasmuch as the entire period form of antecedent and consequent gestures exhibits the sets of tendencies noted, we find a musical analogue to the logical conditional and connection of statements by material implication.

Having delved at length into the musical conditional and inference, we may add a few obvious but important observations on them. Recalling that a gesture may be a formal segment ranging from a simple motive up to major formal sections or even entire movements, we need to remember that musical conditionals also have such extent. Material implication may connect gestures of any contextual scope. This appears clear enough not to detain us now. Rather, certain interrelations of the syntax and pragmatics of musical inference can stand mentioning.

Regarding the relatedness of syntax and inference, one must not overlook the importance of fixed patterns or procedure by rule in composition. Whether predetermined by a style system or emergent within stylistic innovation, formal design offers composers schemata for making logically connected gestures. Accordingly, musical inferences by composer, performer, or auditor may be supported by explicit discursive knowledge about categorical forms such as rondo, fugue, and the like. The homogeneous and heterogeneous classes of forms outlined earlier list those formal bases for musical inferring. For genuinely comprehensive aesthetic experience of any work in a given style, discursive knowledge of the style's categorical designs and inferences based on that knowledge are indispensable requisites. But there also are equally valuable relations of syntax and pragmatics in musical inferrings. Thus, as a categorical design is involved in ordering gestures, control is given not only to gestural statements as schemata, but also control is given to the inferential retrodictions and expectations of performers and listeners. So in playing or listening to gestures of a sonata form, for example, a musically informed person is guided by the larger formal scheme in discerning the logical relations binding gestures together. Because one knows the orderings of theme groups and sections as patterns of thought, he is prepared to recognize the conjunctive gestures, disjunctive or conditional gestures, and negations that are presented to give a cohesive form and coherent experience. One is equipped to infer, recollect, and to intuit with probable accuracy. By these means the composer may communicate with his performers and auditors. Through use of formal schemata and connectives the composer may take advantage of symbolic structures to present his statements logically (or illogically, if he prefers). The presentations give one and all a chance to make the most refined or forceful musical inferences and to enjoy profound aesthetic experience. Such uses of music's forms and connectives seem to correspond in musical thinking as closely as our artistic modes of communication come to the logician's communications, which are based on primitive terms and relations, postulate sets, theorems and rules of inference used in deductive formal systems. So, then, we must acknowledge the aesthetic importance of several syntactic, pragmatic, and inferential matters: (1) the logical operators connecting gestures, (2) their location within formal designs which the operators give coherence, and (3) the control over interpretation that the operators and forms give musical experience.

Without elaboration we now must indicate a further point of significance for the future development of adequate musical aesthetics, particularly affecting musical theory and composition as well as performance and, ultimately, listening. This point is that we need a program for the development of the musical analogues of propositional calculi. Moreover, we need such a program both in rigorous form and in informal account accessible to the average musician and sophisticated music listener.[34] In that theoretical program the musical gesture, as a "well formed formula" or unanalyzed expression, would be treated as in a formal logical system such as advanced by Alonzo Church. Then groupings of gestures would be true solely in virtue of their logical relations or structure. The musical theory accordingly would need to elaborate logical systems. The minimal content of such a system might be couched in exhibition or in listing sets of musical ideas necessary for creative syntax; to wit: (1) symbols for undefined gestural terms and primitive relations, (2) primitive "propositions" or a postulate set, as well as (3) primitive rules of inference, and (4) theorems or inferential operations for forming complex gestural combinations. To a very limited extent discussions in this chapter imply a certain background for such a program and suggest some possible lines for its development. However, substantive pursuit lies outside the scope of this book for the most part.

Here is a good place for us to restate the main points of our discussion of logical relations in music. The main point is that music offers its gestures so that the gestures and their component sign properties are connected in ways which are analogous to the connections signified by certain logical operators. Moreover, the logical modes of connection to which we have drawn attention may be recognized as an autonomous dimension of music. The logical functions operate in music by the exhibition of musical properties: (1) by the display of the properties characterizing feelings of relation and propositional attitudes of belief, doubt, and negation; (2) by the acting out of punctuation meanings common also to speech (*i.e.*, position, pause, emphasis, and inflection); (3) and by the execution in sonorous motion of inferential acts, in which musical properties have functions analogous to inferential schemes of discourse (particularly connection by conjunction, disjunction, negation, and material implication).[35]

Truth and Congeneric Meaning

Before many philosophers were accepting aesthetic experience as (1) not requiring some unique "essence" or property of the art work and (2) *not* based on a special "aesthetic attitude," there often was associated with those notions a doctrine to the effect that artistic expressions were neither true nor false.[36] Although the doctrine persists to some extent as a relic in aesthetic theory, it now must be recognized as poppycock—if we are to accept a semiotic-gestural theory of music. The doctrine failed utterly to account for a number of evident facts. Foremost among these is that there are extensive similarities between the "fictive" or "pictorial" worlds of art as closed systems and the creative linguistic systems of philosophers such as Carnap—not to mention the extensive ramifications of set theory for musical systems such as those of Schoenberg and Milton Babbitt. In addition, the doctrine seems to ignore pragmatic conceptions of truth as fulfillment of expectations—which obviously apply to music. And with acceptance of iconic signs as central to the meaning of art works it is clear that music can and does have sense and reference, signifying symbolically and informally, Mrs. Langer notwithstanding. Accordingly, as musical gestures are matters of fact, so are their significations, so are their logical connections, and so must these involve truth values both in congeneric and extrageneric dimensions of the art work. However, even now aesthetic writings dwell too much upon obvious, if important, features of artistic truth—the age-old problems of "truth about" and propositional functions or being "true to life" (mimesis or verisimilitude).[37] The overemphasis on extrageneric meaning and truth results in an undue neglect of congeneric truth values, the latter being our present concern.

In Willard Quine's book, *Word and Object*, important cues are given us about truth, which apply to congeneric musical meaning.[38] Quine seems to affirm that truth is linked to non-verbal stimuli (which would include musical gestures) and is affected by one's theoretical point of view. He suggests that use of the word "true" (or "false") is best expressed from the viewpoint of a theory and within its terms, complete with the theory's sense of "reality." In addition, truth and falsity are not simply properties of expressions. They are "passing traits" for a person, at a place and time, under conditions bearing upon the utterance. All this seems applicable to musical gestures. Another philosopher, S. F. Barker, points out that there are good grounds for our supposing that a clear-cut distinction between inductive and deductive inference is questionable.[39] This is so especially when inductive inference is conceived, as in this book, to involve problematic, ampliative, and generalizing features. Such inference (as in congeneric musical cases) is based, as is deductive inference, upon relations between statements.[40] Furthermore, according to Arthur Pap, it is possible that even deductive inference may involve gradations of entailment—which suggests that deductive truth also may be a matter of degree.[41] So if we follow those foregoing thoughts, we surely may describe truth and falsity as variable gradients. Truth values seemingly are tied to a lack of clear enough difference between induction and deduction as well as to cases in which truth and entailment are matters of degree.[42] These points need be borne in mind in considering truth and music.

In musical experience our reality is the sensory world of sound, silence, and rhythm known by acquaintance. It is a complex reality. In one sense it is the reality of purely musical events in congeneric gestures and their significations. In another sense it also is the reality of musical gestures that signify extragenerically. In either sense musical reality is apprehended and interpreted just as any other reality, and the interpretation calls for instinctual and rational responses just as other reality does. Our musical realities include musical gestures with logical structuring. So in view of the preceding observations on inference and truth, it may be ridiculous to prescribe some all-inclusive way to verify musical statements and sequences of them, because it appears that all musical gestures may not be shown to be true or false in the same way.[43] Besides, in themselves some musical gestures would have no congeneric truth value beyond their corroboration as stylistically possible stimulus objects by their self-ostensive "definition," *i.e.*, their brute existence before us. Some musical gestures in a work must be accepted as congenerically primitive terms—objective states of affairs—in order that the musical act can be developed. As regards congeneric meaning and syntax, some atomic or simple gestures are presupposed as fact. What makes such basic gestures congenerically true, then, is that the composer has created and presented them and that others have accepted them or assented to them in good faith. In this sense basic gestures should be regarded as simple matters of fact.

We also must acknowledge another sense in which congeneric gestures are true and note how their truth is verified.

One may interpret a gesture itself not only as an individual or fact but as a basic statement. A basic gestural statement is a musical observation-statement: it expresses an attitude and signifies a fact or state of affairs. The fact or state of affairs a basic gestural statement indicates in a congeneric truth is another musical gesture, which in its turn may be interpreted as an individual or congenerically primitive event. Confrontation with the relevant fact—the other iconically signified gesture—is what allows verification of a basic gestural statement's truth. An interpreter's believing in the signification's adequacy and that the signified gesture is a fact is necessary. In addition, the signification and sign must be describable. To verify such a basic gestural statement, then, one must be able to show (1) that the signified gesture exists and may be accepted as an individual or fact, (2) that the basic gestural statement and the signified gestural state of affairs are adequately correlated iconically, and (3) that in normal discourse one can properly say and point out what the correlating properties are.

Basic gestures may in turn be negated or may be combined by logical constants to form other molecular or complex gestures. These other complex gestures are congenerically true or false in virtue of their relation(s) to those presupposed basic gestures and to the extent interpreters affirm belief in those relations. Insofar as they can be called true, the complex gestures are true to a person (1) when faced by certain relevant facts and conditions and (2) in view of his beliefs about the facts. The facts are the basic gestures and the elemental sonic and rhythmic characteristics creating their sonorous motion. One's belief about the elemental facts eventually comes down to one's acquaintance with them or their sense of reality to him—pure and simply, feeling. The belief is essentially pre-linguistic and instinctual—the final court of appeal for truth—although it does take other forms such as expecting and remembering, too. So basic gestures and their sonic-rhythmic properties stand as factual states of affairs in congeneric musical meanings. The logical structure of complex gestures and their syntactic relations to basic gestures determine the truth value of such molecular gestures. The forms of structure and connective relations for the chief kinds of molecular gesture have been examined. However, iconicity or resemblance of other gestures to a work's basic gestures is central to determining truth value. The correspondence of derived gestures to the basic ones constitutes grounds for affirming their truth. But regarding the complex gestures and the syntactic rationale for their truth, the following may bear recapitulation. In disjunctive gestures, if either one or both of the disjunct basic gestures is accepted as true, then the complex whole is true. Otherwise it is false. In the case of the conjunctive gesture, the compounded gesture as a whole is true provided that each of its basic conjunct gestures is believed true. Otherwise, the whole is false. And for the conditionals, the consequent gesture's fulfillments of expectations caused by the antecedent gesture are the grounds for acceptance of the conditional as true. Otherwise, if the consequent thwarts or disappoints one's expectations, then the conditional would be interpreted as false.

One of the outstanding links between syntactics, pragmatics and truth is forged by the instinctual responses to logical structuring that interpretant formation involves. Logical relations may elicit affective (including conative) responses as well as relatively more restricted discursive responses. Our earlier examination of propositional attitudes reveals that a great deal of instinctual stimulus-function is involved in the exhibition of logical constants in music. So the affective force of the truth value of conditionals bears further scrutiny. Here it is important to acknowledge that the negation—explicit or implicit—of one's interpretative inferences or desires draws out affective responses.[44] This is especially so in interpreting conditionals. A consequent's frustration of one's desires or conflict with his expectations may be expected to lead to affective response. Moreover, the intensity and extent of affective-conative response would tend to correlate closely in degree to the gradations of surprise or the thwarting of interests, which the objective stimulus object displays or causes by its apparent improbability. However, when the interpreter regards the probable consequent of an antecedent as a disjunction of two or more probable conclusions, then definiteness of prediction and any attendant degrees of surprise and frustration may be lessened. Corresponding affective-conative response levels might also be milder feeling and satisfaction or aversion. But where predictive antecedent signs are strongest and consequent denial of antecedent tendencies most pronounced, the greatest emotional responses may be the resultants. These remarks hold, with appropriate changes of concepts, for the falsification of other connective relations of gestures by disjunction and conjunction. In short, when not anticipated, negations and complex gestures that do not ring true probably will cause affective responses. In this connection it would appear clear why many listeners and performers unaccustomed to a work or a style may have emotional experiences with them: nearly everything is a surprise; the musical events seem false or altogether unrealistic. Lack of relevant stylistic ("linguistic") acquaintance may place some interpreters in an auditory world of blooming confusion. In that situation stimuli can hardly be grasped as relevant basic facts or gestures, let alone relationships between gestures noticed as existent, gestures understood as true or not.

Should there be a genuine question about congeneric truthfulness, only acquaintance will help; then only such acts as re-hearing, examining the score, and inspecting the given data can satisfy one's doubts. However, if another person is available to aid, he may help to resolve doubts by pointing out relevant facts which we have identified as the basic gesture(s) and their elemental properties. The demonstrative assistance may be supplemented by discursive descriptions and comments. Verbal directions may explain where, how, what, and why certain facts are relevant. In these latter cases, where assistance is involved, the only hope for one's recognition of a congeneric truth or falsehood lies in the person's getting the drift of what is shown or told him. Grasping the congeneric truth of musical gestures requires us to use our senses and reason. There seems to be no uniformly guaranteed way to find such musical truth without aesthetic sensitivity, perspicacity, knowledge of a work's style, a firm acquaintance with the elemental musical properties, discernment of basic gestural facts, and ability to comprehend the functioning of the logical operators and forms in music.

There *is* logic in music. It takes effort and extensive knowledge of music to grasp it.

Notes

1 Charles W. Morris, "Foundations of the Theory of Signs," in *International Encyclopedia of Unified Science*, vol. 1, no. 2, ed. Rudolf Carnap, Otto Neurath, and Charles W. Morris (Chicago: University of Chicago Press), p. 90.
2 Ibid. pp. 95–98.
3 Ibid., p. 86; Bertrand Russell, *An Inquiry into Meaning and Truth* (Baltimore: Penguin Books, 1962), pp. 60–61, 65.
4 William James, *The Principles of Psychology*, vol. I (New York: Henry Holt and Co., 1890), pp. 245–46.
5 Morris, "Foundations of the Theory of Signs," pp. 97–98; Russell, *Meaning and Truth*, pp. 201–02.
6 Arthur Pap, *Semantics and Necessary Truth* (New Haven: Yale University Press, 1958), p. 369.
7 Russell, *Meaning and Truth*, pp. 69–80.
8 Ibid., p. 200. Cf. George Herbert Mead, *The Philosophy of the Act*, ed. Charles W. Morris et al. (Chicago: University of Chicago Press, 1938), pp. 114–15.

9 Russell, *Meaning and Truth*, pp. 276–77.
10 This line of thought was suggested by Dr. Hubert Kessler of the University of Illinois and is outlined in his paper "On the Modes of Connection of Musical Ideas."
11 Irving M. Copi, *Symbolic Logic*, 3rd ed. (New York: The Macmillan Co., 1967), pp. 12–14.
12 Paul R. Halmos, *Naive Set Theory* (Princeton: D. Van Nostrand Co., Inc., 1960), p. 13.
13 Russell, *Meaning and Truth*, pp. 69–80.
14 Copi, *Symbolic Logic*, pp. 9–10.
15 Halmos, *Naive Set Theory*, p. 14.
16 Russell, *Meaning and Truth*, pp. 276–77.
17 Silvan S. Tomkins and Carroll E. Izard, eds., *Affect, Cognition, and Personality* (London: Tavistock Publications Ltd., 1965), pp. 15, 253.
18 Bertrand Russell, *Principles of Mathematics* (New York: W. W. Norton and Company, Inc., 1964), p. 23.
19 Rudolf Carnap, *Introduction to Symbolic Logic and Its Applications* (New York: Dover Publications, Inc., 1958), p. 19.
20 Copi, *Symbolic Logic*, p. 14.
21 J. O. Urmson, ed., "Logic," in *The Concise Encyclopaedia of Western Philosophy and Philosophers* (London: Hutchinson and Co., Ltd., 1960), p. 234–38. A clear account of kinds of inference is given by S. F. Barker, "Must Every Inference Be Either Deductive or Inductive?" *Philosophy in America*, ed. Max Black (London: George Allen and Unwin Ltd., 1965), pp. 58–73.
22 Gilbert Ryle, *The Concept of Mind* (New York: Barnes and Noble, 1949), pp. 232, 300–01.
23 Hubert Kessler, "On the Modes of Connection of Musical Ideas," (manuscript, 1960), pp. 2–5.
24 Ludwig Wittgenstein, *Philosophical Investigations*, trans. G. E. M. Anscombe (Oxford: Basil Blackwell, 1953), pp. 181ᵉ–183ᵉ.
25 Russell, *Meaning and Truth*, pp. 170, 236–37.
26 Pap, *Semantics and Necessary Truth*, pp. 327–80.
27 A. J. Ayer, *The Problem of Knowledge* (New York: The Macmillan Co., 1956), p. 174; Russell, *Meaning and Truth*, pp. 133, 204–05.
28 Morris R. Cohen, *A Preface To Logic* (New York: Henry Holt and Co., Meridian Books, 1956), pp. 65–68; H. H. Price, *Thinking and Experience* (Cambridge: Harvard University Press, 1962), pp. 128–35.
29 See Leonard B. Meyer, *Emotion and Meaning in Music* (Chicago: University of Chicago Press, 1956), pp. 47–79. The best discussion of style and style systems is given by Meyer. His extraordinary book gives painstaking elaboration of the comprehensive meaning of inferential musical experience and includes extensive analysis of the intellectual and affective elements in the music itself (which embody implicative relationships often). Also see Leonard B. Meyer, *Music, the Arts, and Ideas* (Chicago: University of Chicago Press, 1967), chaps. 1, 3, and 7 for related discussions.
30 Susanne K. Langer has argued that music is not a language because, she maintains, it has no, or is incapable of having, a dictionary of musical denotations. The argument that music is not a language is true of music as a whole, but it appears false of music restricted to a well formed style or a style system.
31 James Drever, *A Dictionary of Psychology* (Baltimore: Penguin Books, 1952), p. 290.
32 See Nelson Goodman, *Fact, Fiction, and Forecast* 2nd ed. (Indianapolis: The Bobbs-Merrill Co., Inc., 1965), pp. 59–83 for a clear discussion of these matters of the inductive problem.
33 Wittgenstein, *Philosophical Investigations*, p. 136ᵉ.
34 Significant steps in the direction of propositional calculi are in development, most notably in the theoretical papers of Milton Babbitt and his pupil Michael Kassler. *E.g.*, see Michael Kassler, "Toward a Theory That Is the Twelve-Note-Class System," *Perspectives of New Music* 5 (1967), 1–80.

35 I am not asserting that music, as practiced now, is a vehicle for an unrestricted range of propositional statement making and expression of logical functions. It quite obviously is not. Rather, music remains a vehicle *par excellence* for expressing immediate values but values logically interconnected. Moreover, it must be clear that there are major logical functions music is ill-equipped to handle. Among these, the most apparent difficulty is in what philosophers call "immediate inference": universal quantification, expressing the sense of words like "all," "none" and existential quantification, expressing the meaning that words like "some" do. Thus, music seems at a loss to express propositions such as "All S is P" or "Some S is P." But musical gestures can and do present "S," "P," and seemingly can express by direct presentation the fact that "This gesture is S" or "This gesture is P," "This negates that," or "This implies that."

36 *E.g.*, L. A. Reid, *A Study In Aesthetics* (New York: The Macmillan Co., 1931), pp. 252–56, 261–67. In contrast, valuable comments on the sources of those older views are given by Leonard Linsky, *Referring* (London: Routledge and Kegan Paul, 1967), pp. 28, 74–80, 88–89, 97–98.

37 Discussions that do penetrate into artistically relevant issues of extrageneric reference and truth include: Theodore Meyer Greene, *The Arts and the Art of Criticism* (Princeton: Princeton University Press, 1940), chap. 23; ———, *Moral, Aesthetic and Religious Insight* (New Brunswick: Rutgers University Press, 1957), chap. 4; John Hospers, "Implied Truths in Literature," in *Philosophy Looks at the Arts*, ed. Joseph Margolis (New York: Charles Scribner's Sons, 1962), pp. 199–214; ———, *Meaning and Truth in the Arts* (Chapel Hill: University of North Carolina Press, 1946), chaps. 6 and 7; John Margolis, *The Language of Art and Art Criticism* (Detroit: Wayne State University Press, 1965), chap. 2; Morris Weitz, *Philosophy of the Arts* (Cambridge: Harvard University Press, 1950), pp. 134–52.

38 Willard Van Orman Quine, *Word and Object* (Cambridge: M.I.T. Press, 1960), pp. 12. 23–24, 191, 226–27.

39 Barker, "Must Every Inference . . . ?," pp. 58–73.

40 Morris R. Cohen and Ernest Nagel, *An Introduction to Logic*, Book I, Harbinger Edition (New York: Harcourt, Brace and World, Inc., 1962), pp. 12, 24, 157.

41 Pap, *Semantics and Necessary Truth*, chaps. 11 and 12.

42 Cf. Michael Dummett, "Truth," in *Philosophical Logic*, ed. P. F. Strawson (Oxford: Oxford University Press, 1967), pp. 49–68.

43 See Alfred J. Ayer, *The Concept of a Person* (London: Macmillan and Co., Ltd., 1963), pp. 162–87. Our discussion is indebted to Mr. Ayer's essay on "Truth."

44 Stephen C. Pepper, *Aesthetic Quality* (New York: Charles Scribner's Sons, Inc., 1937), pp. 89–113; Reid, *Study in Aesthetics*, pp. 122–24, 129–31, 160–63.

Extrageneric Musical Meaning

Extrageneric musical meanings are those resultants of a primarily iconic sign situation in which someone interprets a musical work or some portion of it as a sign of some apparently non-musical object. The external objects a musical work or its gestures may signify are multitudinous. For the moment we would but point out two important classes of potential significations, namely organic behavior and extraorganic events or things. We shall return to these shortly. First, however, we should observe that there is not uniform belief in the possibilities or values of extrageneric musical meaning.

Apparently there has always been controversy over whether or not music has extrageneric meaning. Although the controversies have been concerned with extraorganic objects—particularly with the imitation of natural objects such as the sea, bird calls, and the like—the main area of contention has been the expression and signification of affective and conative states on the one hand and the arousal by music of those states in listeners on the other.

We read, on the negative side, of the opinion held by the Epicurean Philodemus (first century B.C.), who reportedly argued to the effect that music is no more an art capable of extrageneric significance, imitative or expressive, no more an affective stimulus, than cookery.[1] And in more recent times Stravinsky has rejected the idea that music is in any fundamental sense expressive:

> I consider that music, by its very nature, is essentially powerless to *express* anything at all, whether a feeling, an attitude of mind, a psychological mood, a phenomenon of nature, etc. . . . Expression has never been an inherent property of music.[2]

And then one can scarcely overlook Eduard Hanslick's famous remarks of disparagement:

> On the one hand it is said that the aim and object of music is to excite emotions, *i.e.*, pleasurable emotions; on the other hand, the emotions are said to be the subject matter which musical works are intended to illustrate. Both propositions are alike in this, that one is as false as the other.[3]

Aristotle believed otherwise. He apparently regarded music as significant of life values and as capable of stimulating one's affective responses.

> It must have such an influence if characters are affected by it. And that they are so affected is proved in many ways, and not least by the power which the songs of Olympus exercise; for beyond question they inspire enthusiasm, and enthusiasm is an emotion of the ethical part of the soul. Besides, when men hear imitations, even apart from the rhythms and tunes themselves, their feelings move in sympathy. . . . Rhythm and melody supply imitations of anger and gentleness, and also of courage and temperance, and of all the qualities contrary to these, and of the other qualities of character which hardly fall short of the actual affections, as we know from our own experience, for in listening to such strains our souls undergo a change. The habit of feeling pleasure or pain at mere representations is not far removed from the same feeling about realities; . . .[4]

And René Descartes, in the opening sentence of his *Compendium Of Music*, expresses what appears to be his very clearly and distinctly apprehended idea that music seeks to stimulate affective responses: "The basis of music is sound; its aim is to please and to arouse various emotions in us."[5]

Proponents of the positive viewpoint have, as Liszt and Wagner did, held that music expresses affective states, and some, notably Smetana and Strauss, have pointed out that music also refers to scenes from life and actions.[6] In our day Aaron Copland sustains the positive view in writing that

> If forced to explain the creative musician's basic objective in elementary terms, I would say that a composer writes music to express and communicate and put down in permanent form certain thoughts, emotions and states of being.[7]

The weight of philosophers' and composers' opinion seems to fall heavily on the positive side, which can be corroborated by reading histories of aesthetic and sources printing composers' comments.[8] This is particularly evident in reading letters of Mozart and Tschaikowsky. In a letter to his father (August 26, 1781), Mozart speaks enthusiastically of how he has signified by specific musical devices such extrageneric objects and events as the emotion rage (made comical), a throbbing heart, the swell of a throbbing breast, whispering and sighing during passages in his opera *The Abduction from the Seraglio.*[9] Tschaikowsky, too, writes to Madame von Meck to tell her with typical zeal about his expression and portrayal through his *Symphony IV* of such extrinsic things as fate in conflict with strivings for happiness, jealousy, lament and despair, joy, a dreamy soul, and a rustic holiday.[10] The "ayes" have it, if any weight is given to sources available.[11] I am aware that autonomistically oriented theorists pop up on such points to argue. Although it may seem a monstrous impertinence to presume that an artist such as Mozart or Tschaikowsky is an intellectual ass who simply doesn't know what he does regardless of what he says he intends, many a critic hesitates not a whit to so presume. But those critics have a point, too. For obviously, if an artist achieves his goals and signifies his intentions, then it would seem that the work itself should on its own reveal whatever was intended, without the crutch of the composer's verbalizations. However, this is not to say that one ought not go outside a work to artists' commentaries. On the contrary, we may advisedly consider a composer's stated intentions. Then in comparing work and intentions, we may choose to rule out as aesthetically irrelevant whatever he has stated that fails in our opinion to correspond with what the work means to us. But what matters in considering the stated intentions of artists is, after carefully comparing the composer's intentions to the work alone and to our own interpretations, whether on returning to hear the work again we find the *work itself* more meaningful, satisfying, or emotionally stirring.

But although a positive majority opinion affords a certain comfort, it is elsewhere that we find cause to believe in the extrageneric meaning of music. It is our own experience that leads to belief (or doubt), and the theories of philosophers and composers that help us to gain understanding. In the present study, music is regarded as extragenerically significant and meaningful. It remains, however, to introduce a number of points in order to explain how and why music has extrageneric meaning and to what extent. I shall, moreover, want to relate extrageneric musical meaning to the congeneric meaning of music. At this point we should note that our attention is largely on music without text and the instrumental accompaniments to dance and vocal music. The admitted external reference of words appearing in vocal music, while aesthetically relevant, is not central to the matter at hand. The difficulties in the extrageneric meaning of music arise most pointedly with music that has no text, as was observed early for musical aesthetics by Plato.[12]

We would say that the extrageneric meaning of music is a resultant of the interaction of listener and music. Extrageneric meaning emerges as the listener responds to a musical gesture or a set of musical properties as signifying something outside the work proper or, for that matter, any other work in the same medium.[13] The musical work as a whole or some part of it may be interpreted as referring to—pointing to, characterizing, or connected with—non-musical objects such as attitudes, thoughts, affective and conative states, physical things and events, or values and properties of such objects. Then music may affect the interpreter by disposing him to respond in ways that usually occur when he is stimulated by such non-musical objects. And the response sequences elicited by the music from an interpreter so disposed are those that are appropriate to things ordinarily regarded as extrinsic to bare musical elements.[14]

Extrageneric musical meaning is possible largely because the musical elements and gestural configurations of them may function as iconic signs. And, as we know, the semantic peculiarity of iconic signs is that they potentially mean whatever they resemble. So the basis of extrageneric meaning consists of the inherent properties of musical gestures that exhibit similarities: music can mean whatever it resembles sufficiently to elicit from an interpreter responses appropriate to that extrinsic object. More specifically, the extrageneric significations of musical icons may be subdivided into the two classes of (1) organic behavior (overt action or intraorganic states) and (2) extraorganic things and events, including those natural and man-made. This is not intended to say that the semantic range of extrageneric musical meaning is anything and everything, but rather that it potentially does include both organic and extraorganic objects.

Local and regional musical properties occupy the role of central importance in extrageneric meaning. These properties are what one interprets as signs having, as the case may be, iconic, indexical, or logical meaning. They make up musical gestures which act as complex signs signifying, primarily iconically, non-musical objects. And we recall in this connection that a prominent feature of icons is that they directly present qualities for our immediate apprehension. Icons embody qualities in the elements and configurations of elements in a significant medium. This is especially valuable to bear in mind in considering the expressivity of music.

Musical Expressivity

Tone and rhythm manifest expressivity.[15] "Directly the inner man presents himself to the ear through the *tone* of his voice. *Tone* is the expression of feeling . . . ," writes Wagner.[16] And, indeed, the roots of sonic and rhythmic expressivity lie in man's brute gestures of voice and movement of body. Our instinctual cries of anguish and pain or pleasure and joy, as well as the revealing qualities of the movements of our bodies, are inseparably tied up with our attitudes. Feeling and desire on one side and the expressive gestural qualities of sounds and movements on the other side reciprocally affect one another at the physiological level.[17] And it is just these things we mean by saying that gestures carry attitude with them. It is something we know by acquaintance. We feel it and notice it in our own behavior, and we recognize it in the overt behavior of others just as well.[18] The qualities of tone and rhythm directly express attitude. And, accordingly, we recognize that those qualities, which are the elements of music, make music expressive. So we know that the sonic and rhythmic elements of music—the local qualities—are inherently expressive of organic sentience. We recognize that musical gestures express attitudes; they carry attitudes with them. "Music is a cry of the soul," as Delius succinctly put it.[19] But, we must remember, that "cry of the soul" is *in* the music itself; the sentient attitudes that music expresses are there objectively in tone and rhythm as such.[20]

Not only are the sonic qualities themselves expressive, they also excite affective responses in us.[21] Sounds directly affect the organism and create the inner commotions of emotion. This may be so because auditory impulses are said to have more extensive pathways to and within the brain than do any of the other sensory systems.[22] But the general significance of sound is that it alerts us and arouses our most primitive instinctual tendencies of behavior.[23] And, moreover, the rhythmic qualities—the impacts and changes in the tensions, stresses, and reposes of sonic qualities—also participate in this affective arousal of the organism.[24] So, then, because the music's sonic and rhythmic elements stimulate affective responses, music itself becomes a powerful affective stimulus; the "emotional reaction to music is normal and basic."[25]

Now we wish to explore the special significance of the points in the foregoing two paragraphs: *because music expresses attitudes and stimulates affective responses, a musical "organism" can engage us in an attitudinal conversation.* This fact has further important ramifications, as we shall see.

Affective and Reflective Responses
to Musical Attitude

But now notice that, when we perform or listen to music, the tone of musical gestures—the attitudes they carry—affect us. Each gesture and attitude of the music is a stimulus to our adjustive behavior. The level of our responses, then, is unreflective, immediate, and unself-conscious. We adjust to the tone of gesture instinctively and without thought or awareness of our adjustment. And at this level the meaning of the musical gesture is our affective response. If the tone of the gesture appears aggressive or angry, our most natural tendencies of response are a physiological mobilization for fight or flight. That sort of primitive response is what the musical gesture means. When our responses in such attitudinal conversation are instinctual and unself-conscious, we are behaving at a pre-linguistic level.

We know, or at least we expect, that the gestures of musical art works are conceived with an attitudinal conversation between music and listener or performer in mind, for we expect that the composer works from both an intuitive and an intellectual point of view. He creates the musical gestures with awareness of the attitudes that various interpreters may take toward the attitudes of the music. Gesture and attitude are selected to elicit certain responses. The sequence of musical attitudes is chosen—hopefully, we take it—by the composer's lending an inner ear to what others' instinctual and intelligent reactions may be. So the composer may, in that way, make a work that controls the performer's and listener's instinctual responses and guides reasoned listening. We may say it is expected of the composer that he conceive the music's gestures and attitudes because he wishes to affect the behavior of performers and listeners as he knows the gestures affect him when he takes the attitudes of other interpreters. Such role taking is needed for musical communication on the composer's part.

But the adjustive responses we tend to make in relation to gestural attitudes hold whether our performing or listening perspective is unreflective or intellectual. However, when we respond at a linguistic and intellectual level of conduct, a big difference is involved. We are socially aware of the attitudes of the musical organism, aware of the attitudes expressed toward our own attitudes. We are self-conscious of both the attitudes of the music and ourselves. And to the extent we are self-conscious, we try to rein in our overt instinctual responses and exert control over the brute tendencies our attitudinal adjustments may set in motion. Nonetheless, even when self-consciously attentive, our attitudes are influenced by the music.

Then we must note that, at a linguistic level of conduct, the composer employs musical gestures and attitudes voluntarily in order to affect interpreters in the same way he himself has been affected. And in that case the musical gestures become potential linguistic symbols. The listener or the performer, if his viewpoint also is self-conscious, may be expected to grasp the symbolic use of the musical gestures. So we may say that, when the musical gestures in fact do explicitly elicit from both composer and others the same response within the same context and on all occasions of use, the musical gestures act as linguistic symbols. And in such situations, an intended jesting attitude and humorous gesture will imply a similar response from interpreter and composer. The listener, from his self-conscious perspective, takes the gesture as making fun and behaves accordingly. If the gesture is funny, he laughs—albeit inwardly, perhaps. In such a situation the humorous gesture implies a specific completion of the aesthetic act: musical joke—the listener's pleasure and laughter. Anyone familiar with Charles Ives' fun-poking *Variations On America* for organ know how truly humorous and linguistically conventional music can be, and he knows what we mean here. But the point is that the symbolic musical gesture stands for a social act. The implicit completion of the social act is a common response to the gesture by composer and listener, which the composer intends and the listener grasps. Hence, the symbolic function of the gesture: the gesture stands for the common interpretation of all involved.

A far-reaching ramification which we should notice is involved in, and begins to emerge from, our present stage of discussion. Because linguistic musical gestures both express attitudes and symbolize a specific sort of completion to the aesthetic act, music and aesthetic experience cannot be confined to a world of autonomous, self-enclosed significance. Music does have reference to extrageneric objects, such as the performer's or listener's behavior, and it does deal with life values. This is, moreover, pertinent both to affective-instinctual levels of behavior and to intellectual levels.

We have seen that musical gestures are inherently expressive: they express attitudes which the composer presumably has tested himself and re-tested from the assumed viewpoints of others. And musical gestures affect others' attitudes, drawing out instinctual tendencies of response. Music is, above all else, addressed to us as listeners or performers and intended to affect us. The reference of musical gestures is to the completions of the aesthetic acts they initiate. And the completions of the acts include resultants of two sorts, those congenerically musical—such as gestures appearing elsewhere in the work—and also those resultants in the interpreters' responses. Musical gestures signify both sorts of resultants. So we find that the musical gestures express attitudes and that the references of music's gestural sign complexes are to other previous, concurrent, or subsequent musical events and attitudes on the one side, and, on the other side, the references of musical gestures and attitudes are to the attitudinal adjustments and other tendencies to respond of the performer or listener. Thus, the comprehensive significance of musical gestures includes (1) congeneric significations and attitudes of the musical organism and (2) extrageneric significations, at least in the sense of the attitudes elicited from interpreters.

The case may be likened to Bertrand Russell's pointing out that the sense meaning of a word is its primary reason for its use rather than the syntactical and semantic relations it bears within language to other words:

> The purpose of words, though philosophers seem to forget this simple fact, is to deal with matters other than words.[26]

I insist similarly that an important purpose of musical gestures, though many aestheticians and musicians forget this simple fact, is to deal with matters other than musical gestures. That other aesthetic purpose of music is to deal with non-musical things. Foremost among these are the attitudes listeners have in response to musical gestures.

Depending on the interpreter's point of view, the meaning to him of a musical gesture may be pre-linguistic or linguistic. If he experiences the musical gesture in an unself-conscious way and responds instinctually, the meaning of the gesture will be what he feels and undergoes; it will be his instinctual, affective response. It is a pre-linguistic meaning. But one may attend self-consciously. And then, if he is aware and notices and recognizes the gesture's attitude and what its effect is on his own attitude and tendency to respond, the meaning of the gesture, although still affective, may be at the communicative and linguistic level. The affective meaning of the gesture is, then, objectively apprehended as such by the self-conscious interpreter. What raises that meaning to the linguistic level is the listener's or performer's successful assumption of the attitude of the composer. If one does entertain within his responses the same attitude toward the musical gesture that the composer did, then the affective meaning of his response may be expected to be at a linguistic level. What matters here is that at both levels of meaning the musical meaning is affective; but in the one case, the meaning is felt, and in the other, it is both felt and objectively known to be affective.

The foregoing observations force us to consider congeneric meaning in another light than that which reflects only upon its apparent autonomous significance. For music clearly involves extrageneric reference and sense: musical experience *presupposes* it. But now a question looms before us about the relation of congeneric meaning to extrageneric meaning. Through considering how the two sorts of musical meaning fit together, we can turn to considerations of some new aspects of extrageneric meaning.

Musical Metaphor

The idea we now need to look into is that congeneric sign complexes may be regarded as metaphors for extrageneric meaning, the *primary* dimension of reference necessarily being congeneric and the *secondary* dimension being extrageneric. In this way of thinking, we would say that music is a metaphor for life values and extrageneric meanings.[27] But this is not to imply that extrageneric meaning is not in itself a valid aesthetic dimension of musical meaning, for it is. But before going on, let us be clear about what we mean by "metaphor."

We may say that a *metaphor* is an icon that links two distinct objects by analogy involving qualitative and structural similarities.[28] The metaphoric sign or sign complex (the primary dimension) is used to signify an object (the secondary dimension) that it does not necessarily symbolize by linguistic convention.[29] The signification holds because the sign and object share certain common properties. The adequacy of the metaphor depends on its extended elaboration of parallels.[30] The elaboration then requires the primary sign complex be a well organized selection and presentation of properties, emphasizing some qualities and relations while suppressing others.[31] And when aptly made, a metaphor itself is pervaded by an aura of the feeling tone peculiar to the secondary object: there is an induced value accruing to the primary object.[32] Thus, in use of metaphor a certain new way of regarding or feeling toward the primary object is offered observers by the artist.

Lest we mistakenly think of metaphor as an inferior way of signifying, let us remember that languages are in their origins metaphoric.[33] And, too, we can bear in mind the observation of I. A. Richards that thinking itself is radically metaphoric.[34] The importance of the idea is in its giving us a way to view the relationship between congeneric and extrageneric meanings of music. Music as metaphor tends to be "live"—it is accepted self-consciously by us as an iconic sign for other literal meanings; and the musical metaphor mostly is not "dead"—so frequently used by many different composers that it has been fully absorbed into conventions of stylistic language.[35] But now let us turn our attention to the situation of music as metaphor.

When we wish to speak of musical metaphor, we keep some specific points in mind. First, and most important of all, we must understand that music serves a social end and that the purpose of music, in this sense, lies in its explicit external reference. The most fundamental sort of reference of a musical work as a whole and of each of its gestures is to the interpreter's behavior. In addition the musical gestures of the work as stimuli address themselves to other, subsequent gestures as internally responsive adjustments and resultants within the work. However, the possibility of the congeneric meanings presupposes the responsiveness of interpreters to the work's gestures and their expressed attitudes. Hence, we acknowledge that a fundamental objective of a musical work is, in general, its extrageneric reference to the attitudes and responsive behavior of listeners and performers, which constitute the basic meaningful interaction of music and listener or performer.

Second, we need to notice that what the interpreter takes as meaningful is the musical gesture, including its congeneric properties and the attitude they carry. For musical works to be effective bearers of metaphoric meanings, they are expected to be adequate sign vehicles, coherently organized in themselves so as to sustain pragmatic, semantic, and syntactic dimensions. Hence, the great—the primary—importance we rightly attach to the congeneric significance of music. It is also presupposed that musical gestures, as complex iconic signs, set up a tissue of internal references and signify other gestures and parts of the work in preceding, concurrent, or later places.[36]

The means that music has for expressing metaphors are the inherent properties of sound, rhythm, and sonorous motion especially. It is, in fact, well known that motion often involves sound and that thus "... sounds announce movement. . . ."[37] And by motion in general we mean change and difference in place or qualitative alteration, such as change in size or shape.[38] As regards motion related to music, Eduard Hanslick pointed out that music exhibits motion and thus has definite reference to a certain sort of extrageneric object.

> A certain class of ideas . . . is quite susceptible of being adequately expressed by means which unquestionably belong to the sphere of music proper. This class comprises all ideas which, consistently with the organ to which they appeal, are associated with audible changes of strength, motion, and ratio: the ideas of intensity waxing and diminishing; of motion hastening and lingering; of ingeniously complex and simple progression, etc. . . . all these ideas being expressible by corresponding modifications of sound.[39]

In considering regional properties of music, we have so far seen something of what value properties are inherently gestural, but we have yet to consider some important ways in which gestures appear and behave. For the way in which an interval occurs, a melody moves, or the particular way the movement of any given context sounds to one is a confirmable regional property of the music. And, because musical gestures involve motion, we ask ourselves what qualities of motion do we hear, and which words can describe them? Many words are universals that can characterize qualities of motion occurring musically as well as non-musically. Such words refer to utterances and movement of gestures that reveal attitude and are gradual and steady in changes, rough and unstable, or vacillating and mercurial in their changes—involving fluttering and quivering, palpitation or throbbing, trembling and shaking, surges and welling up, or abrupt, heavy sinking. And consider the distinctions made by gestures in affective ranges of fear-flight, anger-fight, excitement, or depression. We find contexts with vastly different properties in those dimensions: *i.e.*, whimpers and whines; timorous, yielding, hesitant, flustered, or confused gestures; other acts of aggressiveness, rage, frenzy, and violence with utterances that shriek, snarl, harangue, or rant. Some reveal movement of restlessness, yearning, rapture, or turgidity and utterance that whispers, squeals, or shouts; still other gestures appear with properties of quiescence, apathy, or despair, with sighs, mumbling, or groaning sounds.

Although such descriptives as the foregoing characterize much of gestural attitudes and qualities, the properties of music we discussed a bit earlier have qualities which support the revelation of those gestural attitudes. Intervals inflecting melodic utterance and movement may creep along in small seconds, they may skip in moderate thirds and fourths, or they may tensely stretch leaps of sevenths and ninths in rasping sounds. Harmonic qualities of intervals vary from irritating tightness of conflicting seconds to the richness of mellifluous thirds and sixths or the hollowness of fourths and fifths, the ambivalence of tritones, or the distended tension of large sevenths and minor ninths. Melodies not only go up, down, or hover on a reciting tone, they also declaim in leaps and plunges, soar, slide, tumble on, or whisper in undulations. Harmonies—tonal or atonal—may progress intently to a goal, or they may merely succeed one another in roaming and vacillating here and there. Masses of chords may present volumes and densities that swell and subside, bloat, that tighten up and cram intervals together, or just dwindle away. The rhythmic force of momentum of motion can be a mere impulsive nudge of an accent, and again it might come as a series of jolts that buffet. And, too, note how some motion is so fast as to whiz by, while other motion has a flux in velocity—now hastening, then lingering, and somewhere else faltering or slackening to a drawl of sounds. And, too, on occasion we hear entrances of gestures that jar us by the abruptness of the declamation, while other gestures sneak in. Some scamper on. Still other gestures seem uttered in spurts, to pause or hesitate, and some conclude with conviction just as some mumble and meander away to nothingness.

It is useful to repeat here that the universals considered above are intuitively recognizable properties of gestures, either in bodily movement or utterance. In addition, the words for those universals correctly describe musical gestures inasmuch as those same characteristics are recognizable regional properties of sonorous motion. As we saw earlier, one physiological base for our apprehension of universals lies in sensory isomorphism. That is, the same quality or relationship, occurring in diverse media, may affect several sense organs in a way interpreted intuitively as so alike as to be given the same name. In the case of a universal so named, the embodying stimulus object may vary whereas the response is taken as the same in the relevant respects.

A substantive point to bring out in this connection is the nature of the "regional property." We would follow Monroe C. Beardsley in defining a *regional property* as a characteristic belonging to a complex whole rather than to any of its relatively elemental parts alone.[40] The regional property may be a "summative property" such as weight or length, where the property is a resultant characteristic of adding more of the same. Or it may be an "emergent property"—a *new* property yielded by the peculiar combination of characteristics in a complex object. The universals we listed above are either summative or emergent regional properties. They are properties of complex wholes, belonging to a gesture as an undivided whole rather than to any separate parts of the gesture. So our list of universals spells out a number of regional properties of motion and sound that may inhere in music and exhibit themselves as potential iconic signs of attitude.[41]

Considerations of regional properties and their verbal versus musical expressions take one into interlinguistic translation or synonymy between verbal terms and musical gestures. Without digressing too far, certain points do require serious consideration if we musicians are to refine our ways of discoursing factually and effectively on musical meaning, particularly as that meaning is attitudinal. Here it is important to regard interlinguistic synonymy as being a relation primarily between long enough segments of discourse or expression to stand consideration in separation from a containing context: the relation of synonymy should not be limited to the medium or the scope of the expression in only one or another of the specific sign systems involved.[42] Different linguistic systems require not only different sound sequences, forms, or visual cues, and the like, but they also often require different ranges of length, intensity, and inflection, and so on, to express one and the same universal. So it is with words and with music. In translating the signification of musical gestures into verbalizations, the establishing of a synonymy requires that sufficiently extended musical segments be taken as the formal unit for comparison. This sort of selection is not an easy job even for those well informed both with linguistic and musical knowledge, for often we run up against the problem of music's peculiar use of extended and complex gestures for the expression of a regional quality that a single word captures. Moreover, this problem is intensified as one considers a universal because it may find expression in diverse historic style systems or styles of separate composers, because each such style must be known as a distinct language or dialect of a language known.[43] A second important point in viewing interlinguistic synonymy is that what must come to the fore in musical to verbal translations is synonymy in relevant respects, which means scaling degrees of iconicity.[44] In deciding whether or not a musical gesture "g" expresses a regional property "p" and can be described aptly by a word "w" or words "x" and "y", the concept of synonymy becomes a comparison of gradients. The synonymy of the musical gesture with a word or set of words must be interpreted as a relation by which the musical gesture "g" is more synonymous with a word or set of words "w" than another "x" or still another "y". The regional property or universal "p" is most nearly synonymous in the cases of "g" ≡ "w": the word "w" then properly translates the gesture "g".[45]

Now, in closing our discussion of interlinguistic synonymy, music, and iconic signs, let us say that the foregoing look at the value properties of music, although an extensive digression, has not been at all exhaustive. But it has attended to a number of basic properties that are distinctly intrinsic to music and also expressible verbally.

Because the sonorous motion of musical gestures displays so very many regional qualities of motion, music is well equipped to signify non-musical objects. Musical gestures can present directly an enormous range of such qualities: *e.g.*, regularity, slowness, moderate movement or quick paces, calmness and gentleness, excitement, tenseness, and hesitancy or firmness, disturbance, agitation and violent movement, as well as progressive leading toward goals. These and many other qualities are characteristic qualities that all things in motion may have in various degrees. We know these qualities by acquaintance, and we can recognize them in various surroundings, both musical and non-musical. And because we find these regional qualities of movement on so vast a scale in musical and non-musical objects and events, music potentially becomes iconically significant of whatever else reveals those qualities. Besides often being characteristic of the movement of inorganic bodies, more often than not the regional properties are characteristic of organic actions and particularly of our own inner states. And this fact leads us to accept musical gestures as adequate signs, in a metaphoric usage, for extra-generic objects. We may interpret music as metaphor for, as the sonorous-rhythmic analogue of, organic behavior especially. We also may take music as significant of other non-musical things and actions. In this connection, it bears reiteration that the root metaphor of a musical work as an organism is an extended analogy. Whereas the properties we find expressive and iconically significant are *in* the music itself, musical works are sonorous-rhythmic sign vehicles. The musical organism is not, strictly speaking, flesh and muscle, blood and chemical, bone and nerve—it is sound and rhythm. But what is important is that musical works are organic in the sense that they support signification and expression of organic attitudes as well as other extrageneric or non-musical objects and events.

So as I have tried to bring out, the regional properties of music, which also are life values, occur on a vast scale. Because of that vastness, the many properties support a wide range of musical metaphors for the things we meet in ordinary experience. Some of those metaphors are so precise, so detailed, so conventional, and so obvious that they may be regarded as "dead" metaphors. Among these appear the cases of patent mimicry—the trombone's Bronx cheers in Henry Brant's *Signs and Alarms*, the cuckoo in Beethoven's *Pastoral Symphony*, or the braying of Bottom with the head of an ass in Mendelssohn's *Overture, A Midsummer-Night's Dream*. In this vein, Oliver Messiaen's *Oiseaux Exotiques*, which the composer describes as ". . . an enormous counterpoint of birdsong . . .," is a striking *tour de force*.[46] The songs of some eighteen birds from various continents are represented and combined in an impressive cacaphony. And a well known example of suggesting a machine is put forward by the *Pacific 231* of Arthur Honegger. As Honegger describes the work, his aim was not

> . . . to imitate the noise of an engine, but rather to express in terms of music a visual impression and physical enjoyment. The piece opens with an objective contemplation, the quiet breathing of the engine at rest, the straining at starting, the gradually increasing speed—and finally reaches the lyrical pathetic state of a fast train, three hundred tons of weight, thundering through the silence of night at a mile a minute.[47]

The composer's comments speak clearly for the music, which is well-enough known that we can accept his word and our aural recognition. The piece does give a most literal representation of a train at rest, in motion, accelerating, and slowing down to a stop. However, since the representation is so vividly explicit, we would go one step further than the composer and admit that the work is an imitation of the noise of an engine.

In the immediately preceding discussion the objective has been to call attention to the semantic potential of music to denote extrageneric objects, and we have referred by example to two obvious sorts of such denotable extraorganic objects—natural ones (bird calls) and man-made ones (engines). The importance of such dead metaphor for music is just what it is for verbal language. The dead metaphor is conventional; and, for those listeners familiar with the musical style, the metaphor explicitly denotes the same thing in any instance of its use to all who observe the music and are acquainted in general experience with the object denoted. Thus, the overt musical imitations, the specific bits of mimicry, have the symbolic status of linguistic signs. This sort of conventional denotation by means of musical icons stands as a firm reminder of music's power to symbolize those extrageneric objects that in pronounced ways involve sound-producing motions.

The merit, or lack of it, in particular cases of musical mimicry is frequently questioned, but it seems that it is the aptness of use that really matters. The use of a dead metaphor in music can be adequate or skillful or charming or humorous or inept or trite and so on just as verbal use of idioms can. The main danger implicit in overt imitations has been duly noted by a composer well qualified to speak to the point. Richard Strauss observed that

> . . . one can paint in tones and sounds, particularly motives expressing action, but there always remains the imminent danger of relying too much on the music and falling into the trap of a boring imitation of nature.[48]

The imminent danger of boring imitation, although especially real in use of dead metaphors, does not, however, have any necessarily negative bearing upon aesthetic value or the conventional denotative potential of music itself.

So far we have been observing how in dead metaphors musical gestures rely upon patent mimicry. However, I wish to place the greater emphasis on live metaphor, which relies upon more open iconic signification and is less conventional. The live metaphors that we find most important are those for mankind's gestures and attitudes—the organic metaphors in a more limited sense. What we need to recognize now is that musical gestures can present and represent much of man's bodily movement and attitudes. These gestures can be divided into vocal utterance and other forms of movement.

Vocal utterance underlies much of the expressivity of music. And quite naturally, vocal utterance can be taken over into music, but as music, vocal utterance appears mostly in a heightened form. It is transformed and developed by selective emphasis, especially on tone—the singing tone of voice—but vocal utterance also is developed in the other dimensions of pitch and loudness, rhythm, cadence and tempo, and so on. Through the use additionally of words, the textual matter of vocal music brings with it the full linguistic capabilities of the language, insofar as the composer wishes to employ them. However, it is not song with its verbally linguistic potential that most concerns us in our exploration of music's extrageneric meaning. Besides, as we know, instrumental music and non-textual vocal music can more than reproduce the wide expressive range of vocal utterance. So it is not the direct use of vocal means or the musical reference to vocal utterence with which I wish to deal, since these are already assimilated by music otherwise. Instead, I now wish to examine overt bodily gestures and then inner states as they are metaphorically signified by music.

In signifying bodily gestures music treats movement that is not dominantly characterized by an intimate association with attendant sounds. In one's striking out with a fist at another, sound is made, but sound is not the most characteristic feature. The sudden, forceful movement is. Musical gestures may signify such movements. In these cases music is presenting movement through sonorous motion in a clearly metaphorical way. The musical presentation of metaphors for bodily gestures is, we recognize, an essential function of music for the dance. An example of what I mean by musical signification of overt bodily gestures can be drawn from a score for ballet. For in ballet music (and similarly in most so-called "absolute" concert music) musical gestures significantly refer to the character of, but not all the detailed sounds involved in, such organic acts as running, lunging, striking out, and so forth.

The final "Pas D'Action" from Stravinsky's *Orpheus* affords an example.[49] In some ninety measures of this masterwork, at least three clearly defined sorts of overt gestures are signified. The stage directions simply state: "The Bacchantes attack Orpheus, seize him and tear him to pieces."[50] By reference to some of the more obvious features of the movement we can describe how the music gives the fully aesthetic version of the action by means of live metaphor.

The movement is fast ("vivace, $\quad = 152$") and mainly in duple meter with simple duple subdivisions of the quick beats. While static, the harmonies center about an acrid formation of a minor third above a dissonant minor second (*e.g.*, a′–c″–a² above A♭). The two main gestures of the movement appear in the two opening measures: a pizzicatto, off-beat chord in the strings, ff, is followed by an abrupt and agitated gesture of four notes (♪ ♪ ♪ ♪ ♪), mf, in the lower registers of the pizzicatto strings (Example 10-1, mm. 1–4). In the main the movement

EXAMPLE 10-1   Igor Stravinsky, *Orpheus*, "Pas D'Action," mm. 1–4
The Bacchantes attack Orpheus, seize him and tear him to pieces.

Orpheus by Igor Stravinsky. Copyright 1948 by Boosey & Hawkes Inc. Reprinted by permission.

develops these short, disruptive gestures in extensions, contractions, and reiterations which often are interrupted by silences, so that an irregular— even erratic—movement prevails.

   After the opening gestures set the action and are briefly elaborated, clarinets and bassoons take up, in their lower registers, a further elaboration, gesticulating in a rather uneasy scampering and muttering (Example 10-2, mm. 9–14), which is punctuated by low-register chords in the brass [126] – [129]. This gives way (at [129]) to interruption by spiccatto strings (♪ ♩♪ ♪ ♪), again in their lower registers.   The action continues disjointedly with short gestures by the strings and frequent interspersal of chords briefly held by woodwinds and horns (Example 10-3, mm. 22–25). The strings and woodwinds pass the gestures back and forth, tossing and grabbing the action between them. At the same time, the range of the instruments expands into a wider and higher registration. All the while a number of short crescendoes and decrescendoes extend volumes from soft to loud and back in short bursts, although the main dynamic level is

EXAMPLE 10-2   Igor Stravinsky, *Orpheus*, "Pas D'Action," mm. 9–14

EXAMPLE 10-3   Igor Stravinsky, *Orpheus*, "Pas D'Action," mm. 22–25

soft. Then suddenly the orchestral tutti erupts (Example 10-4, mm. 56–59), fff, into a raucous recurrence of the initial, acrid harmony. In unison durational rhythm, the orchestra lunges into an extension of the opening gestures and in short order tears them down into fragments, while resuming the lower registers, reducing the orchestral tutti to pizzicatto

EXAMPLE 10-4   Igor Stravinsky, *Orpheus*, "Pas D'Action," mm. 56–59

strings and soft dynamic (137 – 140). The clarinets and bassoons scamper and mutter once more briefly (139 – 141). The movement closes with unevenly spaced and held reiterations by the brasses, in their lower registers, of another acrid chord reminiscent of the opening sonority (Example 10-5, mm. 84–90).

The music just commented upon does not attack anyone, nor does it seize or tear anyone to pieces. But the gestures of the music do perform artistic acts that we correctly take as the metaphoric equivalents. We recognize certain characteristics of the music's sonorous motion as giving a fairly extended parallel to attitude and bodily gestures with which we are, for the most part, acquainted. Foremost we notice that the music does have an aggressive attitude to it—in the acrid harmony that dominates the movement; in the disruptive overall movement; in the quick and incisive gestures that jab out in unexpected thrusts; in the excited pace of the movement; in the two main sets of timbral registrations of low, sparse, yet dissonant textures versus the shrilling orchestral tutti; in the covert softness sharply contrasted to quick crescendoes and to sudden extreme loudness. The attitude of the movement is unmistakably antagonistic and emotional, signalling attack.

The attack is not primitive. Rather the musical gestures strike out, now from strings, then from woodwinds and horns. The sections make

EXAMPLE 10-5   Igor Stravinsky, *Orpheus*, "Pas D'Action," mm. 84–90

their attack in quick thrusts and lunges at irregular intervals in alternation. And then (at two measures before 137) the music does burst
out in a sudden and extremely loud series of dissonant chords with a
gripping, syncopated rhythm. The whole orchestra unites in a moment
of violent seizure. And last the main gestures are quickly broken down
and fragmented. The movement of violence and continued force tears
apart into a series of small, punctuated gestures that subside only
partially. The motion is still irregular at the ending, the tone of harmony
still menacing, even bitter. In all, then, the music signifies metaphorically
four extrageneric things: (1) a prevailing emotional attitude of anger and
violence; (2) gestures of attack; (3) an abrupt seizure; and (4) a tearing
into pieces.

So in specific effects the musical gestures present a metaphoric performance for Bacchantes attacking Orpheus, seizing him and tearing
him to pieces. But not one Bacchante nor Orpheus is represented. Only
the angry gestures of the Bacchantes are given in the analogue of sonorous
motion. We might say that only the verbs, only the actions, are implicit in
the musical gestures, along with the pervasive attitude of anger. And that
is what we mean by saying that music can give us metaphors for life values
and extrageneric objects.

Although metaphors for balletic gestures and bodily action constitute a big part of extrageneric musical meanings, musical signification is not tied to the shirttails of dance. Apt musical metaphors for bodily action stand on their own—as we can tell in listening to the Stravinsky or a large amount of music for dance that continues in the concert repertory, and also as we can observe at dance programs choreographed mostly to absolute music. Adequate congenerically meaningful musical gestures assimilate their metaphoric dimensions without any loss of integrity. Music that fails to absorb the metaphoric reference to bodily action is usually dismissed by the contemptuous phrase "Mickey Mouse" music —meaning music that superficially imitates body movements, as the music to cinematic cartoons often does with boring precision. (In such inadequate artistic efforts both congeneric and extrageneric significations usually will be found superficial, in addition to the basic musical gestures' wanting in intrinsic merit.)

If we reflect a moment, we can see that what music does is to perform actions in sonorous motion that we identify and characterize in spoken language mostly by active verbs (or active verb forms such as participles and gerunds). We use our language to name these universals of action, whether the actions appear musically as metaphor or more literally in daily life. Bertrand Russell listed such universals for action among the primitive terms of language, calling them "object words" because they at once express an attitudinal state of the speaker and indicate a fact.[51] In isolation, such words as "run" and "attack" have meanings we have learned directly without needing other knowledge. And, moreover, they express complete sentences in the simplest possible way. We ought to acknowledge that for musical signification in general musical gestures have a cognate function. In its gestural performatives, music can indicate and characterize at once many active organic movements and the atti-tudes they carry with them. Musical gestures express attitude and refer to a fact in one immediate, performative act. The implication is, then, that music does have certain sentential functions, though limited as noted just now. Accordingly, it seems that music can make implicit state-ments of the sort that some object words do. We shall need to return to this point later, for it is rich in its implications for the meaning of music.

The essential fact the foregoing discussion has sought out is that expressive musical gestures can adequately signify bodily action. The straightforward performative nature of music's gestures easily supports metaphors for such actions as running, thrusting, crawling, and so forth. Since we know such actions and their qualitative shadings and differences from doing and observing them, we recognize their analogues given musically. Thus, we find in music the great potential for the metaphoric presentation of, and reference to, the life values of bodily movement.

Quite possibly the most important organic metaphors of music are those significant of our inner states of feeling and desire. In these the gestures not only express but also signify attitudes. This is so because, as we have seen, the sonic and rhythmic elements are themselves expressive. As sheer quality, the elements themselves exhibit their expressivity. They make up gestural sign complexes in multifarious combinations which convey a comparable variety of attitudes. But in terms of iconic sign functioning, the very exhibition of qualities is significant. The exhibition of sonic and rhythmic qualities by gestures is a metaphoric presentation of organic attitude. So inasmuch as musical gestures are expressive to you or me, the gestures also must exhibit qualities which at the same time signify the attitude expressed. As the sonic and rhythmic qualities appear expressive, they also signify iconically: the gestures then signify sentient states. And we take account of peculiar combinations of those qualities as significant of inner states—metaphorically speaking, the inner states of the musical organism. Hence, we see that what is expressed by a significant musical gesture may also be what is extragenerically denoted by it: a feeling, a mood, an emotion, or desire. These are expressed and denoted.

The essence of those affective and conative states of our inner life is qualitative and rhythmic.[52] The fleeting changes, the welling up and waning of excitement, and the massive and sustained tensions we feel in living through experiences are permeated by rhythmic qualities; they are felt as rhythmic. The very passage of our life as we feel it consists in a continual rhythmic flux. We feel the rhythm of life as we feel it consists in a continual rhythmic flux. We feel the rhythm of life in cyclic, but not necessarily evenly measured, phases of accumulating energy and tensions building to phases of stress, when excitation is at its height and when tensions discharge impulsively, emphatically; and these are followed by other phases of relaxation, diminishing strain, repose and recovery of energy that become preparations for still other repetitions of the cycles of excitation, tension, stress, and repose. And, as we know, these cyclic phases of felt rhythms happen in multitudinous ways: some quick, others prolonged and voluminous, but more often than not a number of these inner rhythms of feeling and desire going on at once, so that sometimes we feel them conflicting and competing to dominate our actions.

Similarly, in musical gesture everything sonorous contributes to the generic quality of rhythm as it shapes the metaphor—flux of consonance and dissonance, the thinning out and massing of textures, the goal-seeking progress of melodic strands and harmonies. The properties of directed tonal motion develop tendencies to and from moments of stress and repose, tension and relaxation. The same properties fulfill and thwart those tendencies in overlapping phases and planes of activity, which now all work together and again may create their own conflicts between competing sets of tendencies. In the exhibition of the generic rhythmic qualities lies much of music's expressive power and gestural significance. For just as rhythm—sheer qualitative flux—characterizes emotion as we live through it, so then does the rhythmic flow of musical sound give up gestural metaphors for organic sentience.

We recognize the expressivity of musical gestures because we have the most intimate possible knowledge of attitudes—immediate, direct experience. We recognize the metaphoric signification of attitudes by those same gestures on the same basis, namely because we are acquainted with what and how we feel when we are under the sway of a given attitude. We know both those states and the reciprocal qualities of our vocal and other bodily actions while we are in these states. So when we hear those telltale qualities and sorts of peculiar movement reproduced in music, we identify them as the particular qualities and special combinations that are appropriate to specific attitudes we have felt and ways we and others have behaved. Either we recognize what appears in common to our behavior and the behavior of others, or we fail to see it at all. Similarly, either we recognize the expressive qualities of musical gestures and, hence, recognize the peculiar attitudes revealed and signified, or we fail to grasp any affective-conative meaning of the qualities. So far as we need to say it, it is largely in these facts of experience that extrageneric truth value consists.

The main burden of the foregoing is that we can interpret music as a sonorous-rhythmic analogue of organic behavior. The musical organism directly presents us with expressive behavior through the properties of its sonorous motion. And the enormous number of those local and regional properties and their very many possible combinations make possible a vast array of musical metaphors for organic attitudes. For the simple fact is that bodily activity—especially as it involves instinctual behavior—is permeated with movement and rhythm. Musical gestures can duplicate in striking degree the most characteristic properties of those organic movements. Musical gestures behave in ways closely akin to both our expressive vocal or other bodily gestures and especially the inner movement we feel when we ourselves experience evanescent feelings, when we undergo emotional stress or have strong desires and are driven by passion.[53] Hence, gestures in sonorous motion readily provide metaphors significant of, and comparable to, affective and conative states that we know by experience. And in the sense that musical gestures are saturated with expressive sonic qualities and vital rhythms, we believe Carroll C. Pratt's assertion that *"Music sounds the way emotions feel."*[54]

Notes

1   "Music is irrational and cannot affect the soul or the emotions and is no more an imitative art than cookery"—Philodemus. Quoted by Bernard Bosanquet, *A History Of Aesthetic* (New York: The Macmillan Company, 1932; citations refer to the Meridian Books edition, 1957), pp. 100–01.

2   Igor Stravinsky, *Chronicle of My Life* (London: Victor Gollancz, 1936), p. 91; reprinted in *Composers On Music*, ed. Sam Morgenstern (New York: Pantheon, 1956), p. 442.

3   Eduard Hanslick, *The Beautiful In Music*, trans. Gustave Cohen, ed. Morris Weitz, 8th ed. (New York: The Liberal Arts Press, 1957), p. 9.

4   *Aristotle On the Art of Poetry With A Supplement Aristotle On Music*, trans. S. H. Butcher, ed. Milton C. Nahm (New York: The Liberal Arts Press, 1948), p. 45.

5   René Descartes, *Compendium Of Music*, trans. Walter Robert (Rome: American Institute of Musicology, 1961), p. 11.

6   Oliver Strunk, ed., *Source Readings in Music History* (New York: W. W. Norton and Co., Inc., 1950), pp. 848–49; Richard Wagner, *Oper und Drama, Gesammelte Schriften und Dictungen* (Leipzig: Breitkopf and Härtel, 1871–1873), vol. 4, p. 234; Morgenstern, *Composers on Music*, pp. 206–07, 332.

7   Aaron Copland, "A Modernist Defends Modern Music," *New York Times Magazine*, December 25, 1949, p. 11; reprinted in *Composers On Music*, ed. Sam Morgenstern, p. 548.

8   *E.g.*, see Monroe C. Beardsley, *Aesthetics from Classical Greece to the Present: A Short History* (New York: The Macmillan Co., 1966); Bernard Bosanquet, *A History of Aesthetic* (New York: The Macmillan Co., 1932); Katharine Everett Gilbert and Helmut Kuhn, *A History of Esthetic*, 2nd ed. (London: Thames and Hudson, 1956); Eliseo Vivas and Murray Krieger, eds., *The Problems of Aesthetics* (New York: Rinehart and Co., Inc., 1953); Morris Weitz, ed., *Problems In Aesthetics* (New York: The Macmillan Co., 1959), Julius Portnoy, *The Philosopher and Music* (New York: The Humanities Press, 1954); Strunk, *Source Readings*; Morgenstern, *Composers on Music*.

9   See Morgenstern, *Composers on Music*, pp. 80–83.

10   See Gertrude Norman and Miriam Lubell Shrifte, eds., *Letters of Composers* (New York: Grosset and Dunlap, 1946), pp. 255–57.

11   W. K. Wimsatt and Monroe Beardsley, "The Intentional Fallacy," in *The Verbal Icon* (Louisville: University of Kentucky Press, 1954), chap. 1. Cf. Henry D. Aiken, "The Aesthetic Relevance of Belief," *Journal of Philosophy* no. 9 (1951). Both articles are reprinted in Weitz, *Problems in Aesthetics*.

12   "For when there are no words, it is very difficult to recognize the meaning of the harmony and rhythm, or to see that any worthy object is imitated by them." Plato, *Laws*, Book II, *The Dialogues of Plato*, trans. Benjamin Jowett (New York: Random House, 1937), pp. 669–70.

13 See F. E. Sparshott, *The Structure of Aesthetics* (London: Routledge and Kegan Paul, 1963), pp. 353–58, for a listing of possible extrageneric designata of art works.

14 Charles Morris, *Signs, Language and Behavior* (Englewood Cliffs, N.J.: Prentice-Hall, Inc., 1946), pp. 8–10; Bertrand Russell, *An Inquiry into Meaning and Truth* (Baltimore: Penguin Books, 1962), pp. 11–12, 175–80.

15 See Herbert Spencer, "On the Origin and Function of Music," *Essays on Education* (London: J. M. Dent and Sons, Ltd., 1911), pp. 310–30; Sir Hubert Parry, *The Evolution of the Art of Music* (London: Routledge and Kegan Paul, Ltd., 1893), chaps. 1 and 3.

16 Richard Wagner, *The Art Work of the Future*, in Strunk, *Source Readings*, pp. 880–81.

17 Roy R. Grinker, "The Physiology of Emotions," in *The Physiology of Emotions*, ed, Alexander Simon, Charles Herbert, and Ruth Straus (Springfield, Ill.: Charles C. Thomas, 1961), pp. 7–8.

18 Alfred J. Ayer, *The Problem of Knowledge* (New York: The Macmillan Co., 1956), pp. 233, 242, 249–54; and *The Concept Of A Person* (London: Macmillan and Co. Ltd., 1963), pp. 41–42, 47.

19 Frederick Delius, quoted in Morgenstern, *Composers On Music*, p. 320. See also the comment of Ernest Bloch ibid., pp. 410–11: "Art is the outlet of the mystical, emotional needs of the human spirit. . . ."

20 Spencer, "Origin and Function of Music," pp. 310–30; John Dewey, *Art As Experience* (New York: G. P. Putnam's Sons, Capricorn Books, 1958), pp. 238–39; Carroll C. Pratt, *The Meaning of Music* (New York: McGraw-Hill Book Co., 1931), p. 209; Roger Sessions, *The Musical Experience of Composer, Performer, Listener* (Princeton: Princeton University Press, 1950), pp. 75–76; O. K. Bouwsma, "The Expression Theory of Art," in *Aesthetics and Language*, ed. William Elton (New York: Philosophical Library, 1954), pp. 93–99; John Hospers, "The Concept of Artistic Expression," *Proceedings of the Aristotelian Society* (1954–1955), pp. 313–44.

21 T. C. Ruch, "Motor Systems," in *Handbook of Experimental Psychology*, ed. S. S. Stevens (New York: John Wiley and Sons, Inc., 1951), pp. 126, 144, 186–88; Donald B. Lindsley, "Emotion," in *Handbook of Experimental Psychology*, pp. 487–88, 495–500, 504–09.

22 See Hallowell Davis, "Psychophysiology Of Hearing And Deafness," in *Handbook of Experimental Psychology*, pp. 1132–33.

23 James L. Mursell, *The Psychology of Music* (New York: W. W. Norton and Co., 1937), p. 20. See also G. W. Wyburn R. W. Pickford, and R. J. Hirst, *Human Senses And Perception* (Edinburgh and London: Oliver and Boyd, Ltd., 1964), pp. 56–57: "They [auditory impulses] also initiate such voluntary motor acts as turning the head towards the sound source, and their more widespread diffusion throughout the neighbouring brain territories will be correlated with affective experiences such as recognition, recollection, pleasure, or distress. . . . Auditory impulses also reach the brain by the reticular activating system and as a result sound stimuli can produce arousal reactions."

24 Dewey, *Art As Experience*, pp. 236–39.

25 Mursell, *Psychology of Music*, p. 29. As Mursell says, ". . . music is capable of arousing intense emotional states apart from . . . representation and symbolism. It appears that the material of music itself is a direct emotional stimulus of unique power. It sets up in the body the precise changes which psychology has long recognized as the physiological substratas of emotion."

26 Russell, *Meaning And Truth*, p. 141.

27 The idea is implicit in Charles Morris' early conception of art works as icons (*Signs, Language and Behavior*, 8–10), as well as in Susanne K. Langer, *Philosophy in A New Key* (New York: The New American Library of World Literature, Inc., Mentor Books 1942); Donald N. Ferguson, *Music As Metaphor* (Minneapolis: University of Minnesota Press, 1960); and Leonard B. Meyer, *Emotion and Meaning in Music* (Chicago: University of Chicago Press, 1956), p. 266.

28 Paul Henle (ed.), *Language, Thought, and Culture* (Ann Arbor: University of Michigan Press, 1958), p. 179.
29 Morris, *Signs, Language and Behavior*, p. 136.
30 Henle, *Language, Thought, and Culture*, p. 180.
31 Max Black, "Metaphor," *Proceedings of the Aristotelian Society* 55 (1954–1955), pp. 273–94; citations refer to the reprint in *Philosophy Looks At The Arts*, ed. Joseph Margolis (New York: Charles Scribner's Sons, 1962), p. 233.
32 Henle, *Language, Thought, and Culture*, pp. 180 and 190–91.
33 Lionello Venturi, "Metaphor," in *The Dictionary of Philosophy*, ed. Dagobert Runes (New York: Philosophical Library, 1942), p. 195.
34 I. A. Richards, *Interpretation and Teaching* (New York: Harcourt, Brace and Co., 1938), p. 48.
35 Cf. H. W. Fowler, ed., *A Dictionary Of Modern English Usage* (London: Oxford University Press, 1944), pp. 348–49.
36 In this connection, we might note that Leonard B. Meyer, in *Emotion And Meaning In Music*, seems to pass over the obviously important retrospective and concurrent references within the musical work. While he concentrates admirably on the futuristic, inferential references of music, he appears to neglect the two other sorts of reference, although by no means altogether. (See Meyer, *Emotion and Meaning*, pp. 35–38, on "evident" and "determinate" meanings.)
37 Jean Jacques Rousseau, in Morgenstern, *Composers On Music*, p. 55.
38 James K. Feibleman, "Motion," in *Dictionary of Philosophy*, ed. by Dagobert Runes, p. 202.
39 Hanslick, *The Beautiful in Music*, pp. 22–23.
40 Monroe C. Beardsley, *Aesthetics: Problems in the Philosophy of Criticism* (New York: Harcourt, Brace and Co., 1958), pp. 83–87.
41 For a most penetrating and succinct discussion of music's regional properties and their relations to expression of attitude see Carroll C. Pratt, "The Design of Music," *Journal of Aesthetics And Art Criticism* 12, no. 3 (1954), pp. 289–300.
42 Willard Van Orman Quine, *From a Logical Point of View*, 2nd ed. (New York: Harper and Row, Publishers, 1961), p. 58. The following discussion is indebted to Quine's observations, pp. 48–64.
43 For the most scholarly and readable music history revealing the main aspects of the interlinguistic problem of synonymy from the perspective of the various historic eras, see Beekman C. Cannon, Alvin H. Johnson, and William G. Waite, *The Art of Music: A Short History of Musical Styles and Ideas* (New York: Thomas Y. Crowell Co., 1960). Especially cf. the style systems of the late Renaissance, chap. 7, early Baroque, chap. 8, and later Baroque, chap. 9—pp. 174–286.
44 Quine, *From a Logical Point of View*, pp. 60–63.
45 The respects in which properties of an art work and our responses to the work are "relevant" were covered also in Chapter 4. For an enlightening theory (and criticism of it) of relevancy in art criticism, see Stephen C. Pepper and Karl H. Potter, "The Criterion of Relevancy in Aesthetics: a Discussion," *Journal of Aesthetics and Art Criticism* 16, no. 2 (1957), pp. 202–16.
46 Oliver Messiaen, *Oiseaux Exotiques* (London: Universal Edition, Ltd., 1959), p. x.
47 Arthur Honegger, *Pacific 231* (Paris: Éditions Salabert, 1924), quoted in prefatory notes.
48 Richard Strauss, in Morgenstern, *Composers On Music*, p. 332.
49 Igor Stravinsky, *Orpheus* (London: Boosey and Hawkes, Ltd., 1948), pp. 47–56.
50 Ibid., p. 47.
51 Russell, *Meaning And Truth*, pp. 23, 62, 163, 171, 203.
52 Stephen C. Pepper, *Aesthetic Quality* (New York: Charles Scribner's Sons, 1937), pp. 89–113; Susanne K. Langer, *Feeling And Form* (New York: Charles Scribner's Sons, 1953), pp. 126–29.
53 Pratt, "Design of Music," pp. 294–96; Ferguson, *Music as Metaphor*, p. 11.
54 Ibid.

The Levels of Extrageneric
Meaning and Artistic Truth

In this chapter we shall explore levels of interpretation in the extrageneric meaning of music and outline certain foundations of artistic truth.

Part I, Levels of
Extrageneric Meaning

As we know, an iconic sign may directly present—exhibit or display—a value property for our immediate apprehension. Or an iconic sign may represent indirectly; it may symbolize for our mediated and discursive reflection about it something else beyond the immediate properties it offers as stimuli. In terms of meaning, these two levels of interpretation of signs tend to result, respectively, in either acquaintance meanings or discursive meanings. These levels of interpretation correspond to what Wittgenstein calls the "change of aspect": *i.e.*, we see or hear *this* or *that* as opposed to we see or hear this *as* or *like* something else.[1] What we first need to recognize is that each level of interpretant formation may result in extrageneric interpretants. A musical work may give rise to acquaintance meanings and to discursive meanings, both of

Notes to this chapter begin on p. 202.

the extrageneric class. Thus, we note that for art works there are extra-generic acquaintance meanings and extrageneric discursive meanings—each sort possible largely through iconic signs and musical metaphors.[2]

The weight of what has just been said is that works can be significant of life values in two ways. Depending on our attitude as observers, the work will appear to us in one or another way, a point we now can take up.

If we are disposed at the moment to observe instinctually and to apprehend apparent auditory images, then music can convey life values that have acquaintance meaning. A work offers us immediate experience with its gestures. The gestures themselves are sad or whatever. And if the gestures seem sad, our responses (sympathy, aversion, and the like) are drawn from us without our thinking about them. We feel sympathetic toward, or we feel repulsed by, the sad gestures. But if we are disposed to observe rationally and self-consciously and to think about our observations, then the gestures of the work may indicate life values that have discursive meaning. The gestures seem to point to things other than the immediate images; they suggest ideas metaphorically related to the gestures. A gesture is then taken as referring to conditions causing sadness, or to the effects of sadness on others, and so on.

We can illustrate the idea by referring to the second movement ("Marcia Funebre") of Beethoven's *Symphony III* ("Eroica"). In form the movement is a fairly conventional march (song and trio), including, however, in its recapitulation an exceptionally truncated theme followed by extended and climactic fugal elaboration of material derived from the trio. The first part (mm. 1–68) is dominated by an unmistakably mournful attitude, to which the second part (mm. 69–104) contrasts a prevalent mood of comfort with an alleviation of sorrow and even moments of exultation (mm. 74–79; mm. 92–101). The lament of the song is conveyed in gestures striving to ascend only to fall back (mm. 1–4; mm. 5–8 and again in mm. 8–16; Example 11-1, mm. 1–20), as under the weight of sorrow. The tone of mourning is established by a number of effects: the very slow, fixed pace of the underlying march rhythm; the minor key and long initial reiteration of the tonic triad (mm. 1–4); the formally hesitant gait of accompanying triplet figures (mm. 6–8 and thereafter); the prevailing lower registers of strings in fairly dense sonorities and the nasal wail of the oboe (mm. 8–16); and the suppressed dynamic levels. Although the second thematic strand (m. 17 and on) begins with a more confident mood, moving in the relative major key with firmer, unified rhythm and parallel motion, the mood fails to sustain itself (mm. 17–20).

EXAMPLE 11-1   Ludwig van Beethoven, *Symphony III*, II, mm. 1–20

Example 11-1 *continued*

It breaks off (m. 20), and shifts back to the earlier sadness through a descending gesture (mm. 23–24 . . .) and another plaintive gesture by the cellos (mm. 27–30). After a restatement of the lament of the first thematic strand (mm. 30–65), the first part closes with a downward movement into the subdued gloom of the tonic minor (mm. 65–68).

The second part—the trio or "Maggiore" section—clearly contrasts to the first by giving a relief from distress and a more encouraging attitude. Emphasis is on ascending gestures in triads (winds, imitatively, 69–74; Example 11-2, mm. 69–70) and in steadfast scales rising (lower strings, imitatively). Twice the motion swells into exultant gestures (mm. 74–79; mm. 92–101). But in its close, the second part is punctuated by unison strings in a decisive descent (mm. 101–104) back into the movement's characteristic song of lament (m. 105).

EXAMPLE 11-2   Ludwig van Beethoven, *Symphony III*, II, mm. 69–79

EXAMPLE 11-2 *continued*

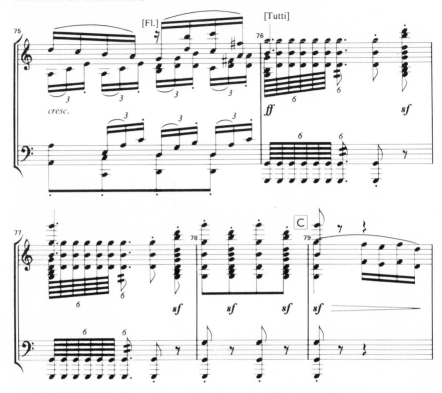

Following the concise reference to the lament (mm. 105–114), the music takes up at length a solemn and resolute pair of simultaneous gestures in fugal texture (mm. 114–150; Example 11-3, mm. 114–120, 140–162). At an episode of climax, the fugue breaks off (m. 150), the music returns to homophonic texture and quickly subsides into a weakened and almost pitiful gesture—perhaps a hopeless yearning conveyed by the violins rising softly, haltingly (mm. 154–157) with a reference to the opening lament. In answer, the lower strings burst out very loudly (m. 159) and a fanfare follows—with an ominous tone (perhaps suggestive of judgement), which tapers off into an ornamental recurrence of the main thematic strand (m. 173). This time the song is accompanied by a restless, quasi-ostinato in basses, echoed by violins and flute. A new and tender gesture of consolation comes with the coda (m. 213) and portions of the first thematic strand return. The movement dies away with a pathetic utterance of the song, its now hesitant rhythms and feeble tones evoking the mood of one broken by grief and despair (Example 11-4, mm. 238–247).

The importance of the movement lies in the perspectives it affords not only of a funeral situation but also of the effects on one of the death of

EXAMPLE 11-3   Ludwig van Beethoven, *Symphony III*, II, mm. 114–120, 140–164

EXAMPLE 11-3 *continued*

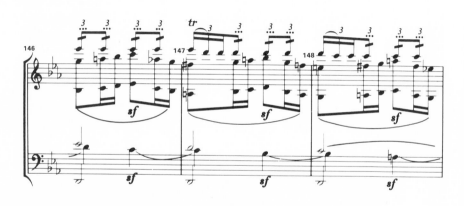

someone for whom one cares. For at the every outset of listening we can find ourselves in the hushed atmosphere pervading a funeral—if we are uninhibited and sensitive enough. We can feel earlier excitement drained and our spirits depressed. The mournful gestures of the music are then

EXAMPLE 11-4   Ludwig van Beethoven, *Symphony III*, II, mm. 238–247

taken as immediate presentations of sorrow, which subdues our excitement, drawing us into a pathetic situation and compelling our instinctive
feelings. And if we are at once strongly affected by the pathos of the gestures, our feelings tend themselves to be saddened. The life values of the
music in this sort of response would appear directly presented—affectively meaningful without our mediated responses—because our attitude
would not be inhibiting straightforward instinctual responses to the de-

spondent situation and the woeful gestures. We may feel the sorrow that death causes.

However, an entirely different sort of aesthetic experience with the movement's opening is possible, one still involving extrageneric meanings. We may reflect upon the musical gestures, and then the movement may begin to take on a new meaning for us: such as the music embodying despair we ourselves feel when everything in life seems to conspire against our happiness, or such as the music signifying the sense of loss and deep regret we know attends the death of one we love or of one for whom we feel the greatest admiration. So, we see that the movement may provide, even at its beginnings, quite different extrageneric meanings on different levels depending on the attitude we have either in coming to the movement or in response to its force. From the aspect of an uninhibited attitude we may have an experience in which self-awareness is absent and which makes us downcast and draws out feelings of unhappiness. But from an intellectualized aspect, we might regard the movement as a metaphor about the sorrow felt at the death of one dear and the inevitable failure of others' efforts to console one broken by grief.

The point is not to belabor what may appear obvious to some; it is to emphasize that there are two levels of response which equally involve extrageneric meanings. Moreover, both levels of response are pertinent to the interpretation of a work; indeed, experiencing the work at both levels is desirable if one is to fully understand it. So we shall say that the life values of a work may appear to us in two ways, according to our attitude or our perspective. The gestures may present life values directly, or those gestures may afford us, by indirection, life values as discursive representations of what the values imply and with which they are involved.

The Extrageneric Importation and Exportation of Values. Equally interesting as the levels at which life values of a work function is the symmetric relationship tying together aesthetic gestures and those values. The relationship intrigues one with its support of an exchange of values. The relationship is, moreover, a function of iconic signs: whatever an icon appears to resemble also resembles the icon. This function of the iconic signs affects the nature of our aesthetic experience in two directions. In one direction life values enlarge the metaphoric meaning that musical gestures have. In another direction the opposite happens: the gestures enrich our experience by revealing additional values of objects and events with which we are acquainted. So we may say that in the one direction of responding to an art work, the observer "imports" life values into the meaning the work holds for him, whereas in the other direction he takes from the work new values for his experience—the work "exports" new perspectives on life values to the observer.[3]

Consider again the "Marcia Funebre". Think what a powerful stimulus the movement can be to one who has suffered the loss of persons dearly loved or others given their fullest admiration, especially if one has taken part in a cortege for a member of his family. For such people could not the movement summon up a welter of memories, some bitterly unpleasant, which to some extent would be imported into the comprehensive meaning of the work? And would not the music afford occasion to reflect upon the more general meanings of death? Of course it could. But in contrast if first hand experience with personal loss through someone's death had not touched one's life, the experience of this movement might well enable one to feel much of the sorrow a funeral carries with it. The work then might—would for a sensitive person—be a source of intuited knowledge, an emotionally charged view of a time of mourning. So in this latter sense of experiencing the "Marcia Funebre," one would find the music exporting values. And, we are wont to add, it is this latter sort of aesthetic experience for which we most prize the extrageneric meaning of music. For it is what we can gain from listening to music that makes it valuable—a point good to pursue.

In musical aesthetic experience the interpretation of iconic signs naturally tends to influence our attitudes and the way we view things. Once we recognize that a work is in some respects similar to value properties of our general experience, that way of seeing the work tends to lead us toward finding extrageneric resemblances in every feature of the work. Creative artists do, of course, capitalize on the observer's tendency, and they develop in their creations new aspects of life values that we can learn to adopt.[5] We expect fine works of art to help us to see our own experience just as orderly, chaotic, or otherwise expressive as the aspects of life shown us by art works.

When we say the musical works give us experience directly or represent experience indirectly, we are aiming at a number of other points as well. One of these was discussed in terms of our responses to gestures being at different levels. Another point brought up was that aesthetic experience opens up new aspects of experience for us. But still another is that musical art goes beyond superficial imitation of extrageneric objects to reveal value properties of what is represented. A few words on the last point should relate all three of these points to the metaphoric nature of extrageneric meaning.

Musical gestures are expressive in the sense that they embody value properties; they outrightly show us the dynamic characters of motion, forces, tensions, tendencies, and consummations.[6] These value properties—the dynamic characters—are certainly *in* music, but they just as surely are properties of extrageneric objects.[7] Thus, they function as iconic signs, supporting symmetric relationships of art to life and life to art.

But it is important to discern that the expressive display of dynamic character in works comes into being through the careful selection and organization of characters by the creative mind. The imaginative efforts of the artist achieve a dynamic character for the work, and the achievement is the skilled product of refinement, condensations and elaborations, intensifications and transformations of artistic elements.[8] But this achievement most often results in a departure from, a variation of, the literal form of objects when they are given in artistic contexts. And so we find that musical works tend to present gestures that are the sensuously heightened product of artistic imagination. For whatever extrageneric content a composer can utilize in a work may appear reworked and formed anew in an aesthetic gesture. And it is in virtue of this that we can say aesthetic experience with music offers us a new perspective on life values.

Now we can see the general significance of the extrageneric meaning of art works: art works, including musical ones, can offer us new experience which is valuable in itself as experience. As Dewey rightly says,

> Tangled scenes of life are made more intelligible in aesthetic experience: not, however, . . . by reduction to conceptual form, but by presenting their meanings as the matter of a clarified, coherent, and intensified or "impassioned" experience.[9]

And, moreover, the very offer of new experience constitutes a communication of life values, which means most decidedly that the musical aesthetic experience gives one information and adds to his store of knowledge.[10]

For the educator one salient point should be derived from these conclusions. In finding that general experience is enriched by aesthetic experience, we have a great deal of the rationale for the importance of musical studies in education. This position stands out against the cries of art for art's sake and of the "autonomy" of art. Such cries tend to suggest that art has no value for general experience, because they in effect assert that art works are devoid of external reference, hence, have no relevance for human affairs. On the contrary, musical art works presuppose intimate relation to life values, through their selective organization and heightened presentation of those very values. Accordingly, we must find that aesthetic experience is wider than autonomistic views allow. And, moreover, we would believe that a substantial value of musical works resides in the metaphoric extrageneric meanings they have, because these meanings can result in expanded knowledge of and about life.

Musical Metaphor and Implicit Acts of Discourse. At this juncture I would like to point out a conclusion to be drawn from the preceding discussions. If we accept (1) that musical elements of sound and rhythm are expressive, (2) that the elements and organized configurations of them are sign complexes or musical gestures, and (3) that organic behavior as well as extraorganic objects are signified by musical gestures conveying attitudes, then it seems to follow that musical organisms can make, or at the least imply, acts of discourse.[11] Moreover, it would seem that such acts of discourse may be about life values, especially gestures and attitudes of mankind.

Acts of discourse may be regarded as communicative utterances, the meaningful uses of verbal gestures, especially in symbolic structures. The semiotic and gestural foundations of meaning and communication in such acts already have been outlined in early chapters. The classification of acts of discourse is quite another matter. (Among those who have developed classifications, C. S. Peirce, Charles Morris, and J. L. Austin seem to have gone furthest.)[12] But the classification process itself is problematic, even though patterns of use seem to generate modes of signifying and discourse. What approach to classification does one take? And how are modes of discourse meaningfully distinguished from uses of acts? Moreover, the great number of modes or uses seems endless. For instances we might consider only the following: the interrogative, exclamative, imperative (including prescriptive, injunctive), the indicative or designative (ostensive, nominative, descriptive, optative, definitive), the formative and systemic, the performative (ceremonial), the valuative or appraisive, and the incitive (inhibitive and facilitative)—to list but a few of the better known sorts of acts in discourse. So to avoid bogging down in the theory of acts of discourse, it seems best to confine to a limited area our discussion of the proposition that music may implicitly present such acts. We can investigate a few representative sorts of act such as designation and interrogation, leaving the bulk of the possible acts to consideration elsewhere.

To begin, we recall our finding that musical art works are, strictly speaking, complex sign vehicles which we regard by a root metaphor as organisms. In their varied constitutions and behavior, the musical organisms exhibit multifarious expressive local and regional properties, and they make gestures which carry attitudes with them.

The many properties of a musical organism and its gestural behavior act as signs. Some properties, singly or in combinations, serve as indices; they seize and direct attention in locating other important objects. Some function as icons which display expressive qualities and characterize congeneric as well as extrageneric objects and behavior. Still other properties hold as logical signs and show the manner of connection and relation between or within the organism's gestures, and they express propositional attitudes.

Interpreted as metaphors, musical gestures signify life values such as organic behavior, although they may signify inorganic objects in terms of their actions. Signification of organic movement and attitudes is of prime importance. What music does is to perform actions in sonorous motion that exhibit the dominant qualities of motion characteristic of organic movement. The performative gestures, moreover, carry with them the attitudes of the musical organism, attitudes expressed by sonic and rhythmic qualities in specifically apt combinations. And to the extent that musical gestures are expressive to us, they exhibit their expressive qualities, and these qualities, then, are iconic signs which signify the attitude expressed. In this frame of reference it can be that sentient states are among the objects signified by musical gestures. Thus, a given gesture may be significant of felt motion that is peculiar to our inner life of affection and conation. And, then, in this situation what is denoted may be identified with what is expressed, which is an attitude, a state of organic sentience. So it seems, then, that musical organisms may be involved in asserting primitive statements (analogues of object words), because their gestures embody the functions of expression and indication that are essential to making statements.

It is not organic acts and affective-conative states alone that music signifies by gestural performances. Music also can present logical signs expressing the connective relations between gestures and can express propositional attitudes. Gestures may be linked in a number of syntactically important ways: by musical punctuation signs (*i.e.*, position, pauses, emphasis, and inflection); by the display of musical properties characterizing feelings of relation or propositional attitudes of belief, doubt, and so on; by the execution through sonorous movement of inferential schemes connecting phases of gestural acts by conjunction, disjunction, negation, and material implication. Therefore, music can give not simply isolated gesture metaphors for organic movements and attitudes, but music also can build up combinations and specific sequences of interrelated metaphors. These may be significant of extended organic acts with a coherent, logical structure and meaning. Hence, musical works may implicitly assert primitive statements, either singly or in logically structured sets.

At this point we should remind ourselves that metaphors import into their comprehension associated clusters of meanings—connotations. Thus, a metaphor expressing a meaning of "running" brings with it the associated aura of feeling that we find pervades our memories of running. One runs to escape or to quickly attain some goal. One runs because of motives and feelings of fear or aggression or self-seeking gain. As apparently appropriate to the instance musically given us, we may import such connotative meanings into the comprehensive meaning of a musical metaphor for "running" or whatever. So what a complex gestural act means to us is the dominant action or attitude it expresses plus the connotative cluster of associations that our acquaintance confers through feeling evoked by that dominant object denoted. These secondary, associated connotations enrich and further qualify the sense of the main musical reference.

We can turn to a theory of Morris Weitz on these matters, for Weitz seemingly suggests—with clear reservations—that music may be capable of implying propositions through metaphor, even complex assertive acts.[13] Let us quote at some length his view as he applies it to a portion of a composition.

> Stated in its positive form, our thesis has been that in some of the arts, especially in literature and painting, among the many elements there are to be found, either directly or indirectly, either stated or gestured, certain asserted propositions which are true or false. The extent of these truth claims in the arts is still an open question, and an invitation to further

aesthetic analysis. . . . That music is a language in the sense of a system of signs that has meaning to listeners, we have already shown, but that music is a language in the sense of a system of signs that contains propositions in the ways that literature or painting do, we do not feel ready to accept. . . . The most I am prepared to say, and this very tentatively, is that some music does contain *musical analogues* of assertions or truth claims. Consider, for example, Beethoven's last quartet, Opus 135. Many critics, even the composer himself, find in it the assertion that life is good or that affirmation of life is the answer to doubt. Perhaps this is too much to find in the music, but what one does find is the sequence of *musical* doubt and affirmation. The fourth and final movement begins slowly and is characterized in this beginning section by irresolution and hesitation within the musical sounds; this is followed by an allegro section in which all the musical doubt and irresolution give way to musical materials that are completely affirmative in their expressive character. Now, if we accept musical hesitation and affirmation as transparent symbols, we may say that this fourth movement embodies the contrast between doubt and affirmation, in which the latter comes after the former, as a kind of *reply* to it. But this is a musical reply, and the whole movement is at most an analogue of the claim that in life affirmation is the answer to doubt.[14]

What Weitz seems to be saying has reference in part to "The Difficult Resolution" (the fourth movement of Op. 135) and to Beethoven's explicitly assigned verbal denotation of the two main thematic gestures: "Must it be?" and the answering resolution formed, "It must be!" (Example 11-5, motto heading movement and mm. 1–15).[15] This analysis of the music's expression of propositional attitudes of doubt and affirmation seems entirely appropriate—a fact that any perceptive listener can easily confirm himself by listening to the movement and studying the score. The opening gestures of the adagio do manifest regional qualities of hesitancy, irresolution, and tenuousness. And the metaphoric signification of doubt through the display of those musical qualities is not dispelled until the allegro and its positive characteristics, which convey an affirmative attitude. What the musical metaphors give us are implicit statements alternately of doubt and affirmation or "the difficult resolution" from the query "Must it be?" to the answer "It must be!" As Weitz contends, then, the question and answer are musical. And, moreover, the most one should make of the analysis is that ". . . in life affirmation is the answer to doubt." But making this much is going rather far toward holding that music potentially can express questions, answers, and so on— so long as it is understood that the significance is metaphoric.

EXAMPLE 11-5   Ludwig van Beethoven, *String Quartet 17*, Op. 135, IV, mm. 1–15

"The Difficult Resolution"

Although some sorts of metaphorically implied statements do seem to fall within the ken of musical signification, it is not at all so plausible that many sorts of statement do. Music may be able to deal with implying statements about the character of motions, especially those involving sound. Such metaphoric expressions as "This is fast", "It is complicated", "Fast moving and complicated events are followed on occasion by simplification and calm", and the like seem possible of musical signification. And, as noted above, music may be able to convey implied statements about life values such as the sequence of attitudes one feels or the progression of propositional attitudes. ("The answer to doubt is affirmation.") However, it seems clear that music falls short of being able to cope adequately with expressions about many qualities, in particular those about colors or hues. It seems problematic whether or not music could signify iconically "redness" or "blueness". And it seems quite clear that music is unable to give an adequate metaphor for many objects such as the moon or a book—not to mention such acts as looking at something (watching or reading) or thinking. Surely there are severe limitations on music's potential to signify much that is common in our experience. And yet it is reasonable to regard favorably the idea that, in limited scope, music may imply some metaphoric statements about life values.

Several more points seem worth noting again in this connection. First, at some point in an effort to clarify the extrageneric meaning of a musical work one must move from description and characterization of musical properties to saying what the meaning is. At this point several assumptions are made in converting descriptive adjectives and performative verbs and phrases into sentences that state that meaning. And it seems easy enough to note several of the assumptions that, as a matter of form, one might often make in so doing an analysis and paraphrase of extrageneric musical meaning. Most important of all one can regard the musical work as an organism, a sort of spokesman who addresses listeners. The musical organism has as its object getting us involved in feeling the qualities of the experience as the music lives through it for and with us. In addition, we can assume that the topic often is life—life values such as our attitudes in relation to events, but more important, in relation to one another. The metaphoric discourse of the music is about our instinctual responses to situations, to what one undergoes as feeling and desire in life. Accordingly, one comes up with metaphoric assertions such as Weitz made that ". . . in life affirmation is the answer to doubt." Given the musical particulars, in paraphrasing the extrageneric meaning we move from the particular qualities and performative acts noted to a generalization about life values. And in order to verify and clarify the claims we may make, we can only (1) make further statements, putting our feelings and thoughts into words as possible, and (2) we must listen to the music and examine the score, noticing and pointing out the properties that singly or cumulatively add up to an implicit metaphor. Moreover, as we noted from Quine's cues, the interlinguistic translation effected must involve sufficiently large segments of musical significations, a point that dictionary-oriented thinkers overlook in considering the whole matter.

We must, perforce, leave the issue unexamined in the main by saying, as Weitz has, that the issue is open. However, in view of some of the evidence, which I have attempted to present in these pages, it seems that a fair case can be made for accepting that music can, potentially at least, give metaphors that imply statements about life values. The lines along which one might seek further understanding of how and why this may be would seem to be those taken here: that is, investigation of music's expressive gestural power and the role that semiotic plays in musical experience.

In any event I trust that the present investigation indicates that a major part of music's meaning lies in its extrageneric sense and reference and that inclusion of this apsect of musical meaning is a necessary part of a balanced theory of musical meaning.

Part II, Artistic Truth

In turning now to artistic truth, we shall briefly consider the meanings of "true" and "truth" in normal discourse, then recapitulate the main features of congeneric truth, after which we can discuss the nature of extrageneric truth and its relation to congeneric truth. Before delving into those matters it is well to be aware of an important challenge to be met in adopting the semiotic-gestural sort of aesthetic theory advanced here. The challenge is articulated by Monroe C. Beardsley in his distinguished book *Aesthetics: Problems in the Philosophy of Criticism.* Beardsley rightly insists that any semiotic theory of music, in order to maintain a valid theory of artistic truth, must give a clear account of the indexical and iconic (characterizing) functions of music.[16] To that challenge I would add the requisites of adequate accounts of the logical operators and interlinguistic translation. All these accounts have been elaborated in foregoing investigations, and some of the foundations for a theory of artistic truth have been mentioned in earlier comments on congeneric truth. But now let us examine the subject of artistic truth more carefully by extending the foundations to cover extrageneric musical truth. It should be borne in mind, however, that the following discussion is not intended as a theory of truth or of artistic truth. It is but a brief discussion aimed at sketching certain points that seem to be central to the development of a theory of artistic truth.

Two matters confront us. One is the meaning of the word "true" as it may be used appropriately in aesthetic analysis. The other is the meaning of "truth" in conjunction with some criteria by which we may attempt to determine the truth value of expressions.

"*True.*"   We may say that in common usage the core meaning of "true" is to be in accordance with either (1) fact or reality or with (2) reason or rule. Some synonyms used in place of true include such terms as real, actual, substantial, authentic, veritable, genuine, well grounded, verified, corroborated; legitimate, correct, accurate, exact, conformable to, and so on. The most basic and important thing to be said about the uses of "true" in discourse concerns the attendant attitude one has in uttering the word. That is, the most fundamental use of "true" is to express one's belief in, or his feeling about the reality of, something. It would seem that this use of "true" not only is primary but also is conjunct with all other uses. There seem to be at least three other empirical uses of "true" worth distinguishing. Another use of "true" is to affirm or assert something directly or to assert *that* something is a fact—the propositional use of "true." In this use one is saying of some state of affairs ". . . is so and so" or, more formally, "It is true that . . ." Still another use of the word is to say "It is true," which is to confirm or attest to some prior statement without repeating it. We might call this the corroborative use of "true," and we should notice the sometimes equivalence of this use to the terms "to warrant," "to guarantee," "to certify" or "to validate." Finally, there is the use of "true" when one means to assent to an expression, when one admits or concedes that something is so. This last use of "true" is rather more of a "yes saying" or agreeing with someone. In all these uses it appears that there is something performatory and ceremonial about them (which is to go against trying to draw a line between so-called performative functions and truth functions of expressions).

"*Truth.*"   Let us turn now to the matter of truth, that which is true, with special reference to possible criteria of verification. That is, we should consider possible principles or standards for belief in and judging of the truth—how to carry out the process of examining and determining grounds for decision. In doing this we shall assume that one may consider musical truth very much as any other truth, except for the medium of presentation and signification being, of course, music.

What makes a statement, whether verbal or purely musical, true depends on what kind of statement it is. The most important kind of statement would seem to be the class of basic statements. *Basic statements* or observation-statements are those directly verifiable by one's confrontation with relevant facts or states of affairs, and we may say that statements are basic provided they contain no other less directly verifiable statements. Basic statements provide the grounds for asserting all other empirical statements which are derivative or relatively complex. A basic statement in music is a simple or atomic gesture.

The *truth* of basic statements seems to depend upon their relation (*i.e.*, correspondence) to some set of facts or state of affairs, whereas the truth of all other statements would depend upon their syntactical structure or relations to basic statements.[17] *Facts or states of affairs* are objects of acquaintance, most specifically those objects acting as stimuli to sensory-perception, *e.g.*, an occurrence or situation directly observed, heard, seen, touched, or otherwise felt. Facts are what can be defined ostensively, that which exists objectively quite independent of whether or not anyone thinks so. It is important to admit that facts or states of affairs include whatever one interprets by means of sensory experience as an individual, and an individual may be divisible into any number of parts.[18] Thus, facts and states of affairs include what some psychologists call gestalts or configurations, what some call sets of stimuli, which we normally interpret spontaneously as entities or individuals. I refer in this book to facts as including such complexes of stimuli and environmental situations which I have named so far "states of affairs."

Confrontation with facts gives rise to observation, belief, analysis, decision, and action. The whole matter of truth and falsehood has to do with brute confrontation by facts and how that experience is interpreted as well as communicated. Discursive signification begins gesturally with physically pointing to a fact, by indexically signifying some object of acquaintance—which is what we mean by saying that facts are what can be defined ostensively or demonstratively. Here, at this step, we relate significatory acts to some state of affairs. Verbal definition, even if ostensive, is itself a step removed. To *say* or otherwise express what a fact is requires one's making a true statement. Thus is language used to say things about observations of immediate or prior sensory encounters. Discourse includes facts in only a derivative form; by their symbolization verbally in true statements facts or states of affairs are operationally but still indirectly contained in discourse. Words, symbolic gestures, and other symbols denote facts by linguistic customs of use, or conventions. The *demonstrative* conventions are verbal (or other linguistic) means of ostensively identifying *particular* facts or states of affairs. The *descriptive* conventions are means of characterizing and saying something about a certain *type*, a kind, of situation or set of facts. We do not "state facts"; facts exist objectively and are independent of statements. Facts appear or present themselves to the senses. We state what the facts are: we state our beliefs, or we make statements about facts. To make a statement is to assert something that is true or false. To express any attitude toward, or to say what a fact or state of affairs is, requires one's asserting a true statement. To misstate one's attitude toward a fact or to misstate the description of a state of affairs, in whole or part, is to make a false statement.

A single fact may give rise to different statements. Statements may be expected to vary as the perspectives of different interpreters do or as the perspectives of the same observer might vary at different places or times. Because of the obvious diversity in interpreters and situations for interpreting one and the same fact, basic statements about gross physical objects may not be verifiable or refutable *solely* by comparison to experience; for surely statements, even basic statements, are intricately interwoven with one's conception of reality, which is a highly conditioned and elaborate set of beliefs.[19] One's beliefs affect his judgement of truth.

Believing in a fact is the pragmatic ground for asserting something or for saying that "———— is true." Truth itself is dependent upon the relation of belief to other things. "True" and "false" then primarily express beliefs and derivatively characterize statements.[20] Among the most important of our beliefs are those about the future, our expectations. And as earlier discussion suggested, the future events to confirm or negate inductive expectations are problematic and do not follow of necessity. Consequently, the chief thing about true predictive statements—whether implicit or expressed—is that expectations based upon such statements will not be disappointed.[21] This is not to reduce truth to probability but to say that the cases of forecasts based on beliefs involve degrees of probability and imply that such statements are verified differently than are juxtadictive or retrodictive statements. Indeed, they are verified by subsequent occurrences that may conform more or less to one's forecasts. They are confirmed by other juxtadictive observation of facts, states of affairs, and statements. That verification may be expressed as a matter of degree, the truth or falsehood in such cases being a matter of the extent that expectations are possible of being fulfilled or thwarted.[22] In this connection we would note further that the truth of empirical statements is not an endemically vagrant value, although variations in conditions of the situation, time, place, and interpreter may differently determine value. Truth is determinable with respect to given conditions. The set of conditions that establish truth value on any particular occasion of a statement may be expected to determine these matters uniformly for the span of the argument concerned.[23]

Iconic presentation or resemblance becomes relevant to truth when selected as the dominant mode of signification.[24] (But iconic signification is not the only mode.) The verification of the truth of "pictorial" and other statements based on iconic signification is effected by comparison of the statements to the possible facts or states of affairs they signify. Provided that both the state of affairs exists and the signification is interpreted as adequate iconically, then the truth of the pictorial statement is established.[25] Complete isomorphism (one-to-one correspondence) to facts is not necessarily assumed or required. Rather, a pictorial statement is adequate if certain conditions are met, to wit: (1) when the facts signified do exist, (2) when the statement can be correlated with the facts by ostensive acts (*e.g.*, demonstrative conventions), and (3) when the facts can be correlated with the signs presenting the statement by other metalinguistic conventions of description.[26]

Congeneric Musical Truth.   From our viewpoint musical reality is a complex world of sound, silence, and rhythm. Its atomistic subparticles are the local sonic and rhythmic properties. Its atomic elements are the intervals making changes in position within the dimensions of pitch, duration, intensity, timbre, and articulation. These intervals constitute sonorous motion, the main regional property of music, which is also manifest as values of tendency. The local and regional properties of sonorous motion are selectively organized into well formed configurations or formal units called gestures. In virtue of their properties, gestures have sign functions, foremost of which are (1) the expression of character or attitude, including propositional attitudes, and (2) the signification of facts. The elemental modes of signifying—indexical, iconic, and syntactic—are present in discrete basic gestures and in complexes of molecular gestures. The dominant aesthetic mode of signifying is the iconic, which admits two main classes of semantic objects—congeneric and extrageneric signs and significations. Of these, the primary semantic dimension for signification of facts and expression of attitudes is the congeneric. A given musical gesture should at once express an attitude and signify another musical gesture that may be prior, subsequent or

concurrent in time. As individual entities, the simple and uncom-
pounded musical gestures are themselves facts or states of affairs. Moreover, the significant local and regional properties of such gestures also
are fundamental facts. All such musical facts are known or knowable on
acquaintance. The very presentation in composition or performance of a
well formed musical gesture is a basic musical statement. A simple musical gesture is what is asserted or stated. That which is asserted is comprised of and about musical facts and states of affairs; it is, most
importantly of all, a congeneric statement. Other complex or molecular
congeneric gestures may be derived and formed through the syntactic
connection of basic gestures by the logical operators.

Regarded as basic statements, simple congeneric gestures may be
true on one or more grounds. When a simple gesture is itself interpreted
as an individual, a fact or state of affairs, it is true by self-ostensive definition: a basic musical gesture is true because of its perceptible existence
before us and our apprehension of it as single entity. Immediate sensory
perception of, belief in, and cognition of a basic gesture establish its
reality and verify our interpretation of it as fact. On the basis of the recognition of basic gestures stated in molecular complexes we can determine
the truth value of derivative congeneric gestures by demonstrative and
descriptive interlinguistic analysis of the syntactic relations between the
molecular and the more basic gestures.

The truth of basic gestural statements may rest on other grounds.
Interpreted as a basic statement, a simple congeneric gesture may be true
also if it iconically signifies another musical fact or state of affairs. Such
a signified musical fact normally would be another basic gesture or a set
of properties of another musical gesture in the same piece. In this view
the truth value of a basic statement obviously depends upon the interpreter's belief in both the basic gesture and the signified gesture as facts in
themselves, as well as his belief in the adequacy of the signification. When
one does believe in these facts and their semiotic adequacy, a basic gestural statement is verified by comparing it to the signified state of affairs,
the other gesture, or set of properties. This grounding for artistic truth
of congeneric statements is patently tautologous in the sense that most
assertions of mathematics are. To a considerable extent congeneric truth
depends upon the syntactic relation of gestural statements by equality or
by equivalence. To establish the truth of basic gestural statements in the
congeneric domain requires (1) the observable existence of the signified
state of affairs (*i.e.*, another basic gesture or set of gestural properties),

(2) the correlation demonstratively of the particular significant basic statement to that specific state of affairs, and (3) the actual or at least possible description in the verbal metalanguage of the foregoing facts, sign functioning and correspondences as a kind or type of situation. On reflection one should see that the earlier discussion of the internal iconic sign functions in the opening section of Beethoven's *Fifth Symphony* establishes just such conditions and can be regarded as a verbal account of the true basic congeneric statements asserted in that section.

The molecular or complex congeneric statements are derived from basic gestural statements by the linking through logical constants of basic statements. The syntactic conditions for effecting the connections and true disjunctions, conjunctions, and material implications were discussed in Chapter 9. The facts that verify these complex gestural statements are other basic congeneric gestures. The truth of such complex statements depends upon their syntactical correspondence to those other basic gestures. The syntactical correspondence is shown by identifying, pointing out, and describing the component statements and the logical connections within the complex gestural statements on the one hand and, on the other hand, the correspondence of those components to the more basic gestures. This requires the same three steps outlined just above for verifying basic statements.

Extrageneric Musical Truth.   It has been held throughout the discussions of musical meaning that congeneric sign configurations are the basic musical statements. They are. Moreover, many—but by no means all—extragenerically interpreted gestural statements are derived from congeneric roots and so may be called metaphors. Thus, the congeneric gestures stand as the primary dimension of reference and support extrageneric metaphors as a secondary dimension of musical meaning. Among such musical metaphors are the implicit acts of discourse. However, not all extragenerically interpreted gestures are derivative. Some extrageneric gestures are proper basic statements. These shall be considered first before turning to the derivative ones.

Two roots of basic extrageneric musical statements should be noticed. First of these is that the musical work and its gestures have a fundamentally external reference in that they are addressed to the instinctual (or rational) adjustive behavior of interpreters. The second is that an inherent property of well formed musical gestures is their expressivity, that gestures carry with them and convey characteristic attitudes. The projective importance of these two root facts is that a leading purpose of musical works is to express attitudes gesturally in order to affect the attitudes of interpreters. Furthermore, we have seen that truth rests upon an interpreter's attitudes including such as belief, doubt, aversion, hesitancy, and expectation. And yet, although attitudes are important to establishing truth, that which is signified as fact becomes central to determining truth.[27] Nevertheless, there is one important class of musical statements in which what is expressed attitudinally begins and remains central: extrageneric statements referring to and expressing the same intraorganic states. In music the gestural performative often is in this class; it may present and signify an attitude that it expresses. Those simple gestures that in one and the same act express and signify an attitude are both extragenerous in sense and reference as well as being basic statements. The truth of these gestures may be determined by the overt fact of their expressive characteristics being dominant and unmistakable on hearing. In an intuitively apprehended sense the basic but extragenerous gestures are true by definition.[28] They are true on appearance alone because of their self-ostensive function and their felt effect on us in directly calling out a sense of belief in them. This, however, may not seem sufficient, even if necessary, for verification. For fuller verification one also may want to test self-consciously for correspondence of the immediate gestural qualities to his own intuitively known acquaintance with those qualities. The joint instinctual-rational testing of appearance may help ground belief further for the reasoning man. Additionally, one may feel the need to point out to himself or others those particular musical qualities that correlate with qualities of his intuitive feelings. He also may want to tie such an intellectual demonstration to a verbal account of his belief and a characterization of the kind of facts and correspondences to them that hold. But the effort may be wasted. Either one directly grasps the relevant facts or else often fails utterly to get such a meaning as basic extrageneric statements offer. Verbal conviction is a poor substitute, if the only one. Although it can lead us to the facts, discursive explanation simply may fail to help us grasp them, let alone be convinced about them.

The sub-class of basic statements stands alone among its larger class of extrageneric statements. Other extragenerous gestures are derivative. Being metaphoric, the latter statements depend for their truth on less direct relations to facts than immediate presentations of facts or identity. Even so, the musical metaphor may be only slightly removed from basic statement. The removal may be to lesser degrees of iconic relatedness between gesture and extragenerous signification. The least degree of removal from fact would be to signifying objects such as bodily actions or vocal gestures by means of musical gestures analogous to demonstrative verbalisms ("the . . . here.") or object-word statements ("Run!"). For example, consider again the "Pas D'Action" from Stravinsky's *Orpheus*. The movement presents several metaphors for bodily actions, including those for an attack, seizure, and tearing to pieces. Concomitant with them is a pervasive emotional tone of antagonism. The music neither represents nor portrays either Orpheus or the Bacchantes. But there are metaphoric gestural statements of action which may be translated by the object words "Attack!"—"Seize (him)!"—"Tear (him) to pieces!" The music's gestures metaphorically assert artistically true statements. Here, in the musical metaphors, we are at the stage of communication analogous in verbal discourse to where one must assert a true statement in order to describe or say something about an external object, event, or action. The musical statements made are derivative and yet as close as possible to more basic statements. Still, the inclusion of extrageneric fact within the comprehensive meaning and truth domain of a musical work is a derivative syntactic operation. In the case of the metaphors carried by the Stravinsky score (and as is normal in adequate musical metaphors) a large number of basic and complex congeneric statements are required to support a relatively few metaphors. Indeed, some ninety measures (taking slightly over two-and-a-third minutes to perform) yield but three metaphors, and these are derived from redundant and varied assertions of small motives one may interpret as basic congeneric gestures. For instance, one may find some thirteen disjunctly connected gestures in the first nine measures alone, and these function merely as the beginning support that leads to establishing the one metaphor of attack.

How do we verify metaphoric musical statements? Since the metaphors are derivative, they must be correlated on the one side to congeneric facts and on the other side to extrageneric facts. The metaphoric statement must be tied to its supporting facts in the primary dimension of meaning, to the basic or molecular congeneric gestures and their properties, including the attitudes expressed. In addition, the metaphoric statement must be correlated with the non-musical objects, events, or actions it resembles. On the congeneric side many basic gestures syntactically connected into larger segments or complex gestures may be required to ground but a single metaphoric statement. This is to say, then, that the metaphoric statement may be a summative or emergent resultant derived from a set of congeneric statements of fact. So all of the relevant congeneric gestures, their connections and properties, must be identified and their correspondence to the summative or emergent metaphor pointed out. The congenerically significant facts and expressed attitudes, then, are correlated with the extramusical facts by translation of relevant interlinguistic synonymy, which requires use of both the (1) demonstrative and (2) descriptive conventions of the verbal metalanguage. These acts must (1) disclose the particular musical and nonmusical facts, (2) show what attitude is expressed, and (3) characterize the sort of facts, musical and non-musical, and their correspondence to each other. Then the artistic truth of the extrageneric statement is established (or not). The sort of demonstrative and descriptive analysis given in Chapter 10 of the "Pas D'Action" is a necessary part of establishing what the facts are, the musical and extramusical facts which may be said to correspond, and, hence, the grounds for belief in the truth of the metaphors discussed.

What makes a musical gesture's extrageneric meaning true? The grounds upon which we establish the truth of an extrageneric interpretant or statement are varied and may include most or all of the following bases:

1. The sense of reality presupposed, hence,
   a. the situational setting or the interpreter's ambiance, plus
   b. the music's internal contextual conditions bearing on the statement's assertion.
2. That which the congeneric gesture or set of gestures itself is—the configuration with its local and regional properties.
3. That which the musical properties express attitudinally, including propositional attitudes.
4. How the gesture or set of gestures signifies, *i.e.*, in which respects the statement signifies
   a. informally as a signal or symbolically by convention, and
   b. indexically, iconically, and syntactically.
5. That which the gesture or set of gestures signifies, the facts to which it refers
   a. congenerically, or
   b. extragenerically.

6. The degree of directness in the signification, *i.e.*,
   a. whether the gestural statement is directly testable and is a basic statement (*i.e.*, contains no less directly verifiable statement), or
   b. whether the gestural statement is indirectly testable and a complex or derivative statement (*i.e.*, relies on relations to other basic statements for its verification).
7. The interpreter's beliefs about the gesture and its adequacy of signification.

In closing the survey of foundations for a theory of artistic truth, it bears comment that overconcern about the metaphoric truth of music may easily lead to the disadvantageous shifting of attention from more important features of artistic truth and aesthetic experience. Within the realm of truth decisions the ones that stand out as the most important artistic values are the congeneric ones. And within the sub-class of extrageneric truths, the basic statements that both indicate and express attitude are the more important extrageneric values. While *what* is stated or implied musically is centermost in analysis and deciding matters of truth, *how* the statement is made commands the greater attention within the total aesthetic act. The immediate values of congeneric gestural quality and structure dominate aesthetic experience, commanding our intuitions and thoughts. Presenting and doing, the expressing of attitude and revealing of dynamic action, permeate the act and draw us into felt union with and understanding of the art work. In this interaction of interpreter and work the signification and attitudes of the music are conveyed. During the aesthetic transaction the musical gesture sustains itself as foremost in import. Showing and overt display of its performative function—not saying or implying something about it—are primary. To treat feeling or quality and structure conveyed directly by the work as something which must have an objective extrinsic correlative to be analyzed for truth value is to misconceive the chief artistic function as representational and pictorial. It is to assimilate artistic truth to derivative extrageneric interpretants when the main artistic function is performative and presentational.[29] However, to avoid being sidetracked by overattention to extrageneric truth values, the interpreter needs to heed the gestures themselves. He needs to give himself over to interaction with the musical organism. Immersion of one's self in the work enables one to be drawn to the aesthetic core and to absorb the most immediate and direct import of the gestures. With this orientation the interpreter may grasp the more general truths of the work. Basic and molecular congeneric expressions and basic extrageneric statements may be comprehended. The fundamental and general truth of gestures—or their falsity—to character and to each other may be understood. All these comments are not, even so, a deprecation of the value of metaphoric truth, for that kind of truth is a major element in aesthetic experience. Moreover, concentration on the immediate properties of the work and absorption of one's self in the larger stream of congeneric experience also yields on reflection awareness of the derivative truth of a work to its extragenerically interpreted significations. But these extrageneric truths of metaphors emerge only through the accumulation of the longer flow of presentations by congeneric gestures. Hence, the focus of attention—even if to come to knowledge about extrageneric truth—must remain primarily on congeneric meaning and truth, out of which grow the dependent metaphoric meaning and truth.

Notes

1   Ludwig Wittgenstein, *Philosophical Investigations*, trans. G. E. M. Anscombe (Oxford: Basil Blackwell, 1953), pp. 193ᵉ–214ᵉ.

2   Charles W. Morris, *Signs, Language and Behavior* (Englewood Cliffs, N.J.: Prentice-Hall, Inc., 1946), pp. 192–96. See also Theodore M. Greene, *The Arts and the Art of Criticism* (Princeton: Princeton University Press, 1940), pp. 229–35.

3   Paul Henle, ed. *Language, Thought, and Culture* (Ann Arbor: University of Michigan Press, 1958), pp. 189–92.

4   See E. H. Gombrich, "Meditations On A Hobby Horse Or The Roots Of Artistic Form," in *Aspects of Form*, ed. Lancelot Law Whyte (London: Lund Humphries, 1951; citation refers to the reprinting in Morris Philipson, ed., *Aesthetics Today* (Cleveland: The World Publishing Co., 1961), p. 124.

5   F. E. Sparshott, *The Structure of Aesthetics* (London: Routledge and Kegan Paul, 1963), p. 376.

6   John Dewey, *Art As Experience* (New York: G. P. Putnam's Sons, Capricorn Books, 1958), pp. 273–74, 288–97; Rudolf Arnheim, *Art and Visual Perception* (Berkeley: University of California Press, 1957), pp. 425–43; and Sparshott, *Structure of Aesthetics*, p. 151.

7   Dewey, *Art As Experience*, pp. 238–39; R. G. Collingwood, *The Principles of Art* (New York: Oxford University Press, 1938), pp. 225, 228–38; Sparshott, *Structure of Aesthetics*, pp. 426–30.

8   Dorothy Walsh, "The Cognitive Content of Art," *Philosophical Review*, 52 (1943): pp. 433–51; citations refer to the reprint in Eliseo Vivas and Murray Krieger, eds., *The Problems of Aesthetics* (New York: Rinehart and Co., Inc., 1953), p. 607; Susanne K. Langer, *Problems of Art* (New York: Charles Scribner's Sons, 1957), chap. 7, especially pp. 98 and 104.

9   Dewey, *Art As Experience*, p. 290.

10 Dewey, *Art As Experience*, pp. 273–74, 288–97; Arnheim, *Art and Visual Perception*, p. 205; Langer, *Problems of Art*, pp. 23–24, 60, 70–74; Morris, *Signs, Language and Behavior*, p. 138.

11 See Greene, *Arts and the Art Of Criticism*, p. 424; Morris, *Signs, Language and Behavior*, pp. 192–96 and chaps. 5 and 6.

12 Charles S. Peirce, *Philosophical Writings of Peirce*, ed. Justus Buchler (New York: Dover Publications, 1955), pp. 98–119; Morris, *Signs, Language and Behavior*, chaps. 5 and 6; J. L. Austin, *How To Do Things With Words* (London: Oxford University Press, 1962).

13 Morris Weitz, *Philosophy of the Arts* (Cambridge: Harvard University Press, 1950), pp. 134–52.

14 Ibid., pp. 151–52.

15 Ludwig van Beethoven, *String Quartet 17, F major, Opus 135* (London: Boosey and Hawkes, n.d.), mm. 1–15.

16 Monroe C. Beardsley, *Aesthetics: Problems in the Philosophy of Criticism* (New York: Harcourt, Brace and Co., 1958), pp. 367–99, especially pp. 372–73, 377–78.

17 Bertrand Russell, *An Inquiry into Meaning and Truth* (Baltimore: Penguin Books, 1962), p. 272; A. J. Ayer, *The Concept of a Person* (London: Macmillan and Co., Ltd., 1963), pp. 169–72.

18 Nelson Goodman, *The Structure of Appearance*, 2nd ed. (Indianapolis: The Bobbs-Merrill Company, Inc., 1966), pp. 36–47.

19 Willard Van Orman Quine, *Word and Object* (Cambridge: M.I.T. Press, 1960), pp. 22–24. For a discussion of the role of belief in the quest for certainty and a criterion of truth, see Philip D. Jacklin, *Certainty and Criteria of Truth*, Ph.D. dissertation (New Haven: Yale University, 1967), pp. 22, 33–34, 89–102 passim. Jacklin offers an unusual amount of analysis of the role of belief.

20 Russell, *Meaning and Truth*, p. 215.

21 Morris, *Signs, Language and Behavior*, p. 121.

22 A. J. Ayer, *The Problem of Knowledge* (New York: The Macmillan Co., 1956), p. 174.

23 Quine, *Word and Object*, pp. 226–27.

24 Ludwig Wittgenstein, *Tractatus Logico-Philosophicus*, trans. and ed. D. F. Pears and B. F. McGuinness (London: Routledge and Kegan Paul, 1963), 2.1, 2.1515, 2.171, 2.21, 2.22, 2.223, 3 = pp. 15–19; Ayer, *Concept of a Person*, p. 183.

25 Ayer, *Concept of a Person*: "If the symbolism is pictorial [*i.e.*, iconic], it is the resemblance of the signs to some possible state of affairs that determines what they signify; but then what decides the question of their truth or falsehood is whether or not this state of affairs exists."—p. 183.

26 J. L. Austin, "Truth," *Symposium on Truth, Proceedings of the Aristotelian Society*, 24 (1950), pp. 111–16. Cf. P. F. Strawson's attack on Austin's formulation of the correspondence theory and Austin's response, pp. 117–72. A firm defence of Austin and the correspondence theory is given by G. J. Warnock, "Truth and Correspondence," in *Knowledge and Experience*, ed. C. D. Rollins (Oberlin: University of Pittsburgh Press, 1962), pp. 11–20.

27 Russell, *Meaning and Truth*, p. 203.

28 Ibid., pp. 204–05.

29 Susanne K. Langer, *Mind: An Essay on Human Feeling*, vol. 1 (Baltimore: Johns Hopkins Press, 1967), pp. 113–20.

12

Structure and Quality of
Affective Musical Meanings

This chapter will delve into what provides psychological coherence and organization for successive affective states elicited by sequences of musical gestures.[1] Although musical syntax as a stimulus factor is a major part of what we must consider, it is not a syntax of music alone with which we must deal. Rather the investigation seeks more to call attention to factors in the pragmatic dimension of meaning which are operative in structuring affective responses into coherent aesthetic experiences. In doing this, however, we do not want to fall into the trap of isolating affective responses from the musical stimulus and then puzzle aimlessly over what causes the responses to be related. Finding principles of psychological coherence for affective states is possible only in considering musical stimulus events and organic responses in conjunction.

So far, our most concentrated inquiries have been directed to the musical work. A composition in performance is the stimulus control object for aesthetic musical experience. The major factors that provide for meaningfulness, intelligibility, and coherence *within* a composition have been discussed in some detail. They include the expressivity of sonic and rhythmic elements, the sensuous surface of sound in motion, the functioning of the local and regional properties as iconic signs, indexical

Notes to this chapter are on p. 213.

signs, and logical signs, the gestural performative role of syntactic and semantic units, the congeneric reference and attitude of gestural statements and their truth values, the categorical formal designs, the logical connection of gestures, principles of patterning, and so on. In addition, considerable attention has been given already to the relations of those factors to responses.

In turning more to responses it is valuable to uncover at once a fundamental presupposition in aesthetic theory: *i.e.*, different people tend to respond to the same thing in closely similar or the same ways, all other things being equal. This idea may be far from obvious truth, because it involves gross inference from one's particular case to many other people's cases, but it is an inescapable presupposition. So far as ways of responding go in general, two have been described—the instinctual-affective and the rational. Although individuals may tend to either disposition according to circumstances, they do respond in both ways. It also is good to remember that dispositions and responses do fluctuate between affective and rational states and that these often fuse. But what most concerns us is that there is similarity and predictability in dispositions and responses within given contexts. So much so, I believe—if extraordinary conditions are not supervening—that the sorts of responses made to the same stimulus by different normal people will be quite alike. If this were not so in a general sense, then we could not hope that an interpreter's experience will resemble the composer's expectations for him. Communication, too, is similarly dependent.

A focal term is the "interpreter's experience." Experience includes events having affected one through the senses in the interaction of the organism and its internal or external environments and which continue to influence the organism's subsequent behavior. Experience surely includes acquaintance knowledge (*e.g.*, knowledge of qualities, relations, memories, habit, and inference) and discursive knowledge (*e.g.*, knowledge about others, physical objects, propositions, and logical structures).

In obtaining experience, whatever the role of the stimulus, the organism exerts its own internal control over stimuli by an organizing activity. Just as we know that the nervous system works as a selective and integrative process through facilitation and inhibition of impulses, we know also that this is true for all levels of activity from the most rudely biologic through the most refined intellectual.[2] Life itself is, in a physiological sense, organization. Life exhibits purposive character in its selective and integrative functions; it is, above all, an organized system of activities.[3]

The internal dispositions and responses are not at all random but are in themselves systemic and discriminatory, tending to discern organization in, or impose it on, experience. These facts directly bear upon our spontaneous interpretation of musical experience.

In hearing music our acts of sensory perception involve dual organizing functions: they confer order upon our responses to auditory stimuli, and they allow us to recognize relationships between stimuli. Being inherently an organizing process, hearing is adapted to sorting and grouping stimuli, whether or not those stimuli are in themselves well formed structures. Therefore, whereas music is the control stimulus to our responses on the one side of experience, on the other side our perceptual activity integrates selected impulses. The organizing functions extend to those of interpretant formation, the pragmatic aspects of sign functioning.[4]

We can uncover still another important presupposition tucked away in the term "interpreter's experience"; that is, responses of most normal people are to both the quality content and the relational structure of events or objects. This is to be seen in that our past experience includes acquaintance knowledge of qualities and relations as well as discursive knowledge about logical structures. But more important than what we know is how we grasp the knowledge. The key fact here is that we at once apprehend from a given situation both the quality and texture or structure of contexts. Experience involves the inseparable apprehension of qualitative and relational contents.[5] The significance of our simultaneous apprehension of quality and structure lies in their two-fold affective force. There is the essential affectivity of the qualitative directly apprehended; there equally is the immediate affective force of structure. In our present discussion the latter needs emphasis. Indeed, even the more assertive formalists among aestheticians will acknowledge the affective impact of structural characters on aesthetic experience.[6] The basic formal coherence of art works is known not alone by rational processes but by the purely intuitional as well.[7] We must acknowledge that the formal characters of the stimulus exert a direct control over affective musical experience. Together with the affective power of structure is found the affectivity of the qualitative content of experience. The primary meaning of quality is affective; the quality of events is what we say we feel.[8] In the felt qualities of experience we have another element of direction and regulation which gives musical experience coherence through intuition. Intuition of coherence is stimulated by the sensuous surface of musical motion. As disposition and response, the intuition of coherence consists in the organism's biologic processes of immediate selection or rejection of impulses, by which acts the quality of events is taken as feeling of rightness or wrongness about the events themselves or about the sequence of events. We usually are unaware of the processes and do not tend continually to focus attention on specific stimuli felt in the normal flow of experience. We tend simply to feel something or to intuit a felicity or malaise in the situation. The quality of the larger process is felt and constitutes a regional quality of felt aptness or whatever for spans of experience. Qualitative characters of a stimulus object produce a feeling, and the sequences of events in sets also produce generalized feelings, including those of sensed wholeness and coherence or the lack of it. In the process of intuition organic selection gives some gestural qualities the power of organization over affective states in the sense of those states being felt to be apt and cohesive or not. Thus, the qualitative characters of a composition constitute a direct control over affective musical experience. Moreover, this sense of rightness or wrongness is not one associated only with our affective states, but it also is the background to intellectual reasoning. As propositional attitude it enters into thought processes; it is attached to, or charges, the whole process of inference[9] as we comprehend the complex meanings of successive gestural statements.

The musical experience is unified by the interaction of the organism and its sonic-rhythmic environment. The experience is bound to the structural and qualitative characters of the music. Thus, just as we cannot fully separate the structural and qualitative properties of the stimulus, so we cannot easily and totally separate the structure and quality of the affective responses from each other. All are strands in the texture of a common context, the musical experience. But although the quality and structural texture of events (either musical stimuli or our responses) are not apprehended in separation from each other, either the qualitative or relational characters of the musical stimulus may appear dominant in given situations. And if one is dominant, it tends to be the qualitative, because the directly apprehended qualitative characters of sense presentations are most quickly taken on instinct as signs of value.[10] The qualitative characters are prized simply because they most command our interest and act as cues to the meaning of the stimulus, as indications of appropriate dispositions and responses to musical gestures and the attitudes they convey.

The temporal natures of music and responses are primary controls for musical experience. G. J. Whitrow has pointed out the temporal nature of mind, comparing it to a tune.[11] The comparison may be extended by saying that especially through its temporal characteristics music displays its profound likeness to life, because through temporal characteristics both music and life achieve organization. Sensory perception, and hearing in particular, is temporally characterized by present organic adjustments occurring in response to the stimulus of already past events, or, from another perspective, by present events calling forth future behavior.[12] This temporal dimension under examination reveals the peculiar transitory quality of the musical present. What we call the "present" of auditory perception is specious: it can be viewed as comprising something of both past and coming sounds. Thus, one main characteristic of musical experience is that the present is always a changing spread of sonorous events extending from, and merging together, an immediate past into an imminent future. The essence of aesthetic interest is in that temporal spread of passing away-now-coming into being.

Because of the temporal spread of the musical "present," our acts of hearing take in spans of sound and rhythm, organizing the passing events into emerging responses. We can say metaphorically that hearing has a mercurial liquidity: as sounds pass on, the process of hearing blends one event with the following, quickly running together events of well formed syntactic units as droplets into a stream. Hence, the perceptual import of pauses; they articulate and bound the spans of temporally merged sound motions. The organization occurs in a rhythmic blending of the perceptual contents. We see in audition, then, that both the successive presents as well as the qualitative contents tend to merge. The characteristic spreading of the perceptual present and the corresponding merging of the sensed contents is a temporal process known as *fusion*.[14]

Fusion is of the essential nature of sensory perception and organization of responses, particularly the more biologic and undisputedly affective responses. Fusion is inherent in auditory perception, and it may be regarded as the primary mode of perceiving and hearing music.[15] Fusion unifies the contiguous immediacies and sensations; it is involved in relating the segregated gestures discerned in self-conscious levels of attentive listening, especially as attention relaxes between successive completed gestural acts and their perception as well formed configurations. Most important, however, fusion is involved in intuitions of consummative quality, for in musical experience, as in life generally, the merging of perceptual immediacies is bound up with our feeling for the larger rhythmic sweep and structuring of complex gestural acts.[16] Here we are face to face with the basic affective values of musical experience as temporal process—with cyclic relaxation-tension-impulsion-relaxation in the primal anticipations of impending import and consummation caused by the rhythmic acts of gestures.

Fusion of the temporal dimension of musical experience, then, constitutes a principle of affective coherence, a principle providing a foundation also for the intellectual acts of discerning objective stimulus coherence. The overriding importance of the temporal dimension of musical experience is in its unifying and regulatory effects, in the sustained control given over that experience by the spread of the present. In the perceptual process of fusion the regulation of our responses is at once a determination in two directions, forward and backward. Events impinging upon the future edge of our experience exert their dominance through our primal, unself-conscious anticipations, while events slipping past retain their sway through their familiarity in our immediate retrospection and recall. And rhythm is involved. The rhythmic quality of musical gestures evokes in our responses a rhythm of feelings. The rhythm of the musical events is felt as tensions bringing us to consummations and emphasis; it is felt as withdrawals from passing stresses and relaxations. What we feel often is imminent and emerging, just ahead. So we feel and know that there is a control to our feelings in the future events; e.g., the release from stress is coming. But there also is something present in qualities felt that has been controlled by passing sounds. The tensions give way; the feeling of strain is going and the emphasis past. So, similarly, through our feeling we know there is control in the passing. The touchstone for understanding the coherence of successive affective states is that our responses and dispositions are controlled by the fusion of the musical present. The coherence of successive affects exists in the control of the aesthetic present, in the past-future fusion within the spread of the stimulating sensuous surface of sounds and the merging of our affective responses.[17]

Another important part of the temporal musical experience is the focusing and waning of attention. In the case of man alone among organisms does there seem to be the continuing capacity of voluntary attending to objects, of isolating and selecting from among stimuli present environmentally those stimuli to which disposition to respond will be actualized in response.[18] This has important bearings upon intelligence, or self-conscious conduct, because voluntarily attending is a creative act: voluntary attention determines one's environment and the situation in which he will act by eschewing some stimuli and interacting with others. It then is directly involved in interpretant formation, in the sorting out of musical characteristics that have significance.

Not all attention is voluntary. In listening to music one's attitude may be a completely relaxed and unself-conscious sensitivity, but the music may not be equally free from tension and dynamic events. Musical gestures may seize attention forcibly and sharply focus it—albeit involuntarily on the part of the listener. In such cases the response is markedly affective, in fact emotional, since the startle mechanism of the brain is tripped. Emphatic, unexpected, greatly contrasted or extreme stimuli may call forth involuntary attention and emotion. The musical properties with such stimulus force are, we recognize, reckoned among the index signs. And, as we know, indexical properties of musical gestures may demand involuntary attention even in the face of one's disposition being intellectualized and his listening already involving voluntarily focused attention. We have, then, two sorts of attention—one involuntary, unself-conscious, and inherently emotional; the other voluntary, self-conscious, and affective.

The important fact about attention and the temporal in regard to the coherence of affective sequences lies in the focusing and waning of attention. The alternation is rhythmic, giving a cyclic fluctuation between relaxed or relatively passive hearing and the more tensed and active attending to musical gestures. Attention may be now voluntarily focused; again it may be caught by the unexpected or extreme stimulus; or at another instant attention may pass over into a submissive attitude. Only with strong interest and sustained effort do we focus and maintain attention voluntarily on gestures or their attitudes. Without a highly motivated disposition, the normal tendency is to vacillate between attentiveness and passiveness.

Whenever attention is focused voluntarily or involuntarily, a memorable environment is created and the commanding stimuli of that environment elicit specific responses. Thus, in the normal fluctuation of attention and passive receptivity, acts of attention structure experience, and they are, moreover, fused together by spans of less focused but qualitatively differentiated experience. The acts of attention most important to our account of affective coherence are the involuntary ones, for, in their directed focus on specific indexical gestural properties, the emotional acts of involuntary attention establish referential points in the framework, or mark off segments, of the musical experience. When attention is seized by intrusion of specific indexical characters of gestures, quiescent responses cease just as voluntary attention does, and configurations of gestures are shaped up in emotionally charged interpretants. In short, the involuntary act of attention is a focal point, a prominence of structure in the sequence of affective responses; it dominates and regulates its context in the whole musical experience. The total sequence of these emotional moments of involuntary attention caused by indices become an intraorganic structure of emotive stresses that control and impart coherence to the totality of the affective responses.

We need to note carefully the rhythmic fluctuation between focusing and waning attention: it comprises a succession of felt stresses and relaxations, qualified by welling and subsiding tensions. In the emphases and tensions of involuntary attentiveness we find the structural rhythmic promontories of the sequence of our affective responses. In the fusion of perceptual immediacies in the moving spread of the present, we have the qualitative contents filling out those affective sequences. Involuntary attention is a psychological principle or mode of structuring and giving coherence to affective responses. Fusion is another such principle of affective organization. Fusion and involuntary attention together structure and organize a rhythm of affectivity in our musical experience.

In consequence of the foregoing discussion and earlier conclusions, a number of observations on affective responses and their musical stimuli should be drawn together. First of all, a musical work—although it is an extended sequence of stimuli—is bounded and stands as an autonomous, congenerically meaningful entity or sign vehicle. The observable local and regional characteristics of the self-contained work are signs whose first effect is affective. The sensuous surface qualities are stimuli to which we respond directly (although responses also may be mediated). Perceived qualities of the music such as loudness or softness, highness or lowness of pitch and tone color all have immediate affective force. The qualities of musical gestures are identifiable with the affective. Moreover, in the case of structural stimuli a similar situation exists. The formal or relational properties of gestures have affective force—*e.g.*, the inclusion of one element in a configuration, the equality of stimuli, one sound being more tense than another, and the like. Either qualitiative or relational properties of gestures may become indices. Indexical properties of congenerically interpreted gestures may, in particular, elicit emotional responses associated with their primal demand for one's involuntary attention. Furthermore, entire congeneric statements that may involve degrees of surprise—*i.e.*, negations, false conditionals, disjunctions, or conjunctions—similarly have affective force. In addition, metaphoric gestures, whether their extrageneric interpretation is predominantly at the instinctual or rational level, import into their meanings the aura of their externally signified objects and situations. This imported aura of significance also may draw from us the normal intuitive dispositions and emotional responses that are inextricably bound up with the significations' associated cluster of connotations. But the most significant fact is that we tend to respond affectively to the virtually inseparable totality of a gesture's quality and relational texture in a given context. We are affected most by the overall character or dispositional attitude of the musical work and its main parts. This is not to say that by careful analysis and discrimination we cannot isolate and consider qualities or relationships of gestures in themselves. We can. Nor is it to hold that our unselfconscious perceptual acts do not select now one then another from among the available structural or qualitative stimuli. They do. It is, rather, to say that in a given situation our affective responses are largely to what normally appears as the grouped structure and content of qualities belonging to a gesture or a whole work. It is to the holistic regional character, the gestural attitude, that we most readily respond with feeling, emotion, or mood.

But to return to the main point of our discussion: the factors giving coherence to the succession of affective responses to a musical work. Let us summarize. The affective musical experience is an interaction between interpreter and music, an interaction during which the quality and structure of the interpreter's affective responses are controlled doubly. The interpreter's feelings, emotions, and moods are guided and shaped by the attitude, the quality and texture, of the musical sequences; the same affective responses are formed also by our innate organic tendencies to give attention, voluntarily and involuntarily, and by our normal fusion of perceptual immediacies into well shaped interpretants. Those tendencies to affective response are general, and they cannot be sundered from higher, cerebral responses of thought. Consequently, the general power of the musical stimulus to control affective experience would seem to be asserted equally over instinctual and rational levels of response. There is control of affective responses into coherent experience. There is interaction of interpreter and music. In that interaction is the control that accounts for the coherence of affective states.

Notes

1   Recent and subtle questioning of the possibility of a rationale for successive extrageneric interpretants and affective states in response to music is posed by Leonard B. Meyer in *Emotion and Meaning in Music* (Chicago: University of Chicago Press, 1956), pp. 270–72 as well as chap. VIII in general. The earlier and traditional questioning of extrageneric meanings is perhaps best given by Edmund Gurney, *The Power of Sound* (London: Smith, Elder and Co., 1880), chaps. 14 and 15.

2   Sir Charles Sherrington, *The Integrative Action of The Nervous System*, 2nd ed. (New Haven: Yale University Press, 1947), pp. 308–52.

3   Edmund W. Sinnott, "The Creativeness of Life," in *Creativity And Its Cultivation*, ed. Harold H. Anderson (New York: Harper and Brothers, 1959), p. 15.

4   Clarence I. Lewis, *An Analysis of Knowledge and Valuation* (La Salle, Ill.: The Open Court Publishing Co., 1946), pp. 11–15.

5   Stephen C. Pepper, *World Hypotheses* (Berkeley: University of California Press, 1942), p. 238; A. J. Ayer, *The Problem of Knowledge* (New York: The Macmillan Co., 1956), pp. 234–37.

6   *E.g.*, see Roger Fry, *Transformations* (Garden City: Doubleday and Co., Anchor Books, 1956), pp. 4, 266–67.

7   De Witt Parker, *The Principles of Aesthetics*, 2nd rev. ed. (New York: F. S. Crofts and Co., 1947), pp. 69–70.

8   John Dewey, *Experience and Nature* (New York: Dover Publications, Inc., 1958), pp. 258, 266–67, 299.

9   Ibid.

10   Lewis, *Knowledge and Valuation*, p. 260.

11   G. J. Whitrow, *The Natural Philosophy of Time* (London: Thomas Nelson and Sons, Ltd., 1961), p. 113. For analogy relating the central nervous system and music, see George Herbert Mead, *Mind, Self, and Society*, ed. Charles W. Morris (Chicago: University of Chicago Press, 1934), p. 86.

12   George Herbert Mead, *The Philosophy of the Act*, ed. Charles W. Morris et al. (Chicago: University of Chicago Press, 1938), pp. 135, 141.

13   Ibid., p. 338.

14   Stephen C. Pepper, *The Work of Art*, p. 152ff; John Dewey, *Art As Experience*, pp. 35–36, 122–24.

15   Stephen C. Pepper, *The Work of Art* (Bloomington: Indiana University Press, 1955), p. 163.

16   John Dewey, *Art As Experience* (New York: T. P. Putnam's Sons, Capricorn Books, 1958), pp. 34–38.

17   Mead, *Philosophy of The Act*, pp. 339–40.

18   Mead, *Mind, Self, and Society*, pp. 25, 95.

Appendix
Affect: Feeling, Emotion, and Mood

Although discussions of aesthetics abound with references to affect, emotion, feeling, attitude, tendency, and such topics, few of the discussions delve into the literature of physiologists and psychologists on those topics. This appendix is aimed at providing a survey of some of the more prominent and accessible theoretical accounts of affective processes.

In the vast literature of contemporary psychology two complementary approaches to the theory of affective phenomena are readily discernible. One approach may be characterized as that of physiological psychology and the other as that of phenomenological psychology. Whereas the first approach emphasizes physiological mechanisms of activation and response, the latter places importance on the subjectivity and introspective nature of emotional experience.[1] In the field of the physiological theories there are two complementary sorts of theories, the so-called thalamic-excitatory ("head") theories and the visceral-muscular ("body") theories. Without attempting a detailed survey of any one approach or sort of theory, one can consolidate some salient features of common agreement among them.[2]

Most theorizing about affect, emotion, feeling, and mood is characterized all too easily by a certain endemic vagueness and a confusing pro-

Notes to this chapter begin on p. 231.

fusion of senses given to key terms. This makes one all the more hesitant to add to the confusion and emptiness of many of the discussions. Rather than be hopelessly vague let us seek out some core concepts and terminology that can serve our interests here. Through them some consolidation of theory seems possible.

We need to be clear about what we mean by feeling, emotion, affection, and related terms because of their particular involvement in discussions of musical experience. For the common character shared by feeling and emotion—the generic concept—we shall use *affect* or *affection* (and, as appropriate, its forms: affective, affectivity, and affective experience).[3] *Affection* is a normal physiological process of the organism.[4] According to Lawrence K. Frank,[5] the organism sustains itself by continuous, unself-conscious adjustment to its environment. Varied situations and events call out momentary functional alterations of the organism, especially those such as secretions of endocrine glands. It is the immediate, introspective awareness of the qualities in relation of the organism's condition in normal ranges of flux that is called feeling. *Feeling* is the privately known quality of constantly and regularly changing bodily adjustments to the environment.[6] The quality of feeling may be said to range over the moderate and less intense portions of affective dimensions (*e.g.*, pleasure-pain, excitement-depression, tension-relaxation, and their innumerable shadings or mixtures).[7]

However, we find in situations of extraordinary stimulation such as startle, threat, incitement to aggression, or conflicts of internal tendencies that the organism's normal physiological processes undergo enlargement, prolongation, and acceleration in a mustering of the full resources of the organism to meet such emergencies. It is this most characteristic massiveness, intensity, molar extension, and amplification of the affective processes that we call *emotion*.[8]

But emotion is not different in kind from feeling; emotion is "more," a matter of degree and relation.[9] The patterns of physiological functioning are essentially the same, but in emotion they are characterized by encompassing qualitative and quantitative extremes of such affective dimensions as pleasure-pain, excitement-depression, and tension-repose.[10] The emotional reactions are voluminous, intense, and fused with the situation to the extent that emotion colors everything experienced with it.[11] Thus, emotion takes possession of the whole organism; it cannot be confined to a part of the body, cannot be located specifically.[12] So we may say that *emotion* is a complex state, involving widespread adjustments that include mental agitation and bodily disturbance with intense, persisting feeling; emotion mobilizes the entire organism to meet stress and usually disposes the organism toward some definite action.[13]

There are numerous causes of emotional arousal, some coming from the external environment and others from within the organism.[14] External excitation, although it may be moderate, most often is in some way or ways extraordinary. It may be singly or jointly, intense, persistent, widespread, sudden, or it may be a competing set of stimuli. But the excitation is such that it decidedly startles, surprises, threatens, perplexes, pleases, or pains. The internal causes may be intraorganic conflict between, or inhibition of, various rational and instinctual functions. Instinctual tendencies may conflict or inhibit one another, as may rational tendencies. Or instinctual tendencies may conflict with rational tendencies, and one sort may inhibit or dominate the other. But whatever the origin of the excitation, the stimulus places the organism under profound stress and disrupts its normal homeostatic equilibrium.

The salient feature of *mood* is the pervasive, generalized spread of a quality of feeling. This may be taken as a persisting residue of subsided emotion or as an intrusion of a dominating and steady feeling tone.[15] In contrast to emotion, mood, although pervading awareness, is not felt to be as intense, as massive, or as concentrated as emotion.[16] Like emotion, mood has a molar, unifying affect on the entire organism; but unlike emotion, mood does not take possession of the organism and, with a surfeit of quality, drive the organism. We may think, more often than not, of *mood* as the after effect of emotional experience, as the long rhythmic pause complementing life's most emphatic moments of stress, tension, and discharge of energy.

Theories about affective processes usually are based on the common ground of the concept pair, "stimulus-response." A *stimulus* may be regarded as any object, event, or situation within the external or internal environment of an organism that causes a change in the organism's activities. In terms of the biology lab we might say that any unit of energy or change in energy that excites a receptor is a stimulus. And in corresponding definition, a *response* is any change, usually adaptive, within the activities of an organism that occurs as a result of stimulation. More specifically, a response may be regarded as change in muscular or glandular activity.

According to Tomkins, Izard, *et al.*, reporting findings of the

American Psychological Association 1964 symposium on affect, any stimulus may initiate a sequence of perceptual-cognitive (rational) and affective-conative (instinctual) responses.[17] It is most important to acknowledge that *both* instinctual and rational systems of behavior play roles in defining the results and meaning of a stimulus. The affective component, however, is primary in determining motivational behavior; learning, perception, and performance vary only as instinctual states are altered. The interpretation, the way one perceives and represents the stimulus and situation to himself, is a critical determinant of his subsequent behavior. The main variables, then, are three: (1) the stimulus, including situation, which is causal, (2) the physical, affective-conative, processes, and (3) the perceptual-cognitive processes.[18]

Physiological Mechanisms in Affect. In its more general nature the physiological activation for affective responses is well known to specialists, and, although somewhat technical, it bears outlining here. The locus of activation is the nervous system, particularly the central nervous system.[19] The nervous system works as a master integrating system for the organism; it receives, facilitates or inhibits, and organizes the input and output of neural stimuli in innervating muscles and glands. It maintains a harmoniously balanced state of the organism by continuously effecting adjustments of the internal environment in response to stimuli of the external environment. In the most general sense the nervous system converts sensory impacts into *acts*.[20] The flexible and dynamic process of the nervous system in sustaining a steady state of the organism is called *homeostasis*.[21] No act occurs, no muscle or gland functions, except when innervated. Although usually activated when stimulated, receptors in themselves may be spontaneously active.[22] But in their turn, neural impulses may fail to activate, may affect glands or muscles directly (reflex arc), or may either facilitate or inhibit other activity.[23]

The two major portions of the nervous system are the central nervous system (brain and spinal cord) and the peripheral nervous system (all else). All activities but those under chemical control are regulated by the central nervous system (c.n.s.). The brain acts as the general regulatory center in receiving and integrating impulses and in discharging to glands and muscles motor, inhibitive or facilitative impulses; it is the seat of consciousness, sensation, emotion and feeling, voluntary acts, and higher mental processes. The spinal cord acts as the conducting pathway for impulses to and from the brain. The peripheral nervous system connects the body to the spinal cord and brain. Interaction of the peripheral nerves is mainly in the central nervous system. The peripheral system includes the twelve pairs of cranial nerves, among them the eighth or auditory nerve, as well as thirty-one pairs of spinal nerves and the sympathetic portion of the autonomic nervous system. The locus of activation for affect is the central nervous system which has outflows into at least three major sub-systems. The first is the voluntary nervous system, which innervates the striated muscles as well as receives impulses from specialized sensors. The second is the autonomic nervous system, which innervates the smooth muscles and glands. The third is the endrocrine system connected with the pituitary body, through which reciprocal influences control glands of internal secretion. All three sub-systems of the c.n.s. interact so that none is independent either of each other or of the external and internal environment. Accordingly, any change in either surroundings (*e.g.*, stimuli such as music) or sub-systems of the c.n.s. has an effect on every other part—hence, the generally widespread effects of affective arousal.[24]

The autonomic nervous system (a.n.s.) is a functional, not anatomical, unit. It automatically and involuntarily activates processes of digestion, respiration, circulation, elimination, perspiration, and endocrine secretion—*i.e.*, the essential life functions. The entirely motor functions of the a.n.s. are carried on within the c.n.s. and may be inhibited or facilitated by impulses from receptors or the higher centers. The two complementary divisions of the a.n.s. are the sympathetic and the parasympathetic branches, which both activate most visceral organs but with reciprocal and opposing effects. The sympathetic branch mostly starts or increases activity, whereas the parasympathetic branch stops or retards it.[25] It is the balanced function of the two branches that largely constitutes homeostasis. Whereas the effects of the parasympathetic branch are specific and selective, the effects of the sympathetic branch are simultaneous and widespread. The sympathetic branch acts rapidly in bringing generalized changes, such as are required in situations of high stimulation or emergency. Specific effects (affective symptoms) of sympathetic innervation involve decrease in salivation and digestion, increase in respiration, heartbeat, blood pressure, flow of blood sugar, enlargement of respiration, dilation of pupils and blood vessels of muscles, erection of hair and so on.[26] By contrast the parasympathetic branch acts to delicately adjust effector organs and takes place during periods of rest, when its innervation of the viscera directs restorative replenishment of energy

expended during prior sympathetic activity. The specific effects of parasympathetic domination include increase in salivation and digestion,
decrease in perspiration, contraction of pupils and small blood vessels,
and the activation of bladder and lower colon to expel waste.[27] The
general importance of the a.n.s. is that whenever stability is threatened,
receptors warn the c.n.s., which in turn sends impulses through the sympathetic system, innervating the viscera and preparing the organism for
extreme situations such as fight or flight and other primal instinctual acts;
the parasympathetic branch reciprocates in preventing overexertion and
allows the organism to build up energy in rest periods. In states of normal
stimulation neither branch is dominant; a state of constant flux and usual
minor adjustments of adaptation to the environment continues.[28] We
can summarize the physiological data as they relate to affection in three
statements. The normal flux of the organism in relatively undisturbed
homeostatic balance corresponds to states of potential "feeling." The
profoundly moving conditions for which the sympathetic nervous system is emphatically in control correspond to "emotion." States in which
the parasympathetic nervous system is most active correspond in considerable degree to "mood." We see, then, that actions of the autonomic
nervous system are intimately associated with defining differentia of
affection, although the physiological responses and most detailed
correspondences of those responses to affective states are still too little
understood.[29]

Physiology of Hearing and Affection

Knowledge of hearing is sketchy. Some details of the anatomy of the ear
are known, but no more than hypothesis exists to explain the translation
of sound waves into neural impulses.[30] Our present interest is to establish
the relationship between hearing (and by containment, music) and affection, from the standpoint of physiology. We shall pass over matters of
anatomy to an outline of the auditory neural pathway and its bearing
upon affection.

The ear contains the organs for hearing and for equilibrium and
acceleration. Fortunately, while all the organs of the ear share certain
neural tracts, the senses of balance and acceleration are served by the
seventh cranial nerve, which apparently functions separately from the
auditory (eighth cranial) nerve.[31] In hearing, the ear gathers, transmits,

and ultimately translates sound waves into afferent impulses traveling to the brain. The sound waves pass through areas of the ear: *the external ear*, the *middle ear*, and the *inner ear*.

The external ear merely picks up sound waves and conducts them, as air vibrations, through the *auditory canal* to the middle ear. In the middle ear the waves activate the *tympanic membrane* ("ear drum"), setting up vibration in the air-filled *tympanic cavity*. Inside the cavity the three auditory ossicles, small bones which work as levers, are activated. The ossicles—the *malleus* ("hammer"), *incus* ("anvil"), and *stapes* ("stirrup")—decrease wave amplification and increase wave force as they transmit waves to the *fenestra vestibuli*, which connect to the inner ear.[32]

The true sensory receptors for hearing (and for equilibrium and acceleration) are in the inner ear. The inner ear is a complex passage way, an *osseous labyrinth* enclosing a fluid-surrounded *membranous labyrinth*. The labyrinths have three regions—*vestibule, semicircular canals*, and the *cochlea*. Within the cochlea is the *cochlean duct* (and semicircular ducts), and the cochlean duct encloses the *basilar membrane*, upon which rests the *organ of corti*.

Motion of the stapes at the fenestra vestibuli sets up vibrations which pass through the fluid (*perilymph*) outside the membranous labyrinth and the fluid (*endolymph*) within the membranous labyrinth. The vibrations are transferred at last to the basilar membrane and organ of corti, the auditory receptor. The organ of corti contains about 24,000 hair cells which wrap around and connect to the peripheral endings of auditory nerve fibers. When agitated by the movement of the basilar membrane, the cells set up—in some yet unknown way—impulses in the auditory nerve.[33] The impulses go through a set of nuclei and tracts in the brain stem to the auditory areas of the cerebral cortex, where they are interpreted as sounds.

The auditory nerve makes uninterrupted connections of the ear to the brain.[34] And although the nerve is very short (about 5 millimeters), its arrangement of fibers is extraordinarily orderly: the nerve enters the lower brain stem (medulla oblongata) at the edge of the pons varolii; the fibers divide, one branch of each afferent fiber going to the dorsal (back) and another to the ventral (front) portion of the cochlear nucleus (which is in the *tectum* of the midbrain); the fibers make first synaptic connections there, preserving the original identity and order of arrangement they had in the cells of the basilar membrane.[35] The basilar membrane is selectively and specifically responsive to different frequencies.

Hence, the basilar membrane's frequency selectivity is viewed as mapped into—"unrolled" in—the nuclei of the brain.[36]

The essential pathway of the auditory nerve proceeds from the organ of corti (on the basilar membrane) to the nuclei in the lower brain stem, the cerebellum, the inferior colliculus, the medial geniculate body, and the auditory area (temporal lobe) of the cerebral cortex.[37]

According to Steen and Montagu, the acoustic nerve emerges in the lower brain stem from the groove separating the pons varolii from the medulla oblongata.[38] Sensory nuclei for the cochlear branch of the acoustic nerve are in the tegmental portion of the pons. The auditory pathway passes upward from nuclei in the tegmental portion of the pons through the cerebellum to the inferior colliculus, which is located within the tectum of the midbrain (mesencephalon). Here occur the first synaptic connections; the colliculus acts as a mediating reflex center. From the inferior colliculus the pathway continues, still in the midbrain, on up to the medial geniculate body, a portion of the thalamus. The thalamus relays impulses on to the temporal lobe of the cerebral cortex. In fact, the thalamus and cerebral cortex form a functional unit by means of an interplay between themselves and within each.[39] The projections of one area into the other affect each other and form, by their interactions, reverberating circuits, one of which is betwen the medial geniculate body and the cortex.[40] Indeed, the auditory cortex is regarded as a phylogenetic outgrowth of the medial geniculate body of the thalamus.[41] With the exception of the medial geniculate body, fibers of the auditory nerve from each ear synapse (interconnect) with each other at each level from the lower brain stem upward; hence, each ear projects impulses equally into each hemisphere of the cerebral cortex. Of course, the autonomic nervous system is activated from the frontal areas of the brain, effecting the more obvious symptoms of affective ("emotional") behavior.

Besides the main projection pathway into the cortex via thalamic relay, there is another, diffuse projection pathway. Exteroceptors and proprioceptors (e.g., fibers of the acoustic nerve) passing through the lower brain stem give off collateral fibers into the reticular formation, which extends from the lower brain stem through the tegmentum into the hypothalamus and thalamus.[42] The reticular formation fills interstices among the longer tracts and their nuclei; its nerve cells are scattered through the tracts of interwoven fibers.[43] The reticular formation also completes a path between cortex and motor neurons, and it has widespread inhibitory as well as certain facilitative functions.[44]

In the diffuse projection pathway the effects of sound achieve genuine affective ("gestural") force because of the stimulation of the hypothalamus.[45] Diffuse projection initiates autonomic reflex effects in the hypothalamus, and at the same time direct thalamic-cortical efferent projection facilitates or impedes hypothalamic initiation of effects. Generally, the stimulation of various areas of the hypothalamus evokes sympathetic and parasympathetic activity involved in affective states. The hypothalamus integrates sympathetic and parasympathetic activities into patterns; indeed, it appears to be the lowest center of integration for the autonomic nervous system.[46] The hypothalamus, by reason of its sympathetic-parasympathetic effects, is believed to be involved not only with emotion but with mood.[47]

The hypothalamus also is extensively interconnected with the thalamus and cerebral cortex, and it acts largely as the efferent relay *down* from the cortex and thalamus.[48] However, some afferent discharge from the hypothalamus is believed to project *up* through the thalamus into the cortex—*i.e.*, into the thalamic-cortical reverberating circuits.[49] Hence, under auditory stimulation the diffuse projection pathway activates extraordinarily complex and important functions that doubly bear upon affective processes: auditory stimuli unmistakably are inherently affective in force, and they definitely activate emotional patterns.[50]

A further effect of importance for affection and the physiology of hearing is that acoustic stimuli, even in simply attracting attention and especially in conditions of startle, suppress the brain's alpha rhythm.[51] The suppression of the alpha rhythm is closely related to emotional arousal (and waking) and hence, contributes to establishing the specifically affective force of sound. Indeed, the very alteration of brain waves by sound stimuli is in itself evidence of the affective arousal and general alerting action. The suppression of alpha waves apparently is related to stimulation of the hypothalamus; at least it is related to thalamic area stimulation. Some of the more specific rhythmic processes (breathing, pulse, sleep cycle, fluid levels, menstruation, and temperature) are definitely controlled by the hypothalamus.[52] As briefly suggested above, it is important that the suppression of alpha waves depends more either upon attention and set under conditions of anticipation-expectation or upon suddenness, surprise, and unexpectedness rather than upon sensory stimulation itself. Inasmuch as suppression of alpha rhythm is apparently a necessary concomitant of affection, the dependency is most significant for any theory of affection. The implications for the psychology of affection seem to be that (1) an attentive preparatory set of belief in one's situation, either as primal unself-conscious anticipation or as self-conscious expectation, may be a sufficient threshold for affective arousal; and (2) sudden or unexpected stimuli evoking conditions of startle, such as surprise, astonishment, or alarm, may be sufficient for affective arousal.

We now may summarize and generalize the material investigated into an adopted theoretical position, one which is adequate to account for affective processes and which especially treats the nature of emotion. It is a position supported by comparatively recent experimental findings about the interaction of the cortical and subcortical nervous structures.

According to Lindsley, affective states are marked by a generalized activation pattern, involving both the peripheral and central nervous systems and their sub-functional unit, the autonomic nervous system. Collaterals from the direct projection pathway give off afferent impulses into the nuclei of the reticular formation in the area of the lower brain stem; the impulses travel through the tegmentum into the hypothalamus, causing affective excitement and activating autonomic and motor discharge; from there some impulses feed on up into the thalamus and are relayed to the cortex; from the reverberating circuits of the thalamus and cortex efferent impulses are directed back through the hypothalamus, again activating autonomic structures, and down the lower brain stem and spinal cord, to innervate the viscera.[53]

We note that the general activation pattern for affection does not necessarily depend upon the involvement of the direct spinothalamic afferent pathway.[54] Rather, the generalized pattern is caused by impulses shunted from the direct pathway into the diffuse projection pathway. Moreover, we should add, visceral and somatic afferents also send up impulses over the reticular formation. Thus, afferent impulses reach the cortex via both direct and diffuse projection pathways, and they activate the waking center in the hypothalamus in the process. This means that a condition of alertness and self-conscious concern is involved in affection, particularly in more strongly stimulating situations. In the general activation pattern both reflex and mediated reactions are initiated; they include autonomic innervation and stimulation of the corticothalamic reverberating circuits. Autonomic activations by stimulation of the hypothalamus may complete reflex patterns and not reach awareness in the cerebral cortex. However, some afferent impulses surely do affect the thalamus and, through its reverberating relays, the cortex.

The higher order of reflex adjustment, which is most important for our consideration, is the *startle pattern*. The startle pattern involves both somatic and visceral reactions and is the mechanism accounting for activation of affective processes. Intense, sudden, extensive, or unexpected auditory stimuli produce generalized (emotional) bodily responses such as anxiety, surprise, astonishment, or alarm, and at the same time the stimuli produce cortical activity, too.[55]

Not only the more powerful but also the moderate auditory stimuli of low intensity or frequency and normal expectancy affect the cortex generally via the diffuse projection paths.[56] And simultaneously, too, afferent impulses along the auditory nerve affect the highest brain centers by direct projection through the lower brain stem, cerebellum, inferior colliculus, and medial geniculate body in the thalamus. The importance of direct projection into the cortex is that it allows recognition of the nature of the stimulus. But before discrimination occurs, diffuse projection blocks (suppresses or abolishes) the corticothalamic alpha rhythm. As we have seen just above, this suppression is evidence of affective arousal and general alerting of the organism. Further affective reactions involve complex combinations of intracortical, intrathalamic, thalamocortical, and corticohypothalamic connections. In the milder affective states of feeling the degree of activation is less; the thalamocortical rhythms are not destroyed, and the synchronizations of the waves are not interrupted. Only moderate autonomic adjustment occurs, with perhaps only some sympathetic dominance.[57]

Phenomenology of Affect

Above we recounted the psychophysiological theory of emotion set forth by Donald B. Lindsley, and we attempted in citations to corroborate its components. The mechanism of affective arousal that Lindsley described, especially for emotion, is the *startle pattern*. Moreover, we found that mere awareness of sound stimuli is sufficient to evoke feeling and emotion. Because the arousal mechanism is an important key to accounting for the affective meaning of art works, we shall extend our original physiological explanation by presentation and adoption of further phenomenological corroboration.

In the 1880s the French psychologist Frédéric Paulhan published a general theory of affection.[58] However, it seems that although the James-

Lange and, later, Cannon-Bard theories were well known and accepted by 1925, the Paulhan theory apparently never became well known in professional circles outside France until after the English publication in 1930.[59]

Paulhan's hypothesis is that the "arrest of tendencies" causes affection: an affective state occurs whenever a more or less complicated reflex action is blocked.[60] The tendencies of the organism's systems to organize stimuli and neural reactions into the completion of an act may be obstructed variously. The obstruction may be the simultaneous existence or the out of phase emergence of competing tendencies within the organism, even such as those processes organized ultimately by the higher levels of homeostasis. Or from another point of view the source of impediment might be other sets of internal or external stimuli than present ones, and the sets of stimuli compete and conflict to control the responses of the organism.[61] The important fact is that the normal process of the organism to organize stimuli and impulses and to release them in an expressive act, a gesture of sound or movement, is interrupted or delayed by the interference of other stimuli or by the conflict of sets of stimuli, or by the conflict of different organizing systems within the organism.[62] This pattern of the arrest of tendencies is a sufficient cause for all kinds of affective states, especially emotion.

Several qualifications are important also. For one, an affective state may last as long as the arrest of tendencies does.[63] While sets of stimuli compete for dominance or interfere with each other and the complete organization of impulses by the various systems, the affect may continue. Another qualification, more important for music, is that stimulus qualities (such as relative intensity, duration, or suddenness of appearance) as well as organizing characteristics (such as relative completion and drive of impulses to discharge) strongly bear upon the success of tendency arrest. The relation of stimulus character and response patterns seems to be proportional.[64] Greater intensity, persistence, or abruptness of stimulation cause greater arrest and, in turn, more extreme affective states.[65] Moreover, the greater or lesser degree of organic systematization and force toward completing an act, when arrested, correspondingly results in more or less massive emotional states.[66] In the case of emotion the violence or felt intensity is proportional to the suddenness and force of the arrest and the strength and organization of the arrested tendencies.

To note simpler facts, we find that both internal and external stimuli produce affective states. Among internal stimuli, the most significant for aesthetics are mental. Paulhan emphasizes that cerebration involves feeling or self-awareness of the act, but also, he says, the causal stimulus to an act or an act itself may be entirely cerebral.[67] He finds this especially the case for what is known as "aesthetic emotion."[68]

The relationship between affection and thought is fundamental in Paulhan's theory. Paulhan regards both as manifestations of the same essential condition, the arrest of tendencies. Arrest is not peculiar to affects; an idea, which is simply intellectual, is also the result of the arrest of a tendency.[69] Consequently, any mental event appears as a tendency, and of course what is called consciousness is seen as stemming from the arrest of tendencies.[70]

But the relationship of thought and affection is more extensive; they both arise as complementary processes from the same matrix of inhibition of organic tendencies, and their distinction is more a matter of degree than kind. From the initiation of tendency, thought is comparatively the more systematized, involves effects of less intensity, and its character is marked by problem solving, by distinctly expectational and distant ends-pursuing traits. Affection is, especially in first stages or on lower levels of homeostatic process, less completely systematized, is more intense, massive, and molar, and its character is more immediately referential and anticipatory.[71] Although we cannot fully pursue the important distinctions and interrelations involved, we can note the substantial fact of Paulhan's thought: both thought and affection arise from the arrest of organic tendencies.

For brief corroboration of Lindsley and Paulhan, we turn to Stephen C. Pepper, who holds that emotion is caused when a pattern of action is obstructed, when it is blocked from a natural completion.[72] In the behavior of others and ourselves and in introspection we can actually observe the conflicts of tendencies, feelings, and ideas as they give rise to affective states. And so, Pepper notes, the blocked patterns *exhibit* the very internal conflict of tendencies.[73] In addition, Pepper points out that certain sorts of stimuli are especially evocative of affective states, since they enter into affection; these include sudden stimuli, widely contrasted ones (intense to weak), and those unexpected. We note, then, that Pepper reaffirms in general the theories of Paulhan and Lindsley as to the causes of affect. Hence, we can assume (1) that any arrest of organic tendency is sufficient to produce affective states; and (2) consequently, because they act as stimuli, the structure and the quality of experience have inherent affective force.

Other recent writings on the phenomenology of affection corroborate the foregoing observations on arousal mechanisms while also laying emphasis on the importance of stress and anxiety, the roles of belief-doubt and desire-interest regarding one's situation, and the positive as well as negative differentia of affect.[74] And by way of a synthesis of views we may advance a hypothesis on the phenomenology of the mechanism of affective arousal.

We may say that inhibition or facilitation of a disposition or an act is sufficient to cause affect. A causal inhibition may occur as resistance to, suppression of, or conflict of intraorganic tendencies, whereas facilitation may appear as acceptance of, or selective attention toward, stimuli. In addition to inhibitive or facilitative causes, affect is causally related (1) to internal or external stimuli, including one's situation, and (2) to the prior dispositional set, comprising especially beliefs or doubts, needs and desires.

Affective stimuli may be grouped into three classes according to their range of intensity or extensity, and these classes may be correlated to kinds of affective response.[75] The classes of stimulus activators are (1) increasing stimulation, (2) sustaining stimulation, and (3) decreasing stimulation. If stimulation range increases suddenly, then the result will be interest, startle, or fear. If the range of stimulation sustains at a high level, distress or anger will result. If stimulation quickly decreases, the result will be relief or joy. Whatever its level or range some stimulus acts as the target or object of response, governing the form of response in relation to prior disposition.

In relation to the organism's prevailing disposition, the causal stimuli may be interpreted variously. The stimuli activating inhibition or facilitation may offer confirmation or surprise, threat or reward in relation to dispositions of belief and doubt. In relation to dispositions of desire and need, activating stimuli may offer deprivation or gratification. In any event, according to the extent to which the dispositional beliefs, doubts, or desires are fulfilled, adequately replaced, or not, the value of the resulting affect will emerge as either positive or negative. Moreover, the values of the affect tend to be tied to the level or range of the stimulation. Both positive and negative affects are evoked by stimulation increase. Unprolonged peak stimulation similarly may be either positive or negative in affective value. But only negative affect tends to be elicited by unrelieved high or minimal threshold levels of stimulation. And only positive affects are called out for the most part by decrease of stimulation. (The musical implications of these tendencies are obvious enough not to need spelling out.) Some of the most basic affects and their dimensions within positive or negative value include: pleasure (comfort-joy), satisfaction (relief-delight), sexual arousal (pleasure-ecstacy), and cognitive arousal (interest-excitement) among positive affects, and anxiety (uneasiness-anguish), pain (discomfort-agony), anger (annoyance-rage), fear (apprehension-terror), shame (embarrassment-humiliation), and disappointment (bafflement-grief) among negative affects.[76]

Because it accompanies most other emotional states, the most significant emotion is said to be anxiety.[77] *Anxiety* may be regarded as an affective state of mixed uneasiness, desire, and concern that is intolerable enough to evoke defensive maneuvers to restore equanimity and avoid overexcitation. A concomitant of organic homeostatic flux, anxiety alerts the organism to potentials of impending threat or reward, deprivation or gratification. It is a symptom of disturbance and breaking down of integration of neural impulses. Moreover, anxiety appears to be related to primal memory, falls on the unpleasant side of affect, and involves awareness of the stimulus. However, at an optimum it heightens efficiency, although in excess it is destructive to emotional balance and overdrives or depresses the organism. Anxiety may be elicited by signals of stress in the internal somatic processes, by psychological stimuli—*e.g.*, by desire or doubt regarding musical tendencies—or by conflicts and resistance in making social adjustments (as in interacting with musical gestures).

Cognitive (*i.e.*, self-conscious–discursive) states also involve affectivity and lead to affective arousal, as we have seen. Among the dispositional sets entering prominently into aesthetic experience, the cognitive states such as belief, doubt, and wishes are quite important, with expectancy probably being the most significant influence on arousal.[78] In discursive inferential acts, such as comprehending the meaning of a musical conditional, experiencing gestural tendencies may elicit belief and a state of expectancy about logical connection of gestures, continuation and completion of the molecular act of statement. When the stimulus of gestural tendencies in the earlier phases of the act are strong enough to educe expectancy and discursive forecast about impending completions of that musical act, then the interpreter is disposed cognitively so that actual forthcoming events will tend to require his affective response. In relation to the situation of an interpreter in a state of expectancy about gestural tendencies, further musical stimuli that either inhibit or facilitate the interpreter's mental disposition are sufficient to cause affective response. The affective response will arise conjointly with cognitive surprise or confirmation as the stimulus of musical tendencies completes the act by, respectively, thwarting or fulfilling the interpreter's discursive forecast. Confirmation of cognitive disposition tends to result in positive affect directed toward both the putative stimulus and one's self, thus promoting preferential behavior toward the stimulus (musical act) and satisfaction.[79] Conversely, refutation of one's predictive belief tends to issue in negative affect and resistance or suppression, directed also against the stimulus as aversion and felt by one's self as disappointment. Both the character of affect as positive or negative and the intensity and extent of the dimension of affect are matters of degree determined by the interpreter's conception of the nature of the stimulus properties. In the case of complete confirmation of expectation, when conceived stimulus properties are not at all different in detail or in kind from predictive belief, the negative effect of ennui may result. This is especially so with redundant events and with stimulus patterns disposed to consummate perceived source tendencies with great uniformity. Abundance of readily forecast musical events, gestures, and operations tends to bore. Small or gradually emergent discrepancies between belief and stimulus source should produce positive affect, while great or sudden discrepancies tend to produce negative affect. Of course, the quality of the affect (whether positive or negative) within its own dimension diverges in degree from feeling into emotion as the stimulation is interpreted as diverging from lesser and more gradual fluctuations into greater and more abrupt contrasts.

Aesthetic Emotion

The term "aesthetic emotion" may be given several meanings. It may mean affective qualities expressed or revealed within the art work itself.[80] Or it may mean any feeling or emotion of an interpreter while he experiences an art work, especially if his attitude toward the work is contemplative.[81] Moreover, aesthetic emotion may mean either thing or both. The main body of this book treats the first possibility of defining aesthetic emotion in terms of attitudes conveyed by gestures and signified as extrageneric objects. The stimulus-oriented sense of the term is acknowledged but will not be developed further here. And in the chapter on aesthetic relevance the second and third senses of the term are considered, although obliquely to one not used to reading in aesthetics. Here we can focus on what appears to be the most commonly received view and relate it to the foregoing view of affection.

We react to the properties of musical gesture, especially to the attitudes they express. Our interpretive responses may be wholly instinctual and affective; they may be largely discursive and rational; they most likely may be a flux between those two modes of response or a blend of affective-rational response. But our responses need not be overt. Far from it. When music seems to make aggressive, threatening motions, we naturally tend to be aroused and to react emotionally with our bodies instinctually mobilizing for fight or flight. If the music appears to strike out at us or state gestures in an angry tone, we are alerted and poised, but we do not strike back or run, even though we may find ourselves grimacing, clenching fists, shuffling our feet, or the like. Rather, in musical experience we are aware that the aesthetic object, however organic we take it, is an art work designed to affect us. It seems that our first instinctual impulses to overt behavior are consciously or semiconsciously inhibited and suppressed. As an urge to outright, active reaction wells up, we exert self-control. We hold in abeyance our instinctual drives. We stop short of running away or hitting back. It would be silly. (However, if the tone of gestures is continually annoying, we may walk out on the performance.) In applying voluntary control and delaying our initial biological impulses we obviously inhibit a disposition and create a subjective conflict of intraorganic tendencies; we set off the mechanism of affective arousal. The agency of inhibition is discursive; the conflict is between intuition and thought. The affective response aroused in this suspension of an act from instinctual completion is what may be called "aesthetic emotion."

Through the intentional inhibition and delay of immediate response to a musical gesture, we have precious moments to imagine alternate responses. The inhibition of instinct by thought permits both further conceptualization and intuition of still newer interpretants. And, fortunately, the rapidity of the nervous system's activity, its temporal dimension and capacity for delaying response patterns, allow us to test ways of answering to the challenge of gestures. In the moment of delay we can savor the diverse feelings and ideas engendered. We can anticipate the appropriateness of alternative responses as well as the possible further action of the musical organism. In short, our deliberate inhibition of the immediately felt tendency affords us a critical contemplative moment in which the rational and affective dispositions blend together in the aesthetic present. This moment has the value of creating a psychical distance, making it possible for us to reflect and feel while we maintain ourselves somewhat apart from total immersion in affectivity.[82]

Notes

1 Carroll E. Izard *et al.*, "Affect, Awareness, and Performance," in *Affect, Cognition, and Personality*, ed. Silvan S. Tomkins and Carroll E. Izard (London: Tavistock Publications Ltd., 1965), p. 2.

2 For an excellent compendium outlining the main sorts of theory of affection along with bibliography see James Hillman, *Emotion*. London: Routledge and Kegan Paul, 1960.

3 Dagobert Runes, ed., *The Dictionary of Philosophy* (New York: Philosophical Library, Inc., 1942), pp. 6–7 suggests this usage, as does Tomkins and Izard, *Affect, Cognition, and Personality*.

4 See William James, *The Principles of Psychology* (New York: Henry Holt and Co., 1890), Vol. II, pp. 442 and 449–54; cf. Donald B. Lindsley, "Emotion," in *Handbook of Experimental Psychology*, ed. S. S. Stevens (N.Y.: John Wiley and Sons, 1951), pp. 473–81, 501–9.

5 Lawrence K. Frank, *Feelings and Emotion* (Garden City, N.Y.: Doubleday and Company, Inc., 1954), pp. 2–5, 18–19, 27.

6 See Felix Krueger, "The Essence of Feeling," in *Feelings and Emotion*, the Wittenberg Symposium, ed. Martin L. Reymert (Worcester, Mass.: Clark University Press, 1928), p. 58. Cf. also Charles Stevenson, *Ethics and Language* (New Haven: Yale University Press, 1944), pp. 54–79.

7 Krueger, "Essence of Feeling," p. 69.

8 Frank, *Feelings and Emotion*, pp. 4–5. See Stephen C. Pepper, *Aesthetic Quality* (New York: Charles Scribner's Sons, 1937), reprinted in *The Problems of Aesthetics*, ed. Eliseo Vivas and Murray Krieger (New York: Rinehart and Co., Inc., 1953), p. 377; also Sir Charles Sherrington, *The Integrative Action of The Nervous System*, 2nd ed. (New Haven: Yale University Press, 1947), p. xviii.

9 Ibid. See Hillman, *Emotion*, pp. 81–86.

10 George M. Stratton, "Excitement As An Undifferentiated Emotion," in Reymert, *Feelings and Emotions*, p. 235; Hillman, *Emotion*, pp. 66, 72, 81, 85–86.

11 Felix Krueger, "Essence of Feeling," p. 73; Pepper, *Aesthetic Quality*, p. 377.

12 Hillman, *Emotion*, p. 105. See Sherrington, *Nervous System*, pp. 256–68 for a clear expression of the "mind-body" relationships involved.

13 Cf. James Drever, *A Dictionary Of Psychology* (Baltimore: Penguin Books, 1952), pp. 80–81; Hillman, *Emotion*, pp. 8–9, 243–89.

14 Lindsley, "Emotion," pp. 496–98, 504–9; Hillman, *Emotion*, pp. 102, 110–12, 202–3; Roy R. Grinker, "The Physiology Of Emotions," in *The Physiology Of Emotion*, ed. Alexander Simon, Charles C. Herbert, and Ruth Straus (Springfield, Illinois: Charles C. Thomas, 1961), pp. 16–19; H. W. Magoun, "The Neurophysiological Correlates Of Emotion," *The Physiology of Emotion*, ed. by Simon, Herbert and Straus, pp. 32–35; Hudson Hoagland, "Some Endocrine Stress Responses In Man," *The Physiology of Emotion*, ed. by Simon, Herbert and Straus, p. 40.

15 Philip L. Harriman, *An Outline Of Modern Psychology* (Ames, Iowa: Littlefield, Adams, and Co., 1956), p. 116.

16 Pepper, *Aesthetic Quality*, p. 377.

17 Izard *et al.*, "Affect, Awareness, and Performance," p. 22.

18 Anthony Kenny, *Action, Emotion, and Will* (London: Routledge and Kegan Paul, 1963), p. 51.
19 Grinker, "Physiology of Emotions," pp. 7–9.
20 Edward W. Dempsey, "Homeostasis," in *Handbook of Experimental Psychology*, ed. S. S. Stevens (New York: John Wiley and Sons, Inc., 1951), pp. 209, 223. See Susanne K. Langer, *Philosophical Sketches* (Baltimore: Johns Hopkins Press, 1962), pp. 12–13, 20–22.
21 M. Abercrombie, C. J. Hickman, and M. L. Johnson, *A Dictionary of Biology* (Baltimore: Penguin Books, 1951), p. 113.
22 Ragnar Granit, *Receptors and Sensory Perception* (New Haven: Yale University Press, 1955), chap. 3.
23 M. Abercrombie *et al.*, *Dictionary of Biology*, p. 159.
24 Grinker, "Physiology of Emotions," pp. 7–9; Edwin B. Steen and Ashley Montagu, *Anatomy and Physiology* vol. 2 (New York: Barnes and Noble, Inc., 1959), pp. 63, 80, 83, 102, 108, 113, 114.
25 Dempsey, "Homeostasis," pp. 215–17, 223–25.
26 Daniel H. Funkenstein,"The Physiology of Fear and Anger," in *Emotion: Bodily Change*, ed. Douglas K. Candland (Princeton: D. Van Nostrand Co., Inc., 1962), pp. 208–10.
27 Funkenstein, "The Physiology of Fear and Anger," pp. 208–10; Steen and Montagu, *Anatomy and Physiology*, p. 123.
28 Dempsey, "Homeostasis," p. 210.
29 Izard *et al.*, "Affect, Awareness, and Performance," p. 13.
30 Georg von Békésy and Walter A. Rosenblith, "The Mechanical Properties of the Ear," in Stevens, *Experimental Psychology*, p. 1075; Hallowell Davis, "Peripheral Coding of Auditory Information," in *Sensory Communication*, ed. Walter A. Rosenblith (Cambridge: M.I.T. Press, 1961), p. 255.
31 Hallowell Davis, "Psychophysiology of Hearing and Deafness," in Stevens, *Experimental Psychology*, p. 1117.
32 Steen and Montagu, *Anatomy and Physiology*, pp. 171–77. See also John R. Pierce and Edward E. Davis, Jr., *Man's World of Sound* (Garden City, N.Y.: Doubleday and Co., Inc., 1958) for a full account, as well as Békésy and Roseblith, "Mechanical Properties of Ear," and also Hallowell Davis, "Psychophysiology of Hearing and Deafness," in Stevens, *Experimental Psychology*.
33 Davis, "Psychophysiology of Hearing and Deafness, in Stevens, *Experimental Psychology*, p. 1116.
34 Ibid., p. 1118.
35 Ibid., p. 1119. See also Békésy and Rosenblith,"Mechanical Properties of Ear," p. 1097; Pierce and Davis, *Man's World of Sound*, p. 157.
36 Pierce and Davis, *Man's World of Sound*, p. 157.
37 Davis, "Psychophysiology of Hearing and Deafness," p. 1119.
38 Steen and Montagu, *Anatomy and Physiology*, pp. 86–89.
39 T. C. Ruch, "Sensory Mechanisms," in Stevens, *ExperimentalPsychology*, pp. 126, 144.
40 Ibid., pp. 145 and 147. See Clinton N. Woolsey, "Organization of Cortical Auditory System," in *Sensory Communication*, ed. Walter A. Rosenblith (Cambridge: M.I.T. Press, 1961), pp. 235–58.
41 Davis, "Psychophysiology of Hearing and Deafness," p. 1120–21.
42 Lindsley, "Emotion," p. 487.
43 T. C. Ruch, "Motor Systems," in Stevens, *Experimental Psychology*, p. 186.
44 Ibid., pp. 186–88. See Raúl Hernandez-Peón, "Reticular Mechanisms of Sensory Control," *Sensory Communication*, ed. Walter A. Rosenblith (Cambridge: M.I.T. Press, 1961), pp. 497–520.
45 Lindsley, "Emotion," pp. 506–8; Grinker, "Physiology of Emotions," p. 21.
46 Dempsey, "Homeostasis," pp. 227–29.
47 Lindsley, "Emotion," pp. 495–96.
48 Dempsey, "Homeostasis," pp. 227–29.
49 Lindsley, "Emotion," pp. 495–500.

50   Ibid., pp. 506–8.
51   Davis, "Psychophysiology of Hearing and Deafness," pp. 1132–33.
52   Lindsley, "Emotion," pp. 495–98.
53   Ibid., especially pp. 504–9.
54   Ibid., p. 506–8; Magda B. Arnold, "An Excitatory Theory of Emotion," *Feelings and Emotions*, The Moosehart Symposium, ed. Martin L. Reymert (New York: McGraw-Hill Book Co., Inc., 1950), pp. 18–19.
55   Lindsley, "Emotion," pp. 506–8.
56   Ibid., p. 508; William D. Neff, "Neural Mechanisms of Auditory Discrimination," in Rosenblith, *Sensory Communication*, pp. 259–78.
57   Lindsley, "Emotion," p. 509.
58   Frédéric Paulhan, *The Laws of Feeling*, trans. C. K. Ogden (New York: Harcourt, Brace and Co., 1930).
59   Ibid., pp. vii–xiv.
60   Ibid., pp. 16–17.
61   Ibid., p. 32.
62   Ibid., pp. 21–22, 30–31, 35–36, 56.
63   Ibid., p. 19.
64   Ibid., pp. 35–36 and 76. Cf. Granit, *Receptors and Sensory Perception*, pp. 10–12.
65   Paulhan, *Laws of Feeling*, pp. 35–36.
66   Ibid., p. 76.
67   Ibid., pp. 23–24, 32, 42.
68   Ibid., pp. 23–24.
69   Ibid., p. 43, 141, 149.
70   Ibid., p. 44.
71   Ibid., pp. 41–44, 56–57, 78, 141–49, 179.
72   Pepper, *Aesthetic Quality*, p. 377.
73   Ibid., p. 378.
74   See Reymert, *Feelings and Emotions*; Hillman, *Emotion*; Izard, "Affect, Awareness, and Performance"; and Simon, Herbert, and Straus, *Physiology of Emotions*.
75   Tomkins and Izard, *Affect, Cognition, and Personality*, p. 16.
76   Tomkins and Izard, *Affect, Cognition and Personality*, p. 15; M. A. Wenger, F. N. Jones, M. H. Jones, *Physiological Psychology* (New York: Henry Holt and Co., 1956), pp. 344–47.
77   Grinker, "Physiology of Emotions," pp. 3, 15–20; Sigmund Freud, *The Problem of Anxiety*, trans. Henry Alden Bunker (New York: The Psychoanalytic Quarterly Press and W. W. Norton and Co., Inc., 1936), pp. 20, 69–70.
78   O. J. Harvey, "Cognitive Aspects of Affective Arousal," in Tomkins and Izard, *Affect, Cognition, and Personality*, pp. 251–53.
79   Ibid.
80   R. G. Collingwood, *The Principles of Art* (New York: Oxford University Press, 1938), pp. 115–19, 279, 292–94.
81   Curt John Ducasse, *The Philosophy of Art* (New York: The Dial Press, 1929), pp. 189–201; C. I. Lewis, *An Analysis of Knowledge and Valuation* (La Salle, Ill.: The Open Court Publishing Co., 1946), chaps. XIV–XV.
82   Edward Bullough, "Psychical Distance," in *Aesthetics*, ed. Elizabeth M. Wilkinson (London: Bowes and Bowes, 1957), pp. 93–97; George H. Mead, *The Philosophy of the Act*, ed. Charles W. Morris *et al.* (Chicago: University of Chicago Press, 1938), pp. 174–75, 190, 343–49, and 454–59.

Bibliography

Abell, Walter. *Representation And Form.* New York: Charles Scribner's Sons, 1936.

Abercrombie, M., Hickman, C. J., and Johnson, M. L. *A Dictionary of Biology.* Baltimore: Penguin Books, 1951.

Aiken, Henry D. "The Aesthetic Relevance of Belief." *Journal of Aesthetics and Art Criticism* 9 (1951): 301–15.

———. "Art as Expression and Surface." *Journal of Aesthetics and Art Criticism* 4 (1945): 87–95.

———. "Some Notes Concerning the Aesthetic and the Cognitive." *Journal of Aesthetics and Art Criticism* 13 (1955): 378–94.

Albersheim, Gerhard. "Mind and Matter in Music." *Journal of Aesthetics and Art Criticism* 22 (1964): 289–94.

———. "The Sense of Space in Tonal and Atonal Music." *Journal of Aesthetics and Art Criticism* 19 (1960): 17–30.

Aldrich, Virgil C. *Philosophy of Art.* Englewood Cliffs, N.J.: Prentice-Hall, Inc., 1963.

———. "Pictorial Meaning, Picture Thinking, and Wittgenstein's Theory of Aspects." *Mind* 67 (1958): 70–79.

Allport, Gordon W. "Attitudes." In *Readings in Attitude Theory and Measurement,* edited by Martin Fishbein. New York: John Wiley and Sons, Inc., 1967.

Ames, Van Meter. "What is Form?" *Journal of Aesthetics and Art Criticism* 15 (1956): 85–93.

———. "What is Music?" *Journal of Aesthetics and Art Criticism* 26 (1967): 241–49.

Amyx, C. "The Iconic Sign in Aesthetics." *Journal of Aesthetics and Art Criticism* 6 (1947): 54–60.

Anderson, Harold H., ed. *Creativity and Its Cultivation.* New York: Harper and Row, 1959.

Apel, Willi, ed. *Dictionary of Music.* Cambridge: Harvard University Press, 1944.

Aristotle. *Aristotle On the Art of Poetry With a Supplement Aristotle On Music.* Translated by S. H. Butcher. Edited by Milton C. Nahm. New York: The Liberal Arts Press, 1948.

Aristoxenus. *The Harmonics of Aristoxenus.* Translated and edited by Henry S. Macran. Oxford: The Clarendon Press, 1902.

Arnheim, Rudolf. *Art and Visual Perception.* Berkeley: University of California Press, 1957.

———. "The Gestalt Theory of Expression." *Psychological Review* 56 (1949): 156–71.

Arnold, Magda B. "An Excitatory Theory of Emotion." In *Feelings and Emotions,* The Moosehart Symposium, edited by Martin

L. Reymert. New York: McGraw-Hill Book Co., Inc., 1950.

Arnstine, Donald. "Shaping The Emotions: The Sources Of Standards For Aesthetic Education." *Journal of Aesthetic Education* 1 (1966): 45–70.

Aschenbrenner, Karl. "Aesthetics and Logic: An Analogy." *Journal of Aesthetics and Art Criticism* 23 (1964): 63–79.

Aschenbrenner, Karl and Isenberg, Arnold. *Aesthetic Theories*. Englewood Cliffs, N.J.: Prentice-Hall, Inc., 1965.

Asenjo, F. G. "The Aesthetics of Igor Stravinsky," *Journal of Aesthetics and Art Criticism* 26 (1968): 297–305.

———. "Polarity and Atonalism." *Journal of Aesthetics and Art Criticism*. 25 (1966): 47–52.

Austin, J. L. *How To Do Things With Words*. London: Oxford University Press, 1962.

———. "Other Minds." In *Logic And Language*, 2nd series, edited by A. G. N. Flew. New York: Philosophical Library, 1953.

Austin, William W. "Espressivo." *Journal of Aesthetics and Art Criticism* 12 (1954): 509–17.

———. "Santayana as a Critic of Music." *Musical Quarterly* 40 (1954): 497–508.

Ayer, Alfred J. *The Concept Of A Person*. London: Macmillan and Co., Ltd., 1963.

———. "Names and Descriptions." *Thinking and Meaning in Logique et Analyse* (1962): 199–211.

———. *The Problem of Knowledge*. New York: The Macmillan Co., 1956.

Babbitt, Milton. "Twelve-Tone Rhythmic Structure and the Electronic Medium." *Perspectives of New Music* 1 (1962): 49–79.

Bach, Carl Philipp Emmanuel. *Essay on the True Art of Playing Keyboard Instruments*. Translated and edited by William J. Mitchell. New York: W. W. Norton and Co., Inc., 1949.

Baensch, Otto. "Art and Feeling." *Logos* 12 (1923–1924): 1–28. Reprinted in Langer, Susanne K., *Reflections on Art*, q.v.

Ballard, Edward G. "In Defense of Symbolic Aesthetics." *Journal of Aesthetics and Art Criticism* 12 (1953): 38–43.

Barford, Philip. "Feeling, Emotion and Imagery as Dimensions of Harmonic Space." *Music Review* 27 (1966): 313–23.

———. "Philosophical Problems in Musical Criticism." *Music Review* 25 (1964): 1–16.

Barker, S. F. "Must Every Inference Be Either Deductive or Inductive?" In *Philosophy in America*, edited by Max Black. London: George Allen and Unwin Ltd., 1965.

Barthes, Roland. *Elements of Semiology*. Translated by Annette Lavers and Colin Smith. London: Jonathan Cape Ltd., 1967.

Barzun, Jacques. "Music into Words." *Score* 10 (1954): 50–65.

Bayer, Raymond. "The Essence of Rhythm." *Revue d' Esthétique* 6 (1953): 369–85. Reprinted in Langer, *Reflections on Art*, q.v.

Beardsley, Monroe C., and Schueller, Herbert M., eds. *Aesthetic Inquiry: Essays on Art Criticism and the Philosophy of Art*. Belmont, Cal.: Dickenson Publishing Co., Inc., 1967.

———. *Aesthetics from Classical Greece to the Present: A Short History*. New York: The Macmillan Co., 1966.

———. *Aesthetics: Problems In The Philosophy Of Criticism*. New York: Harcourt, Brace and Co., 1958.

———. "The Limits of Critical Interpretation." In *Art and Philosophy*, edited by Sidney Hook. New York: New York University Press, 1966.

Beethoven, Ludwig van. *String Quartet 17, F Major, Opus 135*. London: Boosey and Hawkes, n.d.

———. *Symphony No. 3*. Vienna: Wiener Philharmonischer Verlag, n.d.

———. *Symphony V*. Scarsdale, N.Y.: Edwin F. Kalmus, n.d.

Békésy, Georg von and Rosenblith, Walter A. "The Mechanical Properties of the Ear." In *Handbook of Experimental Psychology*, edited by S. S. Stevens. New York: John Wiley and Sons, Inc., 1951.

Bell, Clive. *Art*. New York: G. P. Putnam's Sons, Capricorn Books, 1958.

Bennett, Victor. "An Analogy of Music and Experience." *Music Review* 13 (1952): 34–40.

———. "The Theory of Musical Expression." *Music and Letters* 17 (1936): 106–17.

Bentley, Arthur F. "The New 'Semiotic'." *Philosophy and Phenomenological Research* 8 (1947): 107–31.

Beranek, Leo L. *Music, Acoustics and Architecture*. New York: John Wiley and Sons, Inc., 1962.

Berenson, Bernard. *Aesthetics and History.* Garden City, N.Y.: Doubleday and Co., Inc., 1948.

Berger, Arthur. "New Linguistic Modes and the New Theory." *Perspectives of New Music* 3 (1964): 1–9.

Berry, Wallace. *Form in Music.* Englewood Cliffs, N.J.: Prentice-Hall, Inc., 1966.

Bertrand, Paul. "Pure Music and Dramatic Music." *The Musical Quarterly* 9 (1923): 545–55.

Birkhoff, G. D. *Aesthetic Measure.* Cambridge: Harvard University Press, 1933.

Black, Max. "Metaphor." *Proceedings of the Aristotelian Society* 55 (1954–1955): 273–94.

———, ed. *Philosophy in America.* London: George Allen and Unwin Ltd., 1965.

———. "The Semiotic of Charles Morris," In *Language And Philosophy.* Ithaca, N.Y.: Cornell University Press, 1949.

Blanshard, Brand. *The Nature of Thought.* 2 vols. New York: Humanities Press, 1939.

Blom, Eric, ed. *Grove's Dictionary of Music and Musicians.* 5th ed. New York: St. Martin's Press, Inc., 1954.

Blum, Frederick. "Santayana's Music Aesthetics." *Journal of the American Musicological Society* 11 (1958): 20–28.

Boomsliter, Paul and Creel, Warren. "The Long Pattern Hypothesis in Harmony and Hearing." *Journal of Music Theory* 2 (April, 1961): 2–31.

Boretz, Benjamin. "A Note on Discourse and Contemporary Musical Thought." *Perspectives of New Music* 4 (1966): 76–80.

Bosanquet, Bernard. *A History of Aesthetic.* New York: The Macmillan Co., 1932.

———. *Three Lectures on Aesthetics.* New York: The Macmillan Co., 1915.

Bouwsma, O. K. "The Expression Theory of Art." In *Aesthetics And Language,* edited by William Elton. New York: Philosophical Library, 1954.

Brahms, Johannes. *Symphony IV.* Vienna: Wiener Philharmonischer Verlag, n.d.

Brelet, Gisèle. "Music and Silence." *La Revue Musicale* 22 (1946): 169–81. Reprinted in Langer, *Reflections on Art,* q.v.

Britton, Carl. "Feelings and Their Expression." *Philosophy* 32 (1957): 97–111.

Broudy, Harry S. "Aesthetic Education In A Technological Society: The Other Excuses For Art." *Journal of Aesthetic Education* 1 (1966): 13–24.

Brown, Calvin. *Music and Literature: A Comparison of the Arts.* Athens: University of Georgia Press, 1948.

Brün, Herbert. "Against Plausibility." *Perspectives of New Music* 2 (1963): 43–50.

Buck, Percy C. *The Scope of Music.* 2nd ed. London: Oxford University Press, 1927.

Buelow, George J. "The *Loci Topici* and Affect in Late Baroque Music: Heinichen's Practical Demonstration." *Music Review* 27 (1966): 161–76.

Bukofzer, Manfred F. *Music in The Baroque Era From Monteverdi to Bach.* New York: W. W. Norton and Co., Inc., 1947.

Bullivant, Roger. "Word-Painting and Chromaticism in the Music of J. S. Bach." *Music Review* 20 (1959): 185–216.

Bullough, Edward. *Aesthetics.* Ed. Elizabeth M. Wilkinson. London: Bowes and Bowes, 1957.

Burke, Kenneth. *Counterstatement.* 2nd rev. ed. Chicago: University of Chicago Press, 1957.

———. *A Grammar of Motives and A Rhetoric of Motives.* Cleveland: The World Publishing Co., 1962.

———. *The Philosophy of Literary Form.* Rev. ed. New York: Vintage Books, 1957.

Busoni, Ferruccio. *The Essence of Music.* Translated by Rosamond Ley. London: Rockliff Publishing Corporation, 1957.

Cage, John. *Silence.* Middletown: Wesleyan University Press, 1961.

Calvocoressi, M. D. *The Principles and Methods of Musical Criticism.* New York: Oxford University Press, 1923.

Campbell, Ivy G. "Basal Emotional Patterns Expressible in Music." *American Journal of Psychology* 55 (1942): 1–17.

Candland, Douglas K., ed. *Emotion: Bodily Change.* Princeton: Van Nostrand Co., Inc., 1962.

Cannon, Beekman C. *Johann Mattheson: Spectator in Music.* New Haven: Yale University Press, 1947.

Cannon, Beekman C. Johnson, Alvin H., and Waite, William G. *The Art of Music: A Short History of Musical Styles and Ideas.* New York: Thomas Y. Crowell Co., 1960.

Carnap, Rudolf. *Introduction To Semantics and Formalization Of Logic.* Cambridge: Harvard University Press, 1961.

———. *The Logical Syntax of Language.* Translated by Amethe Smeaton. London: Routledge and Kegan Paul, Ltd., 1937.

Carpenter, Patricia. "But What About the Reality and Meaning of Music?" In *Art and Philosophy*, edited by Sidney Hook New York: University Press, 1966.

"The Musical Object." *Current Musicology* 5 (1967): 56–86; with responses by Leo Treitler, Rudolf Arnheim, Ruth Halle Rowen, Edward T. Cone, Bernard Stambler, and David Burrows: 87–116.

Carritt, Edgar F. *Philosophies of Beauty.* New York: Oxford University Press, 1950.

Carver, George A. *Aesthetics and the Problem of Meaning; The Application of the Logical Positivists' Verifiability Criterion of Cognitive Meaning.* New Haven: Yale University Press, 1952.

Cassirer, Ernst. *Language and Myth.* Translated by Susanne K. Langer. New York: Dover Publications, Inc., 1946.

The Philosophy of Symbolic Forms. Vol. I. Translated by Ralph Manheim. New Haven: Yale University Press, 1953.

Castelnuovo-Tedesco, Mario. "Music and Poetry: Problems of a Song Writer." *Musical Quarterly* 30 (1944): 102–11.

Cazden, Norman. "Towards a Theory of Realism in Music." *Journal of Aesthetics and Art Criticism* 10 (1951): 135–51.

Chandler, Albert R. *Beauty and Human Nature.* New York: Appleton-Century-Crofts, Inc., 1934.

Chavez, Carlos. *Musical Thought.* Cambridge: Harvard University Press, 1961.

Cherry, Colin. *On Human Communication.* 2nd ed. Cambridge: M.I.T. Press, 1966.

Chomsky, Noam. *Syntactic Structures.* The Hague: Mouton and Co., 1957.

Church, Alonzo. *Introduction to Mathematical Logic.* Princeton: Princeton University Press, 1956.

Clarke, Henry Leland. "The Basis of Musical Communication." *Journal of Aesthetics and Art Criticism* 10 (1952): 242–46.

Cohen, Morris. *A Preface To Logic.* New York: Henry Holt and Co., Meridian Books, 1956.

Cohen, Morris R. and Nagel, Ernest. *An Introduction To Logic*, Book I. Harbinger Edition. New York: Harcourt, Brace and World, Inc., 1962.

Collingwood, R. G. *The Principles of Art.* New York: Oxford University Press, 1938; Galaxy Books, 1958.

Colwell, Richard. "The Theory of Expectation Applied to Music Listening." *Council for Research in Music Education* 5 (1956): 17–23.

Cone, Edward T. "Words into Music: The Composer's Approach to the Text." In *Sound and Poetry*, English Institute Essays. New York: Columbia University Press, 1957.

Cooke, Deryck. *The Language of Music.* London: Oxford University Press, 1959.

Cooper, Grosvenor and Meyer, Leonard B. *The Rhythmic Structure Of Music.* Chicago: University of Chicago Press, 1960.

Copi, Irving. "A Note On Representation in Art." *Journal of Philosophy* 52 (1955): 346–49.

Symbolic Logic. 3rd ed. New York: The Macmillan Company, 1967.

Copland, Aaron. "A Modernist Defends Modern Music." *The New York Times Magazine* (December 25, 1949).

Music And Imagination. New York: The New World Library of World Literature, Inc., 1959.

What to Listen for in Music. Rev. ed. New York: McGraw-Hill Book Company, Inc., 1957.

Cowley, Malcolm, ed. *Writers at Work.* New York: The Viking Press, 1958.

Croce, Benedetto. *Aesthetic As Science of Expression and General Linguistic.* Translated by Douglas Ainslie. 2nd ed. London: The Macmillan Company, 1922.

Crocker, Richard L. "Pythagorean Mathematics and Music (Part I)." *Journal of Aesthetics and Art Criticism*, 22 (1963): 189–98.

"Pythagorean Mathematics and Music (Part II)." *Journal of Aesthetics and Art Criticism* 22 (1964): 325–35.

Daitz, Edna. "The Picture Theory of Meaning." *Mind* 62 (1953): 184–201.

Darack, Arthur. *Aesthetics of Music: Early Greek Views.* Ann Arbor: University Microfilms, 1951.

Darwin, Charles. *The Expression of the Emotions in Man and Animals.* Chicago: The University of Chicago Press, 1965.

Davis, Hallowell. "Peripheral Coding of Auditory Information." In *Sensory Communication*, edited by Walter A. Rosenblith. Cambridge: M.I.T. Press, 1961.

"Psychophysiology of Hearing and

Deafness." In *Handbook of Experimental Psychology*, edited by S. S. Stevens. New York: John Wiley and Sons, Inc., 1951.

Davis, R. C. "Motor Effects of Strong Auditory Stimuli." *Journal of Experimental Psychology* 38 (1948): 257–75.

Dempsey, Edward W. "Homeostasis." In *Handbook of Experimental Psychology*, edited by S. S. Stevens. New York: John Wiley and Sons, Inc., 1951.

Demuth, Norman. *An Anthology of Musical Criticism from the 15th to the 20th Century*. London: Eyre and Spottiswoode, 1948.

Descartes, René. *Compendium Of Music*. Translated by Walter Robert. Rome: American Institute of Musicology, 1961.

De Selincourt, Basil. "Music and Duration." *Music and Letters* 1 (1920): 286–93.

Detweiler, Alan. "Music and Poetry." *British Journal of Aesthetics* 1 (1961): 134–43.

Dewey, John. *Art As Experience*. New York: G. P. Putnam's Sons, Capricorn Books, 1958.

——. *Experience And Nature*. Reprint. New York: Dover Publications, Inc., 1958.

Dickinson, George S. "Analogical Relations in Musical Patterns." *Journal of Aesthetics and Art Criticism* 17 (1958): 77–84.

Doob, Leonard W. "The Behavior of Attitudes." In *Readings in Attitude Theory and Measurement*, edited by Martin Fishbein. New York: John Wiley and Sons, Inc., 1967.

Dräger, Hans Heinz. "The Concept of Tonal Body." *Archiv für Musikwissenschaft* 9 (1952): 68–77. Reprinted in Langer, *Reflections on Art*, q.v.

Drever, James. *A Dictionary of Psychology*. Baltimore: Penguin Books, 1952.

Ducasse, Curt John. *The Philosophy of Art*. New York: The Dial Press, 1929.

Duncan, Elmer H., ed. *Twenty Year Cumulative Index to the Journal of Aesthetics and Art Criticism*. Vols. 1–20, 1941–1962. New York: ANS Reprint Co., 1964.

Edman, Irwin. *Arts And The Man*. New York: W. W. Norton and Co., 1939.

Einstein, Alfred. "The Conflict of Word and Tone." *Musical Quarterly* 40 (1954): 329–49.

——. *The Italian Madrigal*. Princeton: Princeton University Press, 1949.

Elton, William, ed. *Aesthetics And Language*.

New York: Philosophical Library, 1959.

Emery, Walter. "Bach's Symbolic Language." *Music and Letters* 30 (1949): 345–54.

Epperson, Gordon. *The Musical Symbol*. Ames: Iowa State University Press, 1967.

Erickson, Robert. *The Structure of Music*. New York: The Noonday Press, 1955.

Esper, Erwin. "Max Meyer and the Psychology of Music." *Journal of Music Theory* 10 (1966): 182–99.

Farnsworth, Paul R. "Sacred Cows in the Psychology of Music." *Journal of Aesthetics and Art Criticism* 7 (1948): 48–51.

——. "A Study of the Hevner Adjective List." *Journal of Aesthetics and Art Criticism* 13 (1954): 97–103.

Feibleman, James K. "Motion," In *The Dictionary of Philosophy*, edited by Dagobert Runes. New York: Philosophical Library, 1942.

Feigl, Herbert and Sellars, Wilfrid, eds. *Readings In Philosophical Analysis*. New York: Appleton-Century-Crofts, Inc., 1949.

Ferguson, Donald N. *Music As Metaphor*. Minneapolis: University of Minnesota Press, 1960.

Fishbein, Martin, ed. *Readings in Attitude Theory and Measurement*. New York: John Wiley and Sons, Inc., 1967.

Flew, A. G. N., ed. *Logic And Language*. 2nd series. New York: Philosophical Library, 1953.

Ford, Donald H. and Schadé, J. P. *Atlas of the Human Brain*. Amsterdam: Elsevier Publishing Company, 1966.

Forte, Allen. *The Compositional Matrix*. Baldwin: Music Teachers National Association, 1961.

——. *Contemporary Tone-Structures*. New York: Bureau of Publications, Teachers College, Columbia University, 1955.

——. "Context and Continuity in an Atonal Work: A Set-Theoretic Approach." *Perspectives of New Music* 1 (1963): 72–82.

——. "Schenker's Conception of Musical Structure." *Journal of Music Theory* 3, (1959): 1–30.

Fortune, Nigel. "Solo Song and Cantata." In *The Age of Humanism*. Vol. 4. *The New Oxford History of Music*, edited by Gerald Abraham. London: Oxford University Press, 1968.

Fowler, H. W., ed. *A Dictionary Of Modern English Usage*. London: Oxford University Press, 1944.

Frank, Lawrence K. *Feelings and Emotion*. Garden City, N.Y.: Doubleday and Company, Inc., 1954.

Frank, Paul L. "Realism and Naturalism in Music." *Journal of Aesthetics and Art Criticism* 11 (1952): 55–60.

Frege, Gottlob. "A Critical Elucidation of Some Points in E. Schroeder's *Vorlesungen Ueber Die Algebra Der Logik*." *Philosophical Writings of Gottlob Frege*. Edited by Peter Geach and Max Black. Oxford: Basil Blackwell, 1960.

  The Foundations of Arithmetic. Translated by J. L. Austin. 2nd rev. ed. Oxford: Basil Blackwell, 1959.

  "On Sense and Nominatum." In *Readings In Philosophical Analysis*, edited by Herbert Feigl and Wilfrid Sellars. New York: Appleton-Century-Crofts, Inc. 1949

Freud, Sigmund. *The Problem of Anxiety*. Translated by Henry Alden Bunker. New York: The Psychoanalytic Quarterly Press and W. W. Norton and Co., Inc., 1936.

Frohoe, Franz, Brödel, Max, and Schlossberg, Leon. *Atlas of Human Anatomy*. New York: Barnes and Noble, Inc., 1961.

Fry, Roger. *Transformations*. Garden City: Doubleday and Co.,1926, Anchor Books, 1956.

Frye, Northrup. *Anatomy of Criticism*. Princeton: Princeton University Press, 1957.

Funkenstein, Daniel H. "The Physiology of Fear and Anger." In *Emotion: Bodily Change*, edited by Douglas K. Candland. Princeton: D. Van Nostrand Co., Inc., 1962.

Gaburo, Kenneth L. *Studies in Pitch Symmetry in Twentieth Century Music*. Ann Arbor: University Microfilms, 1962.

Gallie, W. B. *Peirce And Pragmatism*. Harmondsworth: Penguin Books, 1952.

Garvin, Lucius. "Emotivism, Expressionism, and Symbolic Meaning." *Journal of Philosophy* 55 (1958): 111–18.

  "The Paradox of Aesthetic Meaning." *Philosophy and Phenomenological Research* 8 (1947): 99–106.

Gehring, Albert. *The Basis of Musical Pleasure*. New York: Putnam, 1910.

Geiringer, Karl. *Symbolism in the Music of Bach*. Washington, D.C.: The Library of Congress, 1956.

Ghiselin, Brewster. *The Creative Process*. New York: Mentor Books, 1955.

Gilbert, Katherine Everett and Kuhn, Helmut. *A History of Esthetic*. 2nd ed. London: Thames and Hudson, 1956.

Goddard, Joseph. *The Deeper Sources of the Beauty and Expression of Music*. London: W. Reeves, 1905.

Goetschius, Percy. *Lessons in Musical Form*. Philadelphia: Oliver Ditson Co., 1914.

Gombrich, E. H. "Meditations On A Hobby Horse Or The Roots Of Artistic Form." In *Aspects of Form*, edited by Lancelot Law Whyte. London: Lund Humphries, 1951.

Goodman, Nelson. *Fact, Fiction and Forecast*. 2nd ed. Indianapolis: The Bobbs-Merrill Co., Inc., 1965.

  The Structure of Appearance. 2nd ed. Indianapolis: The Bobbs-Merrill Company, Inc., 1966.

Gotshalk, D. W. "Form." In *The Problems Of Aesthetics*, edited by Eliseo Vivas and Murray Krieger. New York: Rinehart and Co., Inc., 1953.

Granit, Ragnar. *Receptors and Sensory Perception*. New Haven: Yale University Press, 1955.

Green, Douglass M. *Form in Tonal Music*. New York: Holt, Rinehart and Winston, Inc., 1965.

Greene, Theodore M. *The Arts And The Art Of Criticism*. Princeton: Princeton University Press, 1940.

  Moral, Aesthetic, And Religious Insight. New Brunswick, N.J.: Rutgers University Press, 1957.

  "The Problem of Meaning in Music and the Other Arts." *Journal of Aesthetics and Art Criticism* 5 (1947): 308–14.

Grinker, Roy R. "The Physiology of Emotions." In *The Physiology of Emotions*, edited by Alexander Simon, Charles Herbert, and Ruth Straus. Springfield, Ill.: Charles C. Thomas, 1961.

Grout, Donald Jay. *A History of Western Music*. New York: W. W. Norton and Co., Inc., 1960.

  A Short History of Opera. New York: Columbia University Press, 1947.

Gurney, Edmund. *The Power of Sound*. London: Smith, Elder and Co., 1880.

Guthrie, E. R. "Association by Contiguity." In *Psychology: A Study of a Science*, Vol. 3, edited by Sigmund Koch. New York: McGraw-Hill, 1959.

Guyau, Jean Marie. *Problems of Contemporary Aesthetics*. Los Angeles: De Vorss and Co., Inc., 1947.

Hall, Robert W. "On Hanslick's Supposed Formalism in Music." *Journal of Aesthetics and Art Criticism* 25 (1967): 433–36.

Halmos, Paul R. *Naive Set Theory*. Princeton: D. Van Nostrand Co., Inc., 1960.

Hampshire, Stuart. "*A Composer's World (Paul Hindemith)*." *Score* 7 (1952): 58–62.

Hanslick, Eduard. *The Beautiful in Music*. Translated by Gustave Cohen. Edited by Morris Weitz. 8th ed. New York: The Liberal Arts Press, 1957.

——. *Music Criticisms, 1846–1899*. Translated and edited by Henry Pleasants. Baltimore: Penguin Books, Inc., 1963.

Harding, Rosamond E. M. *An Anatomy of Inspiration*. Cambridge: W. Heffer and Sons, Ltd., 1940.

Harrah, David. *Communication: A Logical Model*. Cambridge: M.I.T. Press, 1963.

Harrell, Jean G. "Issues in Music Aesthetics." *Journal of Aesthetics and Art Criticism* 23 (1964): 197–206.

Harriman, Philip L. *An Outline of Modern Psychology*. Ames, Iowa: Littlefield, Adams and Co., 1956.

Hartshorne, Charles. "The Monistic Theory of Expression." *Journal of Philosophy* 50 (1953): 425–34.

Harvey, O. J. "Cognitive Aspects of Affective Arousal." In *Affect, Cognition, and Personality*, edited by Silvan S. Tomkins and Carroll E. Izard. London: Tavistock Publications, 1965.

Hauser, Arnold. *The Social History of Art*. New York: Alfred A. Knopf, Inc., 1951.

Haydon, Glen. "On the Problem of Expression in Baroque Music." *Journal of the American Musicological Society* 3 (1950): 113–19.

Heeb, Donald O. *The Organization of Behavior*. New York: John Wiley and Chapman and Hall, 1949.

Henderson, Isobel. "Ancient Greek Music." In *Ancient and Oriental Music*, Vol. 1, *The New Oxford History of Music*, edited by Egon Wellesz. London: Oxford University Press, 1957.

Henle, Paul, ed. *Language, Thought, and Culture*. Ann Arbor: University of Michigan Press, 1958.

Hevner, Kate. "The Affective Character of the Major and Minor Modes in Music." *American Journal of Psychology* 47 (1935): 103–18.

——. "Experimental Studies of the Elements of Expression in Music." *American Journal of Psychology* 48 (1936): 246–68.

——. "Expression in Music: A Discussion of Experimental Studies and Theories." *Psychological Review* 42 (1935): 186–204.

Heyl, Bernard C. "Artistic Truth Reconsidered." *Journal of Aesthetics and Art Criticism* 8 (1950): 251–58.

——. *New Bearings in Esthetics and Art Criticism*. New Haven: Yale University Press, 1943.

——. "Relativism Again." *Journal of Aesthetics and Art Criticism* 5 (1946): 54–61.

Hiller, Lejaren and Bean, Calvert. "Information Theory Analyses of Four Sonata Expositions." *Journal of Music Theory* 10 (1966): 96–138.

Hillman, James. *Emotion*. London: Routledge and Kegan Paul, 1960.

Hindemith, Paul. *A Composer's World*. Cambridge: Harvard University Press, 1952.

Hines, Robert Stephan, ed. *The Composer's Point of View*. Norman: University of Oklahoma Press, 1963.

Hocutt, Max Oliver. "The Logical Foundations of Peirce's Aesthetics." *Journal of Aesthetics and Art Criticism* 21 (1962); 157–66.

Hofstader, Albert. "Significance and Artistic Meaning." In *Art and Philosophy*, edited by Sidney Hook. New York: New York University Press, 1966.

Honegger, Arthur. *Pacific 231*. Paris: Éditions Salabert, 1924.

Hook, Sidney, ed. *Art and Philosophy, A Symposium*. New York: New York University Press, 1966.

Hospers, John. "Art and Reality." In *Art and Philosophy*, edited by Sidney Hook. New York: New York University Press, 1966.

——. "The Concept of Artistic Expression." *Proceedings of the Aristotelian Society* (1954–1955): 313–44.

——. *Meaning And Truth In The Arts*.

Chapel Hill: University of North Carolina Press, 1946.

Howes, Frank. "The Foundations of Musical Aesthetics." *Proceedings of the Royal Musical Association* 83 (1957): 75–87.

Hsu, Delores Menstell. "Ernst Kurth and His Concept of Music as Motion." *Journal of Music Theory* 10 (1966): 2–17.

Hughes, Dom Anselm. "Music in Fixed Rhythm." In *Early Medieval Music Up To 1300*, Vol. 2, *The New Oxford History of Music*, edited by Dom Anselm Hughes. London: Oxford University Press, 1954.

Hull, Clark L. *A Behavior System*. New Haven: Yale University Press, 1952.

Humphreys, Louise and Ross, Jerrold. *Interpreting Music Through Movement*. Englewood Cliffs, N.J.: Prentice-Hall, Inc., 1964.

Hungerland, Isabel Creed. "The Iconic Sign and Expressiveness." *Journal of Aesthetics and Art Criticism* 3 (n.d.): 15–21.

Hutchinson, William R. "Aesthetic and Musical Theory: An Aspect of Their Juncture." *Journal of Aesthetics and Art Criticism* 24 (1966): 393–400.

Irvine, Demar B. *Expression of Ideas and Emotion in Music*. Ph.D. dissertation, Harvard University, 1937.

Isenberg, Arnold. "Critical Communication." In *Aesthetics and Language*, edited by William Elton. New York: Philosophical Library, 1954.

Ives, Charles. *Essays Before a Sonata and Other Writings*. Edited by Howard Boatwright. New York: W. W. Norton and Co., Inc., 1964.

———. *Nineteen Songs*. Bryn Mawr, Pa.: Merion Music, Inc., 1935.

Izard, Carroll E. with Gerald M. Wehmer, William J. Livsey, and J. Rex Jennings, "Affect, Awareness, and Performance." In *Affect, Cognition, and Personality*, edited by Silvan S. Tomkins and Carroll E. Izard. London: Tavistock Publications, 1965.

Jacklin, Phillip D. *Certainty And Criteria of Truth*. Ph.D. dissertation, Yale University, 1967.

Jacobs, Robert L. "A Gestalt Psychologist on Music." *Music Review* 17 (1956): 185–88.

———. "Music as Symbol." *Music Review* 21 (1960): 226–36.

James, William. *The Principles of Psychology*. 2 vols. New York: Henry Holt and Co., 1890.

Jones, Daniel. "An Attempt to Formulate General Aesthetic Principles Through Music—Aesthetics." *Score* 11 (1955): 33–52.

Kainz, Friedrich. *Aesthetics the Science*. Translated by Herbert M. Schueller. Detroit: Wayne State University Press, 1962.

Kant, Immanuel. *Critique of Judgement, First Book, Analytic of the Beautiful*. Translated by J. H. Bernard. New York: Hafner Publishing Co., 1951.

Kaplan, Abraham. "Referential Meaning in the Arts." *Journal of Aesthetics and Art Criticism* 12 (1954): 457–74.

Kassler, Michael. "Toward a Theory That Is the Twelve-Note-Class System." *Perspectives of New Music* 5 (1967): 1–80.

Katz, Adele. *Challenge To Musical Tradition*. New York: Alfred A. Knopf, 1946.

Kaufmann, Henry W. "Vincentino and the Greek Genera." *Journal of the American Musicological Society*, 16 (1963): 325–46.

Keil, Charles M. H. "Motion and Feeling Through Music." *Journal of Aesthetics and Art Criticism* 24 (1966): 337–49.

Keller, Hans. "Deryck Cooke's Achievement." *Music Review* 22 (1961): 34–38.

Kennick, W. E. "Form and Content in Art." In *Art and Philosophy*, edited by Sidney Hook. New York: New York University Press, 1966.

Kenny, Anthony. *Action, Emotion and Will*. London: Routledge and Kegan Paul, 1963.

Kessler, Hubert. "On the Modes of Connection of Musical Ideas." Paper read before the Midwest Chapter meeting of the American Musicological Society, St. Louis, Missouri, April, 1960.

Kiesow, Federico. "The Feeling-Tone of Sensation." In *Feelings And Emotions*, The Wittenberg Symposium, edited by Martin Reymert. Worcester, Mass.: Clark University Press, 1928.

Kivy, Peter. "Charles Darwin on Music." *Journal of the American Musicological Society* 12 (1959): 42–48.

———. "Mainwaring's *Handel*: its Relation to English Aesthetics." *Journal of the American Musicological Society* 17 (1964): 170–78.

Knox, Israel. *The Aesthetic Theories of Kant,*

242   Music and Meaning

Hegel, and Schopenhauer. New York: The Humanities Press, 1936.

Koffka, Kurt. "Problems in the Psychology of Art." In *Art: A Bryn Mawr Symposium*, ed. by Richard Bernheimer, Rhys Carpenter, Kurt Koffka, and Milton C. Nahm. Bryn Mawr, Pa.: Bryn Mawr College, 1950.

Köhler, Wolfgang. *Gestalt Psychology.* New York: Liveright Publishing Corp., Mentor Books, 1947.

Kostelanetz, Richard. "Modern Music Criticism and the Literate Layman." *Perspectives of New Music* 6 (1967): 119–33.

Krueger, Felix. "The Essence of Feeling." In *Feelings And Emotion*, The Wittenberg Symposium, edited by Martin Reymert. Worcester, Mass.: Clark University Press, 1928.

Lang, Paul Henry. *Music in Western Civilization.* New York: W. W. Norton and Co., Inc., 1941.

Langer, Susanne K. *Feeling And Form.* New York: Charles Scribner's Sons, 1953.

———. *Mind: An Essay on Human Feeling.* Vol. 1. Baltimore: Johns Hopkins Press, 1967.

———. *Philosophical Sketches.* Baltimore: Johns Hopkins Press, 1962.

———. *Philosophy in a New Key.* New York: The New American Library of World Literature, Inc., Mentor Books, 1942.

———. "The Principle of Assimilation." *Score* 24 (1958): 42–53.

———. *Problems of Art.* New York: Charles Scribner's Sons, 1957.

———, ed. *Reflections On Art.* Baltimore: Johns Hopkins Press, 1958.

Langfeld, Herbert S. *The Aesthetic Attitude.* New York: Harcourt, Brace and Howe, 1920.

La Rue, Jan. "On Style Analysis." *Journal of Music Theory* 6 (1962): 91–108.

———. "Significant and Coincidental Resemblance Between Classical Themes." *Journal of the American Musicological Society* 14 (1961): 224–34.

Laszlo, Ervin. "Aesthetics and Live Musical Performance." *British Journal of Aesthetics* 7 (1967): 261–73.

Lee, Harold N. *Symbolic Logic.* London: Routledge and Kegan Paul, Ltd., 1962.

Lee, Vernon. *The Beautiful.* Cambridge: University Press, 1913.

———. *Music And Its Lovers.* London: George Allen and Unwin Ltd., 1932.

Leichtentritt, Hugo. "Aesthetic Ideas as the Basis of Musical Styles." *Journal of Aesthetics and Art Criticism* 4 (1945): 65–73.

———. *Musical Form.* Cambridge: Harvard University Press, 1951.

Lenneberg, Hans. "Johann Mattheson on Affect and Rhetoric in Music." *Journal of Music Theory* 2 (1958): 47–84.

———. "Johann Mattheson on Affect and Rhetoric in Music (II)." *Journal of Music Theory* 2 (1958): 193–236.

Lewis, Clarence I. *An Analysis Of Knowledge And Valuation.* La Salle, Ill.: The Open Court Publishing Co., 1946.

———. "The Modes of Meaning." In *Semantics and the Philosophy of Language*, edited by Leonard Linsky. Urbana: University of Illinois Press, 1952.

Lewis, Clarence I. and Langford, Cooper H. *Symbolic Logic.* 2nd ed. New York: Dover Publications, Inc., 1959.

Licklider, J. C. R. "Basic Correlatives of the Auditory Stimulus." In *Handbook of Experimental Psychology*, edited by S. S. Stevens. New York: John Wiley and Sons, Inc.. 1951.

Ligeti, György."Metamorphoses of Musical Form." *die Reihe* 7 (1965): 5–19.

Lindsley, Donald B. "Emotion." In *Handbook of Experimental Psychology*, edited by S. S. Stevens. New York: John Wiley and Sons, 1951.

Linsky, Leonard. *Referring.* London: Routledge and Kegan Paul, 1967.

———, ed. *Semantics and the Philosophy of Language.* Urbana: University of Illinois Press, 1952.

Lippman, Edward A. "The Esthetic Theories of Richard Wagner." *Musical Quarterly* 44 (1959): 209–20.

———. "Hellenic Conceptions of Harmony." *Journal of the American Musicological Society* 16 (1963): 3–35.

———. *Musical Thought in Ancient Greece.* New York: Columbia University Press, 1964.

———. "The Problem of Musical Hermeneutics: A Protest and Analysis." In *Art and Philosophy*, edited by Sidney Hook. New York: New York University Press, 1966.

———. "The Sources and Development of the Ethical View of Music in Ancient

Greece." *Musical Quarterly* 49 (1963): 188–209.

"Spatial Perception and Physical Location as Factors in Music." *Acta Musicologica* 35 (1963): 24–34.

"Symbolism in Music." *Musical Quarterly* 39 (1953): 554–75.

"Theory and Practice in Schumann's Aesthetics." *Journal of the American Musicological Society* 17 (1964): 310–45.

Lissa, Zofia. "Aesthetic Functions of Silence and Rests in Music." *Journal of Aesthetics and Art Criticism* 22 (1964): 443–54.

"On the Evolution of Musical Perception." *Journal of Aesthetics and Art Criticism* 24 (1965): 273–86.

Lloyd, L. S. "The A Priori Theorist and Music." *Music and Letters* 26 (1945): 97–102.

Lodge, Rupert. *Plato's Theory of Art*. New York: The Humanities Press, Inc., 1953.

MacCurdy, John T. *The Psychology of Emotion*. New York: Harcourt, Brace and Co., Inc., 1925.

MacDowell, Edward. *Critical and Historical Essays*. Edited by W. J. Baltzell. Boston: Arthur P. Schmidt, 1912.

Machlis, Joseph. *The Enjoyment of Music*. New York: W. W. Norton and Co., Inc., 1955.

Mackerness, E. D. "Edmund Gurney and 'The Power of Sound'." *Music and Letters* 37 (1956): 356–67.

Margolis, Joseph. "Aesthetic Perception." *Journal of Aesthetics and Art Criticism* 19 (1960): 209–13.

The Language of Art and Art Criticism. Detroit: Wayne State University Press, 1965.

ed. *Philosophy Looks At The Arts*. New York: Charles Scribner's Sons, 1962.

Martin, F. David. "The Power of Music and Whitehead's Theory of Perception." *Journal of Aesthetics and Art Criticism* 25 (1967): 313–22.

Martin, Richard M. *Intension and Decision*. Englewood Cliffs, N.J.: Prentice-Hall, 1963.

Toward A Systematic Pragmatics. Amsterdam: North-Holland Publishing Co., 1959.

Mauron, Charles. *Aesthetics and Psychology*. London: Hogarth Press, 1935.

McAlpin, Colin. "Is Music the Language of the Emotions?" *Musical Quarterly* 11 (1925): 427–43.

McMullin, Michael. "The Symbolic Analysis of Music." *Music Review* 8 (1947): 25–35.

Mead, George Herbert. *Mind, Self and Society*. Edited by Charles W. Morris. Chicago: *University of Chicago Press*, 1934.

The Philosophy Of The Act. Edited by Charles W. Morris *et al.* Chicago: University of Chicago Press, 1938.

Messiaen, Oliver. *Oiseaux Exotiques*. London: Universal Edition, Ltd., 1959.

Meyer-Baer, Kathi. "Nicolas of Cusa on the Meaning of Music." *Journal of Aesthetics and Art Criticism* 5 (1947): 301–08.

"Psychologic and Ontologic Ideas in Augustine's *De Musica*." *Journal of Aesthetics and Art Criticism* 11 (1953): 224–30.

Meyer, Leonard B. *Emotion and Meaning in Music*. Chicago: University of Chicago Press, 1956.

"Meaning in Music and Information Theory." *Journal of Aesthetics and Art Criticism* 15 (1957): 412–25.

Music, the Arts, and Ideas. Chicago: University of Chicago Press, 1967.

"On Rehearing Music." *Journal of the American Muiscological Society* 14 (1961): 257–67.

"Some Remarks On Value and Greatness in Music." *Journal of Aesthetics and Art Criticism* 17 (1959): 486–500.

Mitchell, Joyce. "Aesthetic Judgment in Music." *Journal of Aesthetics and Art Criticism* 19 (1960): 73–82.

"Criteria of Criticism in Music." *Journal of Aesthetics and Art Criticism* 21 (1962): 27–30.

"A New Approach to an Aesthetic of Music." *Journal of Aesthetics and Art Criticism* 15 (1956): 227–31.

Moles, Abraham. *Information Theory and Esthetic Perception*. Translated by Joel E. Cohen. Urbana: University of Illinois Press, 1966.

Morgan, Douglas N. "Must Art Tell the Truth?" *Journal of Aesthetics and Art Criticism* 26 (1967): 17–27.

Morgenstern, Sam, ed. *Composers On Music*. New York: Pantheon, 1956.

Morris, Charles W. "Esthetics and the Theory of Signs." In *Journal of Unified Science*, vol. 8, edited by Rudolf Carnap and Hans Reichenbach. Chicago: University of Chicago Press, 1939–1940.

———. "Foundations of the Theory of Signs." In *International Encyclopedia of Unified Science*, vol. 1, no. 2, edited by Rudolf Carnap, Otto Neurath, and Charles W. Morris. Chicago: University of Chicago Press, 1938.

———. "Science, Art and Technology." *Kenyon Review* 1 (1939): 409–23.

———. *Signification and Significance*. Cambridge: M.I.T. Press, 1964.

———. *Signs, Language and Behavior*. Englewood Cliffs, N.J.: Prentice-Hall, Inc., 1946.

Morris, Charles W. and Hamilton, Daniel J. "Aesthetics, Signs, and Icons." *Philosophy and Phenomenological Research* 25 (1965): 356–64.

Morris, R. O. *The Structure of Music*. London: Oxford University Press, 1935.

Munro, Thomas. *The Arts and Their Interrelations*. New York: The Liberal Arts Press, 1949.

———. "Evolution and Progress in the Arts: A Reappraisal of Herbert Spencer's Theory." *Journal of Aesthetics and Art Criticism* 18 (1960): 294–315.

———. *Towards Science in Aesthetics*. New York: The Liberal Arts Press, 1956.

Mursell, James. *The Psychology of Music*. New York: W. W. Norton and Co., 1937.

Myers, Rollo. "Music and Human Personality." *Score* 19 (1957): 27–33.

Nagel, Ernest and Brandt, Richard, eds. *Meaning and Knowledge: Systematic Readings in Epistemology*. New York: Harcourt, Brace and World, Inc., 1965.

Nahm, Milton. *Aesthetic Experience and Its Presuppositions*. New York: Harper and Brothers, 1946.

Nallin, Walter E. *The Musical Idea*. New York: The Macmillan Company, 1968.

Neff, William D. "Neural Mechanisms of Auditory Discrimination." In *Sensory Communication*, edited by Walter A. Rosenblith. Cambridge: M.I.T. Press, 1961.

Newman, William S. "The Climax of Music." *Music Review* 13 (1952): 283–93.

Norman, Gertrude and Shrifte, Miriam Lubell, eds. *Letters of Composers*. New York: Grosset and Dunlap, 1946.

Ogden, C. K. and Richards, I. A. *The Meaning of Meaning*. 8th ed. New York: Harcourt, Brace and Co., 1946.

Ogden, C. K. Richards, I. A., and Wood, James. *The Foundations of Aesthetics*. 2nd ed. New York: Lear Publishers, 1948.

Oliver, Alfred R. *The Encyclopedists as Critics of Music*. New York: Columbia University Press, 1947.

Olson, Harry F. *Music, Physics, and Engineering*. 2nd ed. New York: Dover Publications, Inc., 1967.

Ortmann, Otto. "Types of Listeners." In *The Effects Of Music*, edited by Max Schoen. New York: Harcourt, Brace and Co., Inc., 1927.

Osborne, Harold. *Aesthetics and Criticism*. London: Routledge and Kegan Paul, 1955.

———. *Theory of Beauty*. London: Routledge and Kegan Paul, 1952.

———. "Wittgenstein on Aesthetics." *British Journal of Aesthetics* 6 (1966): 385–90.

Osgood, Charles E. and Thomas A. Sebeok, eds. *Psycholinguistics, A Survey of Theory and Research Problems*. Bloomington: Indiana University Press, 1965.

Overton, Richard K. *Thought and Action*. New York: Random House, 1959.

Palisca, Claude V. "Vincenzo Galilei and Some Links Between 'Pseudo-Monody and Monody'." *Musical Quarterly* 46 (1960): 344–60.

———. "Vincenzo Galilei's Counterpoint Treatise." *Journal of the American Musicological Society* 9 (1956): 81–96.

Pap, Arthur. *Semantics and Necessary Truth*. New Haven: Yale University Press, 1958.

Parker, DeWitt H. "The Nature of Art." *Revue Internationale de Philosophie*, Première année (July, 1939): 684–702.

———. *The Principles of Aesthetics*. 2nd rev. ed. New York: F. S. Crofts and Co., 1947.

Parkhurst, Winthrop. "Music, the Invisible Art." *Musical Quarterly* 16 (1930): 297–304.

Parry, Sir Hubert. *The Evolution Of The Art Of Music*. London: Routledge and Kegan Paul, 1893.

Paulhan, Frédéric. *The Laws of Feeling*. Translated by C. K. Ogden. New York: Harcourt, Brace and Co., 1930.

Payne, Elsie. "Emotion in Music and in Music Appreciation." *Music Review* 22 (1961): 39–50.

Peirce, Charles S. *Philosophical Writings of*

Peirce. Edited by Justus Buchler. New York: Dover Publications, 1955.

Pepper, Stephen C. *Aesthetic Quality.* New York: Charles Scribner's Sons, 1937.

——— *The Basis of Criticism in the Arts.* Cambridge: Harvard University Press, 1945.

——— *The Work of Art.* Bloomington: Indiana University Press, 1955.

——— *World Hypotheses.* Berkeley: University of California Press, 1942.

Pepper, Stephen C. and Popper, Karl H. "The Criterion of Relevance in Aesthetics: A Discussion." *Journal of Aesthetics and Art Criticism* 16 (1957): 202–16.

Perl, Carl Johann. "Augustine and Music." *Musical Quarterly* 41 (1955): 496–510.

Philipson, Morris, ed. *Aesthetics Today.* Cleveland: The World Publishing Co., 1961.

Pierce, John R. *Symbols, Signals and Noise.* New York: Harper and Brothers, 1961.

Pierce, John R. and Davis, Edward E., Jr. *Man's World of Sound.* Garden City, N.Y.: Doubleday and Co., Inc., 1958.

Pike, Alfred. "Perception and Meaning in Serial Music." *Journal of Aesthetics and Art Criticism* 22 (1963): 55–61.

——— "The Theory of Unconscious Perception in Music." *Journal of Aesthetics and Art Criticism* 25 (1967): 395–400.

Pirie, Peter J. "The Predicament of Musical Aesthetics." *Music Review* 19 (1958): 130–36.

Pitts, Carl Estes. *Affective Arousal To Music As A Function of Deviations In Perceived Complexity From An Adaptation Level.* Ann Arbor: University Microfilms, Inc., 1964.

Portnoy, Julius. *Music in the Life of Man.* New York: Holt, Rinehart and Winston, 1963.

——— *The Philosopher and Music.* New York: The Humanities Press, 1954.

——— "Similarities of Musical Concepts in Ancient and Medieval Philosophy." *Journal of Aesthetics and Art Criticism* 7 (1949): 235–43.

Pousseur, Henri. "Music, Form and Practice." *die Reihe* 6 (1964): 77–93.

Powell, Mel. "A Note on Rigor." *Perspectives of New Music* (1963): 121–24.

Prall, David. *Aesthetic Analysis.* New York: Thomas Y. Crowell Co., 1936.

Pratt, Carroll C. "The Design of Music." *Journal of Aesthetics and Art Criticism* 12 (1954): 289–300.

——— *The Meaning Of Music.* New York: McGraw-Hill Book Co., 1931.

——— *Music as the Language of Emotions.* Washington, D.C.: Library of Congress, 1952.

Price, H. H. *Thinking and Experience.* Cambridge: Harvard University Press, 1962.

Price, Kingsley B. "Is the Work of Art a Symbol?" *Journal of Philosophy* 50 (1953): pp. 485–503.

Quantz, Johann Joachim. *On Playing the Flute.* Translated by Edward R. Reilly. New York: The Free Press, 1966.

Quine, Willard Van Orman. *Elementary Logic.* Rev. ed. New York: Harper and Row, Publishers, 1965.

——— *From a Logical Point of View.* 2nd ed. New York: Harper and Row, Publishers, 1961.

——— *Word and Object.* Cambridge: M.I.T. Press, 1960.

Rader, Melvin. *A Modern Book of Esthetics.* 3rd ed. New York: Henry Holt and Co., 1960.

Ransom, John Crowe, ed. *The New Criticism.* Norfolk, Conn.: New Directions, 1941.

Ratner, Leonard. *The Listener's Art.* New York: McGraw-Hill Book Co., 1957.

Rawlins, Ian. *Aesthetics And The Gestalt.* London: Thomas Nelson and Sons Ltd., 1953.

Read, Herbert. *The Forms of Things Unknown.* London: Faber and Faber Ltd., 1960.

——— *The Meaning of Art.* Harmondsworth: Penguin Books Ltd., 1931.

Reese, Gustave. *Music in the Renaissance.* New York: W. W. Norton and Co., Inc., 1954.

Regener, Eric. "Layered Music-Theoretic Systems." *Perspectives of New Music* 6 (1967): 52–62.

Reid, Louis Arnaud. "Knowing in Music." *Proceedings of the Aristotelian Society* 41 (1940–1941): 113–26.

——— *A Study In Aesthetics.* New York: The Macmillan Co., 1954.

——— "Symbolism in Art." *British Journal of Aesthetics* 1 (1961): 185–91.

Reti, Rudolph. *The Thematic Process in Music.* New York: The Macmillan Company, 1951.

Révész, G. *Introduction To The Psychology Of Music.* Translated by G. I. C. de Courcy. London: Longmans, Green and Co. Ltd., 1953.

Reymert, Martin L., ed. *Feelings and Emotions,* The Moosehart Symposium. New York: McGraw-Hill Book Co., 1950.

——— ed. *Feelings And Emotions,* The Wittenberg Symposium. Worcester, Mass.: Clark University Press, 1928.

Richards, I. A. *Interpretation and Teaching.* New York: Harcourt, Brace and Co., 1938.

——— *Principles of Literary Criticism.* New York: Harcourt, Brace and Co., 1924.

Rieser, Max. "On Musical Semantics." *Journal of Philosophy* 39 (1942): 421–32.

——— "The Semantic Theory of Art in America." *Journal of Aesthetics and Art Criticism* 15 (1956): 12–26.

Rigg, Melvin. "The Expression of Meanings and Emotions in Music." In *Philosophical Essays in Honor of E. A. Singer,* edited by F. P. Clarke and Milton C. Nahm. Philadelphia: University of Pennsylvania Press, 1942.

——— "Musical Expression: An Investigation of the Theories of Erich Sorantin." *Journal of Experimental Psychology* 21 (1937): 442–55.

Ritchie, Benbow. "The Formal Structure of the Aesthetic Object." *Journal of Aesthetics and Art Criticism* 3 (n.d.): 5–14.

Rochberg, George. *Duo Concertante.* Bryn Mawr, Pa.: Theodore Presser Co., 1960.

——— "Duration in Music." In *The Modern Composer and His World,* edited by John Beckwith and Udo Kasemets. Toronto: University of Toronto Press, 1961.

——— "Indeterminacy in the New Music." *Score* 26 (1960): 9–19.

——— "The New Image of Music." *Perspectives of New Music* 2 (1963): 1–10.

Rollins, C. D., ed. *Knowledge and Experience,* Proceedings of the 1962 Oberlin Colloquium in Philosophy. Oberlin: University of Pittsburgh Press, 1962.

Rosenblith, Walter A., ed. *Sensory Communication,* Contributions to the Symposium on Principles of Sensory Communication. Cambridge: M.I.T. Press, 1961.

Ruch, T. C. "Motor Systems." In *Handbook of Experimental Psychology,* edited by

S. S. Stevens. New York: John Wiley and Sons, Inc., 1951.

Rudner, Richard. "On Semiotic Aesthetics." *Journal of Aesthetics and Art Criticism* 10 (1951): 67–77.

——— "Sign Process and Valuation." *Journal of Philosophy* 55 (1958): 340–44.

——— "Some Problems of Non-Semiotic Aesthetic Theories." *Journal of Aesthetics and Art Criticism* 15 (1957): 298–311.

Runes, Dagobert D., ed. *The Dictionary of Philosophy.* New York: Philosophical Library, Inc., 1942.

Russell, Bertrand. *Human Knowledge.* New York: Simon and Schuster, 1948.

——— *An Inquiry Into Meaning And Truth.* Baltimore: Penguin Books, 1962.

——— *The Problems of Philosophy.* London: Oxford University Press, 1912.

Ryle, Gilbert. *The Concept Of Mind.* New York: Barnes and Noble, 1949.

——— *Dilemmas.* Cambridge: Cambridge University Press, 1954.

Sabine, Paul E. "Acoustics." In *The Encyclopedia Americana,* Vol. 1. New York: Americana Corporation, 1956, pp. 97–102.

Sachs, Curt. *The Commonwealth of Art.* New York: W. W. Norton and Co., Inc., 1946.

——— *Rhythm and Tempo.* New York: W. W. Norton and Co., Inc., 1953.

——— *The Wellsprings of Music.* Edited by Jap Kunst. New York: McGraw-Hill Book Co., 1965.

Salzer, Felix. *Structural Hearing.* Vols. 1 and 2. New York: Charles Boni, 1952.

Santayana, George. *The Life of Reason.* New York: Charles Scribner's Sons, 1954.

——— *The Sense of Beauty.* New York: Charles Scribner's Sons, 1896.

Savill, Agnes. "Physical Effects of Music." *Music and Letters* 39 (1958): 16–28.

Schenker, Heinrich. *Neue Musikalische Theorien und Phantasien.* Vol. 3. *Der Freie Satz.* Vienna: Universal-Edition, 1935.

Scherchen, Hermann. *The Nature of Music.* Chicago: Henry Regnery Co., 1951.

Schiller, Friedrich. *On the Aesthetic Education of Man.* Edited and translated by Elizabeth M. Wilkinson and L. A. Willoughby. Oxford: The Clarendon Press, 1967.

Schneider, Marius. "Primitive Music." In *Ancient and Oriental Music,* Vol. 1, *The New Oxford History of Music,* edited by Egon Wellesz. London: Oxford University Press, 1957.

Schoen, Max, ed. *The Effects of Music*. New York: Harcourt, Brace and Co., Inc., 1927.

———. *The Understanding of Music*. New York: Harper and Brothers, 1945.

Schoenberg, Arnold. *Fundamentals of Musical Composition*. Edited by Gerald Strang. New York: St. Martin's Press, 1967.

———. *Style and Idea*. New York: Philosophical Library, 1950.

———. *Theory of Harmony*. Translated by R. D. Adams. New York: Philosophical Library, 1948.

Schrade, Leo. "Music in the Philosophy of Boethius." *Musical Quarterly* 33 (1947): 188–200.

Schueller, Herbert M. "Correspondences between Music and the Sister Arts." *Journal of Aesthetics and Art Criticism* 11 (1953): 334–59.

———. "'Imitation' and 'Expression' in British Music Criticism in the 18th Century." *Musical Quarterly* 34 (1948): 544–66.

———. "Schelling's Theory of the Metaphysics of Music." *Journal of Aesthetics and Art Criticism* 15 (1957): 461–76.

Schwadron, Abraham A. *Aesthetics: Dimensions For Music Education*. Washington D.C.: Music Educators National Conference, 1967.

Schwartz, Elliott and Barney Childs. *Contemporary Composers on Contemporary Music*. New York: Holt, Rinehart and Winston, 1967.

Schweitzer, Albert. *J. S. Bach*. Vol. 2. Translated by Ernest Newman. New York: The Macmillan Company, 1935.

Scott, Cyril. *The Philosophy of Modernism In Its Connection With Music*. London: Kegan Paul, Trench Trubner and Co., Ltd., (n.d.).

Seashore, Carl E. *In Search of Beauty in Music: A Scientific Approach to Musical Aesthetics*. New York: Ronald Press, 1947.

———. *Psychology of Music*. New York: McGraw-Hill Book Company, 1938.

Seeger, Charles. "On the Moods of a Music-Logic." *Journal of the American Musicological Society* 13 (1960): 224–61.

Sessions, Roger. "The Composer and His Message." In *The Intent of the Artist*, edited by Augusto Centeno. Princeton: Princeton University Press, 1941.

———. *The Musical Experience of Composer, Performer, Listener*. Princeton: Princeton University Press, 1950.

Sherburne, Donald W. "Meaning and Music." *Journal of Aesthetics and Art Criticism* 24 (1966): 579–83.

Sherrington, Sir Charles. *The Integrative Action of the Nervous System*. 2nd ed. New Haven: Yale University Press, 1947.

Shifrin, Seymour. "A Note from the Underground." *Perspectives of New Music* 1 (1962): 152–53.

Shirlaw, Matthew. "Aesthetic—and Consecutive Fifths." *Music Review* 10 (1949): 89–96.

Sibley, Frank. "Aesthetic Concepts." In *Philosophy Looks At The Arts*, edited by Joseph Margolis. New York: Charles Scribner's Sons, 1962.

Simon, Alexander Herbert, Charles, and Straus, Ruth, eds. *The Physiology of Emotions*, Springfield, Illinois: Charles Thomas, 1961.

Sinnott, Edmund W. "The Creativeness of Life." In *Creativity and Its Cultivation*, edited by Harold H. Anderson. New York: Harper and Brothers, 1959.

Smith, Robert C. *Esthetic Theory and the Appraisal of Practices in Music Education*. Ann Arbor: University Microfilms, 1964.

Smither, Howard E. "The Rhythmic Analysis of 20th-Century Music." *Journal of Music Theory* 8 (1964): 54–88.

Sorantin, Erich. *The Problem Of Musical Expression*. Nashville, Tenn.: Marshall and Bruce Co., 1932.

Sparshott, F. E. *The Structure of Aesthetics*. London: Routledge and Kegan Paul, 1963.

Spencer, Herbert. *Facts and Comments*. New York: D. Appleton and Co., 1902.

———. "On the Origin and Function of Music," *Essays On Education*. London: J. M. Dent and Sons, Ltd., 1911.

Stallman, Robert W., ed. *Critiques And Essays In Criticism*. New York: The Ronald Press Co., 1949.

Stambaugh, Joan. "Music as a Temporal Form." *Journal of Philosophy* 61 (1964): 265–80.

Stechow, Wolfgang. "Problems of Structure in Some Relations Between the Visual Arts and Music." *Journal of Aesthetics and Art Criticism* 11 (1953): 324–33.

Steen, Edwin B. and Montagu, Ashley. *Anatomy and Physiology*. Vol. 2. New York: Barnes and Noble, Inc., 1959.

Stevens, S. S., ed. *Handbook of Experimental Psychology*. New York: John Wiley and Sons, Inc., 1951.

Stevenson, Charles. *Ethics And Language*. New Haven: Yale University Press, 1944.

———. "Interpretation and Evaluation in Aesthetics." In *Philosophical Analysis*, edited by Max Black. Ithaca: Cornell University Press, 1950.

Stockhausen, Karlheinz. "Music and Speech." *die Reihe* 6 (1964): 40–64.

Stolnitz, Jerome. *Aesthetics and Philosophy of Art Criticism*. Boston: Houghton Mifflin Co., 1960.

———. *Aesthetics: Sources in Philosophy*. New York: The Macmillan Co., 1964.

Stratton, George M. "Excitement as an Undifferentiated Emotion." In *Feelings and Emotions*, The Wittenberg Symposium, edited by Martin Reymert. Worcester, Mass.: Clark University Press, 1928.

Stravinsky, Igor. *Chronicle of My Life*. London: Victor Gollancz, 1936.

———. *Orpheus*. London: Boosey and Hawkes, Ltd., 1948.

Stravinsky, Igor and Craft, Robert. *Conversations with Igor Stravinsky*. Garden City: Doubleday and Co., Inc., 1959.

———. *Expositions and Developments*. Garden City: Doubleday and Co., Inc., 1962.

———. *Memories and Commentaries*. Garden City: Doubleday and Co., Inc., 1960.

Strawson, P. F. *Individuals*. Garden City: Doubleday and Co., Inc., 1963.

Strunk, Oliver, ed. *Source Readings in Music History*. New York: W. W. Norton and Co., Inc., 1950.

Sullivan, J. W. N. *Beethoven, His Spiritual Development*. New York: Alfred A. Knopf, Inc., 1927.

Taylor, C. A. *The Physics of Musical Sounds*. London: The English Universities Press, Ltd., 1965.

Taylor, Eric. "Rousseau's Conception of Music." *Music and Letters* 30 (1949): 231–42.

Tenney, James. *Meta + Hodos*. New Orleans: Tulane University Press, 1964.

Thomson, Virgil. *The Art of Judging Music*. New York: Alfred A. Knopf, 1948.

Tischler, Hans. "The Aesthetic Experience." *Music Review* 17 (1956): 189–204.

Toch, Ernst. *The Shaping Forces in Music*. New York: Criterion Music Corp., 1948.

Tolstoy, Leo N. *What Is Art?* Translated by Aylmer Maude. New York: The Liberal Arts Press, 1960.

Tomas, Vincent A. "The Concept of Expression in Art." In *Science, Language, and Human Rights*. Philadelphia: University of Pennsylvania Press, 1952.

Tomkins, Silvan S. and Carroll E. Izard, eds. *Affect, Cognition, and Personality*. London: Tavistock Publications, 1965.

Tovey, Donald Francis. "Words and Music: Somer Obiter Dicta." In *The Main Stream of Music and Other Essays*, edited by Hubert Foss. New York: Meridian Books, Inc., 1959.

———. *Musical Articles from the Encyclopaedia Britannica*. London: Oxford 1944.

Towneley, Simon. "Early Italian Opera." In *The Age of Humanism*, Vol. 4, *The New Oxford History of Music*, edited by Gerald Abraham. London: Oxford University Press, 1968.

Treitler, Leo. "Musical Syntax in the Middle Ages: Background to an Aesthetic Problem." *Perspectives of New Music* 4 (1965): 75–85.

Urmson, J. O., ed. *The Concise Encyclopaedia of Western Philosophy and Philosophers*. London: Hutchinson and Co., Ltd., 1960.

Ushenko, Andrew P. *Dynamics of Art*. Bloomington: Indiana University Press, 1953.

Uvarov, E. B. and Chapman, D. R. *A Dictionary of Science*. Rev. ed. Baltimore: Penguin Books, 1951.

Valentine, C. W. *The Experimental Psychology of Beauty*. London: Methuen and Co., Ltd., 1962.

Van Den Borren, Charles. "The French Chanson." In *The Age of Humanism*, Vol. 4, *The New Oxford History of Music*, edited by Gerald Abraham. London: Oxford University Press, 1968.

Venturi, Lionello. "Metaphor." In *The Dictionary of Philosophy*, edited by Dagobert Runes. New York: Philosophical Library, 1942.

Vinton, John. "Bartók on his Own Music." *Journal of the American Musicological Society* 19 (1966): 232–43.

Vivas, Eliseo and Krieger, Murray, eds. *The Problems of Aesthetics*. New York: Rinehart and Co., Inc., 1953.

Wallaschek, Richard. "On the Origin of Music." *Mind* 16 (1891): 375–86.

Warnock, G. J. "Truth and Correspondence." In *Knowledge and Experience*, edited by C. D. Rollins. Oberlin: University of Pittsburgh Press, 1962.

Webern, Anton. *Konzert*. Vienna: Universal Edition, 1948.

　　　The Path to the New Music. Translated by L. Black and edited by W. Reich. Bryn Mawr, Pa.: Theodore Presser Co., 1963.

Webster, J. H. Douglas. "Golden-Mean Form in Music." *Music and Letters* 31 (1950): 238–48.

Weiss, Paul. *The World of Art*. Carbondale: Southern Illinois University Press, 1964.

Weitz, Morris. *Philosophy Of The Arts*. Cambridge: Harvard University Press, 1950.

　　　ed. *Problems In Aesthetics*. New York: The Macmillan Co., 1959.

　　　"The Role of Theory in Aesthetics." *Journal of Aesthetics and Art Criticism* 15 (1956): 27–35.

Welch, Paul. "Discursive and Presentational Symbol." *Mind* 64 (1955): 181–99.

Wellek, Albert. "The Relationship Between Music and Poetry." *Journal of Aesthetics and Art Criticism* 21 (1962): 149–56.

Wenger, M. A. "Emotion as Visceral Action: An Extension of Lange's Theory." In *Feelings and Emotions*, The Moosehart Symposium, edited by Martin Reymert. New York: McGraw-Hill Book Co., 1950.

Wenger, M. A. Jones, F. N., and Jones, M. H. *Physiological Psychology*. New York: Henry Holt and Co., 1956.

Werner, Heinz. "Motion and Motion Perception: A Study in Vicarious Functioning." *Journal of Psychology* 19 (1945): 317–27.

Westergaard, Peter. "Some Problems in Rhythmic Theory and Analysis." *Perspectives of New Music* 1 (1962): 180–91.

　　　"Webern and 'Total Organization': An Analysis of the Second Movement of Piano Variations, Op. 27." *Perspectives of New Music* 1 (1963): 107–20.

Wever, Ernest Glen and Lawrence, Merle. *Physiological Acoustics*. Princeton: Princeton University Press, 1954.

Whitehead, Alfred North and Russell, Bertrand. *Principia Mathematica to * 56*. Rev. ed. Cambridge: Cambridge University Press, 1962.

Whiteley, C. H. "On Understanding." *Mind* 58 (1949): 339–51.

Whitrow, G. J. *The Natural Philosophy of Time*. London: Thomas Nelson and Sons, Ltd., 1961.

Wienpahl, Robert W. "Zarlino, the Scenario, and Tonality." *Journal of the American Musicological Society* 12 (1959): 27–41.

Wimsatt, W. K. and Beardsley, Monroe C. "The Affective Fallacy." *Sewanee Review* 57 (1949): 31–55.

　　　"The Intentional Fallacy." In *The Verbal Icon*. Louisville: University of Kentucky Press, 1954.

Winold, Charles A. *The Effects of Changes in Harmonic Tension Upon Listener Responses*. Ann Arbor: University Microfilms, 1963.

Wittgenstein, Ludwig. *Lectures and Conversations on Aesthetics, Psychology and Religious Belief*. Edited by Cyril Barrett. Oxford: Basil Blackwell, 1966.

　　　Philosophical Investigations. Translated by G. E. M. Anscombe. Oxford: Basil Blackwell, 1953.

　　　Tractatus Logico-Philosophicus. Translated by D. F. Pears and B. F. McGuiness. London: Routledge and Kegan Paul, 1963.

Woolsey, Clinton N. "Organization of Cortical Auditory System." In *Sensory Communication*, edited by Walter A. Rosenblith. Cambridge: M.I.T. Press, 1961.

Wyburn, G. W. Pickford, R. W., and Hirst, R. J. *Human Senses And Perception*. Edinburgh and London: Oliver and Boyd, Ltd., 1964.

Youngblood, Joseph E. "Style as Information." *Journal of Music Theory* 2 (1958): 24–35.

Zink, Sidney. "Is the Music Really Sad?" *Journal of Aesthetics and Art Criticism* 19 (1960): 197–207.

　　　"Poetry and Truth." *Philosophical Review* 54 (1945): 132–54.

Zipf, George Kingsley. *The Psycho-Biology of Language*. Boston: Houghton Mifflin Co., 1935.

Zuckerkandle, Victor. *The Sense of Music*. Princeton: Princeton University Press, 1959.

　　　Sound and Symbol. Translated by Willard R. Trask. New York: Pantheon Books, Inc., 1956.

Index

Index